NEVILLE SARONY is an Anglo-Irish barrister who served in the 7th Gurkha Rifles, graduated LLB (Hons) at the London School of Economics and was called to the English Bar. He spent two years in the UK's Foreign Office before establishing the first foreign law practice in Nepal. He practised in London until 2000. From 1986 to 1998 he was chairman of a group of travel companies in Kathmandu. He is now a practising silk in Hong Kong and also has a home in Spain.

Also by Neville Sarony

The Max Devlin Series
The Dharma Expedient
Devlin's Chakra

Memoir
Counsel in the Clouds

THE CHAKRATA INCIDENT

Neville Sarony

BLACKSMITH BOOKS

For Jason and Brandon Dhakhwa

The Chakrata Incident
ISBN 978-988-75546-7-7

Published by Blacksmith Books
Unit 26, 19/F, Block B, Wah Lok Industrial Centre,
37-41 Shan Mei Street, Fo Tan, Hong Kong
Tel: (+852) 2877 7899
www.blacksmithbooks.com

Dramatis Personae

Max Devlin. Major, Royal Gurkha Rifles (RGR), seconded to SIS.
Major-General Macrae. Deputy Adjutant-General, Ministry of Defence.
James Chalmers. Dir of Operations (Asia), Secret Intelligence Service (SIS).
Prabhat Yonjon. Company Sergeant-Major, RGR, signals.
Kesarsing Limbu. Sergeant, RGR, explosives & weapon training.
Deepraj Rai. Sergeant, RGR, unarmed combat.
Herman Durwachter. Lieutenant-Colonel, US Rangers, seconded to CIA.

Indian Cabinet:
Arvind Kaur. Prime Minister.
Amitab Roy. External Affairs Minister.
Sakhrani. Home Minister.
Dilconda. Defence Minister.

External Intelligence Bureau, aka, Research & Analysis Wing (RAW), India:
Major-General Narayan Mullick. Special Secretary, aka, the Chief.
Francis 'Freddie' Fernandes. Senior Officer.
Flight-Lieutenant Ulan. Mongolian pilot, Aviation Research Centre (ARC).
Flight-Lieutenant Linka. Tibetan pilot, aka the Mad Monk, ARC.

Indian Army:
General Chaudhari. Chief of Defence Staff (CDS).
Colonel Sidartha Chopra. Ex-5th Gurkha Rifles.
Major Manek Jha. Indian Army officer, Camp Commandant, Baniyana.
Captain Shanaaz Khan. Indian Army Medical Corps.
Nisha Khan. Younger sister of Captain Khan.

All-Tibetan Specialised Unit of the Special Frontier Force (SFF, aka, the 22s):
Dapon Lhendup Penjo. Commanding Officer.
Norbu Khamba. Company Commander.
Jhampa. Company Commander.
Paljor. Company Commander.
Pema. Company Commander.
Choden. Team leader of Jigme, Jamsung, Sonam.
Choki. Team leader.
Kalsang. Team leader of Dawa, Loshay, Tenzing.
Palden. Team leader.
Lobsang Gyaltsen. Intelligence Officer.
Si-thar. Paramedic.

PLA & 128 Mountain Rapid Reaction Regiment (128 MRRR):
Lieutenant-General Liu Peng. Shigatse Regional Commander.
Colonel Wei Zhongxi. Commanding Officer, 128 MRRR.
Major Xan. 128 MRRR.
Sergeant Guo. 128 MRRR.

Officers' Mess
1st Battalion, The Royal Gurkha Rifles
Shorncliffe, Kent

The Black Bear's melody played at 140 paces to the minute normally stirred the adrenalin, but Major Max Devlin's mind was not on the piping. Instinctively, he joined the other officers beating time on the tabletop as the Pipe-Major marched steadily around them.

The music died after the Gurkha piper left the room to the roar of appreciation. Returning minus his pipes, the Gurkha smiled as he registered the quantity of Glenmorangie that he would have to down in one; this was his farewell performance before going on pension and the commanding officer wanted him to know how much he would be missed. He lifted the quaiche in salute and swept the table with his eyes, acknowledging the old familiar faces as well as those less well known as he drank in the warmth of their applause to counteract the wrench of knowing that his years of service were all but over. They all raised their glasses, faces still burned Helmand-brown above the high collars of their mess kit. He had to take a deep breath to calm himself. The whisky would be a balm. He stood to attention facing the colonel-saheb, raised the quaiche in both hands, his voice not as steady as his piping when he said, '*Sab sahebharulai tagrarahanuhaus.*'

As the response roared out, Devlin let his mind drift, wondering, not for the first time, why the grammatically incorrect toast had never been corrected? History, he reflected, was littered with the corseted detritus of tradition and Gurkha service in the British Army had almost two centuries of tradition. What would the future hold for the Gurkha piper once he was no longer an immediate member of the tightly knit family of the battalion? Nowadays, unlike in the past, Gurkha soldiers on pension rarely returned to the challenging demands of farming in the Himalayas.

Futures were very much on Max's mind. He took a polite sip of his port, a drink of which he was not particularly fond. Maintaining a façade of sociability, he had toyed with a glass of the excellent Margaux throughout dinner, declining the frequent efforts of the mess waiters to recharge it. He allowed his eyes to track everyone seated around the oblong mahogany table, taking in the faces animated by the generous amount of alcohol consumed.

No hard drinking for him tonight.

The flames from the candles caught the silver centrepieces making the figurines appear to move. The mess waiters hovered in the background, the more angular Tibetan profiles of the Sherpas and Tamangs set in concentration. Max turned to the young second-lieutenant on his right and asked, 'Hugh, as a Scot, how did you find the piping?'.

'Bloody marvellous, sir.'

'It's Max, you can drop the sir.'

'Eh, but you're a Major…,' the young officer's mouth formed to tack 'sir' on the end as his eyes flicked to the medal ribbon for the Military Cross, then he stopped himself. 'I mean Max.'

Devlin smiled encouragement, 'This is a mess dinner night, I prefer informality.'

Catching the colonel's eye, Max raised his glass. The smile of response was as fulsome as ever. With only half an ear attuned to the young Scotsman's knowledgeable critique of the piping, his eyes quartered the room: the walls heavily brocaded with oil paintings of Gurkha VCs, rows of medals of illustrious former Gurkhas framed in glass cases, memorabilia of nearly 200 years of Gurkha regiments serving the British crown. Two old and bold majors, Peter Standish and Miles Anderson, were heavily engaged discussing their pensions, something Max gave little thought to. But it served as a reminder, he chided himself, his career path had been spectacular so far, despite an unmilitary streak of iconoclasm. But even assuming he made lieutenant-general, these days people retired early and there would still be life after the army.

He let his mind wander to fantasising about his ideas for Nepal.

'Who'll be the next Pipe-Major?'

The question registered in time for Max to respond. 'Dillikumar, I imagine,' he said. 'He's far and away the best piper.'

'True sir…Max, but he's relatively junior in rank.'

'The modern army is less fixated with years of service. Merit has its own value.'

Even as he said it, Max realised that this must sound self-serving. As the youngest substantive major in the Brigade of Gurkhas, he was under close scrutiny by one or two more senior majors who were comparing their diminishing prospects of commanding one of the two Royal Gurkha Rifle battalions. He inhaled the atmosphere. Being posted to a staff job in the Ministry of Defence had divorced him from that aspect of soldiering that he most relished – daily command of men he considered the world's best combat troops and the bond with them and various of his brother officers.

At the far end of the table, Bruce Rose's face was creased in laughter, his eyes reduced to narrow slits but the image that stuck in Devlin's mind was the controlled fury with which Bruce had led B Company to track down an Afghan army captain attached to the battalion who had murdered three of the company's men whilst they slept and then escaped into the night. No one would have associated tonight's blond-haired, fun-creased face with the remorseless, diamond-hard eyes between the rim of his helmet and the edge of his face scarf in Helmand province. The company's Gurkha 2i/c had confided to Max that Bruce had stood by whilst the men extracted their revenge. Anxious about repercussions from Brigade HQ, Max had persuaded Bruce to report that though they were certain they had shot him, the Afghan had disappeared.

The incident had strained their close relationship as Devlin argued against revenge killings only to be met by Rose's incendiary retort: 'I was sending them a message, "Don't you ever, ever fuck with my men!"' In human terms, it had been a potential end to an outstanding officer's career. But they both knew that any investigation would have been met by a wall of silence. B Company needed closure and Bruce had willingly connived at it.

When Gurkhas closed ranks, they presented an impenetrable wall to the outside world. A journalist making a TV documentary had once asked Max to define what it was about the relationship between the Gurkhas and their British officers that worked so well. He had embarked on a historical analysis, but she interrupted him, wanting a quotable response, preferably in a sentence – one that it was beyond him to provide. Devlin had joked with her that he was Irish, so how would he know?

From time to time, he had recalled the question and tried, in his mind, to distil the essence of what was, in most cases, a symbiotic relationship that defied a succinct definition. It nagged at his need to be able to express it. In a conscious endeavour to divorce his personal opinion, he had studied most of the memoirs written by 19th-century Gurkha officers as well as books by leading anthropologists on the peoples of the Himalayas. But articulating the intangible quality eluded him and he fell back onto the wholly unacademic realisation that it was rather akin to falling in love – you knew when it happened and until then it remained a mystery.

So, that was it, a soldier's love story.

Max nodded as he saw the colonel stand up signalling the end of the dining phase of the evening. As he made his way out towards the anteroom, he felt a restraining hand on his arm.

'Max, hang back a moment, will you.'

Lieutenant-Colonel Richard Neal was the finest commanding officer he had ever had. Indicating the empty chairs beside the dining table, Neal sat down, followed by him.

'About your appointment with the DAG tomorrow,' the colonel began, 'my informant in Wilton did me the courtesy of telling me.' Noting the worry lines on Max's face, he smiled reassuringly, 'No, it's nothing bad. That, I can say.

'I'm under strict orders not to disclose the nature of the meeting but I just want to assure you that whatever your decision,' Neal added, 'I will be pulling every string I know to have you take over command of the battalion in due course.'

'I'm grateful, Colonel.'

'No, not only do you deserve it,' Neal said, 'the battalion deserves you.' Devlin gave a modest shake of his head, but the colonel went on,

'The powers that be are fully aware of your linguistic skills and special knowledge, they make you a highly valuable commodity. More than which I am not at liberty to divulge.' He frowned for a second before continuing, 'I sense that timing may not work in your favour but that's just guesswork on my part.' Rising to his feet, Neal added, 'Just remember that you remain an integral member of the brigade.' Pointing towards the anteroom, he said, 'Now let's join the others. I gather the Pipe-Major has a treat for us.'

The rest of the evening passed too slowly for Devlin's liking. He felt curiously detached, more spectator than participant, his thoughts running riot with speculation as to what the morrow would bring.

There was something surreal about these occasions, those he was accustomed to seeing with sweat running down their camouflage-paint distorted faces, intense with the focus of their responsibility for the men under their command were transformed into elegantly rifle-green-clad boys who had never grown up. The two Nepalese officers' behaviour indistinguishable from the Brits. It was the *yin* and *yang* of their work and play, one where death or disastrous injury was a hair's breadth away and the other a decorous alcohol-fuelled abandon. The common thread being the brotherhood of soldiering with the best. Tonight, his staff job set him slightly apart and he resented the artificial distancing. No sooner had Colonel Neal taken his leave than Max thanked the president of the mess committee and walked briskly out into the car park and his vintage Austin-Healey 3000.

The drive back to London was uneventful and though he put on an Oscar Peterson disc with Ray Brown, part of his mind subconsciously following the interplay, he considered the hours before the meeting a waste of time. He could not shake off the feeling that despite Neal's reassurance, perhaps even because of it, he might not be comfortable with whatever it proved to be. The fact that the appointment was on a Saturday only increased his concerns – nothing important usually happened on Saturdays.

His intuition was not giving a clear signal.

Office of the DAG
The Ministry of Defence
Wilton, Wiltshire

'Major Devlin, I'd like you to meet Mr. James Chalmers.'

The other man in Major-General Macrae's office stood up and shook hands with Max. He put Chalmers in his late 40s, distinguished greying hair over a face that seemed to be enjoying a private joke and a discreetly well-tailored dark blue suit, the effect of which was tempered by louche dark brown suede brogues. No question, the man was a spook.

Major-General Macrae, the deputy adjutant-general at the Ministry of Defence, indicated the other chair in front of his desk. Max waited to discover what Chalmers's presence meant and he was already composing a polite refusal.

'Tea or coffee, gentlemen?' Both declined. The DAG leaned back in his chair and steepled his fingers. 'I'll not beat about the bush,' he began, 'the Secret Intelligence Service of which Mr. Chalmers is a senior officer want the army to second you to them for a specific operation.' One of his eyebrows shot up for a second, then he continued, 'Please don't say anything until you have heard Mr. Chalmers's request and my own observations.' Max nodded acquiescence. 'James?' The general inclined his head forward in Chalmers's direction.

'General Macrae doesn't mince matters,' observed the SIS director of operations (Asia). His professional smile was disarming. 'Major, I know that you signed the Official Secrets Act when you were posted to the SAS,' Chalmers said, 'but I hope you will pardon the scanty account I am about to give you. You are well aware of the need-to-know principle that governs all intelligence work and given the political sensitivity of what we have in mind, I can only give you the broadest of pictures.' He gave a little dismissive wave of his hand before adding, 'What you divine from what I tell you is, of course, a matter for you.' He half-turned towards the general's desk and opened a fat file. 'You have been on SIS's radar for some time. Your language skills, particularly for the Indian subcontinent as well as Tibet first brought you to our attention.'

Max recalled being approached by a captain in military intelligence who had asked him to make discreet inquiries of a Pakistan army officer with whom he had been on a Commonwealth Combined Services Course. 'Captain Herbert, as I remember?'

Chalmers nodded, 'Then you added *Dari* when you served in Afghanistan and according to the head of station in Kabul.' Turning over several pages in the file and running his finger down a page, he continued, 'you so impressed an Afghan warlord by conversing with him in his own tongue that he refused to allow the Taliban to operate in his area.'

'It was more a gesture of courtesy,' Max responded quietly. 'What really impressed him was the ability of our men to communicate with the villagers under his control.'

'I see,' said Chalmers, closing the file. His head slightly inclined forward as he shot the question, 'How would you feel about working with the Indians?'

'Forgive me, Mr. Chalmers but that's too vague a question to merit a considered response.' It did not seem to matter that his tone carried the 'so put that in your spook's pipe and smoke it' sense, save that he did want to avoid offending the DAG. Chalmers nodded but whether in acknowledgement that the question was ill-composed or because it confirmed some other observation in his file that recorded an atypical disregard for authority, Max could not tell.

'*Touché*. I deserved that,' Chalmers smiled. Max noticed the crinkles at the corners of the director's eyes. 'You have excellent relations with some of the Indian Army officers with whom you have crossed paths,' Chalmers said, 'but do you share the low opinion that many Nepalese have of their southern neighbours?'

'With respect, sir, that's too general an observation.' Out of the corner of his eye, Devlin was watching Macrae's expression to see whether he disapproved. So far, neutral. Reassured, he continued, 'When Indian customs officers abuse their powers to steal from Nepalese at the borders or their politicians take unfair advantage of the fact that Nepal is a landlocked country, yes, I agree with them. But if you put me in a room full of Europeans, Americans and Indians, I would almost certainly find a great deal more common ground with the latter.'

'And their bureaucrats?'

Max was not going to be drawn. 'I judge individuals,' he said, 'not categories.'

'Mm.' Chalmers glanced away for a moment and Max had the impression that the spymaster had reached a critical juncture in his sales pitch. When the director turned to face him again, Max had the impression that Chalmers was about to cross a line that he had set for himself.

'Together with the Indian Research and Analysis Wing...,' he resumed only to be interrupted by Max, 'You mean the Indian External Intelligence Bureau.'

'Yes, it is a bit of a euphemism,' the SIS man acknowledged. 'We and the CIA have set up a centre in northern India to provide specialist training to their Special Frontier Force.' Max maintained what the Mongol people called 'a cold face', giving nothing away. 'For obvious political reasons, it has to be under the nominal control of the Indians,' Chalmers continued, 'but SIS and the CIA provide the directing staff. The Americans are putting in a great deal more money than we are but it's a shared command.'

It was sorely tempting to point out that this was a recipe for endless problems but a quick look at Macrae's raised eyebrows signalled that he obviously shared this opinion.

'We would like you to head up the British team.' So, there were to be others. 'If you accept the job, you get the right to vet our contingent.'

Chalmers looked briefly towards Macrae, who spoke directly to Max. 'It's a brevet lieutenant-colonel's post.' Aha, so the army were sufficiently interested to offer an inducement, but Max guessed that his pay would come out of the Secret Vote, so it would cost the army nothing.

'When would the posting take effect?' he asked.

'Immediately.'

The inviting prospect of leaving his desk job at the MoD almost overrode his reservations about the unknown aspects of the post, let alone the effect on his career. He focused on practicalities. 'The British team?'

'Four, you and three British Army NCOs go as instructors in signals, explosives, weapon training and unarmed combat,' Chalmers said, 'for potential cross-border operations.'

In his mind's eye, Devlin selected his candidates for these posts, all Gurkhas. But timing was the crux of the matter. He had no intention of losing his prospects of commanding one of the RGR battalions.

'And for how long would it be, the posting?' He noted the way that the spook's eyes seemed to lose focus for a fraction of a second – he was unsure of his answer.

'As I said, it's a tripartite project among the Indians, the Americans and ourselves.' Chalmers paused, frowned and his glance took in Macrae before squaring up to Max. 'It's politically sensitive within the Indian administration itself…so it's been given the greenlight for a trial period of 18 months.' Max nodded his understanding. Why was there such a gulf between politicians and soldiers?

'I take it that these *potential* cross-border operations would be unattributable?'

'Obviously the Chinese will assume that they are CIA with complicit Indian support but the Tibetans in exile have various groups acting independently of western backing,' Chalmers said.

'And neither the American nor I will be venturing into Tibet,' Max said, making it as a statement.

Chalmers shook his head sharply as he confirmed, 'No. Nor any of the Indian members of the team.'

On the one hand, Max was intrigued by the prospect but once again he would be away from soldiering in the battalion. The army must have approved of the job; otherwise, he would not be here now.

'I'd appreciate 24 hours within which to decide, sir,' he said, standing up to face the DAG before adding, 'If that is acceptable, General.'

Macrae tapped his phone. 'Call me.'

Chalmers stood up to shake Max's hand. 'It's been a pleasure, Major.'

*

Max had only been back in his office five minutes when the phone rang. He recognised the voice. The tone was neutral, so he concluded that he was not about to be given a bollocking.

'Come up, will you.' Macrae did not wait for a reply.

Max made a quick note on a sheet of paper before heading back to the DAG's office. Back there, Max took a seat whilst Macrae walked over and sat on the windowsill. 'There's one hell of a lot of you scratch my back and I'll scratch yours about this.' His smile was thin, almost as though he was none too comfortable about the situation. 'I'll give you my take on this, but it doesn't leave this office.' The general stared out of the window for a moment before spelling out his observations. 'The Joint Intelligence Committee wants us to get closer to the Indians. The White House wants to counter China's global aspirations in Asia and the CIA believe that despite our colonial history we get on better with the Indians than they do.' The irony of the situation was not lost on Max, given how much pressure the Americans brought on the British post-war government to grant Indian independence.

Turning round to face Max, and in an earnest tone, he went on, 'If the collaboration works well, we all earn credit with New Delhi and, in turn, they feel reassured about our support against Beijing.' Max was well aware that Downing Street's current incumbent had a soft spot for the Tibetans but could not afford to offend the Chinese and prejudice trade relations. 'Initially, Chalmers wanted us to second a SAS team for the project,' Macrae said, 'but the chief of general staff believes that the sensitivity of the politics demands a specialist team under an officer with your sort of credentials.' The wry smile escaped the general for a second before he added, 'Credentials like yours don't grow on trees, so we don't have a large field to choose from.'

Macrae stood up, took a deep breath and looked Max in the eye. 'You're worried about the effect on your prospects of command.' He turned, gave a little throwaway gesture with his right hand. 'So would I be, in your shoes.' Walking back to his desk, the general pointed to what Max recognised as his own military service file. 'This posting would count as staff-cum-regimental, almost an ideal combination and it would enhance your profile but,' he said, sitting down heavily in his chair, 'anything political carries risks.' He left it in the air.

Max knew there was little point in asking the risks to be spelled out, most professional soldiers regarded politicos as the kiss of death. Equally, he knew that no senior officer was going to give him any sort of guarantee about his future, no matter how candid he might be. When he had walked back to his office after meeting the SIS director, Max had more or less decided to accept the offer. Nothing the DAG had said had changed that.

'May I select all Gurkha NCOs?'

'We rather expected that you would.'

Max allowed himself a smile as he handed over the sheet of paper. 'These are the men I need for my team, General. Sergeant-Major Prabhat Yonjon, signals expert, Sergeant Kesarsing Limbu, explosives and weapon training and Sergeant Deepraj Rai, unarmed combat.'

'They all speak English and Tibetan,' he added. 'Deepraj grew up in Darjeeling which has a large Tibetan community. Prabhat is a Tamang, their language is closely akin to Tibetan. Kesarsing is married to a Bhutanese girl. His life would be a disaster if he couldn't communicate with his beautiful wife.'

'You're in then?'

'Sir,' Max nodded.

Queen Anne Street
Westminster, London

He stood for a moment outside St. James tube station and looked across the road at the architecturally graceful building, estimating it to be about 200 years old. The stone of its exterior façade managed to convey a sense of aged stolidity, a far cry from the high-tech glass-curtain-walled edifice that he had anticipated would house part of the Secret Intelligence Service. A spot of rain fell on his forehead and he took a quick look at the sky: grey and overcast, London at its unloveliest. He allowed himself a smile of satisfaction, he could almost feel the fetal embrace of India, catch the eddy of burning charcoal in his nostrils, velvet nights and brick oven days.

The building was anonymous, no signage of any description, better he thought than some absurdly named import/export company. The heavy oak door swung open almost as though whoever was inside could see him.

'Colonel Devlin?' The door was opened by a member of the Corps of Commissionaires, lending a wholly neutral air to the building. Max produced his ID card and was ushered in with that corset-straight manner that commissionaires exhibited. He signed in and was given a visitor's pass to wear. 'Take a seat, sir. Someone will be down to collect you shortly.'

The edge of his visual field detected movement on the staircase and Chalmers strode across, his hand outstretched. 'Colonel, good to see you. Please.' The SIS director indicated the staircase and led the way up two floors and along a corridor to a small room, modestly furnished with two battered wooden desks, unmatched chairs that looked as though they had been purchased in an impoverished country house auction.

'Please take a pew. Coffee?' Max smiled appreciation. 'Thanks.'

Whilst Chalmers operated a coffee machine, Devlin examined the map of Northern India, Tibet and China on the wall behind the desk. Beneath the map was a bookcase. He scanned the titles, recognising Sun Tzu's *The Art of War*, Jan Morris's *Heaven's Command: An Imperial Progress* and both volumes of Sven Hedin's *To the Forbidden Land*.

'You've spotted my little reference library,' said the SIS man, holding out a cup of coffee. 'Actually, they're my own copies, not the firm's. See anything you'd care to borrow?' Devlin shook his head politely.

'Max,' Chalmers began, 'I hope you don't mind the familiarity, but we all use first names in the office, top to bottom.'

'I have no problem with that, James.'

'Good.' The spy chief pointed to the other desk in the room and said, 'Temporarily, that's yours, and all the junk on it.' He laughed before continuing, 'I'd appreciate it if you'd read yourself in as quickly as possible.' He opened a drawer in his desk and took out a pass. 'This is yours. It gives you access to this building at any time, night or day but you'll need to log in and out,' he said. 'Now that you're here, I'll explain the setup. The project is codenamed Camelot. It's under my directorate.' Chalmers paused and stared out of the window, giving Max the impression that the SIS director was still trying to decide how to put it into words.

Chalmers turned to face Max and grimaced, 'What we have is a sensitive situation.' Max sipped the coffee, waiting. 'Over the years, the CIA have blown hot and cold about Tibetan resistance. The cousins, that's what we call them,' the spook added as an aside. 'They're in one of their hot phases, have been for the last couple of years as the Indians are trying to woo them away from the Pakistanis.

'The yanks are funding a specialised unit of the 22s whose purpose is intelligence gathering within Tibet. The Indian Army wants detailed information about the PLA's dispositions and strengths in those areas immediately adjacent to the disputed territories in the Himalayas,' Chalmers added. 'The only reliable intel is what these Special Frontier Force personnel gather; it's old-fashioned human intelligence, boots on the ground.' The SIS director's eyes rolled up momentarily. 'But it's also high risk for the 22s, they're tortured and executed if caught,' he added, in a tone as grim as his expression.

'It doesn't seem to deter them. They've lost over 40 since this was set up,' Chalmers continued. 'It's been hinted that these high losses are one of the reasons that we've been asked to help. But we're told that there's opposition to the infiltration from within the Indian cabinet; the chief of defence staff is desperate for the intelligence, but the prime minister is equally anxious not to upset Beijing.'

He twisted his mouth as if finding the words was difficult. 'This is where it gets complicated. SIS's opposite number in Indian intelligence, Narayan Mullick, is designated special secretary of the Research and Analysis Wing. He's an Indian Army major-general who was transferred into the Indian Civil Service to counter inter-service rivalry, I gather it's been successful. Mullick reached out to us because there's a school of thought that the CIA's methods are, how shall I put it, a little insensitive?'

Devlin was familiar with the criticism.

'The CDS, General Chaudhari, is ex-Sandhurst and Staff College,' Chalmers continued. 'He had a chat with our CIGS who happens to have been a contemporary of his and the rest, as they say, is history.'

'I can't imagine the CIA being overly enthusiastic at being given a nanny,' Max said, shaking his head.

'It's been sold to them as part of the Five Eyes joint intelligence project.' James flicked his eyebrows. 'I think they've bought it,' he said, 'but...' His face hardened. 'We'll have to walk on eggs,' Max interjected.

'Your CIA opposite number is Lieutenant-Colonel Herman Durwachter,' Chalmers resumed. 'We'll leave it to you how you manage the joint command. The camp commandant, Major Manek Jha, is a figurehead really, because the whole project is the brainchild of the RAW.

'As you probably know, the status of the RAW is unique, in theory it reports to the Indian joint intelligence committee but it's answerable directly to the Cabinet Secretariat and is not subject to parliamentary oversight,' he added. 'Narayan Mullick is reckoned to be brilliant and fiercely protective.' The SIS man frowned. 'We're all supposed to be on the same side but there are a number of seriously powerful egos in play here and, as usual the Brits play the Cinderella figure, eminently dispensable, on top of which our most formidable adversaries are the

Chinese.' Leaning forward, Chalmers rested his elbows on the desk. 'This project is largely a suck-it-and-see operation, you'll be making up the rules as you go along. It's quasi-military, but from our perspective, above all it's an intelligence operation.'

'At which I'm a novice,' Max said.

'But what is it actors say, a quick read?' James said with a smile before looking at his watch. 'We've arranged for your Gurkha signals instructor to report to GCHQ to be brought up to date. Tomorrow, the other two Gurkhas will report to the Tower, our training centre outside Brighton, to select your weapons and unattributable kit. The guys you'll be training are armed with a ragbag of weaponry that can't automatically be traced back to the UK or the US. You need to familiarise yourselves with the same kit. In the 1960s the CIA supplied the Khamba guerrillas with bloody rubbish, poor devils. This time round it's all good stuff, mainly Israeli, Russian and Croatian. Not that the Chinese will be fooled for a nano-second, but London and Washington can delude themselves and it will be that much more of a problem for Beijing to run in front of the United Nations.

'I suggest you spend today going through the files and ask me any questions that arise from them, then go down to the Tower this evening so you can brief them and make up your list of stores and equipment,' Chalmers added. 'We'd like to fly the team out on Thursday.'

Max had to remind himself that today was only Monday. Everything was being rushed, which made him feel uncomfortable. It went against the basic military principle of prioritising preparation but somehow he doubted whether James would be happy to be told that prior preparation prevents piss-poor performance. Nonetheless, as he was about to move into a potentially fractious territory where he would be responsible for his team, he needed to cover the ground comprehensively. A little feigned humility was called for.

'Look, James, as I said, quick read or no, I'm a novice in your field and I'm about to become responsible for my team in what has all the makings of a political minefield,' Max said. 'But I know a little about the RAW and particularly about the 22s. They developed from the Special Frontier Force. It started out as the Indo-Tibetan Frontier Force. I believe they keep one unit composed entirely of Tibetans?' Chalmers nodded. 'It's all supposed to come under Mullick's command,' Max went on, 'they refer to him as the Chief. A bit like C in SIS, I imagine, but because he answers directly to the Indian cabinet, various cabinet members think they're entitled to commandeer the services of RAW. Even within New Delhi, it's a political football. My guess is that given the sensitivities of some Indian politicians, this Anglo-American sideshow is virtually certain to offend someone. All of which is my justification for asking for sufficient time to study the proposal, the logistics and, top priority, the individuals involved.'

James's expression was inscrutable as he stared at Max. He reached forward and selected a Balkan Sobranie cigarette from a carved box, snapped a handsomely wrought lighter, drew in a lungful and exhaled it slowly. Max glanced at the NO SMOKING sign on the wall. James gave a dismissive wave. 'Provided I don't set off the smoke alarm, no one's the wiser.'

As the powerful aroma began to fill the room Max was tempted to say 'You must be joking' but thought better of it. James looked at the end of his cigarette for a second, breaking off eye contact. 'I ought to have known, you really do know your Indian scene, don't you?' He gestured with the cigarette. 'I made a serious error in characterising you as merely a military type with out of the ordinary linguistic skills, for which mistake I apologise,' Chalmers said. 'Might I suggest that having read yourself in, you dictate the operational schedule?'

Max was pleasantly surprised. 'I'd appreciate that.'

'Good.' Chalmers lifted his cigarette hand interrogatively. 'Still OK for the Tower this evening?'

'Certainly.'

The meeting broke up and Max settled himself into the spare desk to study the files. He accepted the offer of a sandwich at his desk and was relieved that Chalmers had a lunch appointment outside. By the time the SIS director returned, Max had his supplementary questions framed.

'Their HQ is in Chakrata but the location of the training camp is not disclosed.'

'Yes, they're very touchy about this, its location will be revealed to you after you get to Chakrata.'

Max felt that this was carrying the need-to-know principle to absurd extremes. 'I do *need* to know the terrain and climate, that dictates our clothing and equipment.'

'Fair point,' Chalmers nodded. 'You'll need both temperate and alpine gear.'

If anything, that annoyed Max even more, the SIS man obviously knew but was adhering to his need-to-know mantra.

'You also told me that the camp commandant was Major Jha but you omitted to mention that the unit commander is Dapon Lhendup Penjo,' Max said. '*Dapon* is the Tibetan equivalent rank of a brigadier-general, so he outranks both me and the American, which raises the rather awkward question of who really is in command?'

'Of the training? You and Durwachter, but operationally, Brigadier Penjo.'

'Now that you've brought up operations, who authorises the cross-border incursions?' Max pressed on. 'Forgive me, but in my limited experience, intelligence organisations have a remarkable capacity for passing the buck when the balloon goes up and I have no intention of playing midwife to an Indian…'

'Cock-up,' James supplied. 'SIS and CIA personnel are forbidden to cross any borders and we, that's us and the CIA, insisted that every cross-border operation requires a specific mandate signed by Mullick and countersigned by the secretary to the Indian cabinet.'

Max shook his head in disgust. Training these people, earning their trust and then sending them off on their own to be disowned if they were caught ran against his basic concept of combat philosophy. This was turning out to be a shitty job that he disliked more with each revelation.

'When SIS and the MoD ran cross-border ops into Indonesia under Operation Claret, our officers and NCOs went in with the Dayaks that we trained,' Max reminded the SIS director.

'But that was a British political decision. We're governed by New Delhi on this one,' Chalmers countered, adding, 'It will be your job to make sure that the people you train are fully capable of operating off the leash.'

Max was tempted to hit back angrily at what he judged a demeaning description, but all his objections were being met with the political defence. It was crunch time, either acquiesce or get off the pot.

'Very well, but if it all goes pear-shaped…'

'It will be your job to make sure it doesn't.'

SIS Training Centre
Sussex

It turned out to be a converted Napoleonic era Martello tower perched on a raised stretch of deserted shoreline. A number of more modern buildings had been added and the whole surrounded by a high security wall constructed of stone and topped with razor wire. The southern side was protected by the seashore and there was a single two-lane road that approached it through the low bushes atop the sand dunes. From the outside, it was as alluring as Stalag Luft III, even the entrance was through a pair of tall timber gates reminiscent of prisons. Once he had negotiated his way past the armed security barrier set halfway down an approach tunnel, he turned into an enclosed area topped in razor wire and set in a red brick wall. An armed guard in a nondescript government blue uniform waved him through and he parked in a white-lined bay to the left of what he guessed would have been the moat around the original tower. Mounting the stone steps leading up to the entrance, which was about 10 feet above ground level, he pushed open the heavy wooden door. Inside, a spiral iron staircase took him up to what must have been the original flat roof but which was now glassed in all round, providing a 360° viewing platform.

Two Gurkhas in smart rifle-green regimental blazers and grey trousers stood to attention and Max shook hands with each one in turn. They were the pick of the crop.

'Good evening, gentlemen.' A tall, lean man with a pronounced limp came up the stairs. He turned a prematurely aged face towards Max. 'Colonel Devlin, I'm Charles Denning. Welcome to the Tower, of which I'm the humble caretaker. An old buffer Her Majesty's government has kindly put out to autumnal grass.'

'Colonel.' Max shook hands and indicated the Gurkhas. 'May I introduce two members of my team. Sergeant Kesarsing Limbu, explosives and weapon training, and Sergeant Deepraj Rai, unarmed combat. They both speak English.'

They exchanged grins. Denning's smile was genuine, albeit tired. Max guessed that whatever the cause of his limp, the man was probably in permanent pain. Denning waved them all over towards a table that was laid for dinner. 'We play by SIS rules here, they pay the bills, so everyone's on first-name terms and there's no rank discrimination,' he said, pointing to a sideboard loaded with drinks. 'Help yourselves, there's beer in that fridge.'

Denning pointed to the chair beside him for Max to sit down.

'I've been briefed on your venture, not the whole thing, of course, only what I need to know to give you whatever you require,' he said. 'I'm the Quartermaster for these covert operations. Don't know how long SIS'll be allowed to run this type of sideshow, damn politicians keep sticking their nose in where they shouldn't.

'Anyway, give me a list of all the kit you need,' he added. 'I suspect you'll find a hundred and one things that no one has thought of but prove necessary once you get there, so just signal me and it'll be my job to make sure you get it.'

'Thank you,' Max nodded his appreciation. Speaking quietly, he went on, 'You'll have to forgive my men, Charles, this first-name business, it won't work. They'll continue to address us as *saheb*, it's part of our culture.'

Denning nodded slowly, 'I defer to your expertise.'

'Thank you. I guessed you'd understand.'

'After we've eaten, come along to my office, we can sort out the mechanics.'

*

Denning was on the phone in his office which, though small, was tastefully furnished with an unmatched pair of Captain's chairs in front of a handsome Victorian oak desk. The air was heavy with a sweet-smelling tobacco emanating from an ancient cob pipe balanced in an ashtray that looked like a partly hollowed shard of honey-coloured stone. Max settled into one of the chairs but his study of the room was interrupted by the telephone conversation coming to an abrupt halt.

Denning grabbed his pipe. 'Filthy habit, I know. But it beats painkillers,' he grinned, then pointed at the ashtray with the stem of his pipe. 'A memento, part of the building that blew apart just as I stepped into it.'

'I wondered, about the limp.'

'A gift from the Taliban. There was so much metal embedded, the quacks offered me the choice of living with it or a prosthesis. I confess I'm rather attached to it, despite the bloody nuisance.' He sucked on the pipe. 'But you didn't come here to listen to this nonsense.'

'Far from nonsense, a lot of us carry a sense of guilt at having escaped.'

'But you were hit twice.'

'Flesh wounds.'

'Bollocks!' Denning laughed. 'Your MC didn't come up with the rations! What can I do for you?'

'The people we'll be training are armed with a ragbag of weaponry that can't automatically be traced back to the UK or the US. We need to familiarise ourselves with the same kit.' Denning nodded and picked up the thread: 'Unattributability.' Max nodded.

Denning reached behind him for a file which he handed across the desk. He pulled on his pipe and rocked his chair back a little. 'This is for your eyes only. I have my own resources in India. My father was Indian civil service and after '47 some of his young protégés kept in touch with me,' he explained. 'First-class minds, way above my pay scale, but good friends and they give me insights into Indian affairs. I asked them to give me the lowdown on the people running the 22s from Delhi.' He tapped the file. 'I think you'd be well advised to look at what they say about the political setup, you'll need to watch your back.'

Max reached forward for the file but Denning kept his hand on top.

'I'd appreciate it if the file did not leave this room.' Max nodded. 'I'll leave you in peace,' Denning said. 'Put the file in the top drawer of my desk when you've finished reading and drop the latch on the door.'

The man got up to leave the room but paused in the doorway. 'You and your chaps can have a free run in the armoury tomorrow morning at sparrow-fart. Anything you want and we don't have, I can get hold of within 24 hours. The range is bang next door, if you'll pardon the pun'.

*

A little over an hour and a half later Devlin left Denning's office, turning over the information in his mind. The Indian Research and Analysis Wing attracted a mixed bag of people, seen as an accelerated route for promotion for those who succeeded but a career graveyard for those who didn't. It made unwelcome reading.

India

5 days later

The Atlas A400M touched down with barely a bump and taxied to a remote corner of Delhi's Palam airfield. The night sky prevented Max from assessing the level of pollution through the window and there was very little illumination at the point where the aircraft came to a halt. The attractive WRAF corporal who had acted as their inflight attendant looked up from where she was bent forward peering through the spyhole in the exit door.

'Going somewhere interesting, sir?'

'As far away from Delhi as I can get,' he grinned as he pulled his Bergen out of the overhead compartment. The Gurkhas were joking amongst themselves as they grabbed their kit.

'Can I give you a hand with that?' Max pushed himself forward and grabbed hold of the door.

'Thank you, sir,' she grinned.

'Thanks for taking care of us.' Max gave her a smile.

'Good luck, sir.'

He turned and waved the Gurkhas towards the exit. They were going to need more than good luck. During the flight, he had settled in to reading *The Noodle Maker of Kalimpong* to refresh his memory of previous CIA involvement with Tibetans in exile. As the Indian night wrapped itself around him, he wondered whose graves he was stepping on. With his Bergen slung over one shoulder and his canvas valise in the other hand he walked down the staircase.

'Welcome, Colonel.' The tall Tibetan dressed in camouflage smock and trousers had his nameplate on his left chest, American style, just the surname: 'Penjo'.

'Thank you, Dapon.' Max made a clumsy *namaskar* then dropped his valise and shook hands.

'Plain Penjo, please. Max, if I may?'

'Please.'

'I'm afraid we still have some travelling ahead of us.' Penjo indicated a helicopter parked some 100 metres away, its rotor turning slowly. As they got closer Max peered through the dark.

'An Mi-17, what we in NATO call a Hip, if I'm not mistaken.'

'Correct,' Penjo said. 'We'd prefer an Apache or even a Black Hawk but the demands of unattributability dictate that we use Russian equipment and the Mi-17 approximates to our needs.' Max felt that it would have been undiplomatic at this stage to disclose his opinion of the machine. The Gurkhas tossed their kit into the helicopter and climbed in.

'Come up front with me, Max.' Penjo led the way forward and pointed to the bench seat on which the pilot was sitting.

'Welcome on board, sir.' The pilot turned a deeply sunburned Mongol face towards Max. 'Flight-Lieutenant Ulan, responsible for this piece of Russian garbage, but I will do my best to get you safely to your destination.'

'Shut up and fly, Ulan.' Penjo turned towards Max. 'Ulan fancies himself as our resident comedian. If it were not for his remarkable flying skills he would have been cashiered long ago.'

The pilot craned around to look into the rear of the machine. 'All aboard who're coming aboard…close the gate, we have clearance.' A uniformed figure slid the door shut and Ulan spoke to the control tower over the radio. 'Make sure you dozy buggers keep all those gin and tonic celebrity pilots out of my way.'

'Ulan is in the Aviation Research Centre,' Penjo explained, 'there's some friction with the Indian air force pilots. Basically, he's jealous of them.'

'No, Dapon,' Ulan retorted, 'not jealous, frustrated because I'm condemned to fly this piece of shit whilst they ponce around in their Hal Suvs.'

'Pay no attention, Max, we managed to have Ulan transferred from the Garud Commando Force where he was a combat star but otherwise a pain in the arse.'

The helicopter lifted and tilted forward suddenly so that they all had to brace themselves.

'Oh, I'm so sorry, Dapon, our load must be out of balance.'

Penjo just shook his head ruefully. Max smiled to himself. There could not be too much wrong with a unit that included an iconoclastic joker, provided that he proved to be a truly excellent chopper pilot.

*

A light touch on his arm woke him up.

'We're just coming into our base.' Penjo pointed towards an illuminated LZ cut out of a forest of tall trees. Max glanced towards the back of the aircraft where the Gurkhas were peering out of the side windows to catch sight of their destination. The helicopter set down as light as a feather.

'Ladies and gentlemen, you may switch on your mobile phones now,' Ulan called out. Max clapped him on the shoulder and said, 'Thanks for the ride.'

'Any time, sir.'

The scent of pine filled his nostrils as he jumped down and he guessed the temperature must be about 10° as a gust of cold air blew out of the tree line. Penjo led them away along a broad, well used track that ran at 90° to the LZ. Some uniformed figures materialised out of the darkness and the Dapon gave instructions, pointing at the members of Max's party.

'We'll get you all into your respective billets and then I suggest we meet in the Command Mess at...,' he paused, looking at his watch, '...22.15 for a nightcap and a bite to eat. The rest of the directing staff will be there.'

Penjo led Max to a neat wooden building about the size of a small cottage, set back in a clearing amongst the trees. A control panel was set into the door. 'You can set your own code, it's on 1234A now.' The door opened directly into a comfortable sitting area with two armchairs identical to British army officers' mess furniture, arranged in front of a small fireplace set into the right-hand wall with a small stack of logs beside it.

The Tibetan pointed to the door at the back of the room. 'Bedroom and bathroom. I apologise for the lack of a minibar.' He grinned, closed the front door, switched on a lamp between the armchairs and indicated for Max to sit down.

'I hope you will forgive me, Max, but I have done my homework on you,' Penjo began. 'You have, if I may say so, impeccable credentials in the exiled Tibetan community. Before he died, Hugh Richardson had commended you to us and we were delighted to learn that you would be posted here.' He frowned and took in a long breath before continuing, 'Our unit is quite separate from the rest of the 22s. We are a clandestine organisation whose principal role is infiltration into Tibet in both an intelligence gathering role and providing support to the resistance movement.' Penjo glanced towards the window. 'I don't want to sound ungrateful. The Indians have been outstanding hosts, we would be bereft without their assistance.' He paused and compressed his lips for a moment. 'But candidly, we never know from one day to the next what their attitude is going to be.' He paused again as if changing his mind about whether to go on. Max saw sudden definition in his eyes. 'When the 22s were first formed, it was expressly to train our people to return to Tibet, run guerrilla operations against the Chinese,' Penjo said. 'Using Mustang as the base in Nepal, we were airdropped in and achieved some success. Then we were given more sophisticated tasks, planting monitoring devices to feed information back to the Indians to help them keep abreast of Chinese nuclear and communications advances.' He gave a little dismissive shake of his head. 'But I think you know all this.'

Max nodded and picked up the thread of the narrative, 'You provided the resistance that enabled your people to hope against hope that the Chinese could be driven out. Forgive me for saying it but I thought it had much more psychological than military value.'

Penjo gave him a rueful smile, 'So did the Indians, until we were deployed during the war that led to the creation of Bangladesh. Though we were never given public recognition for our contribution, India did acknowledge our utility and we were put on a more conventional footing. That's also when they started to second Indian Army personnel into the 22s. The Gurkhas, Garhwalis and Kumaonis blended in easily but not so the non-hill soldiers.' He grimaced uncomfortably. 'There are still some tensions, even though we have learned to work together over time, after a fashion.'

'Surely there was no plan to send Indian nationals into Tibet?'

'That was what I kept asking but getting no definite answers. You have to remember that we were the bright idea of our founder. Then when some influential politicians regarded it as politically dangerous to offend Beijing, suddenly we were surplus to requirement.'

'So bringing in the racial mix was to give the 22s a more conventional role as counterterrorism special forces?'

'That's how I interpreted it, until we acquired our new special secretary, Narayan Mullick. He rebuilt the Special Frontier Force for cross-border penetration. That's why the SFF is exclusively composed of our people.' He shot a quick uncomfortable glance at the window before continuing, 'This may sound ungrateful…' Max shook his head encouraging the Tibetan to continue. 'The Americans have been generous, providing us with weapons, money, training…' Penjo broke off, shaking his head before adding, 'but we have lost too many.' He left the sentence hanging in mid-air. Max let the various reasons for attributing these losses to the Americans run through his head.

'You think they are responsible in some way?'

Penjo shook his head slowly and said, 'I cannot put my finger on it but morale is low, as though the next mission will be another disaster.'

The idea that the CIA would deliberately send people to their death had to be dismissed out of hand and yet, just suppose that they wanted a way to cut their losses without losing face? No, he could not accept such duplicity. So, what was causing a loss of morale? Everything he knew about the Tibetan resistance fighters argued for an unwavering determination to regain their country, their religion, no matter what the odds.

'That was the idea behind bringing your team in,' Penjo said. 'The training regime, somehow it is bringing our differences to the fore instead of binding us together, you will see for yourself.'

'It was my idea,' he continued. 'I confided in General Chaudhari, the CDS, pointing out that the British had a unique achievement with the Brigade of Gurkhas, perhaps we could build the SFF through this philosophy. The general jumped at the idea and persuaded a reluctant prime minister.' Penjo gave a little grin before adding, 'I also recommended that they ask for you.'

'I'm flattered.'

'We have to have someone who understands our philosophy, our history, our culture.' The Tibetan became pensive. 'Fernandes, he is the RAW's director of this operation, he does not...,' he paused, searching for a word, 'empathise with us. Don't misunderstand me, he's extremely intelligent, but...' He opened his hands expansively. 'You will see.'

'I think you give me too much credit.'

'No.' Penjo stabbed the air with his finger. 'You will see, you will understand.' He paused, thinking, then suddenly looked as though he had made up his mind. 'But there is more. The hard truth is that Colonel Durwachter is unpopular, very, extremely unpopular. I have caught snatches of conversations.' He compressed his lips and shook his head. Max sensed that he could interpret the body language.

'You have a *geshe* amongst your people?' Penjo nodded. Max said softly, 'He's put a curse on the American?'

'I think so.' Penjo had laced his fingers tightly together. 'Some of our people are *Bon-pa*.' This came as no surprise to Max. The old shamanic ways were deeply rooted. He smiled, 'I doubt the good colonel would lose any sleep, even if he knew. It really only works on those who believe.'

'True, but what if they become impatient, we have a complete range of weaponry and...' Penjo held his hands in a gesture of despair. That, Max was forced to concede, would alter the odds. Even if they kept the strictest control over the armoury and ammunition, all it would take would be one determined man with a knife and all of them would have at least one or more knives. The quandary was that informing the American risked the CIA pulling the plug on the entire enterprise. But if the Ranger was not warned, his life was at stake. On the other hand, sending the *geshe* away would only aggravate the problem and there was bound to be more than one of them.

'I think you have to take the company commanders into your confidence,' Max advised. 'Be up front with them, tell them that you know about the opposition. 'Let them spread the message, if anything happens to Durwachter, the unit will be disbanded. Reassure them that our team will be reviewing the training regime.'

Even as he spoke Max knew that he was taking a chance by committing himself to a new broom approach before he had even set foot on the ground. Worse still, on the face of it he was accepting that there was something wrong with Durwachter's style. He also admitted to himself that his reaction was arrogant. He shrugged his shoulders mentally, if his years working with and learning from the inhabitants of the high Himalayas had not equipped him for the job, the chances of someone without any such background making a pig's arse of it had to be higher. He knew rather than assumed that he could do a better job, but that did not mean he would.

'I need time to feel out the situation and try to shift their focus.'

The worry lines on Penjo's face eased fractionally. 'I appreciate this, truly.' The Tibetan allowed himself a wry smile, 'It was such a relief when I heard that you would be coming.' He frowned and added, 'I realise that this is a far greater responsibility than you were led to believe.'

'I hope I can justify your confidence.'

The grim expression re-occupied the Tibetan's face. 'I must also tell you that on top of our internal problems, suddenly two days ago the government imposed a ban on us getting within 10 kilometres of the Chinese border,' Penjo said. 'Ordinarily I would have been frustrated but I welcome this break, it comes at the most appropriate time, coinciding with your arrival.' He smiled grimly.

Max was not sure where all this was going, the secondment was starting to look like a series of bridges too far, way beyond what he had anticipated. No one had informed him about the ban before he left the UK.

'Could this be an internal Indian Army issue? Someone jealous of General Chaudhari? As secretary for RAW, Mullick presumably still has a seat in the cabinet secretariat?'

'Oh yes, and he's very much onside,' Penjo said. 'It's true that previously the Indian Army would have liked to see us disbanded.'

'Regular armies have a long history of conflict with any form of special forces,' Max smiled. 'It's the conventional mind running up against the unconventional. But you have General Chaudhari on your side, don't you?'

'Yes, but…we, I mean the Tibetans in exile, have our own sources and they tell us that there is a power struggle in the cabinet. Way above my pay scale.' Penjo looked at his watch. 'I think we'd better get along to the mess but I had to brief you on the politics before you met the others. I should also mention that Herman wants to meet you in the mess at 06.00 tomorrow morning.'

Devlin got to his feet. 'He won't be there tonight?' Penjo shook his head. 'OK. That's my problem,' Max said. 'My instinct is to tackle the morale problem first, deal with what is within our control. We can do little about the politicians.' Penjo seized his hand with both his and shook it. 'Thank you.'

Max gestured towards the door. 'Please go ahead, I'll just wash my face and follow on.' Penjo stood up. 'Turn left out of here and just follow the track, you can't miss it.'

Left alone, Max reflected on what he had got himself into. First there had been Chalmers's diplomatic etching of the Indian politics. Then the very useful, but no less disturbing data that Colonel Denning's Indian civil service contacts had gathered for him and now that he was on the ground he had learned the real motive behind his secondment. Had there been a breakdown in the train of communications? It was inconceivable that SIS were unaware of the personnel problems on the ground, so what purpose was served in leaving him in ignorance? Surely, Fernandes would have communicated this to Mullick? Ostensibly, the British team had been put together to train the SFF for clandestine cross-border operations but according to Penjo these had been ruled out now. Most disturbing of all was the morale issue and the animosity to the CIA's man on the ground. All of a sudden, the Chinese seemed less of a problem than the setup in India, let alone those to whom he was responsible in London.

Kipling's lines ran through his head: '*But when it comes to guns and slaughter. You will do your work on water. An' you'll lick the bloomin' boots of 'im that's got it.*'

Was the whole game worth the candle?

*

All the heads turned towards him as Max entered the mess. The tension was palpable, a mix of curiosity and apprehension floating on a bed of dissatisfaction or was it suppressed anger? It was not difficult to identify the major players in the room. The only Indian face presumably belonged to the camp commandant, Major Jha. Apart from Penjo there were five ethnic Tibetans. One, he noted, was a strikingly attractive woman. She had the classic aristocratic diamond-shaped face, deep dark eyes set in a pale skin, her hair braided and worn in a circle like a tiara. A voice broke into his thoughts.

'Colonel Devlin, may I call you Max, I'm Manek Jha.' Of average height, his dark hair brushed back severely from his forehead and the almost obligatory clipped military moustache, Jha was the epitome of a career Indian Army officer. His handshake was firm and his dark brown eyes held Max's steadily.

'Please do.'

'You've met Brigadier Penjo, of course.' There was the slightest pause before he continued, 'Colonel Durwachter has asked if you would meet him here at 06.00 tomorrow morning.'

'I look forward to meeting him.'

A young Tibetan came up beside them and made a formal greeting, hands steepled together in front of him before sticking his hand out to Max. '*Keh-rahng ku-su de-boy yin-peh?*'

'I'm fine and privileged to be here,' Max replied in Tibetan, watching the young man's face light up.

'We were told that you spoke our tongue but not that you are so fluent,' the Tibetan said, holding himself momentarily to attention. 'Lobsang Gyaltsen, sir, unit intelligence officer. May I offer you a drink?'

Max looked around to see whether there was a bar and saw two racks of spirits behind a countertop. 'I'd appreciate a glass of Black Dog Centenary, no ice, but I think we had better speak in English for the benefit of the Major.'

Lobsang's face lit up. 'You know it, sir?'

'Indeed.'

Jha smiled at Lobsang. 'If we can't supply Max with a good Irish whisky, I'm betting he'll stick to the Black Dog,' he said. 'The undiluted spirit is blended and matured in Scotland but bottled in India to avoid the scandalous duty.'

Max quartered the room searching for the Gurkhas, noting that they were already in conversation with the Tibetans. He turned towards Jha and said, 'Thank you for looking after my people.'

'It's my privilege. My father was a Rajputana rifleman. I, to his enormous annoyance, went into the engineers.'

'Always a home for the brightest.'

'Hmm, there are exceptions,' the Indian smiled.

Max walked across to the knot of Tibetans and Gurkhas. Prabhat, his signals expert, made the introductions, allowing Max time to get his first impressions.

'This is Pema, she's one of the four company commanders.' Almost a foot shorter and of slim build, nonetheless she conveyed an air of authority as she gave an almost imperceptible nod of her head, her expression formal but her eyes penetrating. The men all wore the full length *chuba* with its high mandarin collar whilst she was dressed in a traditional brocade *bhaku* and silk *hongchu*. She addressed Max in Tibetan, 'We welcome you, sir, and we look forward to the changes you will bring.' He smiled to himself, he had forgotten how direct these people could be. No messing about here. She intended to impress, and she had.

'This is a big change for me. I'm accustomed to these rogues,' Max said, waving his hand towards the Gurkhas, sparking laughter from all of them except Pema. Anxious not to get into a heavy discussion at this stage he thanked her for the welcome, looking around so as to include them all but she continued to address him, 'You speak like a highly educated Tibetan.'

'You are kind but it is thanks to my teacher.'

Lobsang handed him a glass and gestured to an older man whose dark brown face was deeply lined. 'Norbu is our most distinguished fighter, he's from Kham. He commanded the last cross-border op onto the Siachen Glacier.' They assessed each other, the Tibetan making a formal little bow.

'When was that?' Max asked Norbu directly.

'Two years ago, *Kushog-saheb*.' Addressing him as the headman was a nice touch, welcome to Max's ears.

'We must talk,' he nodded acknowledgement and turned to the next man.

'This is Jhampa, he's from Ladakh.' The eyes that stared at him out of a deeply sunburned face held not a trace of warmth and the greeting was as close to minimal as consistent with necessary formality.

Max spoke first. 'I have trekked up the Stok Kangri, the view is magnificent.' Jhampa's eyebrows twitched. 'You are a climber?'

'No,' Max gave a rueful smile. 'Not so skilled. I prefer to trek the mountains to find peace.' This earned him a grunt of reluctant approval, the eyes blinked.

'So, you are a mountain man…Kushog-saheb.' That Jhampa followed Norbu in according him this status was a step in the right direction, even if it had been hesitant.

'Finally, I would like you to meet Paljor.' Tall, with striking features, it was the crow's eyes that Max noted immediately, as well as the broad smile, the deep bow and the firm handshake.

'We are most happy meeting you, sir.' Paljor spoke English with an Indian accent. 'I went to school at St. Augustine's in Kalimpong.'

'Would the holy fathers approve of your career?' Max asked.

'Well, they were always talking about forgiveness, so I suppose it doesn't matter.' They both laughed.

Max reverted to Tibetan, 'Please.' He raised his glass in a toast and they drank, except Pema. He raised an interrogatory eyebrow. 'You don't drink, Pema?' She gave a snort of disapproval. 'I can drink these men under the table, if I wish.' The men roared in protest which lit the tiniest of smiles on her face.

'Unfortunately, true.' Penjo had caught her words as he joined them.

A shaft of a smile lit her face for a second as she turned towards Penjo to say, 'I have an 04.00 start, Dapon-saheb, my company starts a three-day endurance exercise. Have I your permission to leave now?' Penjo gave Pema a cheerful wave which she acknowledged by straightening her shoulders. As she turned away, she caught Max's eye. 'Good night… Kushog-saheb.' He was amused that she appeared to have accepted his designation as reluctantly as Jhampa. 'Good luck.' She gave him that almost imperceptible nod of the head, turned and left.

Max looked at his watch, then at Penjo. 'I think the rest of us have an early start tomorrow. I'm turning in.' He raised his glass in a salute to all of them, bid them goodnight and walked back through the trees to his cottage.

The wind blew fitfully through the branches and the musty scent of the moss-covered ground rose to meet the flat musk of the pines overhead. He sucked it in, content to be in countryside with which he was familiar. The welcome had been friendly enough if a bit formal. But in addition to the undercurrents to which Penjo had referred, he detected contained animosities amongst the company commanders. It was a pity that Pema would be away for a few days, it would make it that much more difficult to assess the situation.

He put considerable weight on his ability to judge people from a first impression. Both the way she carried herself and her speech marked her out as educated and accustomed to commanding, he would need to find the key to gaining her confidence. She was the most difficult to read. He suspected that this was something that she had deliberately cultivated.

Paljor and Lobsang were both well-educated, he anticipated that this was atypical of the majority. Norbu and Jhampa were the most enigmatic. Jhampa's attitude bordered on insubordination but he had touched a chord with him over the mountains, it was too soon to reach a conclusion about him. As a Ladakhi he would be something of an outsider, the others were all Tibetan born. Jhampa's reserve could well be his defence to what he perceived as discrimination by them. The fact that he had been given command of a company was evidence of his abilities, but it was Norbu that they most respected, commander of the most recent operation into Tibet. The Khamba would be a natural guerrilla fighter. The nomads had provided the escort to the Dalai Lama when he had escaped Tibet in 1959. They represented the Tibetan way of life that was most imperilled by the Chinese invasion, wild herders accustomed to wandering the vast steppe, subject to no secular authority and though they owed nominal religious allegiance to the Dalai Lama. Many of them followed the old *Bön* ways. If it was true what Penjo had told him about a curse on Durwachter, Norbu would almost certainly know who the *shaman* was and might even have ordered it. Though he had appeared friendly, according him the title of 'Kushog' could even be a ruse to lull him into a false sense of being accepted.

He stood still and shook his head, sucking in the heavy scented night air as he took a long look up into the darkness of the forest canopy before entering his cabin. Tomorrow would present him with a fuller picture. He stripped off, took a quick shower and was asleep within a minute or two of his head touching the pillow, Pema's face evaporating with his consciousness.

SFF Training Camp
Baniyana Forest

It was still dark when his body clock woke him at 05.00. It was reassuring that despite the changes in time zones, he could still set the time to wake up in his mind. Washed and shaved he was back in the mess by 05.30.

A buzz cut hairstyle that could only have been Herman Durwachter stood up at a table in the corner most distant from the entrance door and waved him over. The room was rectangular in shape with the bar across the rear wall. A door to the left of the bar obviously led to the kitchen but save for the two of them, none of the other members of the unit was there. They helped themselves from a silver-plated coffee pot and a mess orderly took their orders for food. Max decided on a chilli herb omelette and Herman two fried eggs on bread.

They settled themselves facing each other. The American leaned forward, elbows on the table. 'Started out as a Navy Seal but got recommissioned as a Ranger, made me as popular as AIDS with the navy,' he grimaced. 'But I've had my share of covert ops, which is probably why I was detailed for this outfit.'

Max listened appreciatively.

'Langley has its own teams of black ops people, any of which could be doing my job. But my take is that the CIA is nervous about working in India. They don't want to carry the can if the whole damn thing turns sour. Had their fingers burned here in '71 and pulled out of supporting the Tibetans. Seems they up an' changed their minds when the Pakistanis got too close to the Taliban, want to cosy up to the Indians and the Indians want to know what the Chinese are doin'. Guess that's where we come in. The Pentagon likes to have some skin in the game and so it finished up as a joint Army-CIA operation. My minder's stationed in Delhi.' Durwachter wore a tired smile. 'Suits me just fine. Keeps the civilians off my back.' He took a long sip of his coffee.

Max nodded. The file he had been given to read in London recorded that SIS had been involved in the early training camp set up for what was then the Indo-Tibetan Frontier Force and staffed it with ex-army instructors. The CIA had been involved in the Khamba guerrilla operations based in Nepal. As far as he was aware, in those days both the British and American personnel had been ex-military employed by their respective intelligence services. Seconding serving officers broke with the previous practice.

'I can guess at the internal UK politics behind our involvement, much the same as yours I suspect,' Max said, 'but I'm just a soldier, following orders.'

'Yeah,' the American wore his disbelief. 'OK. Now, here on the ground I smell more politics.' He wrinkled his nose and said, 'I guess you know the 22s are based at Chakrata which is where their command headquarters are situated. But we're here in the Baniyana Forest with a bunch of Tibetans organised in two columns each of two companies. Our task is to train them so that we can infiltrate them back into Tibet where they will supply the Indians…and us I guess…with current information on the PLA's activities in Tibet, their preparations for invading India and especially in relation to their siting of nuclear missile silos.' He took a long pull at his coffee. Screwing up his eyes, he asked, 'D'you know about the missing nuclear detection device?'

Max nodded. In his briefing papers in London there had been a detailed account of how a team of 22s had infiltrated into Tibet, planted a device to monitor nuclear activities but when they had gone to retrieve it, the device was missing. The best explanation seemed to be that it had been lodged in an ice crevice, but the ice had melted, and the device had fallen into a deep crevasse. The alternative was that the PLA had discovered it. The equipment itself had been cobbled together from parts drawn from different sources so that its origin would be untraceable, but the PLA would have known that the most likely personnel to have been involved in locating it in the first place would have been SFF members.

Max's instructions were that the intelligence and security committee of the Indian Parliament wanted to place more of these devices, but the prime minister had vetoed the proposal because of sensitive relations with Beijing.

The American tapped the table with his knife. 'The Indian government has a bunch of cockamamie politicos who don't know their asses from their elbows. They've got some young guys who think that everything can be done by monitoring communications and interpreting satellite data. But Narayan Mullick, the top honcho at the RAW wants to get his guys in and out of Tibet to supply reliable HUMINT. Right now, he's under a prohibition against any of the SFF being within 10K of the Tibet border. Don't know who christened them "The Mavericks" but it don't help us.' Durwachter dropped his voice as the mess orderly brought out their breakfasts. Max waited for the man to get back to the kitchen.

'So, our work is dependent on a political change of mind?'

'You betcha.'

'What about the people we have under training, what's their quality?'

Herman rolled his eyes up. 'They're good I guess but Jesus, they're goddamn stubborn and…,' he looked around quickly, screwed his face up before adding, 'They smell.' Max laughed.

'We call it *foetor tibeticus*.'

'That some Tibetan phrase for a goddamn stink?'

Max shook his head. 'It's Latin, a sort of academic joke. Their concept of hygiene is governed by their environment. When you live in temperatures of minus 40° maintaining bodily warmth is more important than our deodorant society and they're not aware of it because they all smell the same.'

'Yeah, but we're not in Tibet here.'

'True but once they go back, they'll need the camouflage of that body odour; otherwise, they'd stick out like Chanel No.5.' Max changed direction. 'How many of them have done a cross-border op?'

'All of them,' Durwachter scowled. 'Even the women.'

'You disapprove?'

'They screw up guys in a fight. First thing they do is protect the fuckin' women instead of stayin' focused on themselves an' their buddies.'

'So, the women aren't their buddies?'

The Ranger gave Max a look of disgust. 'It's not the same.'

Once upon a time he had shared that opinion but experience had taught him better. 'You know, in my experience, Tibetans don't distinguish between men and women except when it comes to sex.' He leaned forward and asked, 'Have you seen any examples of this over-protectiveness in any training situation?'

'Don't have to, it's just natural,' the American grimaced. 'And that Pema, she's such an arrogant bitch...always looks at me like I'm some sorta low life.'

Max smiled, 'Maybe she feels that's the way you think about her.' Durwachter clicked his tongue dismissively. Max pressed on. 'Does she bring her team back in one piece after an op?' The Ranger grunted in frustration, 'The only one who does.'

'Well?'

Shaking his head despondently, Herman said, 'It just ain't right and I think she's undermining my authority with the rest of them.'

'But you and I don't really have any authority, we're here to counsel and train,' Max reminded his American counterpart.

'Goddamn, you know what I mean.' Durwachter glared at him. Max began to sense where the trouble lay. Time to change the topic. 'What's the total active strength?' The Ranger paused, disinclined to shift from his chosen subject. 'Oh yeah. Well, originally there were nearly 200 of them but 32 never made it back from previous missions. We think the last ones were ambushed on their way over the final pass.

'Nobody says anything but I get the idea that the ones who didn't make it deliberately sacrificed themselves for the others,' he continued. 'The PLA would have got all of them if they'd been able to use helicopters but Norbu, he's the ugly one, says that they were only border troops.'

'And the survivors are looking for pay back?'

'You're goddamn right, 'cept that's not what we're training them for.'

Max thought for a moment before delivering what, in reality, was advice. There was no point in getting off on the wrong foot with the man.

'Isn't the trick for us to channel that energy?'

'Hmm.' Durwachter pulled a face. Max decided not to disclose that he had dealt with Tibetan guerrillas before in case the American read it the wrong way.

'I expect that we'll be able to turn them around, together.' Max looked across the empty room. The functional furniture bore all the signs of its colonial heritage but it contrasted with framed photographs of the Dalai Lama and the Potala Palace. What drew the eye was a magnificent *thangka* depicting avenging furies, the strident reds, yellows and blues of the figures set against the border of crudely drawn skulls. Nodding towards it, he said, 'It captures so much of their character, doesn't it?'

Durwachter glanced at the painting, then shook his head. 'I'm just a Presbyterian country boy, don't go for all that hocus-pocus.' Max studied the pale blue eyes in the tanned face. The man's mindset was a barrier against understanding the people he was charged with training. Time to change the subject again.

'What do you make of Lobsang?'

'He's Penjo's XO as well as feeding us with the latest intel out of Tibet,' Durwachter said. He speared some egg and bread on his fork, then raised his knife, waving it like a wand. 'Guy was born in India, got a degree and graduated from Dehra Dun, the Indians' idea of West Point. He's got brains, I give you.' This was said in a way that indicated the American's low regard for any military ability before he added, 'The others only accept him because of Penjo.' Lifting up the egg and toast, he went on, 'He translates for me, but I don't know how accurate he is, sometimes they smile or laugh in the wrong places.' The more he heard, the more Max grasped the gulf between the American and the people he was supposed to be communicating with. At moments like this he wondered whether some lunatic had deliberately chosen Durwachter for the post in order to sabotage the project.

Max looked at his watch and said, 'We're scheduled for a directing staff meeting in Manek's office at 07.30. What do you make of him?'

'Manek? He's probably a good engineer but he knows zilch about special ops. So far he's kept out of our hair. He reports directly to Chakrata, but it's a guy from Delhi, Fernandes, who runs the show.'

'Francis Fernandes?'

'Yeah, I think that's his name, very smooth dude, talks more like an Englishman than an Indian.'

'Not like me?' Max grinned.

'Hell no, sounds more like one of those old-style movie actors, you know, John Barrymore. Calls himself Freddie,' Durwachter said, standing up. 'Better move out.'

*

They turned left out of the mess and walked beneath an overhead canopy of pine branches through which the early morning sun had not yet penetrated. The familiar scent of the morning dew on the pine leaves was a comforting counterpoint to the troubled world into which he was stepping. A wooden signpost beside the path pointed to the Regional Forestry Office.

'Is that where we're headed?' Max asked.

Herman grunted agreement, 'The cover for this whole operation is that this is a forestry research project. There used to be a whole lot of deforestation in this region until the state government got tough on the illegal loggers and started shooting them. Now only the real desperate risk getting their ass shot off for some firewood. Works real good for keeping local folks' noses out of our business.'

Max had wondered how they maintained a secure perimeter. He reflected that until the Anglo-Nepal war of 1813, all of what was now Uttarakhand right up to the eastern border of Kashmir had been part of Nepal. Even now the majority of indigenous inhabitants were Garhwalis and Kumaonis, ethnically the same as the Gurungs and Magars of western Nepal and their geography was virtually identical too.

They emerged into a clearing the size of a football pitch with a functional-looking single storey box-shaped building set against the treeline. Four wooden steps led up to an open veranda which gave onto doors and windows spaced at equal intervals along its length. Herman loped up the stairs and pushed open the main door. They entered an office in which several clerks were already at their desks. Nodding a silent greeting which he was pleased to note they responded to by sitting to attention, he followed Herman into what was obviously a conference room.

'Gentlemen,' Major Jha said as he stood up from his seat to the left of Penjo, who sat at the head of a rectangular table. He indicated the vacant seats on either side of them. Max took his seat. Durwachter sat between Penjo and Lobsang. The three Tibetan officers occupied seats on each side and the three Gurkhas sat next to each other at the far end of the table.

'My role is purely administrative, so I'll not detain you long before handing over to Dapon Penjo,' the camp commandant began. 'As far as the public is aware, this is a top security forestry research facility.

'We occupy about eight square miles of forest, designed to provide maximum secrecy,' Jha continued. 'In order to maintain that secrecy, there is no live firing permitted within this area. All live firing has to be carried out in the Alpine training area north of Munsyari.' The major delivered his instructions in a clipped tone of speech, holding himself erect in his seat. 'Though camouflage overalls are worn in camp, no badges of rank or other identification is permitted,' he added. Giving a little passing gesture with his hand, he continued, 'We get visitors from time to time, you understand. When you go off site, it is essential that you do not wear any items of uniform, anything that would indicate that you are military personnel. As Herman knows, this is particularly important for you, gentlemen.' He looked at Max. 'The presence of foreign military in this region would excite unhealthy interest,' Jha said. 'If anyone inquires what you are doing, just tell them that you are forestry consultants with an NGO.'

He then turned to face the Gurkhas at the far end of the table. 'No visitors of any nature may be brought onto the camp site.' Max caught Deepraj's eye and shook his head. Whether or not Jha had intended to make a special point with regard to the Gurkhas, Max was well aware of Deepraj's reputation, having had to get him out of woman trouble a couple of times when they had served in 22nd SAS together. Out of the corner of his eye he saw Lobsang suppressing a grin. He would have to keep those two apart.

'We have a medical station located in a building 100 metres west of here,' the camp commandant said. 'It's manned by a paramedic for minor injuries. Anything more important, we have a dedicated Indian Army trauma surgeon on call from Chakrata.' Max raised his hand. Jha paused.

'Delay between call and attention?'

'Urgent calls, between 30 to 40 minutes. A chopper is on standby.'

'Friend Ulan?' Max smiled.

'No, Max, we bypass the ARC for medical emergencies, there's an IAF Chinook on standby on the Chakrata pad.' With a little self-satisfied smile, the major continued, 'We have a small motor transport pool and our drivers will act on your instructions.' And report our activities back to you, no doubt, Max mused.

'All communications both outward and inbound must be encrypted. Please familiarise yourselves with the encryption codes that have been provided for your personal mobiles.' He turned to Max. 'The support staff are carefully screened 22s who have volunteered to provide us with cooks, waiters and so on, but I must ask you to bear in mind that they are serving military personnel, not hotel staff.' He looked around at everyone, then continued, 'I do not need to remind you that this is a covert operation and conversations should be guarded in the presence of non-operational personnel.'

He turned to Penjo. 'Have I omitted anything, Dapon?' Penjo shook his head. 'Nothing, thank you.'

The camp commandant stood up. 'I'll take my leave, gentlemen.' The Tibetans and the Gurkhas stood up but Jha waved everyone back into their seats and left the room.

Penjo pulled his chair a little closer to the table and turned to face Max. 'I apologise for Pema's absence. Her company's exercise has taken time to plan. I instructed her to leave with them early this morning. You will have time to get to know her.' Max heard Herman's barely audible grunt.

'Lobsang will take Prabhat to our communications hut and introduce him to the permanent signal staff. We have a direct feed from the National Technical Research Organisation's station at Chakrata.'

Placing his hands flat on the tabletop, Penjo scanned all the faces. 'Any questions, gentlemen?' Heads shook. He continued, speaking to Max and the Gurkhas, 'As I think you know, our unit is divided into two columns, each of two companies, I appointed the company commanders.' He nodded towards the Tibetans. 'I propose that we stick with these teams until we've had time to review the situation in the light of our most recent losses.'

Durwachter lifted his hand to signal that he wanted to speak. Penjo nodded in his direction. 'Now that Max is here, I'd like to suggest that we each supervise one of the columns; get some friendly competition,' the American said. Max would have preferred joint supervision but now was not the time to disagree, he nodded.

Penjo looked down the table at the Gurkhas. 'I hope you will find our people up to your high standards.' They smiled back at him. Turning to face Max, the Dapon continued, 'We can work on the programme. Fernandes will want to see it.'

Indian Cabinet Secretariat
New Delhi

U nder the pretence of organising his papers, prime minister Arvind Kaur observed his closest political colleagues. Major-General Narayan Mullick, the new special secretary of the Research and Analysis Wing, was listening intently to defence minister Dilconda whose voice was too soft for him to hear. The Chief was obviously still feeling his way in the RAW and had been dropped in the deep end with the current cabinet dispute over Tibet. The PM had no doubt that the Rajkumar, as Dilconda was referred to behind his back, was bending Mullick's ear to the military's position. The long-standing rivalry between the army and the external intelligence bureau had only been partially resolved by appointing a major-general as its operational head and Kaur hoped that the defence minister could persuade the intelligence chief to adopt a neutral stance. It was one of those occasions when, ironically, the PM welcomed Dilconda's arrogant aloofness. The princely states had been absorbed into the union and their hereditary rulers officially deprived of their titles; but they continued to use them and they still impressed the general public. But, he mused, Mullick was far from being typical of the general public.

'Shall we start, Prime Minister?'

Amitab Roy, minister for external affairs, lifted his voice above the level of conversation. He had insisted on this meeting knowing that the recent election results in Uttar Pradesh had shaken the PM's authority. Bloody Bengali, always ready to undermine the premier, secure in the knowledge that the Americans and Europeans regarded him as the most skilful diplomat in Asia. Kaur could not afford to sack him.

'Certainly, *Bhaia*,' he said, giving Roy his best prime ministerial smile. 'Please speak to your proposal.'

The foreign minister looked across the table at the other members of this inner cabinet. He knew that he could count on home minister Sakhrani but that arrogant prick Dilconda would vote with the PM, even though he was supposed to represent the army's interests. The unknown quantity was Mullick. As a relative novice, it was highly unlikely that he would oppose the PM who had been voted in on the promise of better relations with their country's two great enemies, Pakistan and China. Still, he reflected, recent border incidents involving both countries had hardened attitudes to their neighbours and he intended to capitalise on this change.

'*Pradhan Mentri-ji*, we dealt with the Pakistani inspired events in Kashmir in our last meeting,' Roy began, smiling at Dilconda. 'Additional military units were rapidly deployed to aid the paramilitary and police and the first results proved the wisdom of aggressive response. The ISI have been given a bloody nose and will have to reconsider their tactics.' His expression changed as he removed a clip of aerial photographs from his file and handed them round the table. Pointing to the top photograph, he said, 'These are the most recent images from our own satellite and underneath...are photographs supplied to us by Washington. This is road building equipment in the disputed border area next to Bhutan.'

Roy tapped the photos. His long fingernail made the PM want to tell him to trim his nails. He pulled out a second batch of photographic images which he distributed as though dealing cards. 'Now, look at these, taken over the Siachen Glacier, the white line marks the border with Arunachal Pradesh and shows that the Chinese have occupied a significant tract of our country.' The foreign minister looked up, the dark boyish features angry.

Kaur gave a dismissive wave of his hand. 'Yes, but this adds little to what we know about the Chinese and their intentions.' There was a gleam in Roy's eye which ought to have told the PM that he had miscalculated.

'Precisely. This is why we need to gather intelligence on the ground in Tibet.'

The PM shook his head. 'I have been working to achieve a *modus vivendi* with Beijing…'

'You call this a modus vivendi?' Roy's rigid finger stabbed at the images, not even concealing the sarcasm.

Kaur was weary of this infighting and deeply frustrated that his overtures to the Chinese leader and his reassurances all seemed to be lying in dust on the floor. He was forced to concede that Roy had a point but sending bodies into Tibet was brinkmanship that they really were not in a position to risk. It had been his decision to prohibit the incursions by the 22s, anxious to avoid anything that could prejudice the secret negotiations with Beijing.

'Permit me.' A dismissive half-smile on his face, Dilconda's suave tones interrupted. 'The army has its hands full dealing with Pakistan's meddling in Kashmir as well as holding the line on the Siachen Glacier and manning the Chumbi Valley as well as pushing back against the Naga terrorists.'

'We're not talking about the army,' Roy corrected the defence minister. 'Isn't this what the SFF was designed to do?'

'My dear friend,' said Dilconda, whose voice was unctuously condescending, 'but this is what we *would be* talking about if we let loose our tame Tibetans.'

'That's no way to describe them,' Mullick observed quietly.

The PM was both surprised and quietly delighted to discover that the Chief had teeth in the defence of his charges. He raised one hand to signal a pause. 'Tell us, Secretary-ji, if we allow your organisation to mount an intelligence gathering operation in Tibet, what are the chances of the Chinese intercepting them, leaving us with all the political repercussions?'

Softly, Mullick replied, 'Mentri-ji, our worst-case scenario is based on interception and capture. All our personnel are, as Dilconda-ji observed, Tibetans, either refugees or the children of refugees. Their equipment cannot be attributable to the government of India and they are unquestionably Tibetan patriots. The Chinese may well believe that they were launched from our territory but there would be nothing to substantiate that.'

'Are you not forgetting the monitoring devices they will be carrying? They are not *unattributable.*' Dilconda did not attempt to conceal the contempt in his voice.

'No, minister, I am not forgetting this,' Mullick said. 'The devices to which you refer are made in Israel.'

The PM noted Sakhrani's slight change of expression. Was the home minister beginning to come around to Roy's side? He could not help asking himself could one ever trust a Scindi? Even if he could count on Sakhrani, he would still lose the vote if Mullick was in favour of lifting the prohibition. Better to be statesmanlike and yield to the inevitable rather than putting it to a vote. Sighing inwardly, Kaur raised one palm to acknowledge submission. 'On your assurance, Secretary-ji, I think we could consider lifting the absolute ban,' the PM said. Roy's face lit up. Kaur continued, 'But only on the basis that each proposed cross-border operation is sanctioned, individually, by this cabinet after we have had time to study the detailed plan.' The PM rubbed his fingers through his beard, something he had a habit of doing when he had outwitted his opponents. It was not lost on the foreign minister.

'I hope, Mentri-ji, that this is not a delaying tactic, our need for intelligence is urgent,' Roy said.

'Duly noted, Bhaia, which is why I am proposing that we lift the ban for the time being on a case-by-case basis and…,' the PM said, lifting his hand again to prevent interruption, '…subject to our approval.' Roy stared at him for several seconds before nodding acknowledgement.

Kaur looked towards his private secretary hovering in the doorway. 'That is that then. Thank you.' The movement of his head embraced them all as he stood up. They gathered their papers. The PM took hold of Mullick's elbow and eased him away from the table.

'You understand that the minutes will record that you have accepted responsibility should anything go wrong,' he said to the Chief, who met his eyes and held them.

'Is that not what I am here for, Mentri-ji?'

'Just so long as you appreciate it,' the PM said, releasing his elbow, and walked away.

Mullick collected his papers wondering whether it was a pyrrhic victory. He had secured a reprieve for his people but lain the sword across his own neck. Roy came up to him wearing an expression that he could not read, a useful trick in a foreign minister. As at this moment they were allies but he had been a soldier too long in government service to trust a politician.

'Watch your back, this place is a viper's nest,' Roy said, nodding darkly towards Dilconda's retreating. 'Put not your faith in princes.' His expression changed. 'Have the British sent their trainers over?'

'Yes, they've been on site for over two weeks now. We got the people I asked for.'

Roy smiled, 'I think Downing Street hopes to sweeten our disposition towards buying their defence equipment. If the Brits can help to resolve your transatlantic problems diplomatically, they'll certainly earn some salami.' A movement behind Mullick's back attracted Roy's attention. 'I think the CDS wants you. I expect he wants to hear the outcome of the meeting,' he said.

Mullick turned to see the ADC to the chief of defence staff standing awkwardly a few feet away. He signalled that he was coming. 'Your support for my SFF unit is much appreciated, Minister-ji,' he said, giving a little bow before joining the ADC who told him that the CDS was in his staff car downstairs.

They walked in silence out of the building and into the forecourt where General Chaudhari's driver stood with his hand on the rear door of the khaki coloured Pajero.

Mullick got in.

'General-saheb.'

'Narayan bhaia.'

The two men understood each other and dispensed with pleasantries. Mullick reported the cabinet decision, stressing that each operation would require specific approval.

'Dammit man, I don't give a monkey's for their approval. What I want is boots on the ground to tell me what the Chinese are up to in Aksai Chin and with their road building in Doklam. We've been starved of that level of intelligence for two years. Can your people deliver?'

There was no air conditioning in the car and Mullick felt the sweat making his shirt stick to his back. Without the CDS's support, there was a real possibility that the SFF would be disbanded but he did not want to commit his people to something beyond their capacity.

'The SFF unit consists of the very best of the 22s and they are all 100% committed,' Mullick said. 'You remember how many we lost on that last operation.' Chaudhari grunted. 'If it's practicable, we'll do it,' Mullick continued.

'That's all I wanted to hear.'

The CDS sat back in his seat, a smile lifting the ends of his moustaches. 'I imagine the Rajkumar was voicing his opposition, claiming to speak on behalf of the army?' Mullick looked puzzled. 'You must learn how to play these bloody politicians. If you want something really badly, sometimes the best way is to oppose it,' General Chaudhari said, inclining his head forward a little as if inquiring whether he was understood. 'Can I give you a lift?'

'No, thank you, General-saheb, I have some more work here.'

Mullick got out of the car, nodded in response to the ADC's salute and headed back into the building. The transatlantic problem was capable of destroying the SFF from within. He hit a pre-set on his mobile. Fernandes answered on the second ring, 'Chief?'

'It's a go. You can brief Penjo.' Mullick cut the connection as soon as his order was acknowledged.

Fernandes was still adjusting to the new chief. Mullick's predecessor had allowed him very wide discretion in his oversight of the SFF. That had enabled him to decide what and how much information to feed back to Chakrata about its progress. He had marked out his career path, successes were to be chalked up to him, but failures must be laid at others' door. He frowned to himself: on his own, the American did not pose a problem but the Britisher had already embedded himself with the Tibetans which made him a potential problem.

Baniyana Forest

Lifting the ban was the first piece of good news in what had felt like a continuous succession of bad luck over the three weeks since they had arrived. Two broken legs, three bullet wounds and two men discharged on discovering that they had incipient TB. Devlin felt that a sense of futility had pervaded the camp and led to people becoming careless. Dividing them into two competing groups had seemed like a good idea at first but as the days progressed, the sharp differences in the training regimes between his and Durwachter's group began to emerge. Most worrying was the undercurrent of hostility to the American. All the senior staff were gathered for a brain-storming session. Herman sat next to his two company commanders, Norbu and Jhampa.

'Your guys are a bunch of pussies,' the Ranger said. The joking manner failed to convince.

'We'll have to agree to differ on that, Herman.' Max gave him a half-smile, making an inclusive gesture to Pema and Paljor.

'You don't push them nigh hard enough,' Durwachter said.

'We all have our own style.'

Max really did not want to get into an open argument in front of the Gurkhas and the four Tibetan officers. He noticed that Paljor was indicating that he wanted to say something. He shook his head. Both his company commanders were capable and highly competent but utterly different personalities. Where Paljor tended to be impulsive, Pema was measured. He liked both of them and they had quickly followed his training methods. All the Tibetans were firmly committed to liberating their homeland, but their enthusiasm often got the better of their judgment, leading to impatience. The loss of so many of them on the last incursion had dented their morale. He had to restore their confidence and that took time, time they had not permitted themselves. It did not help that Pema had brought her company back intact whereas Norbu and Jhampa had both suffered severe losses. His training system was designed to teach them the value of self-discipline and teamwork. Unlike most conventional soldiers who needed to have someone they feared to give them a sense of unity, these people were unified in their dedication to Tibet. This, he was convinced, was the key to building self-reliant teams of specialists. Both Pema and Paljor had observed Max's relationship with the Gurkhas and tried to emulate it. The mutual respect that grew out of this was what distinguished his group from Durwachter's.

'When we get the go-ahead, I guess we'll have to select the guys we send in,' the American frowned. 'Judging by the performance data, I'll give you that generally your guys outscore mine, but my bucks are on my guys to handle stuff when the shit hits the fan.'

Max did not give in to the temptation to point out that none of the broken limbs and bullet wounds had occurred in his group. The Ranger pushed back his forage cap and said, 'What say we shuffle the deck a mite, you take some of mine and I yours?'

'Good idea, for later,' Max responded. 'Let's allow them to go on building their teams and then do some whole team swaps.' He felt that the unity that he had built up in his group needed to be allowed to develop further and that the different styles could interrupt that process.

Durwachter's eyebrows shot up momentarily, then he gave a flick of his head. 'Yeah, I guess that wraps it up for this week.' He gave a loose salute towards the Gurkhas and said, 'Thanks guys, great job.' They smiled in response. The American turned to Max. 'They're so goddamn regimental!' He shook his head resignedly and walked away from the forest clearing that they had commandeered as their debriefing area.

'I'd like to give my teams this weekend off,' Max told the company commanders. 'What do you think?' The four looked at each other and smiled. Paljor's face beamed. Despite Durwachter's criticism, Max had driven his teams hard, testing their resilience and watching for weak links. They had earned a 48-hour break. The American's teams probably needed it even more.

'Tell Herman I'm giving my people a weekend pass,' he said to Norbu and Jhampa, 'and suggest that you all get one too.'

Norbu grinned. Jhampa's facial expression did not change and pointing at Norbu, he said, 'You tell him.' Norbu shrugged his shoulders and loped after Durwachter.

Max raised a quizzical eyebrow. 'He listens to him,' Jhampa said.

'Not to you?'

Jhampa shook his head resignedly. Max nodded understanding. Now was not the time to explore these relationships. He turned to the Gurkhas.

'I'm going to Mussoorie tonight, back on Sunday evening,' he said. 'If any of you want a lift, I've commandeered a vehicle.'

Prabhat glanced at Kesarsing.

'The Dapon-saheb has invited us to go hunting with him,' Kesarsing said. 'We'll accept if it's still on.'

'Great,' Max said, looking at Deepraj who grinned, '*Huzoor.*'

'On your best behaviour,' Max said. They all laughed.

*

Deepraj was a first-class driver and totally at home on the series of hairpin bends that contoured the hill roads. They drove in silence for a while then Max decided to quiz the Gurkha on the rumour of the curse.

'I hear they have one or two *kalo jhakri* in the camp.' As Max expected, the response was non-committal. Deepraj was also a jhakri but to Max's knowledge his powers were benign. 'Do you know who they are?'

'Huzoor.' This was said in a tone that indicated that he was offended that Max would ever doubt his ability to recognise another shaman. Now was the moment to push the competitive spirit.

'If someone put a *sarap* on the American, could you lift it?'

There was a long pause, easily explicable as Deepraj steered them through two tight bends. As they emerged on a short stretch of straight road the Gurkha turned to look at him.

'Saheb, if there was a sarap, should I?'

Clever bastard, as he well knew from past experience, there was a great deal more than met the eye with this taciturn hillman. Max decided to change the subject.

'In your opinion, which are the best teams?'

'In *my* opinion, Choden's and Kalsang's.'

Max laughed, 'I take it that Kesarsing disagrees with you.' Differences of opinion between Rais and Limbus were the everyday stuff of a Gurkha battalion.

'Huzoor. He prefers Choden and Choki.'

So, they were in agreement about the pocket dynamo Choden. By far and away the toughest of the women, not only could she do everything the men could do and usually do it better, but her team was rock solid behind her. As both Choden and Kalsang's teams were in Max's column he could readily concur with the choice. Choki, however, was in Herman's and there had been too few opportunities to assess him.

'What's the problem with Choki?' Max asked. Deepraj took one hand off the wheel and tapped on the dashboard, it was a signal that Max recognised as the man's way of buying time before giving a reply that he knew would be unpopular. He put both hands on the wheel and spoke without turning his head: '*Thangchha*'. It was a good verb. Not only did it mean that Choki cheated but it was said with the quiet disgust with which Deepraj coloured it, the sense embraced virtually all the traits that Gurkhas despised.

'How?'

'Supplies Herman-saheb with girls.'

'Yes, but if Kesarsing thinks he's good, there has to be a basis for that.'

'He's good, but how can you trust him?'

That, Max reflected was sound judgment, assuming that Choki was currying favour with Durwachter. It also meant that he had to reflect on the Ranger's reliability. Could it be behind the hostility to the American, he wondered.

'Does Kesarsing-saheb know?'

'*Thut!* He says it doesn't matter.'

The sound of the engine was all that stood between them for several more kilometres. If girls were being brought onto the site, they'd have to be smuggled in and out and that required complicity amongst the 22s responsible for security as well as breaching their secure status. Despite a professional reluctance to judge another officer's capabilities, there had been several opportunities for him to observe the American covertly. Their approach to training was very similar to each other, basically leading by example but there they parted company. Where Max encouraged, the Ranger cursed those who failed to meet his exacting standards, shouting into their faces and belittling them in front of everyone, a sure sign that he had never worked with Asians before. Nor did it help his equanimity that the handful of women under his command came up to the mark no matter how tough the tasks he set them. Now he understood the anger smouldering amongst the Tibetans. Worse, he had noted Durwachter's resentment towards the women. He would have to find a way to address this, even if it meant uniting all the Tibetans against the American. Their *esprit de corps* was of far greater importance than Herman's ego.

'Do they confide in you, any of you?'

'A bit.'

'Anything I ought to know?'

Deepraj's hand reached out for the dashboard again, fingers drumming. 'Not something they told us but Prabhat-saheb overheard part of an argument. Someone, he didn't identify who, was saying "Don't do anything stupid." His mother tongue is close to theirs so he catches meanings that Kesarsing and I might miss,' the Gurkha said. It struck Max that maybe the curse was the least of the threats to the American. Hopefully this long weekend break would allow tempers to cool. He would have to discuss it with Penjo. Both columns would move to the live firing area on Tuesday, that would create ample opportunities for an accidental misfire.

The warm night air filtered in through the open windows carrying the feral smells of the forest, the headlights caught tiny twin mirrors of light as startled animals were caught momentarily before being swallowed up into the velvet shadow.

'It's a bit like the road from Ghoom, isn't it?'

Deepraj had grown up in the Darjeeling district of the eastern Himalaya. 'Huzoor.'

'Been here before?'

'Uh huh.' A shake of the head. 'My mother-in-law's brother runs a *chiya-dhokan* there.' Max guessed that there would be something more powerful than tea served in the shop.

'Staying with your *mama*?'

'They live over the chiya-dhokan on Library Road. I'll drop off at the Mall, saheb, I can find my way from there.'

'I'm at the Gateway hotel, not too far away. I'll go for a hike up to Kempty Falls tomorrow afternoon, then have a beer at the Writer's Bar afterwards. Fancy joining me?'

Despite the difference in rank, there was a special bond between them which was traced back to the battalion's first tour in Helmand province. They had found themselves isolated from the rest of Max's company, lying side by side in a ditch full of IEDs and surrounded by the Taliban. Deepraj had let rip a tremendous fart and Max found himself shaking with laughter before they fought themselves out of it. When Max was convulsed with laughter as Ian Brown, the battalion doctor, was dressing his wounds, the good doctor thought it was PTSD until eventually, still shaking, Max had explained.

'Going for a hike? Isn't that what you call a busman's holiday, saheb?'

'Not really, I was thinking of swimming in the river up there.' This, Max knew, would make Deepraj think. Gurkhas were not renowned for their ability to swim.

'*Pagal huzoor.*'

Max smiled to himself. Perhaps he was a bit crazy in the Gurkha's eyes.

Ambala Cantonment Railway Station

Fernandes waved irritably at a fly on the rim of his teacup. The station's vegetarian restaurant had been Manek Jha's choice, it was an accurate reflection of the passed-over major's taste. The intelligence officer conceded that had anyone been interested enough to observe them, they would not have attracted attention. Still, it offended his sensibilities to have to put up with the general dirt and dilapidation surrounding them, all so unnecessary. He forced himself to laugh inwardly, would he ever have thought that his British education and Oxford would lead to him sitting in this decaying railway station dealing with an Indian Army officer of limited intelligence? Still, he reflected, Jha's job made no intellectual demands, all he had to do was make these confidential reports on the SFF unit's activities. Though Jha was tasked to report on both the foreign officers, Fernandes's only real concern was with Devlin; whereas the American danced to the tune played by the CIA's Delhi head of station, the Britisher was very much his own man. Fernandes could not shake off the feeling that Devlin had a colonial sense of superiority. Or was it just his own unfounded sense of inferiority?

'How reliable is your Tibetan informant?'

'He's ambitious, you were right,' Jha told Fernandes. 'When I told him that he'd have the chance to be promoted to work in your organisation, he could not hide his enthusiasm. You won't have to pay him.'

Fernandes had been worried that Devlin's ability to communicate directly with the Tibetans could have shut him out of the picture. Jha's recruitment of the Tibetan officer gave them fly-on-the-wall access.

'Tell *Jokhang* not do anything to arouse *Garuda*'s suspicions,' Fernandes said, using code names to guard against a breach of security, 'just keep us informed of everything that is agreed on between him and the Tibetans.'

Jha's forehead creased. '*Texas* is a big problem,' he said with a despairing shrug. 'The Tibetans, well…they all dislike him.' He paused and looked into his teacup before adding, 'I'd say they hate him.'

'All of them?'

'Not quite.' Jha looked nervously around the crowded restaurant but no one was paying them the slightest attention. 'I think he likes Jokhang because his English is so good, so he doesn't feel left out as he does with the others.'

'Texas has gone to Delhi and Garuda to Mussoorie, you say?'

Jha nodded, then fingered his moustache nervously. 'You will put in a good word for me…with the Chief?'

'Of course.' Fernandes almost felt sorry for the man, desperate for a promotion well beyond his capabilities. But he served an essential purpose, providing them with a channel for the flow of information yet being out of the command circle. 'Your work is much appreciated and I'm sure it will be recognised in time.'

Jha's face relaxed into a smile. 'I'm sorry for asking.'

Fernandes gave a dismissive wave of his hand. The information loop was tight, just as Mullick wanted it. Jha signalled the elderly, unshaven attendant. Fernandes stood up and said to Jha, 'Please, I'll settle up. You carry on with your weekend.'

The major raised his arm as if to salute, then let it fall with an embarrassed smile, turned and left. Fernandes left some grubby rupee notes on the stained and chipped marble tabletop and walked slowly out into the station concourse.

General Chaudhari, the chief of defence staff, was demanding intelligence on the Chinese state of readiness in both the hotspots and the CIA wanted intel on missile sites, all of which the SFF unit was best positioned to obtain provided that the cabinet approved an operation. Well, that was beyond his pay scale, but Fernandes wondered how the army chief and the American spooks would react if no approval was forthcoming from Raj Bhawan. There were so many different interests at play, he had to ensure that he had a finger on all the pulses so that any event could be turned to his personal advantage. The intelligence community was intellectually challenging but full of players with their own agenda.

Mussoorie Gateway Hotel

It felt good to have no distractions, just sitting in the morning sunshine, enjoying a remarkably good cup of coffee and gazing out across the Dun Valley. The waiter had told him that the beans came from Nepal and he made a mental note to see if he could buy some in the bazaar. Two large mynah birds perched on the iron balustrade were bickering away in tones extraordinarily reminiscent of the patois of the local Garhwali people, the birds' aggressive attitude giving him a rude reminder of the problems he faced in the Baniyana encampment. Durwachter was proving a more intractable problem than Max had anticipated. It was the potential for disaffection amongst the Tibetans that worried him most. All the training in the world was pointless if the teams were riven with antagonism. His attempts to get alongside the American had yielded little success; the Ranger was an efficiency machine who lacked insight, either into himself or others. Involuntarily, Max shook his head. Time to put aside the problems for a couple of days and just soak up the atmosphere of the lovely hill station. No wonder the Nepalese had annexed Garhwal and Kumaon until the East India Company seized the territory at the end of the Anglo-Nepal war in 1815. The British had a lot to answer for.

*

The Cambridge Book Depot was an Aladdin's cave of literary treasures. Max wandered amongst the racks, initially picking out books that he had seen in London but were so much less expensive here. Turning a corner, he came across shelves of 19th century autobiographies and collections of diaries written by the soldiers and administrators who had lived in the Himalayan foothills when the Indian subcontinent had been part of the

British empire. Disciplining himself as much as possible, he bought six of the most promising works and took his parcel of books back to the hotel.

*

There was something familiar about the sound of the boots on the gravel terrace. Max looked up from the volume of Hodgson's work on the Himalayan languages.

'Huzoor, I'll join you for the hike but not the swim.'

Deepraj's serious expression amused him, it was as though he expected Max to criticise him for refusing the offer of bathing in the river. Closing the pages on the shop's bookmark, he stood up and stretched. 'Good idea.' Pointing at the Gurkha's jump boots, he added, 'I'll get mine.'

His room gave onto the hotel terrace and he walked in leaving the door open. The hotel was constructed against the mountainside and the exposed rock faces were an integral part of its architecture. Deepraj pointed to the bare rock that formed part of one wall. 'It's a bit like the Flintstones.'

'Well, it's an expensive cave.' Max tossed him a bottle of water. 'Catch, Barney! We'll drive part of the way and find somewhere to park, a couple of miles short of the falls, then hike on from there.'

*

It was late afternoon and the last visitors to the falls were leaving as they walked up the main track that contoured the hill down which the mountain stream cascaded. As he caught his first sight of it, Max was struck by the savage beauty of the opalescent water gushing out of the rock and falling like the strands of a wild old witch's hair. He stood aghast at the shoddy observation platforms constructed around the pools, half completed, dirty concrete pilings topped with corrugated iron sheets. A garishly coloured advertising hoarding screamed its message like an ugly whore in a tranquil garden. He could scarcely believe that anyone could have converted something of such striking natural beauty into this cheap fairground.

'Looks more like a collection of Bombay brothels, huzoor.'

Max grunted, lost for words to describe his disappointment. His eye followed the line of the stream up the hillside, noting that there looked to be no structures above what appeared to be the main tourist attraction. 'Let's climb up towards the source,' he said, pointing towards the top of the hill. It was a steep climb and it took them time to reach a point where the force of the water lessened and a small natural rock pool acted as a staging post before, gathering weight, the stream fanned out and down to the next level. Max sat on a rock and peered into the water. Deepraj was looking down from a higher vantage point.

'It's quite shallow,' he said with a laugh. 'I don't think you can swim here, saheb.' Max had already reached that conclusion. He looked around. It was already beginning to get dark. 'Let's go,' Max said. Accustomed though he was to trekking in the hills, it never ceased to amaze him how Gurkhas had a knack of going downhill faster than anyone else. Being that much taller did not help either.

'Getting old, huzoor?'

'I'll beat you on the flat, cheeky bugger.'

It was dark as they headed back along the track which was just visible as the clouds drifted clear of the moon. Max let Deepraj with his uncanny night vision lead and they settled into a fast walk, the stillness of the night broken by the soft sawing of the cicadas and the occasional frog belching. After the barren wilderness of Iraq and the IED nightmare of Afghanistan, it was pure joy to be in the embrace of such savage beauty: the water fracturing the mountainsides and the wild orchids festooning the trees like nature's jewellery. The path dipped, running beside what looked like the ruins of an old fortified tower which loomed some 20 feet above them. Just as Deepraj was about to step onto the makeshift metal bridge, he stopped abruptly, and Max heard what he took to be a muffled cry of distress. They both turned their heads side on to the tower, straining to hear. There it was again – this time a more deep-throated wailing. Deepraj pointed towards the top of the tower and they both ran back up the track searching for some form of access. It was a narrow gap in the vegetation that they had not noticed on their way down and they eased their way carefully forward through it. The gap gave onto the roof of the tower and the panic-stricken moans covered any sound that they might have made as they approached. Max signalled Deepraj to pause as he surveyed the scene.

Two men were half-kneeling, one on each side of a young woman, pinning her arms and legs to the ground. A third man held some cloth over her mouth with one hand and a knife over her face with the other. The fourth was kneeling between her legs, his bare buttocks facing towards them as they approached.

Max held up two fingers and directed Deepraj to the man at the head and on the right, then took a running kick, landing his boot under the man's naked crutch. The force of the kick converted the man up and to the left where he fell screaming on top of the one on that side sending them both sprawling. With his pants around his ankles and doubled over in pain, Max ignored him to deal with the one now trying to scramble to his feet. His boot caught him in the side of the head and there was a satisfying crunch as he collapsed. Turning back to the first man, Max stomped on his head to neutralise him before turning to see that the one who had been at the girl's head was in a classic knife-fighter's stance, holding it low and traversing the blade across his body with short stabbing movements towards Deepraj who was smiling as he faced off against the man. As Max turned towards the first one that the Gurkha had dealt with, the man shouted at him in Hindi, 'Back off or I'll kill this Muslim bitch.' He held a vicious-looking flick knife against her throat. Blood was streaming down from a wound over his left eye, his face contorted into the mask of a fanatic. This was the kind of game changer that troubled Max most, an emotionally unstable zealot with a hostage whose only value to him was as a way out of his troubles. Max smiled and held his arms out wide, moving them a little as he approached the man slowly.

'*Asti, asti bhaia*,' he said softly, making the man face him and move out of a line of sight of Deepraj and his opponent.

'*Rokai!* Don't come any closer.' The man's tone was high-pitched, part threat, part fear. He held the girl in front of him, his left arm around her so as to leave his right hand free to press the point of the knife against her throat. The blood was running over his eyebrow and into his eye. Max gambled on him being blind to his immediate left field of vision. He inched closer to him, talking softly and moving his outstretched arms. It was risky and needed lightening action which could not be telegraphed but it was the best option he had. He pointed to the man's left and shook his head slowly, shrugging his shoulders.

'My friend's gun is pointed at your head.'

As the man turned his head fractionally to the side tracking his eyes, so the point of the knife parted momentarily from the girl's throat and Max sprang across the gap between them and closed his right fist around the blade of the knife, tearing the girl away with his free hand. The man's scream of rage died as Max twisted the knife so that the top of the hilt struck his throat, then he punched the man under the jaw with such force that his head snapped back. The man collapsed onto the ground in an unnatural position. Max heard a sudden explosion of air and turned just as Deepraj's attacker crumpled slowly to the ground, the handle of his own knife sticking out of the side of his neck.

The girl's keening sobs struck his ears and he squatted down beside where she sat trembling on the ground. Her face was buried in her hands, but he assumed from her attacker's words that she was a Muslim. He said to her gently in Urdu, 'It's over, you're safe.' He picked up her jeans which were an arm's length away. 'Here, put these on whilst we deal with these animals.' He pushed the anger out of his voice. Up close he saw that she could not have been more than 16 and in shock. Right now, she needed reassurance more than anything.

'My friend and I are soldiers,' Max said. 'We'll sort this out whilst you get dressed, then get you to a doctor, we have a car not too far away.' She looked up at him nervously, fear still making her eyes bulge. 'My name's Max, would you like to tell me yours?' He squatted down so that he was more or less on the same level as she was. She said something unintelligible through her sobs.

'OK, take some deep breaths.' He glanced over to where Deepraj was checking on the other three, two of whom were breathing nosily. 'I'll be back in a minute.' Deepraj was checking the carotid artery of the one Max had punched. He shook his head. Two dead. The one he had kicked in the head was holding his face and moaning and the semi-naked man appeared to be unconscious. Deepraj tore his jeans off him, kicked his legs apart and began stomping on his genitals with his jump boots. The man must have passed out with the pain because the only sound was of air expelled under pressure.

'Enough.' Max grabbed Deepraj by the shoulder. 'I said enough. We need to get this girl out of here.' For a second or two he was afraid that the Gurkha would ignore him. The light was in his eyes and he had seen this before in combat situations. Pausing to spit on the man, Deepraj straightened up. 'Huzoor. *Saala.*'

'Just leave them here like this,' Max said, 'it looks like a gang fight.' He turned around and was relieved to see that the girl had got her jeans on and was standing up. He smiled at her encouragingly, 'I'm sorry, I didn't catch your name.'

'Nisha.' It was so softly spoken that he almost did not hear it.

'Hello, Nisha. This is Deepraj, he'll lead the way and if you need any help you just lean on me.' Instinctively he wanted to put an arm around her but he remembered being told that some rape victims were terrified of any man touching them. They regained the path and crossed over the narrow bridge after which the track widened so that he could walk beside her. He took his cell phone out of his pocket.

'Is there someone you would like me to call?'

She shook her head quickly and said, 'No. She'll be angry with me.'

'Who will, your mother?'

Again, the quick bird-like shake of the head. 'My sister, Shanaaz.' She began sobbing again and Max risked putting an arm lightly across her shoulders. 'Told me…not to come on my own…'

'Look, it's not your fault, these bastards…,' he stopped in mid-sentence realising that anything he said was liable to bear out the sister's warning. They walked on with Max trying to distract the girl with small talk whilst he also had to decide what to do about the men they had left behind. Once the police were brought in, there was no way of keeping their part in the incident a secret. If Nisha reported it, she would have to explain how she had been rescued and he was not at all sure that the local authorities would be willing to turn a blind eye to the involvement of a

British officer and a serving Gurkha soldier doling out instant justice on the local talent.

'Sir,' she broke into his train of thought.

'Just call me Max.'

'Max, sir, could you call my sister?'

'You're sure you want to call her now?'

She nodded and told him the number. 'Doctor Khan,' a woman's voice answered.

'Doctor, I'm calling on behalf of Nisha, she wants to speak to her sister Shanaaz.'

'Why can't she speak to me herself? Is she in trouble?' There was both anger and anxiety in the voice. 'And who are you?'

Max mouthed silently at Nisha, 'Your sister is a doctor?' She nodded.

'She's not in any immediate danger but she has just been through a terrifying experience,' he said. 'I'm anxious to get her safely home.'

'Put her on.' It was a command. He handed Nisha the phone. 'Your sister wants to talk to you.' Her hand trembled as she took the phone, but she got no further than saying 'Shanaaz' before bursting into tears. Max took the phone gently.

'Doctor, we're close to the Kempty Falls, Nisha can direct us to your home, and you can take over from there.'

'What's happened to her?'

'May I suggest that you let her explain that herself once we get her home?' There was a pause before the doctor's authoritative voice resumed, 'Very well. Please give me your name.'

'Devlin, Colonel Max Devlin.' Hopefully, giving his rank would provide some sort of reassurance.

'Devlin?' There was genuine surprise in her tone. 'Colonel Devlin, the Baniyana Forest?' The anger had left her voice.

'Yes.'

There was a longer pause this time before the doctor said, 'Please call me when you are a few minutes away.'

When they reached the car, Max draped a spare camo smock round Nisha's shoulders and sat in the back seat next to her. She had revived enough to give Deepraj directions and the journey was mercifully short.

Dr. Khan was waiting in the road outside the neat little bungalow and the sisters clung to each other before Nisha was led inside. Max whispered into the doctor's ear, 'She was attacked by some men. I'm sure you'll know what to do.' She nodded.

'Please come inside, my ayah will get you a drink whilst I attend to Nisha.'

'Perhaps we could come back tomorrow?' Now the girl was in good hands, he felt that the sisters would be better off left alone, added to which he needed to think about how to extricate themselves from the mess up at the falls. The doctor thought for a second, still grim-faced, she said, 'Thank you, yes.'

'I'm staying at the Gateway.'

She nodded as she guided Nisha back into the house.

*

An hour later, showered and in a change of clothes, Max and Deepraj were both nursing a drink in the Writer's Bar. They took their drinks out onto the terrace.

'What do we do now, huzoor?'

Max had been thinking of little else. It really depended on Dr. Khan and how she wanted to handle it. From what little he had learned about local politics, in the wake of a local surge of populist nationalism, Muslims would probably be disinclined to make a fuss. From what he could recall the four men had been relatively young and well-dressed, they might be scions of local worthies for all he knew, which would make for a massive furore. His gut instinct was to pretend that they had nothing to do with it. Not having gone straight to the police had already virtually committed them to this course but it could all change dramatically if Dr. Khan chose to do so. From his short encounter with her, she struck him as an obviously professional woman, one who would do what she saw as the right thing, come what may. On the other hand, she would be hyper-protective of her sister. He decided. 'I'm going to call the doctor, then we'll decide what has to be done.'

Deepraj studied him for a moment, then nodded slowly. Max tapped the number on his mobile. Just as he thought it would go to voicemail, she answered, 'Dr. Khan.'

'Doctor, this is Max Devlin. Can you speak freely, or shall I call back?'

There was no hesitation in her response. 'No, now is good. Nisha is sleeping, I gave her something.'

'I don't wish to pry but, how is she?'

'Thanks God, you must have arrived just in time. I…we're so grateful to you.'

The earlier professional detachment had been replaced by a warmer, much more personal tone. Max decided it was time for direct contact. 'I know I proposed that we come back tomorrow but I wonder whether we could come over now, we'd really appreciate the opportunity to talk matters through?'

There was a momentary pause and he wondered whether he had pushed his luck.

'I think I know what you mean.' Suddenly she was business-like again. 'Yes, come now.'

He let Deepraj drive so that he could run over in his mind how he was going to approach the problem. He had not asked her how she knew who he was, or at least where he was working. He had seen the Indian Army Medical Corps cap badge on a beret hanging in the entrance hall of the bungalow from which he deduced that she must be connected to the 22s. That meant that she would be conscious of the secrecy of the work on which he was engaged. Just how that stacked up against the attack on her sister though, was an unknown. In the brief time that he had had to judge her character, he sensed that she would most likely want to raise a storm and though he had no intention of stopping her, he was determined to try and keep his and Deepraj's involvement out of it completely. He outlined his thinking and received a non-committal grunt in response. Finding themselves in less than auspicious circumstances was fast becoming a bad habit.

*

She opened the door herself and ushered them into a softly decorated living room, fresh coloured chintz covers on the three-piece suite of comfortable sofa and chairs.

'I've sent Mina, my ayah, home,' Dr. Khan said. 'I have some Black Label but nothing to cut it. Ice?'

Both of them thanked her and stood whilst she poured out three glasses and added ice cubes from a silver-plated bucket. Handing them over, she indicated the sofa and sat in an armchair next to the empty fireplace. Her dark hair was drawn back severely revealing the sort of classic features that would have graced a cinema billboard. Her colouring was closer to a dark olive and for the first time he noticed that her eyes were blue. She looked straight back at him.

'We're Kashmiris.'

'I guessed as much.' Max leaned forward, the glass held in both hands. 'Was she raped?' There was a quick shake of the head.

'Badly bruised but I don't think he managed to penetrate her. Between her struggling and your timely intervention, she escaped the worst.' She took a sip of her own drink. 'Her recollection is very vague, but she has the impression that her attackers were all sprawled on the ground by the time that you left.'

'Actually, two of them are dead and the other two will need hospitalising.' Max said it quietly and unemotionally, simply stating facts. Her eyebrows shot up for a second and her free hand looked for purchase on the arm of the chair.

'You're sure they're dead?' She paused, then added, 'I imagine, Colonel, in your experience you can tell.'

'They died from their own knives, the ones they threatened Nisha with before turning them on us.'

She stared at him as if she was trying to read his mind. She raised her glass in a toast. 'Good.' He lifted his glass in response and noted the grin on Deepraj's face. 'Filth like them don't deserve to live.' This was said with surgical dispassion. Max allowed himself a shadow of a smile as he responded, 'I take it that this is the sister, not the doctor talking.' He had to hope that what he was about to propose would be met sympathetically.

'Of course,' she smiled and he glimpsed, for the first time, the femininity that she sheltered behind her professional persona.

'As you seem to know about me, I take it that you're aware of our role?'

'I'm the on-call frontline trauma surgeon for the SFF unit. My official post is MO to the ITBP Academy, here in Mussoorie, it provides me with suitable cover,' she explained, referring to the training institute for officers of the Indo-Tibetan Border Police Force.

'Then, I don't need to tell you that it would be a serious breach of your country's national security if our involvement in this incident were to be publicised,' Max said. 'Frankly, I was hoping to persuade you to forget ever having seen us here.' He paused but she just stared at him. He went on, 'If you decide to report the attack on Nisha, it would simplify everything if she had no recall of what happened after she was assaulted.'

'I think that would complicate things, Colonel.'

'Max, please.'

'From your account, the remaining attackers won't be eager to explain how they came by their injuries and I suspect they'll want to distance themselves from their dead friends.' She shook her head and went on, 'It would do nothing for Nisha's reputation to have people knowing about it. You can rely on us to say nothing. With any luck, the local police will think it was some sort of gang feud.'

'I am very concerned about both of you. They knew that Nisha is Moslem. Are there some Hindu extremists active locally?'

'Mussoorie's been allied to Congress since way back and though there are a few fanatics stirring up anti-Moslem prejudices I hadn't felt at risk before today.'

'You'll probably be protected because of your uniform, but Nisha?'

'I particularly asked to be posted up here because I thought she would be safe,' Dr. Khan said. 'Even so I warned her against being out in remote places on her own, but she wants to be a horticulturist and she's always looking for rare orchids.'

Deepraj nodded thoughtfully as he interrupted, 'We saw some beautiful species up near the falls.' Max smiled to himself, there were sides to the man that still took him by surprise.

'India is becoming very insecure for us, especially women, it is our home and I am sworn to defend it but some days I wonder who are our enemies?' She looked up at the ceiling. 'I'll take better care of her from now on.' Again, her smile lifted the worry lines in her face. 'I can't thank you both enough. May I invite you to lunch tomorrow?' She looked at Deepraj, who replied, 'I must spend time with my family, thank you.' Max was about to decline politely then had second thoughts. 'That's kind of you.'

When the storm broke and he was sure that it was when rather than if, he could not rule out some form of revenge attack.

*

He dropped Deepraj off at the mall. 'Keep your ears open for any news about our friends up at the falls. I'll leave the hotel at 18.00 hours.' Suddenly he noticed a bloodstain on the Gurkha's sweatshirt. 'We'd better dispose of our clothes as soon as we get back to camp, just in case.'

Deepraj looked down and nodded, 'It's like Helmand again.'

Baniyana Forest
Monday

E ven before he walked into his office Max sensed the tension in the air. The clerks' greeting was subdued and formal, none of the usual smiles. There was a note on his desk asking him to call Manek Jha as soon as he came in.

'Morning Max,' Jha greeted him. 'I'm afraid we have a problem.' Pointing to the chair opposite his desk, the camp commandant added, 'There's been an unholy row between Choden and Choki. No one will tell me how it started, but Choki's nose is broken.'

'Choden?' Max asked.

'She's OK.'

Max kept a straight face whilst uttering a silent bravo. 'Have you spoken to Dapon Penjo?'

'Well,' Jha paused before blurting out, 'he's not back. Well, I haven't seen him.' He looked uncomfortable and decided, 'As it's an SFF disciplinary matter, I suggest that we leave it to the Dapon to sort out.'

Max gave a short nod and left the office. He had no intention of just leaving the matter to Penjo to deal with.

*

The three Gurkhas were drinking tea in a small room that they had commandeered for themselves. Max accepted the offered mug and lifted it in a salute to Kesarsing. 'Why did Choden break Choki's nose?' he asked. Prabhat laughed before Kesarsing could answer: 'Because she's tougher!'

Max allowed a hint of a smile but knowing that Kesarsing valued both Choki and Choden, he waited on his opinion.

'They argued about Herman-saheb,' Kesarsing began to explain. 'Choden accused Choki of pimping for him. Choki lost his temper, called her a liar and Choden flattened him.'

'Is he pimping?'

Kesarsing grimaced, 'Yes.'

'How bad is the opposition to the American?'

All three exchanged glances then Prabhat replied, 'It's dangerous.' The others nodded.

'Keep your eyes open and your ears peeled,' Max said, 'I need to know what's going on.' He then turned to Prabhat and said, 'Especially you. You're more likely to catch things.'

'Huzoor.'

Penjo could deal with the Tibetans, but the more urgent task was to handle Durwachter.

*

The Ranger was cleaning a handgun that Max recognised. 'CZ85?'

'AT-2000 version, made by the Swiss,' Herman said. 'Best 9-mm there is.'

'15 rounds certainly gives you a winning hand.'

'Yup.' The American continued cleaning the weapon, then said without looking up, 'Somethin' chewin' you up?'

'Yes,' said Max, who decided not to beat about the bush. 'What we do in our off-duty hours is our own business but not if it affects our work here, especially within the camp.'

Durwachter snapped the magazine back into its housing and looked up under his brow. 'I think you're just about to poke your nose into my business.' He paused, put the gun down on the table and stood up. 'That'd be a bad idea.'

Max affected a smile and sat down pointing to the empty chair. 'You and I have a lot in common,' he began. 'We're both foreigners, guests, if you like.' Relieved that Herman had resumed his seat, Max let his voice turn serious. 'We have the authority that goes with our rank but that doesn't automatically command respect, especially with the Tibetans.'

'I get it.' The Ranger's expression turned angry. 'You're the hotshot guy with their language an' all but,' he said, jabbing his finger into Max's chest, 'just so's you don't forget, this is a joint command.' A sneer twisted his face for a moment before he added, 'And Uncle Sam's footin' the bill.'

Max knew that he had to swing this around somehow. Raising both hands in mock surrender, he said, 'Herman, I'm well aware of this but you and I both know that we have a problem and I need your help to solve it.'

The American leaned back, staring at him before he responded critically, 'Like how?'

'As you say, we bring different strengths to the party.' This yielded a twitch of an eyebrow. 'We have our own techniques and you're critical of mine,' Max continued. Said with a crooked smile, this produced another twitch. 'But these people put their lives on the line,' he added, 'knowing that if they're caught, they'll be tortured, their families traced and probably executed as a lesson to others.' Leaning forward, he explained, 'They're people whose country and way of life has been stolen from them. India is supposed to be a temporary refuge but, in their hearts, they fear its permanence and what that means.

'We're the real visitors, we have a home and a country to return to,' Max added. 'Our job is to teach them all the skills to survive. On top of all that, both our governments, as well as India, exploit them for the intelligence that they can bring.' He had the man's full attention now. 'So, can we agree that we owe it to them not to screw things up in such a way that they turn on each other?' Max let the question hang in the air, hoping that it would not be necessary to spell it out in greater detail.

Durwachter stared at him, his facial expression giving nothing away whilst his body language was shouting abuse. 'Man, you should be a politician,' he finally said. 'All those words…just to get me to stop fuckin' the locals.' Shaking his head, he added, 'I do my job, you do yours, stay outta the rest of my life.'

Max tried to put his anger and disgust on a backburner. His objective had been to appeal to the man's professionalism but that had proved a forlorn hope. He was also troubled because there was an element of hypocrisy in the light of events in Mussoorie but, faced with callous indifference and despite the fact that it was Washington that was footing the greater part of the bill, his frustration broke through. He stood up and declared, 'I don't want to ever hear again that you're using a member of the SFF to pimp for you. You're big enough and ugly enough to forage for yourself.' He spun around and strode out of the room.

Indian Cabinet Secretariat
New Delhi

There were beads of perspiration between the edge of his pugaree and the top of his nose. Arvind Kaur made a mental note to get his secretary to remind the public works department to fix the ancient air-conditioning system that was clanking away in a losing battle against the heat. What was the point of being the prime minister of India if he had to conduct the nation's business in a sauna?

The meeting of the inner cabinet had been going on for over half an hour and the PM was having difficulty controlling his impatience.

'I am hearing what you are saying, Mentri-ji, but can we afford to appear to back down in the face of their aggression?' Visibly angry, external affairs minister Roy was dabbing his bald head with a handkerchief as he questioned Kaur.

'It's only posturing,' the PM countered. He had worked for nearly a year in secret negotiations with the Chinese premier to de-escalate the tensions on the border that had led to actual exchanges of fire between Chinese and Indian troops in both the Aksai Chin and Doklam regions, breaking the prohibition against firing. Just when he thought that there was agreement over appointing a joint border commission, Beijing had withdrawn its co-operation, claiming that India was complicit in the Dalai Lama's opposition to the Han migration into Tibet. He sensed the chief of defence staff, General Chaudhari, bristling.

'Tell that to my poor bloody *jawans* with bullets in their gut,' the CDS blurted out.

'General-saheb, what I'm saying is that Beijing is as keen to resolve these issues as we are, so that we can put an end to such incidents,' Kaur said. 'Of course, I deplore such attacks on our jawans, but we cannot afford to provoke the Chinese, which is what we risk if the 22s cross into China.'

'You mean Tibet,' Roy grimaced. This sort of nit-picking was likely to derail the planned cross-border operations.

'Well, yes,' the CDS grunted, and he was not to be mollified.

'Time out, gentlemen,' the PM said as he lifted his hands to make a 'T'. He looked across the top of the polished table at Mullick and asked, 'Secretary-ji, do I still have your assurance that the political risk is minimal?'

The special secretary's forehead puckered. 'Risk is risk, Mentri-saheb,' he said, giving a deprecatory wave of his hand. 'My people are highly trained and, as I have emphasised, even if they are caught, they are unattributable.'

The PM threw himself back in his chair. 'It's not a question of your unmentionables...'

Seeing the anger darken the Chief's face and a bead of perspiration run down the PM's nose, Roy signalled General Chaudhari into his chair and raised his voice: '*Bas!*' Suddenly conscious that he was overstepping himself, the minister for external affairs changed to a conciliatory tone, forcing himself to smile. 'Is it that we are having a border dispute here in Raisina Hill?' he asked, joining his hands together in a soft *namaste* to both Mullick and Kaur. 'Mentri-ji, your achievements in improving our relations with Beijing are part of your legacy to the country,' Roy said. 'But it is our duty to strengthen your negotiating hand when dealing with the integrity of our land and...' Gesturing towards the CDS, he added, '...the full backing of the military.' The minister paused, gauging the PM's reaction to his intervention.

'The electorate responds to bold leadership,' Kaur asserted. He knew a trump card when he saw one and the need to win the upcoming election justified the risk. Nothing united a country so much as external aggression. It was easy enough to clothe political expediency in the apparel of statesmanship. The PM wiped away the perspiration on his nose, looked at Mullick through eyes shut down to slits and spoke in a tone calculated to lend weight to the responsibility he was shifting. 'Bring this inner cabinet your plans for exploratory incursions into both the Aksai Chin and Doklam regions and we will consider them.'

Turning to General Chaudhari, Kaur raised a precautionary finger and said, 'You'd better start quietly strengthening the units deployed on our borders – just in case.' The CDS gave a satisfied nod.

Roy allowed himself to breathe more easily. He guessed that the American ambassador had used some leverage; he would have to tap his own sources in the embassy to find out what they had offered. It was important for his own prospects that he be identified with standing up to the Chinese. He watched Mullick talking deferentially to the PM: the intelligence chief was precisely what he imagined the best of the old Indian civil service must have been, the ultimate professional. But Mullick was wholly committed to the people for whom he was responsible, that was the military side of his character. For both their sakes, Roy hoped that the proposed operation would go off smoothly.

The PM acknowledged Mullick's assurances and hurried back to his office and the comfort of its modern air-conditioning. He ordered a fresh lime-*pani* and sat down to reflect on what he had just agreed to. The generals always wanted to play at soldiers and despite Mullick's attempt to mollify him, the fact was that the Research and Analysis Wing needed an excuse to justify its existence. Months of careful, secret and measured negotiations were being sacrificed so that he could shore up his image before elections. The Americans wanted the intelligence almost as much as the Indian Army did, but the pressure that they brought to bear on him was far more subtle. He did not trust the Chinese any further than he could throw an elephant, but he still believed that he had established a working relationship with their premier.

He decided to use his direct line to Downing Street to emphasise how much he was relying on the British team in Chakrata to keep the Americans in check.

Baniyana Forest

'Kushog-saheb…' Halfway across the parade ground, Max looked back at the office block where a clerk held the entrance door open and said to him, '…telephone for you, urgent.'

His inclination was to ignore it. He had slept fitfully, his mind churning over the problems in the camp and a nagging anxiety about Shanaaz and Nisha. He had woken, feeling even more tired. The clerk looked agitated and announced, 'It's Doctor Khan, in Mussoorie.'

Max retraced his steps, almost running. 'I'll take it in my office.'

Her voice was steady, but he detected the stress in it. 'We…I mean all of us…have a problem,' she began.

'Can you both come here?' he asked, confident that the landline was compromised. The less said over the phone, the better. 'You can fill me in on the details once you get here.'

She paused for a moment before asking, 'Will Nisha be allowed in?'

'I'll authorise it and notify the guards,' Max said. He could just hear some muffled speech as Shanaaz spoke to someone, presumably Nisha. Off the top of his head, he added, 'You'd better both pack a bag.'

'Thank you…bye,' she said, then the line went dead. The fact that she had immediately accepted his suggestion confirmed his fears for their physical safety. One of the attackers must have identified Nisha. Whether he had made the connection to Deepraj and himself Max could only guess, though it struck him as unlikely. The decision not to report the attack and its outcome had been necessary: not only had he wanted to shield Nisha from all the pantomime of an investigation, but his own involvement would have far-reaching political consequences. Not for one second did he regret the deaths. They were vicious fanatics, not just rapists, and men with knives had a bad habit of sticking them in other people. It was highly improbable that they would have left Nisha alive. Killing them had been virtually unavoidable in the circumstances, but it was essential to preserve his and Deepraj's anonymity. For the moment, he needed a cover story to account for Shanaaz's sudden arrival.

The phone rang.

'Kushog-saheb, Dr. Khan asked me to tell you that she will make a surprise medical inspection later today.' He thanked the caller and returned the handpiece to its rest. Worried she may be, but she still had her wits about her. He smiled to himself, he was discovering just how impressive this woman was, not just a beautiful face.

*

Penjo's office was a curious set of contradictions with which Pema was comfortable. The aroma of burnt joss sticks overwhelmed the underlying smells of old files, photocopy chemicals, government polish and machine oil. The walls had photographs of him with an eclectic variety of personalities, a famous Khamba guerrilla leader, a Rinpoche, a group of 22s in combat gear, one of him smiling next to Pema at some sort of reception, a formal studio portrait of himself in Indian Army uniform and, dominating the room, a pair of beautiful *tangkas* framing a picture of the Dalai Lama next to Penjo, the pair of them smiling broadly at the camera. *War and Peace* flashed through her mind, but she was no Anna Karenina. To her parents she was a terrible disappointment. The early brilliance that had secured her a place at MIT for her master's in international relations had segued into a burning passion for the Tibetan cause which, in turn, led to her being commissioned in the SFF.

'What is it, *noo-mo?*' He invested so much more than just 'sister' into his form of address and she, in her turn, calling him uncle contained an intimacy that broke the boundaries of formal kinship.

'*Ah-koo*, the American will never break us but I can't rule out the chance that someone will take it into their head to get at him.'

Penjo wore what she thought of as his pensive face, inscrutable, almost like Marpa, the mythological master of Milarepa. Could, she thought fancifully, a man be described as beautiful? He broke into her thoughts. 'Have you spoken to the Kushog-saheb?'

She hesitated. Even though she trusted Max instinctively, it went against the grain to break the bond of loyalty to her own people. She shook her head apologetically and said, 'Perhaps I ought to…'

He interrupted, 'It's as though he is one of us. I leave it to you to speak to him.'

She was gratified that he left it to her to do, rather than allowing Max to know that she had not trusted him. Penjo steepled his fingers and leaned his face into them before asking, 'Who is most likely to do something?'

It was inevitable that if she reported her worries, she would be asked who she suspected but she had no hard evidence to point the finger at anyone, just a gut instinct and that was not enough. He must have guessed that she found it awkward. 'Norbu?' he asked, looking into her eyes to search for a flicker of recognition.

'Choki?' There, he caught the tiniest movement. Now, that was a surprise. He knew that Choki was pimping women for the American and presumed that there was something in it for him, so why would he do something against his own interests? As against that, he obviously enjoyed Durwachter's confidence and that would give him easy access. Penjo looked up at Pema from under his brow. 'Leave it with me,' he told her, 'but if you learn anything more certain, bring it to me, any time, no matter.'

'*Ah-koo*,' she said, acknowledging the instruction with a graceful nod of the head, turned and left.

He would have had to be blind and deaf not to be aware of the mounting animosity towards the American, but Pema's concerns heightened his fears. The man was an outstanding special forces officer whose experience was invaluable for their purposes. Perhaps with other nationalities he would have been ideal, but Durwachter allowed his inflexible military attitude to offend the Tibetan sense of pride. That, and his refusal to countenance the role of women in a combat role, combined to set him at odds with the people under his command. Not for the first time, Penjo regretted not having been more assertive soon after he realised that the Ranger was a square peg in a round hole. But he doubted whether it would have made any difference, Fernandes had told him that the Chief was powerless to effect a change: Durwachter was Langley's choice and as they were footing the majority of the bill, Chakrata was in no position to question it. At a time when they were about to select the teams to be sent into Tibet, this undercurrent did not augur well.

He looked at the left-hand tangka which had a mandala, at the centre of which, the expression of the supreme Buddha *Amoghasiddhi* conveyed utter serenity. It struck him, not for the first time, that what they were about was far removed from the eight-fold path to enlightenment.

*

The paramedic, Si-thar, set down the tray of tea and coffee cups on the desk. 'Can I get you anything else, doctor?' he asked.

Shanaaz gave him a tight smile and said, 'No, thank you, Si-thar.' He gave a little bow and left, leaving Max alone with the sisters.

'This was pushed under my front door,' Shanaaz said as she unfolded a sheet of paper which she then passed to him.

Someone had cut out the letters from what appeared to be newspaper print and stuck them onto a sheet of lined paper that looked like a school exercise book.

mUsLim BITchiS wE kNOw WHO yoU aRE wE coming kILL yOu

'Why send a warning if this is what they really intend?' Max wondered.

'The dead men were the sons of very influential local politicians in Uttarakhand, so the ones who survived must be similarly connected,' Shanaaz said. 'They're smart enough to know that an attack on Nisha or me now could be seen as revenge and that would make people wonder if there was more to it than was being disclosed. Attacks on women are becoming so common that people will automatically assume it was one that went wrong. I think they want to bide their time until it's safe to kill us, but maybe they couldn't resist frightening us.' She took Nisha's hand and added, 'They succeeded.'

'Well, you're safe here,' Max assured the sisters. He knew that this was only temporarily reassuring but short of posting Shanaaz to another command district, he could think of nothing that would remove them from danger. From newspaper reports and discussions in the mess Max was aware that Congress Party's hold on power was threatened by a rising tide of Hindu nationalism under the BJP and its affiliated parties. The level of political corruption ensured that the surviving attackers would evade justice whereas the death of the Khan sisters would be an inconvenience to be buried swiftly.

'Let's play it simply as a racial issue,' he said. 'I'll see if we can get this back up the chain of command to have you posted out of the state. Meanwhile, I think you should have your things brought here.' Max glanced at Nisha, conscious that she would not be security cleared. 'We'll get a temporary pass for you,' he told her, smiling as he was anxious to set the teenager at ease. 'I think you'll find this a fascinating place.'

Nisha looked at Shanaaz, who nodded. It was obvious that the younger sister was still suffering from post-shock symptoms. The germ of an idea occurred to him.

'I think you should meet Choden, one of the Tibetan officers here, she's only a few years older than you are but she can teach you martial arts,' Max said. 'I'm not suggesting that you'll ever need them in the future, but we live in a time when young women need to be able to defend themselves.' Nisha gave him a half-hearted smile.

'I think that would be excellent,' Shanaaz said, 'I might join the class too.' She gripped Nisha's hand, endorsing the suggestion. Shanaaz looked at Max and said, 'We can both use the flat over the clinic, it's where I usually stay when I'm here on call and there are two bedrooms.'

'Good. Then I'll leave you to settle in whilst I get the admin wheels moving,' he said. The smile that she gave him broke momentarily through her clinical reserve. Appreciation was natural but was there, perhaps, a little something else?

As he walked through the forest, Max pondered how much to reveal to Penjo. His brief trip to Mussoorie now threatened to compromise his future role here but he had acquired a responsibility for the Khan sisters and that could not be ignored.

*

'Shit!'

Penjo's reaction was eminently foreseeable and Max wondered whether he would be told to get on the next flight to London. To his immense relief, the Dapon scratched his head and grinned, 'I was about to shift a pressing command responsibility onto your shoulders but now I see that I seriously underestimated my problems.'

Max shrugged his shoulders apologetically. 'Circumstances conspired against me or should I say, us?'

Penjo nodded. 'First, thank you for putting me in the picture.' Dropping the grin, he continued, 'Until you and I decide otherwise, no one else needs to know about the men you killed. Can I assume that Deepraj will keep quiet?'

'I told him not even to tell the other Gurkhas unless I authorised it.'

'We'll run with the racist attack basis for transferring Dr. Khan out of the state, but I want her to be here until the cross-border operation has been completed, just in case,' Penjo said. 'You know that she's a frontline combat surgeon?'

'So I gather.'

'She could be earning a fortune in the private sector,' Penjo added. There was no disguising the pride in his voice. 'Now I have to turn to your end of the bargain.' He stood up, walked around his desk and stood in front of the right-hand *tangka*. Pointing to the two figures depicted there, he asked, 'D'you recognise these, one rarely finds them in our iconography.'

Max studied the figures. '*Me-lha* and *Chu-lha*, I think. God of fire and goddess of water.'

'Congratulations,' Penjo said. 'Two elements without which we humans could not survive and yet both equally capable of destroying us. They represent, to my mind, the delicate balance that we have to achieve in our life and work.' He walked over to the window and looked out across the parade ground to the edge of the forest in which the spirits gambolled like lambs until more powerful forces took and held them captive.

'We need the Americans' money to sustain an ever-diminishing hope of recovering our land, but we dance to their tune,' the Tibetan said. 'We also need a physical base from which to operate.' He spread his arms wide, embracing the area. 'We're indebted to the Indians and their generosity.' Max guessed what was coming but held his tongue. 'If anything happens to Herman, both our benefactors are likely to reconsider their support.' Penjo turned with his back to the light streaming in through the window so that Max could not see the expression on his face.

'As one specialist soldier to another, could you try to make him understand us?' the Dapon asked Max.

'I have tried but I'll give it another go.'

'Please.' It troubled him that Penjo must have felt unable to isolate the threat to Durwachter. The worry lines returned to the Tibetan's forehead. 'And in the meantime, let's all be alert to anything out of the ordinary.'

Though he agreed with the sentiment, Max had to laugh grimly to himself; in an environment as cuckoo as this, only something remarkably sane would be noticeable.

Baniyana Forest
2 days later

M ax raised his hand and the Gurkhas stopped running. Wiping the sweat off their faces they hunkered in a rough circle cradling their weapons. Mist still hung in the treetops like a wraith and the forest was stretching sleep laden limbs all around them. Their pre-dawn runs gave them the opportunity to compare notes without the risk of being overheard. Max nodded to Prabhat, the signals expert.

'No doubt there's a curse on him, saheb,' the Gurkha confirmed. 'I can identify three *geshe*, two in Herman-saheb's column, one in yours, but some of the people in his column are complaining it's not powerful enough because nothing seems to be happening to him.' Prabhat looked up into the trees as the clatter of wings announced a goshawk taking flight. He paused to enjoy the moment, talking to himself, 'They usually only break cover when they're sure of their prey.'

'The *geshe* or the goshawk?' Deepraj joked.

Prabhat shook his head, he was not in the mood for humour. 'The anger is there,' he told Max. 'You don't have to look for it. They follow his orders, but their eyes disobey. They have great patience.'

This was what worried Max. Tibetans' anger was a slow-burning fuse. It was what kept their belief in recovering their homeland alive when, objectively, no one would give them a snowball's chance in hell. It was also what drove them to run the all too immediate risk of torture if captured. Death, in comparison, was not feared. Now, the same dynamic that made them such effective special forces was being siphoned off in their animosity to someone they felt held them in contempt. Max snorted in disgust.

'Saheb…,' Prabhat looked up at Max from under the brim of his jungle hat and said, 'Can you make Herman-saheb understand?' The lack of conviction in his voice echoed Max's own thoughts. There had been officers posted to Gurkha regiments who were not fit to command any troops, men with such preconceived notions of their ethnic superiority that disaster shadowed their every step. Of those who were not transferred out promptly, a few had not survived their first experience of combat. Were it not for Washington's vital backing, the best solution would have been to get Durwachter replaced but he assumed that Penjo would have gone down this path if it had been an option. Part of the problem for Max was that he knew that the Ranger resented his rapport with the Tibetans. His abilities were a massive advantage for him, but only served to emphasise the American's isolation.

'I might make things worse,' Max said. Seeing the puzzled look in Prabhat's expression, he explained, 'He thinks I'm too close to them already.' Comprehension dawned on the Gurkha's face. Max shrugged and added, 'I'll give it a go.' He had no realistic hope of achieving the sort of change in Durwachter's behaviour that would moderate the Tibetans' feelings towards him. Max needed more inside information.

'Forget the *geshe*,' he said. 'Who has the most influential voice amongst them?' The Gurkhas looked at each other before letting Prabhat, as the most senior, speak first, 'Norbu?' The Gurkha glanced at his colleagues before adding, 'Pema?' The other two nodded and Kesarsing repeated, 'Pema.'

It confirmed Max's opinion. It also raised the distinct possibility that Pema was the driving force behind the hostility to the American; his misogyny alone would have founded her opposition. But would an appeal to her undoubted intelligence be sufficient to get her to use her influence to call off the undeclared war against Durwachter? Putting himself in her shoes, Max considered it unlikely.

HQ Research and Analysis Wing
Chakrata

The file had 'ULTIMATE' printed in bold red letters across the cover. General Mullick slid it across the table to Fernandes. This was the only security classification less restricted than 'YOUR EYES ONLY'. The special secretary's tone left no room for error: 'Return to my safe when you're finished.'

'Chief.' Fernandes gave a little bow of his head.

'It sets out the CDS's requirements for detailed intelligence on China's positions and preparedness in both Aksai Chin and the Doklam Plateau,' Mullick said, then paused, tapping the side of his face. Fernandes wondered whether this indicated that his boss had reservations about something. He waited for him to continue.

'You'll note that they want us to plant more nuclear detection devices,' Mullick said. So, he had accurately interpreted the Chief's body language. Planting the NDDs required much deeper penetration into the Tibetan hinterland and a proportionately higher risk to those ordered to do the job.

'Commit these orders to memory and issue them to Dapon Penjo in person,' Fernandes was told. 'His commanders must be briefed verbally, there can be no other written records.' He wondered whether he would be able to avoid the civil service procedure of leaving his own initials in the margin to note that he had read the orders. Opening the file, he noted it was addressed simply to the 'S/RAW', not to Mullick by name, nor was there a signature in the margin. His superiors were covering their arses in anticipation of the shit hitting the fan. If at all possible, he would follow suit.

'The Dapon will insist on a written order,' Fernandes said.

Mullick looked at the intelligence officer as though he was stupid and pointed at the file. 'Of course, he will,' the Chief snapped. 'You'll draft an "ULTIMATE" classified instruction under the codename "OPERATION CAMELOT". Code all geographical destinations but give the Dapon the actual place names verbally. The NDDs are referred to as "icons" and the written orders will be to remove them.'

Fernandes doubted whether anyone reading the operation order would be fooled into thinking that the 22s had been deployed to steal icons but if that was what those higher up the chain of command wanted, he was not about to prejudice his own career by voicing his opinion. C. P. Snow's phrase rang in his ear: 'the euphoria of secrecy does go to the head'. His time at Oxford had taught him to philosophise.

'When do they want the operation?' he asked.

'As soon as the Dapon judges it best to go.'

Fernandes was surprised that this amount of leeway was being given to the people in the field. Normally, the desk-bound warriors had all the answers.

'Impress on him that the CDS would have liked this information yesterday,' Mullick said.

The Chief tapped his face again before continuing, his tone more curious, 'There's a report from the Indo-Tibetan Border Police at Mussoorie that two men were killed up by the Kempty Falls. They were both sons of very powerful BJP supporters who are screaming for retribution. Apparently, a group of four young men were attacked by two men, one white one local. They claim that it was a totally unprovoked attack.' The Chief took a sheet of paper out of his briefcase and studied it for a moment. 'A woman's broken bracelet was found close by the bodies which suggests that a woman was involved in some way,' he said. 'There've been no reports of an attack on a woman, but I find it strange; why would two men take on twice their number for no apparent reason, nothing was stolen. The involvement of a white man is another factor. Get one of our people to check the registers of all the hotels in Mussoorie for anyone who might answer the description.'

Fernandes squeezed his eyes almost closed in anticipation of what he might hear. Mullick looked at him steadily, his voice neutral as he asked,

'D'you think it could have been one of our foreigners?' The intelligence officer stared across the room in an unfocused way as his superior continued, 'Two men, one a white man, take on four, kill two and disable the other two and then disappear, leaving no trace of themselves. Very efficient. The sort of thing that either of our people could do.'

'But why?' Fernandes stopped midway to answer his own question. 'If a woman was being attacked and they happened to be nearby?'

'My thoughts,' Mullick said, passing the second file over. 'The absence of a report from the woman, assuming that this is what happened, would be understandable, most rapes and sex attacks go unreported.'

Fernandes pressed his boss, 'If one of our people was in Mussoorie at that time, what do you want me to do?' The Chief tapped his face for several seconds and Fernandes could almost see the thoughts behind his eyes.

'Report to me, no one else,' Mullick said. As an afterthought, he added, 'Get one of the CBI's interrogators to interview the two survivors. Their account doesn't make sense.' He looked at Fernandes in a way that explained why he was the head of the Research and Analysis Wing. 'We have to keep these political fuckers off our back, otherwise we're courting disaster.' Fernandes nodded agreement, picked up the 'ULTIMATE' file and stood. General Mullick waved him away.

Fernandes closed the door behind him and walked along the wooden slatted floor toying with the possibilities. That one of their two foreigners might be responsible for the deaths in Mussoorie held unlimited potential for the application of personal leverage. In the shadowy world that he inhabited, knowledge was king. Some judicious inquiries needed to be made.

Baniyana Forest

'There are two strategic objectives: first, reconnaissance and mapping of PLA missile site positions and preparedness in Aksai Chin and the Doklam Plateau and second, planting NDDs in deeper terrain,' the Dapon informed the teams. 'We are relying on American ELINT to fix the best positions for the NDDs.' He turned to face Durwachter and said, 'I would like you to take command of that aspect of the operation, including selecting the teams to carry it out but please be guided by Norbu's knowledge of the geography and local issues.' The Ranger blinked acknowledgement.

'Max will be responsible for planning and deployment of the three Recce teams for each operational area. Because the two NDD teams will penetrate much deeper, I want the team members to be familiar with their respective operational areas, as far as possible, so I'm giving that priority over the Recce teams.' This produced a more affirmative nod from the American.

'It still leaves you a richness of choice, Kushog-saheb,' Penjo smiled at Max. Though he appreciated the nickname they had given him, it did serve to underscore their preference for him over his American counterpart. But the allocation of responsibilities avoided him having to argue with Durwachter and meant that he would have all the women to choose from too.

He allowed his mind to drift as Penjo outlined the details each team would be tasked with. Penjo had briefed him privately beforehand so that they could work out how to avoid a clash of loyalties and individual claims to specialised knowledge of the operational areas. The NDD teams would be exposed to maximum risk and emergency exfiltration would almost certainly be ruled out because of the depth of penetration. All the teams would be delivered by helicopter to their respective jump-off points on the Indian side of the border but from there on they would be on foot. Pre-arranged coded radio signals would cover most emergency situations. Exfiltration by air was only to be asked for in extreme circumstances and would not be guaranteed. Penjo had explained that he would have to get cabinet approval for this, and he had been told that it was highly unlikely. Their exchange had not improved Max's opinion of the politicians. He felt obliged to ask, 'If they're not prepared to rescue our people, why allow the operation at all?'

'I think the prime minister has been sandwiched between the army and the Americans,' Penjo said. 'He's concerned about the prospects for his party in the elections. If we succeed, he can't boast about it but if it all goes disastrously wrong, he'll take the blame at the polls.' The Tibetan's frown deepened as he asked, 'Have you made any progress on the Herman front?'

Max shook his head. 'Prabhat thinks that their patience is running thin, but now that he has to organise the NDD operation, anything I say is likely to be misinterpreted.' It was such an obvious question that Max hesitated before asking, 'Given the respect in which you are held, is it worthwhile you having a quiet word with the senior officers?'

Penjo looked momentarily embarrassed. He stared hard at Max, almost as though trying to decide whether to speak. 'I can't do anything about the *geshe*,' he said, 'this is something so deeply ingrained in our culture.' Looking away, the Tibetan added, 'There was an occasion, a few years ago, I knew a curse had been placed on a young man. I consulted a venerable Rinpoche at Dharmasala, he came and held a meeting, but the *Bon-pa* didn't attend. I had the young man transferred out.'

'Did that work?'

Penjo's expression darkened. 'No. He died,' he said. 'The doctors said that his heart just stopped working but he was only young.' He made a gesture of hopelessness and added, 'At least the curse doesn't seem to have had an effect on Herman.'

'True.'

*

'Max.'

He turned around. Fernandes was standing on the veranda of the mess holding a newspaper in his hand. He tapped the page at which it was folded open and asked, 'Have you read this?'

'What?' Max took the newspaper and read the piece to which he had been referred. It was a lurid account of the murder of the sons of two prominent politicians at the Kempty Falls and some journalistic speculation about the possibility that it may have involved a woman whose bracelet was found at the scene.

'Why ask?'

'You were in Mussoorie when it happened,' Fernandes said.

Max checked the article and said, 'So, presumably, were a large number of other people.'

'Mm.' Fernandes's tone annoyed him.

'What's that supposed to mean?'

'Nothing, just curious.'

Max thrust the newspaper back at Fernandes but as he turned to leave the spook's voice became admonitory as he said, 'But if you were involved, somehow, it would be your duty to inform me.' In his mind Max knew that Fernandes would be the last person he would confide in. Nor did he like it that the man had reached this conclusion so quickly.

'If you intend to accuse me of something, just make damn sure of your facts,' Max told him. 'That apart, I don't appreciate your tone, especially not in public.' Fernandes compressed his lips, momentarily lost for words. Max decided to close it down. Adopting a normal tone of voice, he said, 'Now I have work to do, as I imagine do you.'

Fernandes blew the air out of his cheeks then added as an afterthought, 'Oh, I've approved the temporary pass for Dr. Khan's sister.'

Max walked away with a neutral wave of acknowledgement. Why would Fernandes bring up the event in Mussoorie and immediately refer to Nisha? There was no way he could possibly make a connection. He tried to dismiss it from his mind but his reservations about the man were hardening.

*

Shanaaz was examining the arm of a member of Max's column. The arm was swollen to almost twice its size and from the expression on the man's face, he was in considerable pain. In a clinical white coat, with her hair tied back severely and wearing reading glasses, she looked every inch the physician. She instructed the paramedic, 'Get a bowl of soapy water, we need to wash the arm.' She looked up at Max. 'Come and look at this. It's a giant millipede sting.'

She smiled at the patient who looked at her gratefully. 'We'll soon stop the pain.' Then she turned to Max to ask, 'Colonel, can you go up to my quarters and get a couple of ice cubes from the fridge.'

'It's a bit early for cocktails.'

'Max!'

'Just a poor joke, I've been stung, so I know the drill,' he said, waving an apology.

'Well, hurry up.'

When he came back, she wrapped the ice cubes in gauze and bound it over the site of the sting.

'That should do it,' Shanaaz said before handing the patient over to the paramedic. 'Check on whether his Tetanus is up to date, let him rest in the recovery room for a while, check on him every half hour just to be sure that he doesn't have an allergic reaction.'

She removed her glasses and gave Max the smile he had hoped for.

'I had a message you wanted to see me,' he said.

'Yes.' Her smile died. 'Let's go upstairs.'

As they walked up, he asked her, 'Where's Nisha?'

'She's out looking for birds to sketch.'

They entered the small, simply furnished sitting room with its open plan kitchenette. 'I can offer you a cup of tea.'

'Thank you.' As she busied herself with water and the kettle, Max asked, 'Have you read that newspaper report?'

'The one speculating about the bracelet? Yes, it was in the mess.' She switched the kettle on and turned to face him. 'Nisha lost her bracelet that night. It must be hers.'

'Could anyone identify it as Nisha's?'

'Don't think so, well, perhaps my mother. It was a present from me but I remember my mother admiring it.'

'Where is she?'

'Mummy? Staying with her brother in Pune.'

She spooned loose tea into an old-fashioned brown china pot and poured on the boiling water. He settled himself in one of the army-issue armchairs, watching her position cups, teapot and milk on the stressed wooden table. She had beautiful hands. Anyone who could bring graceful precision to such a mundane task had to be an accomplished surgeon. He picked up the thread of the bracelet.

'What about any of Nisha's friends, might they remember it?'

She shook her head. 'She usually holidays with mummy, the rest of the time she's in school at Loretto in Darjeeling.'

So far so good, he thought, but why was Fernandes hinting at a connection? Max decided not to burden Shanaaz with his concerns. But the political dimension and the fact that the surviving attackers knew where the sisters lived were game changers.

The wall mounted phone rang, and she crossed the room to answer it. Her mouth set in a grim line as she held the handset to her ear. She spoke quietly before replacing it on the wall.

'That was the CO of the ITBP Academy. The assistant commissioner of police reported an attack on my bungalow.' She gave him a reassuring wave of her arm. 'No serious damage, a couple of broken windows which have been boarded up. Some ITBP cadets surprised the vandals and they ran off. The DC wants to know if I've received any threats lately.'

'It's not safe for you or Nisha to return to Mussoorie.'

'But how do I justify a transfer without revealing the whole story?'

'Have you still got that note threatening to kill you?'

She opened her emergency case, took out the folded paper and handed it to him. He read it again.

'On top of the attack on your bungalow this should be sufficient.'

She sighed and sat back on the sofa, picked up her glasses from the table and played with them.

'I was happy in Mussoorie until all this,' Shanaaz said. 'It's the best posting I've had, short of a war, I do more traumatic surgery than I had hoped for.'

Her habit of raising her eyebrows when she was intense had the opposite effect of making her look almost as though she was joking. Max checked himself from laughing.

'Perhaps they could post you to Kashmir.' The words were no sooner out of his mouth than he wished he had kept his mouth shut. Her eyes shut him down. He held his hands up in surrender. 'Stupid and thoughtless of me, I'm sorry.'

There was a sense of despair in the way she shook her head. 'No, it was logical, trauma surgeons go where their skills are needed and, my God, the people there need us.' She lifted her head; the anger had left her eyes. He felt a flicker of hope. She reached out and patted the top of his hand. 'I'm truly grateful to you, I know you're trying to protect us.' She looked out of the window. 'Maybe you're right and the note will work.'

'I'm sure we can arrange for you to stay here until things get sorted.'

'But I need to collect my things, all we have is an overnight bag each.'

For a moment she was just a woman separated from her necessities, he found it a delightful change. 'Can someone pack for you, I'll go and collect them.'

'No, I need to be there.'

'OK, I'll organise an escort, we'll go tonight and come back straight away, but Nisha stays here.'

Suddenly she looked deflated, the brisk doctor was nowhere to be seen, replaced by a vulnerable woman. Max checked his watch.

'I'll pick you up at 18.00 hours.' He looked down at his untouched cup of tea. 'Sorry.'

Hurrying out of the clinic he ticked off the reports that needed to be made and what arrangements were necessary. The attack on top of the death threat justified an escort party and that also gave him an idea.

The road to Mussoorie

'They're still there.' Deepraj was in the rear seat looking back. Max glanced in the rear-view mirror. The Pajero clung tightly to the mountain bends but Penjo had taken the other Pajero to Chakrata to expedite Shanaaz's temporary posting to Baniyana Forest, so Choden and her team were in a camouflaged Mahindra 550. The copy of the WW2 jeep's low suspension meant that it coped well with the roads that contoured the hills but in other respects its performance could not match the Pajero.

'We're about five minutes away from the outer part of town,' Shanaaz said in a voice that betrayed her nervousness.

'Right,' Max said. He looked for a space where the two vehicles could stop without blocking the road and found one over a culvert. What had troubled him was not the message about the attack on Shanaaz's bungalow but that it came from the assistant commissioner of police. Why would a relatively mundane incident of hooliganism command interest from the most senior police officer in the region?

Inquiries of Manek Jha indicated that the senior police posts were in the gift of influential BJP politicians. To date, no one had revealed the identities of the two men killed at the Kempty Falls, but rumour had it that they were relatives of powerful local politicians. The two survivors would doubtless have concocted some colourful story to account for their injuries and the fact that they knew who Nisha was and where she lived made the sisters prime targets for revenge killings.

When he had outlined his plan to Shanaaz she seemed torn between her instinct for survival and the prospects of him succeeding.

'But if they've boarded up the broken windows, surely the police will keep an eye on the place?' she said.

'How sure are you that the Uttarakhand police in Mussoorie are not under the influence of these people?' For a moment she had looked almost desperate. Quickly, Max added, 'I'm not saying they are, it's just that India has more than the usual crop of criminal politicians and it looks as though the two dead men were related to people of influence.' She had looked as though she wanted to disagree but somehow felt obliged to go along with his idea.

*

From their observation position, the men watched as two figures in headscarves got out, leaving the Pajero parked in front of the bungalow. The women stood looking at the front of the building for a minute, pointing at the boarded-up windows, then walked up to the front door and let themselves in.

'It's them,' said the civilian as he turned his bandaged face towards the uniformed figure beside him.

'You're sure?'

'You can see they're Muslim bitches, can't you? And they have the key to the door, what more do you need?'

The man's voice was hoarse and partly muffled where the bandage crossed his mouth. His interlocutor still paused. These people controlled all the important local posts. In the meeting conducted in the closed shop premises he had been assured that his future career was all mapped out to the top. Still, he reflected, if he gave the signal now, he would cross the line and there would be no room for looking back. He did not believe the story about the four men having just teased the girl and then been attacked by armed men shouting '*Allahu Akbar!*' There was no history of Muslims attacking people locally but there had been an increasing number of reports of sexual harassment of girls by the young members of influential businessmen. His informant was hissing with impatience. He did not have to spend time wondering why they had chosen him, he had the biggest network of criminal informants in the area, manpower was never going to be a problem. Mentally he shrugged, it was his *kismet*, what had they taught him at school, 'Man proposes, the Gods dispose.' His walkie-talkie hissed.

'Go?'

'*Ha ji, go!*' There, it was done. His orders were to get the informant out through the rear of the premises and deliver him to where a car would be waiting at Gandhi Chowk.

'Come, we must go.'

'No, no, I want to watch it.'

He had anticipated this and signalled to the two constables behind them in the room. They took hold of the informant who began to struggle, protesting in a hoarse whisper. He put his mouth close to the man's unbandaged ear, 'You want them to hear you, Bhaia?' That part of the man's face that was visible through the bandages was twisted in fury. One of the constables clapped his hand over the man's mouth and they dragged him out of the room towards the rear of the house, he followed. His driver could drop him off at the Welcome Hotel to establish an alibi for himself in the bar. His informant was still struggling, and he had to resist the urge to kick him in the arse.

*

Shanaaz turned on the light and wished she hadn't. She stood stock still, her legs felt weak. The room had been trashed. She felt a firm grip on her arm.

'I know this is awful,' Choden said, 'so let's just get your things and get out of here like the Kushog-saheb told us.'

Shanaaz closed her eyes and took some deep breath before opening them again. 'There's not much here, just those books,' she said, pointing to a bookcase the contents of which had been thrown on the floor.

'Okay. Let's get your suitcases or bags and you just point to what you want, I'll fill them.' Choden's quiet, business-like voice steadied her. She led the way up the stairs to the box room and took out some duffel bags. Shanaaz pointed to an old leather suitcase and said, 'That's for the books.'

A sudden explosion of noise below them made her heart stop. The crash of breaking glass preceded a growing bubble of shouts and curses, she was paralysed. Choden grabbed her arm and shoved her violently through the nearest door which she closed behind them. There was a small brass bolt which she shot into position. She took in the room in a second: there was a bed, a chest of drawers and a heavy-looking old wooden wardrobe that stood next to the door.

'Help me,' Choden said as she began to push the wardrobe so as to block the door. Shanaaz snapped out of her stupor and together they manoeuvred the heavy piece across the doorway. She could hear men shouting to each other and doors banging against walls. Someone started to pound on the bedroom door. Choden put her finger to her lips, she had a cell phone in her hand and hit a pre-set number. Then she looked at Shanaaz and grinned, 'Two minutes, maximum.'

The sound of something metallic striking the door was accompanied by a torrent of abuse. They both leant against the wardrobe, the force of the blows against the door transmitting through the piece of furniture. Choden glanced across the room towards the window. It faced the street in front of the bungalow, not a promising exit. The wardrobe inched towards them. With her eyes, she measured the bed against the space between the wardrobe and the far wall and discarded the idea of trying to jam the barricade, it fell short and they did not have enough time to manoeuvre it into position. The top of the wardrobe tilted towards them then rocked back but it had been shifted sufficiently far away from the door to allow an arm to pass through and get a grip on the side panel. She withdrew the K-bar from its sheath strapped to her leg and hacked at the fingers. The scream of pain drowned out the shouting and the arm disappeared.

'Push!' Choden ordered and they put their shoulders against the wardrobe, almost closing the gap. She knew that it only bought them momentary respite, the damage done to the hand would incite their attackers into a greater frenzy.

The voices in the corridor reached an animal pitch and she knew that they would be overwhelmed once the barrier was gone. How many could she take out before they got her too? The wardrobe rocked and one side moved towards them creating a narrow gap. This time the barrel of a pistol was pointed through and the sound as it was fired left a ringing in her ears. She ducked down and peered round the side of the wardrobe. A man's body was halfway through the gap, the pistol waving in the air. A leg was already through the gap and within arm's reach. She stabbed the K-bar into the knee and was rewarded with a shriek of pain and the leg was withdrawn. Another shot was fired, the bullet hitting the far wall causing the plaster to crack. She glanced again at the window, quite suddenly it presented a better option than remaining in the room. She signalled towards it with her head. 'Go!' Shanaaz took a second to register, then sprang across the room, unlatched the window and swung it inside. Choden waved. 'Go! I'll follow.'

Shanaaz looked down into the little garden, measuring the distance with her eye. Sudden movement in the road caught her attention. Several figures were running towards the bungalow. She felt crushed of breath as her escape route was cut off. There was another explosion and the window shattered. In desperation she swung a leg over the sill and looked down. Unbelievably, she realised that it was Max looking up at her.

'Don't jump!' He disappeared from view. Suddenly, the sounds inside the bungalow changed and moved away from outside the bedroom.

'Give me a hand, doc.' Choden was squeezed between the door and the wardrobe, trying to make enough space to get through. Shanaaz hesitated. 'C'mon.' Half comprehending what the Tibetan was trying to do, she pulled against the side of the wardrobe until Choden had slipped out. The character of the shouting had changed to commands that she recognised to be in Tibetan. Her legs felt weak and she sat down on the bed suddenly aware that she was hyperventilating. She made herself breathe deeply to bring her heart beats under control.

There was a grating sound as one side of the wardrobe began to move towards her. 'Shanaaz?' Max appeared in the gap. 'It's over.'

She looked up at him and realised that she must have tears in her eyes. He put his hand on her shoulder. 'Get your stuff and let's get the hell out of here.'

Shanaaz resisted the desire to throw her arms around his neck and cling to him. Summoning all her self-control she looked him squarely in the face and said, 'You took your time.'

She saw the surprise on his face, then a slight twitch of his head and a look of resignation. He gave her a little mock bow and muttered, 'My apologies, Ma'am.'

He eased himself out of the room and almost bumped into Choden. 'There's six of them,' she said. 'All badly injured but nothing fatal.'

'Bind, gag and blindfold them, load them into the Pajero and then dump them at the guardhouse to the ITBP Academy,' Max said. 'Tell the guard commander to turn them over to the Uttarakhand police in the morning. Just say that they were caught breaking into Dr. Khan's bungalow. Then get back here asap.' The Tibetan gave him her slow grin, turned and disappeared down the staircase.

Max was convinced that the police were involved somehow. The bungalow ought to have had a guard on it and whoever had kept the place under surveillance seemed to be able to move with impunity. At least, this time he did not have to conjure up a story to cover their actions. Choden's team had followed their orders to the letter, there had been no fatalities – as yet, he added to himself.

There was a grain of truth in Shanaaz's criticism. He had delayed sending the team in until he was reasonably certain that there were no more of the bastards in the vicinity. Operational necessity trumped her momentary discomfiture, but her professional persona had reasserted itself as she organised the packing. He was satisfied with the outcome but did not fool himself into thinking that this lesson would halt the malign forces at play. Religious fanaticism coupled with the rising propensity for violence to women was too powerful a combination to be stifled by a couple of setbacks. But with Shanaaz and Nisha taken off the board, at least he could return to focusing on the purpose for which he had been posted here. The irony that his American counterpart shared the misogyny of so many of their host nation did not escape Max.

Why the hell couldn't they all just concentrate on what they were supposed to be doing, combatting Chinese aggression?

Baniyana Forest

Penjo was smiling, something that had become a rare event.
'I spoke to the Chief this morning after Max gave me a report on yesterday's events and he asked me to pass on his congratulations to all those involved in the rescue of Dr. Khan,' the Dapon said. 'He also assured me that he will have inquiries made into the possible involvement of the Uttarakhand police in Mussoorie.' He smiled at Shanaaz, 'You are most welcome here, Doctor-saheb.' She inclined her head in appreciation.

'Choden and her team did a first-rate job,' Max said.

'Well now, she's in your column, so I guess it's no surprise that you're rootin' for her,' Durwachter said, 'but I've no reason to doubt that one of the guys would've done as well.' The Ranger's eyebrows twitched up to colour his words with a hint of sarcasm.

'She personally saved me from being killed,' said Shanaaz whose eyes flashed a warning at the American. 'But there again, if I'd been a male doctor, I imagine you would have expected me to defend myself.'

Max wondered whether Shanaaz was hypersensitive to gender discrimination or if she had already diagnosed Herman's misogyny. Registering that he had shown his preference too openly, the American raised both hands in surrender and looked around at the others. 'I'm not underrating what Choden did, just sayin' that I'd've expected any of the teams to perform well, under those circumstances.' Max shook his head, why did the man have to qualify his words? He saw the expression on Pema's face and decided to chip in.

'I think Herman's argument is more reasoned than discriminatory, it's not as you may think.' He looked hard at Pema, willing her to silence. She compressed her lips and Max continued, 'It's based on the perception that men have a natural tendency to protect women. The thinking is that in combat, if a woman is wounded, the men would give priority to attending to her rather than focusing on their mission.' He looked hard at Pema again as he went on, 'It's a fair comment in a Caucasian setting but some female combatants in Asia contradict the stereotype...' Max turned to Durwachter before adding, '...and our Tibetans are an exception to the norm.'

The American waved a hand in token submission and said, 'Thank you, Kushog-saheb.'

Penjo nodded at Max, his face betraying his fear that the issue might break into open argument. 'Now I have the news we have been waiting for. We have orders to deploy two intelligence gathering operations across the Line of Actual Control before the monsoon breaks,' the Dapon revealed, referring to the notional demarcation line separating territories controlled by India and China. 'As the Chief has to submit our operational plans for ministerial approval, he wants them on his desk by the end of this week.'

Max did a swift mental calculation, based on an exfiltration before the heavens opened, he surmised that the teams would need to move very quickly across their allotted areas if they were to gather sufficient information to make the operation worthwhile. He raised his hand and asked, 'How do we go in?' All heads turned towards him in surprise. Max corrected himself, 'How do *they* go in?'

Penjo allowed a glimmer of a smile before replying, 'Helicopter up to our side of the LAC and on foot thereafter.'

'And the exfiltration?'

'The same. We're interdicted from violating Chinese airspace.'

'What about an emergency extraction?'

'Same,' Penjo frowned.

Durwachter pointed at Max and asked, 'So, the LAC is our border?' The Dapon nodded. Herman stared at Max as he said, 'We sure as hell wouldn't leave our folk to make their own way out of enemy territory if something went wrong, I guess neither would you.' The American leaned back in his chair, his grating tone adding to its critical delivery.

Max nodded agreement and looked at Penjo for an explanation. The Dapon's head twisted apologetically, his tone a little defensive. 'I communicated my view which…,' he looked at both of them and said, '…agrees with yours, but the cabinet believes China would simply use it as an excuse to roll over our border and the government is afraid of the shit they would face.'

It struck Max as totally unworldly. The Chinese could always manufacture an allegation of hostile intrusion if they really wanted to attack. Durwachter stood up and shook his head in exasperation. 'Hell, what about the real shit that our people would face on the ground?'

Max saw the Tibetans whispering amongst themselves. A sense of perspective was needed. He used Penjo's rank to restore order. 'Dapon, of course, we have to make contingency plans, but our priority is to get our teams in and out without detection and that is what they are trained to do.' He glanced at Herman before looking straight at the company commanders and dropping into Tibetan. 'You're all going into your own country, your own territory and your own people, it's not the same as if it was Herman or me,' Max said. 'The odds are in your favour to get in and out without arousing suspicion, added to which you'll be working in your usual teams, all specially trained personnel. It's very different from a bunch of American or British soldiers doing the same thing.'

Max felt uncomfortable. He could utter the words, but it almost felt like betrayal. 'You've all done it before, it's what you signed up to do.'

Suddenly, Norbu laughed out loud. 'The Kushog-saheb is right, we're like *chah*.' He flapped his hands and the others joined in the laughter. Durwachter looked at Max for a translation. 'Norbu says they're like birds.'

The American sat down, put his head in his hands and shook it. 'I swear to God, they're a bunch of crazies.'

Max decided to capitalise on the change in mood. He grinned at the Tibetans, 'He says you're all *nyom-pa*.' They all joined in the joke but Max thought he detected a coldness in Norbu's eyes, even though there was laughter at the edges.

Focus restored, Penjo thanked Shanaaz for attending the meeting and she took the hint. Standing up, she scanned them all before saying, 'On behalf of my sister and myself, I just want to say thank you for the way that you have looked after us.' Looking directly at Max, she continued, 'At first, I thought Colonel Devlin's plan was unnecessarily cautious.' There was some laughter. 'I was wrong,' she said and turned to face Herman before adding, 'My presence here today is primarily thanks to Choden, an outstanding soldier to whom I am indebted.' She stood to attention, saluted, turned and left the room.

Max turned to Herman. They had to get down to business.

'We have to select the teams to be deployed to each of the target areas. Company commanders know best who are familiar with which areas. I suggest that people go into their own home territory as far as possible without breaking up the established teams.' He looked at Penjo who nodded his approval. Max decided not to interfere with their choice though he hoped they would seek his advice on which teams would be tasked to which objective. He also hoped that the preparations would distract them from their animosity to the American and that Durwachter would do nothing to exacerbate the situation in the meantime.

'Carry on.' Penjo signalled to Max with his head and they walked out of the room together. Max deliberately avoided looking at Herman, hoping that he would just get on with the job. Once outside the room, Penjo talked as they walked along.

'I've asked Herman to bring me his team selections. I'll try not to interfere with them,' said Penjo as he half turned his face towards Max, 'but it's my head that will roll.'

Max did not envy the Tibetan his responsibility, nominally in command, he was trapped in an in-running nip between those for whom he was responsible and the political-administrative monolith that made the strategic decisions and, worse, how they were to be executed. But he did not have the luxury of time to commiserate, the final pre-operational exercise was about to start, and the hope was that it would identify any weaknesses in the command and control structure.

Alpine training area north of Munsyari

The moon threw an insipid light onto the landing zone cut out of the forest, but even with the flares they would light when the helicopter approached, it would require considerable skill to drop it into the space, without fouling the encircling trees. Max had been tempted to tell Jhampa to widen the area but decided against it. Two earlier bits of advice had been met with a defensive: 'But that's not how Herman-saheb does it'. On this occasion, concern for the helicopter and its crew almost won out over challenging Durwachter's authority. Max walked back into the forest, making his way to where Prabhat was supervising the communications. Up close, he raised his eyebrows interrogatively.

'Nothing yet, saheb,' Prabhat whispered. They were supposed to maintain radio silence, but the Gurkha signals expert could encode a message that would go out in no more than a second.

'Tell Ulan he's got zero tolerance on the LZ.' Prabhat nodded and busied himself with his transceiver. Max's eyes felt gritty from lack of sleep. Both columns had been engaged on this exercise for the last 10 days and though he had grabbed the odd occasion to get his head down, the demand to assess the abilities of the teams had kept him on his feet almost continuously. Reluctantly, he had agreed to Durwachter's proposal that they swap columns for the exercise. There was force in the American's argument that they would approach their task without any preconceived judgments about respective strengths and weaknesses, but he could not suppress a niggling sense of concern, entrusting his column to someone whose methods he disapproved of. On the other hand, he conceded, what better way to test their resilience and coherence? Durwachter's column, as he still thought of them, had been assigned as Blue Force, tasked to penetrate two facilities held by Red Force under Pema and Paljor. After some limited success, Blue Force had withdrawn into a defensive position from which they were tasked to be extracted by helicopter. The exercise had been designed to create maximum difficulties for the extraction, the Blue Force personnel were static, their position would be identifiable once the choppers came in. Add to this that the Mi-17 and its sister ship the South African Rooivalt had very limited troop-carrying capacity which meant repeated flights to lift all Blue Force, even assuming that they could continue to land.

'Acknowledged,' Prabhat whispered to him. Max nodded. From what he had observed, Ulan would handle the task competently, he was less sure of the other assigned pilot, Desmond Morris. A handsome Anglo-Indian who had transferred to the IAF from Indian Airways and flew by the rule book, something Max found curiously out of character with the demands of the SFF. Speaking softly, Max gave Prabhat his orders, 'Stay with the Blue Force HQ until they're lifted out, then meet me at the RV with the vehicles.'

He jogged back along the track to where Norbu and Jhampa had sited their command post on a rise in the floor of the forest which gave them as good a view of their position as the trees permitted. Norbu greeted him with his quizzical look, the opposite to the scrunched expression that Max had decided was the Khamba's excuse for a smile.

'This is a shit position,' Norbu spat his disgust. 'We should have been long gone, on foot.'

Max hunched his shoulders. 'I agree with you,' he said, 'but we have to practise the air extraction drills in a hostile setting.'

Norbu jerked his thumb in the direction of Red Force and said, 'Those bastards will be on us before the chopper sets down.'

'Then you'll have to fight your way out...again,' Max grinned.

After a moment's hesitation, Norbu gave him the scrunch: 'I'm going forward to control the withdrawal.' Pointing at Jhampa, he added, 'He's got the LZ.' Norbu picked up his Uzi and disappeared into the trees. Max had already checked on the Blue Force positions of which he approved.

'It's coming in,' Choki said softly to Jhampa, his Maxar transceiver held close to his ear. Jhampa signalled to those holding the flares and they ignited them, temporarily blinding Max with the intensity of light.

Then as he heard the 'thump, thump, thump' of the rotor blades, a series of explosions and small arms fire announced the Red Force attack. Still worried about the inadequacy of the LZ, Max moved to where he could watch what was going on. The Mi-17 appeared suddenly, virtually at treetop height and stopped directly above the gaping hole in the canopy before descending almost as though it was falling out of the sky. Leaves, pine needles and bits of twig showered down on him and he sheltered his eyes so that he could continue to observe. The chopper landed as gracefully as a giraffe sitting down, the side doors were open, and Ulan shouted through the cockpit window, 'Move your arses, the Disneyland express is here!'

Jhampa stood bent over under the revolving rotor blades shouting at the first teams to board. He almost threw the last one on as the machine began to lift off. No sooner had it cleared the LZ space overhead than the second Mi-17 hove into view, filling the empty space in the sky and manoeuvring to position itself directly over the landing zone. It descended slowly, almost feeling its way between the trees that enclosed it. Unlike Ulan's hedge trimming, its descent was faultless but, Max reflected, so mind-numbingly slow that it presented a juicy target for any RPG.

Jhampa was back under the rotor blades directing the second group of teams on board but this time he had to tell the pilot to take off: 'Go! Get the fuck out of here.' He shook his fist at the ascending machine then ran back to where Max was standing.

'Stupid bastard, he'll have us all killed, flying like that,' Jhampa said. 'Where does he think he is, fucking Santa Cruz?'

Max managed not to smile but the Ladakhi was 100 per cent correct. Any further commentary on the quality of the air service was interrupted by a loud explosion near at hand. Norbu came running out of the treeline, followed by an extended line of troops. He shouted at Jhampa, 'We're getting out on foot.' Pointing at Choki, he yelled, 'Your teams are rear-guard, hold them off as long as you can.'

Then he waved the remaining teams onto the path leading away from the LZ. Jhampa pointed to the positions for Choki's team and punched him playfully on the arm, announcing, 'No upgrades for you today, not even cattle class.' Then he set off at a run after Norbu.

Max stood back in the treeline and observed Choki positioning his team. Despite Deepraj's disregard for him, Choki's dispositions were well thought out, one team on each side of the track, well concealed in a classic ambush configuration and an unobstructed escape route. Max watched as two men ran forward and buried dummy claymore mines on each side of the track leading into the LZ clearing before resuming their firing positions. He stood far enough inside the treeline to be hidden from view whilst he kept the position under observation. An umpire in a live firing exercise was the most vulnerable to being shot as the troops fired over the heads of where they expected their enemy to be. True, it was risky but the lesson that his Gurkhas had instilled into the SFF operatives was never to waste a shot and the yellow band around Max's jungle hat clearly identified him as directing staff. Slowly and as soundless as a silent movie, shapes began to separate from the undergrowth. He adjusted his binoculars in an attempt to identify individuals.

'Well done,' Max mouthed silently as one of the figures found a claymore and identified it to those in the immediate vicinity before dropping flat to the ground. He was fairly certain it was Choden.

'Fire!' Choki's voice carried through the trees and pieces of bark started to rain down on the approaching Red Force. Max saw a couple of flash-bang grenades fly through the air and then bark and twigs started to fall on him as the attackers opened fire. The defenders on his left were already pulling back under covering fire from the team on his right, then they too disappeared into the forest.

Bang! One of the dummy claymores on the left of the approach track exploded, throwing soot into the air. Calculated to delay the pursuit, it succeeded. By the time the Red Force teams had swung wide to approach from the flanks, Choki's teams were long gone. Max moved forward as he saw Durwachter walk into the empty LZ space. The American looked angry and thundered, 'Why've they gone?' He threw his hands up in despair.

Max told him, 'Norbu made a tactical decision to withdraw on foot when he heard you so close.' The American glared at Max through slitted eyes and asked, 'Why didn't you stop him? The objective is to give them experience of an airborne extraction.' Max looked pointedly at the troops behind the Ranger and said, 'Let's discuss this after we get back to base.'

'Goddamn!' Durwachter glowered at him and looked about to argue it there and then but must have had second thoughts as Pema came up to him with the question: 'They've escaped?'

Max put her in the picture, and she grinned, 'Woos!' Max refrained from commenting. Pema turned back towards Paljor and he heard them laughing. Turning to Durwachter, Max said, 'Why don't we take the opportunity to extract Red Force by air, the choppers will be returning, even though it's not a tactical extraction…?' He left the question in the air. The Ranger gave a dismissive wave and shouted back as he walked away, 'Do what you like.' His body language expressed his anger.

Penjo appeared from behind the Red Force troops. He nodded approvingly at Pema and Paljor as he walked up to Max. He gave a quick glance towards Durwachter's retreating back.

'What's up?'

'Disapproves of Norbu abandoning the air extraction,' Max explained. 'We should discuss it when we're all back.' Penjo raised one eyebrow. The whoomph of the approaching rotor blades prompted Max to tell him that the Red Force should use the opportunity for a chopper lift. Penjo nodded, 'Good idea. You coming back by road?'

'Yes.'

'We'll go together.' They stood and watched the choppers land, Penjo observing Desmond's balletic manoeuvring, shook his head as he commented, 'Ulan may be a rogue but you're far more likely to get out alive with him than our test pilot.' He paused, as if reflecting before continuing, 'As we're prohibited from extracting our people by air, this is all a bit academic anyway.'

'Mm.' Max decided that it was diplomatic not to seek clarification.

'Huzoor.' Deepraj trotted up to them wearing a broad grin. 'The last team will go with Ulan the Warrior!' They all smiled but Max's tone was serious as he said to Deepraj, 'You and Prabhat-saheb make sure that the live grenades don't get mixed up with the dummies before they're returned to the armoury.' The yellow paint that distinguished the dummies from the live Mills grenades tended to wear off and everyone was tired, a potentially dangerous scenario.

'Huzoor.' It was not that Max did not have confidence in the company commanders but from past experience he knew that the rivalry in the field often carried over after the training exercise and that could lead to a relaxation of focus on the basics.

As he and Penjo walked back through the forest they compared notes on the comparative performances, both agreeing that the individual teams worked exceptionally well together, but because they were not designed to be deployed in larger units, there had been insufficient work done on command and control of companies.

'I think it served a useful purpose in showing up the wrinkles,' Penjo said, sounding constructive.

'True but our planning is still based on deployment of the individual teams, that's where our strength lies,' Max observed.

'Initially they'll go in as companies, and only splinter once they're well inside.'

Max was far from convinced that this strategy would achieve the level of covert penetration that the teams would need. He decided to argue his point.

'Mobility, speed and the smallest possible silhouette are the keys to survival and success,' he told Penjo. 'My preferred plan would be to move them up close to the LAC under company command but then have them cross in individual teams.'

The Dapon was silent in thought, the quiet *tud tud* of their boots seeming to blend with the natural voices of the forest. The Tibetan had the worst of all jobs, he had to select the people to go in but had to remain behind and maintain communications with Chakrata and Delhi, where a potential hornet's nest of politicians and senior officers would be hovering ready to pounce on the slightest mistake. Max did not envy him. During the entire time that the teams were in Chinese territory, other than the encrypted map references they sent, they would be out of contact, unless disaster struck and then Penjo would be under the gravest of responsibilities, aware of their vulnerability but impotent to help. Max probed for an update. 'It's still academic?'

Penjo gave him a sideways look as though he was feigning indifference. 'Delhi still has to approve the plan.'

'Chances?' Max pressed him.

'Fifty-fifty. There was a report in the Times of India that the Chinese foreign minister will make an official visit soon,' Penjo said. 'It's common knowledge that Kaur wants to cosy up to Beijing.'

Max allowed himself an impatient click of his tongue. 'He's forgotten that the last time they did the *Hindi-Chini bhai bhai* thing, it was closely followed by a Chinese invasion.'

'True.' Penjo's response was pensive. He stopped and faced Max. 'I'd like you to continue overseeing Norbu's and Jhampa's companies. I know that you have developed a close affinity with Pema and Paljor, but Herman's people are seething with anger. He makes no allowances for our cultural differences, just reduces everything to his military work ethic.'

Max's initial reaction was concern for Pema's company, why should Durwachter's *modus operandi* be permitted to risk disaffecting them when they were now an effective operational group? He pressed Penjo, 'You think Pema will take any more kindly to his attitude than Norbu?'

Penjo gave him a wry smile. 'Well, it will give us time to work on a solution.'

Events, however, were soon to interrupt that.

Prime Minister's Office
Raisina Hill, New Delhi

Arvind Kaur surveyed the faces at the table whilst his mind digested the information that the party's managers had served up for his breakfast table. His popularity, so they said, had dropped significantly following his meeting with the Chinese deputy foreign minister, Jiang He. The press had been highly critical, querying why he would waste time with a mere deputy. Ignorant swine, he had muttered to himself. Jiang was the key intermediary between himself and the Chinese premier in their aim to effect a fundamental change in Sino-Indian relations. A fickle electorate and a disruptive press and now, here he was with his most important ministers, each one of whom fancied themselves in his chair. Defence minister Dilconda's supercilious tones ruptured his thoughts.

'If they can get in and out undetected, I grant that the information will greatly assist our defence forces,' Dilconda said.

'And buy us considerable clout in Washington,' added Roy, the foreign minister.

Kaur shook his head and asked, 'And if they don't?'

'They're unattributable and we'll deny any involvement,' said Mullick as he tapped the folder in front of him on the table.

'You seriously think the Chinese will believe that bullshit?' the PM thundered.

Mullick bowed his head a little apologetically. 'The point, Mentri-ji, is that they will not be able to prove it,' the special secretary said.

Kaur sat silently pondering this, why had he not considered the problem from this angle before? When the CIA had armed and trained the Khamba guerrillas after the flight of the Dalai Lama, their base had been in Nepal, but the Chinese never openly criticised the Nepalese government. In theory, at least, the inevitable antagonism would be directed principally at the USA, he could plead ignorance as well as anyone, just as Beijing pretended to know nothing of its soldiers' incursions into Indian territory. But he still had to protect his legacy. His gaze took in both Dilconda and Roy.

'Let me have a cabinet minute from you, confirming that any operations by the 22s across our border will be fully deniable,' Kaur said, 'then I'll sign off on the plan.'

Dilconda raised one quizzical eyebrow in Roy's direction. Looking directly at the defence minister, Roy said, 'We can do that, Mentri-ji.'

Mullick left the room as soon as it was polite to do so. In the corridor, hé pressed a pre-set on his mobile.

'Speak!' General Chaudhari answered.

'It's a go.'

'*Tik hei.*'

Then the line was cut.

Baniyana Forest

'Max,' Penjo called as he waved some papers at Max who was about to walk into his office. 'The Chief is coming up this evening. He didn't say much but he gave me the impression that the operation has been given the green light.'

'Doubtless he'll fill us in when he gets here.'

'Here. Your copy of the joint assessment,' Penjo said as he gave Max a plastic folder containing several sheets of paper. 'Is Herman in his office?'

'I haven't checked.'

They walked together along the corridor and the Dapon knocked on the Durwachter's door. There was no response.

'I'll leave his copy in his desk drawer, it's confidential stuff.'

Max stood in the open doorway as Penjo tugged at the left-hand top drawer.

'Is it locked?'

'No, just a bit stuck.'

Penjo pulled harder and the drawer suddenly came free. Max heard a familiar metallic clink, but it was a good second before his mind registered the significance of it.

'Grenade! Down!'

Max flung himself at Penjo, driving the Tibetan to the floor, landing sprawled across him, then the explosion blew the desk apart and the force of the blast momentarily knocked him senseless.

He was conscious of hands rolling him over and faces appeared, their mouths moving but he heard nothing apart from a constant whine in his ears. He experienced a sense of disembodiment, a detachment that relieved him of any responsibilities. He felt himself smiling. Then the pain in his head hit him and his hand felt wet. He looked down and noted a darkening stain on his camo pants over his left thigh and blood running over his hand. His mind came back into focus like a set of tumblers in a lock falling slowly into place.

'Penjo?' His voice echoed in his head. He tried to see through a thinning cloud of dust or was it smoke? The smell was a confusion of gunpowder, burnt paint, charred wood and the stench of a room that had been torn open. His vision was blurred but he could see a face, its lips moving soundlessly. He felt himself being lifted and closed his eyes to enjoy the rare feeling of not having to take charge.

Drifting in and out of consciousness, he saw Deepraj's worried face for a second, then nothing.

*

'Max? Can you hear me, Max?'

He came to, with Shanaaz's face filling his vision, then everything receded a little against a background of white ceiling and walls.

'Yes.' He heard his own voice.

'OK, I'm going to examine you for brain damage.'

'Too late, I was born this way.'

'Ha-ha. Just shut up and do what I tell you.'

He could read nothing from her expression, just a typical business-as-usual doctor's face as she went through the initial tests. He was disappointed that she showed no sign of special concern for him, even though he had concluded that apart from whatever wound there was to his thigh, he was perfectly fit and well. Plainly, there was to be no emotional sympathy. He dutifully counted the fingers held in front of his face and followed her index finger as it swept left and right, right and left across his field of vision.

'No nystagmus, no apparent signs or symptoms,' she tallied them off. 'Headache?'

'Mm'. He moved his head gently side to side with no ill effects.

'I'm going to clean up the wound on your thigh and stitch you up,' Shanaaz said. 'You'll stay here under observation for 24 hours.'

Max was suddenly aware that under a cellular blanket he was naked apart from a large blood-stained field dressing over his left thigh.

She turned away and walked to a wash-hand basin, talking as she went, 'Si-thar, remove the dressing and give me 1% lidocaine.' The paramedic smiled at Max as he wheeled over a trolley. Now he was conscious of a dull ache in his head and the wound hurt when the dressing was peeled away, re-opening the jagged six-inch gash which began to bleed. He ignored it. They knew what they were doing. Time to catch up.

'Penjo, is he OK?'

She turned towards him as she snapped on her surgical gloves. 'Thanks to you, yes.' He thought he detected criticism of himself, the way she said it. 'He has mild concussion but insists on pretending that he's fit and well.' She injected some local anaesthetic around the site of the wound. 'Tell me if you can feel anything.' She pricked the skin above and below the gash.

'Uh-huh.'

'Is that a yes or a no?'

'No.'

She leaned close over him and he caught the scent of her body as she began exploring the wound for fragments. 'I think you were lucky: it was a shard of metal from the desk that hit you, not shrapnel from the grenade, the metal drawer must have directed most of the force upwards,' she said. 'It's not too deep either. I don't see any major damage to arteries, nerves or sinews.' He heard the sound of a suction tube as the paramedic cleared the blood away. She knew her explosive theory too, smart girl.

'Good. I'm closing you up now.'

'Any other casualties?'

'No, thank God. Who would do such a thing?' She sucked her teeth as she tied off the stitches. 'Someone must really hate Durwachter.' She stood up and gave him a look that he could not interpret, a sort of reluctant half-smile. 'Penjo says he doesn't know how you knew it was a grenade. Some of them think you're invested with magical powers.'

His laugh was cut short because it made his head hurt. 'No magic. Some years ago, a British Gurkha officer in Hong Kong was killed in precisely this way,' Max said. 'I heard the sound of the release lever on

the grenade as it was dislodged, and it triggered the memory...luckily.'
He watched her hands as she spread ointment on the wound and covered
it with gauze before wrapping another dressing over it. There was a
contradictory choreography to her movements, fiercely professional and
yet almost tender.

'Thanks, doc'.' He leant on his elbows as he began to sit up.

'Where do you think you're going?'

'I need to sort out this mess quickly.'

'Over my dead body,' she said. 'Provided you promise to stay here in
bed I may allow you to go to the lavatory.' Max looked at her, inviting
an explanation. 'Otherwise, you'll have to use a bedpan. I'm not having
those stitches pulled.' She paused and grinned at him, 'It's too good a
job to waste on a hopeless case like you.' She turned and despite the fact
that she was wearing military fatigues, she managed to flounce out of the
room.

'Madam is a *yi-dag*!' The paramedic laughed as he disposed of the
soiled dressings and threw the needle into a sharps box.

'*Phö-cha kesho*!' Max requested. 'With two spoons of sugar.' Doctors
knew everything about stitching and dressing but nothing so revived a
soldier as a cup of hot sweet army tea and right now he was in dire need
of revival.

The attempt on the American's life put the whole setup in jeopardy.
Regardless of the CIA's reaction, they had an emotionally disturbed SFF
operative on the loose. He – or she – had to be identified and taken out
of play. The likelihood was that most if not all the Tibetans approved
of the objective, even if they disapproved of the method. Just as the
Gurkhas had closed ranks around the man responsible for the British
officer's death, he anticipated that the Tibetans would clam up to protect
whoever was responsible.

'Shit!' He slammed his palm down on the metal bedstead. General
Mullick was due to arrive this evening. Even if they had wanted to
conceal the event from the special secretary, they would need a solid
explanation for why Max was confined to a sick bed. His head hurt, the
effects of the anaesthetic had already started to wear off and he had rarely

felt so useless. He wanted to shout but disciplined himself just to mutter, 'Where's my bloody tea?'

*

'It was Choki,' Prabhat spoke across the top of his mug of steaming tea.

'How do you know?' Kesarsing asked, looking at Deepraj and Prabhat.

The three Gurkha instructors had taken themselves off into the forest and brewed up some tea on a Tommy cooker.

Prabhat began softly, 'The saheb told us to make doubly sure that none of the live grenades were mixed with the dummies, so we had to account for all the remaining live ones. Choden and Kalsang had kept an accurate record of the live ones that had been used.' He nodded to indicate that this is what he had anticipated before continuing, 'So, the tally of dummies was done by elimination.' His forehead creased in a frown. 'Choki accused Pema's team of having thrown one more than their ration. Pema insisted angrily that they had only thrown the number issued.

'Choki showed her the receipt chit with her initials on it,' he continued. 'When I came across them arguing, I examined the chit and saw it supported Choki, but I also noted that the entries were only in pencil.'

Looking at Kesarsing, Prabhat added, 'I know you're the expert on explosives and you think he's good, *bhai*, but I agree with Deepraj, thangchha.'

Kesarsing nodded slowly. 'He impressed me with the way he handled explosives, but if as you say he cheats?' he said, looking at his colleagues. Words were unnecessary.

Deepraj looked at his watch. 'The doctor said we could visit the saheb after five, it's nearly time.'

Prabhat pointed to the enamel jug on the Tommy cooker and said, 'Better bring that along, you know what he says about the healing power of *masala chiya*.'

They all laughed and Deepraj checked to make sure there was enough tea left in the pot.

As they walked back along the forest path towards the clinic, Kesarsing asked Deepraj, 'What did the doc' say, will he be OK?'

Deepraj was slow to answer. 'You know what these doctors are like, never tell you the truth. But when we were carrying him to the clinic, he opened his eyes and said, "Get me out of here, you little bastard." I think he's going to be OK.'

*

The room smelled strongly of burning butter lamps, their tiny flames illuminating the face of the small bronze-gilt statue of *Chenrezig*, the patron of Tibet, that stood on the low altar table. All four company commanders knelt, their heads touching the ground before the embodiment of compassion, their voices low but unified in prayer.

Pema tried to concentrate on the words, but her mind was a roiling turbulence of dark thoughts, the black faces of the demons kept thrusting their way through her attempts to rationalise events. She had more reason than the other company commanders to loathe the American, who demonstrated his contempt for women at every possible opportunity. She allowed herself to imagine how she would be feeling if the grenade had killed or seriously injured the man for whom it was intended, and she recognised that any prayer she would have been offering would have been of thanks. But it did not justify the attempt or its method, the result had been to injure the man she cared about most and as for the Kushog-saheb, she was still barely able to believe that he threw himself on top of the Dapon. Now she respected Max more than any foreigner she had ever met. But she was furious, such a stupid trap which had nearly killed people wholly committed to their cause. She half wanted to think that it had been set by a Chinese agent but had that been the case it was far more probable that the target would have been Penjo or one of the four company commanders. No, it was one of their own people and the assassin had to be rooted out – they could not afford to have a loose cannon.

She sensed Norbu raising himself up and leaning back before he said, 'Now, enlightenment?'

They re-arranged themselves in a tight circle, sitting cross-legged on the rugs that provided the only decorative colour in the wooden shed that they had converted into a temporary *gompa*.

Paljor steepled his fingers and bowed his head a little before he said, 'Lobsang?'

Norbu stared at him for a moment or two before replying, 'He is not as we are.'

They all understood what he meant: they were all seasoned fighters having led missions into Tibet, theirs was a confrerie of risk and survival, the basis of their trust for each other, whereas Lobsang, despite being the unit intelligence officer, had never crossed the border. Paljor nodded acquiescence.

Jhampa gave a little cough to indicate that he wanted to speak. 'We can all agree that we would wish to be free of the American but not like this,' he said. 'Everyone was put at risk. We cannot have such a person working with us.'

Pema and Paljor nodded. Norbu's expression was unreadable. He looked down at his hands for a second or two, then sat up. 'Who is it?' he asked.

They looked at each other, no one wanting to be the first to speak. Pema stared steadily at Paljor who sighed, 'Alright.' She had shared the information from the Gurkhas with him and he had agreed to break the news to Norbu. She was uncomfortable accusing a senior officer in Norbu's column and had gone with Prabhat to tell Paljor what the Gurkhas had discovered. Closely questioned, Prabhat had set out the facts and Paljor had reached the same conclusion. He looked straight into Norbu's eyes and said, 'Choki, it was Choki.'

Norbu just stared back at him. A slight lifting of the eyebrows signalled his first reaction. Paljor recounted what he had learned from Prabhat and Pema.

'But he was…' Norbu started.

'His friend?' Pema interposed.

Norbu nodded before adding, 'Perhaps he had begun to resent being used as some sort of servant, he's a proud man.'

They all recognised this sentiment, each of them had been criticised in front of their subordinates and the resentment had built up.

'It doesn't matter why he did it, what are *we* going to do about it?' Norbu asked.

Paljor's face was dark with anger. He drew his hand across his throat.

Pema tried to restore a sense of reality. 'We are members of the Indian defence forces,' she said, 'we can't exact our own justice.'

'In Tibet we can, and we have,' Norbu pronounced gravely before pinching his nose between his fingers, then added, 'But we are not in Tibet.'

'What do we do if they call in the military police?' Pema frowned but Paljor interrupted, 'We don't want those fuckpigs here, have you seen the way they march? Like a bunch of chickens with a hernia.'

Norbu's face smiled but his eyes remained neutral. He waved his hand to counsel restraint. 'We need to deal with this ourselves,' he said, looking at Pema. 'You and I will talk to Penjo-la. In the meantime, say nothing about what we know to anyone else. Can we count on the Gurkhas to remain silent?'

'Prabhat said they would only tell the Kushog-saheb,' Pema said.

Norbu nodded. 'Good.'

Pema looked at him, her face a study of concern. 'Do you think they will cancel the operation now?'

Norbu inclined his head a little towards her. 'It will be out of our hands,' he said, 'but we must do everything to reassure higher command that our effectiveness is not compromised.' He spoke authoritatively but she knew that he nursed the same doubts that she did.

'If it could be passed off as an accident, a defective grenade...?' She let the idea float in the air.

Norbu grunted, 'Jha wouldn't know the difference, doesn't know his arse from his elbow.'

She nodded agreement. 'Still, worth a try.'

The clinic

He woke instantly, his hand feeling for his CZ75 and not finding it. He tried to catch the sound that had alerted him and opened his eyes just enough to be able to see without appearing to be awake.

'It's only me,' she said, sitting on the side of the bed. 'Are you always expecting the worst?' He opened his eyes fully. Her features were not clear and for a second he wondered whether his sight had been affected, then he realised that the room was dimly lit by some form of night light. He let his head sink back onto the pillow.

'I've always had the knack of waking fully.' He paused for a moment. Her question deserved a proper answer. 'In Afghanistan, we had several incidents of Afghan soldiers with whom we were embedded suddenly changing sides,' he said. 'They'd wait till we were asleep then murder us in our beds.' In his mind's eye he saw again the fractional paralysis before reality kicked in and he reacted, too late to save Tim Pike, it was his recurrent nightmare. 'It becomes instinctive.' Now he could smell her, nothing more than a scented soap but it managed to be both fresh yet heady.

'How's the leg?' she asked. He gave a non-committal grunt. 'Why won't you take the Tramadol, it will ease the pain,' she said, shaking her head in despair, but her tone was jesting. 'I think you're more than a little crazy. Putting up with pain is the least of your worrying characteristics.'

'Meaning?'

'Look how you jumped in to save Nisha…and now this,' she said, gesturing at his thigh. 'You court danger.'

'I reacted. It's what soldiers do,' he said.

'Not all of them.' She leant over him and brushed his hair away from his forehead. 'I've not thanked you for all that you did for Nisha and me.'

'It's…' She put her finger across his lips, then removed it and kissed him. It was much more than a Thank-you and he held her head as they explored each other's mouth. She pulled away, breathing heavily and took his hand in both of hers. Shaking her head slowly, her expression serious.

'Not yet,' she said. 'I have to get you fully fit.' Was she holding out the promise of more or had he misjudged the warmth of her response?

He grinned, 'I can take any amount of R & R.'

'Well, that's all you're getting,' she said, standing up and looking down at him, 'for now.'

Next morning

They were all in the clinic's large casualty receiving area, Max seated in a large chair with a cellular blanket across his knees and everyone else ranged around him in a semi-circle.

Penjo tapped his pencil on the arm of his own chair. 'We managed to postpone the Chief's visit for 24 hours,' he said, 'which means that by this afternoon, latest, we have to decide how we are going to handle this.'

Durwachter had taken a seat as soon as he had walked in but other than a nod of acknowledgement to Penjo and Max, he had spoken to no one. Now he surveyed them all and said, 'Don't know what you all have in mind, but I want the motherfucker who tried to get me.'

Penjo nodded gently. 'Of course, of course.' He looked straight at the Ranger and said, 'We have a choice. Put in the hands of the military police, all the work that you have done here will be for nothing. We are a clandestine unit, the involvement of you, Max and the British Gurkhas is politically highly sensitive: an investigation by outside forces at this point wouldn't just scupper our planned operation, it would most probably pull the plug on the SFF and its objectives. We're out of the ordinary, and as such, the conventional forces are suspicious of us, even a bit envious.' He saw Durwachter about to interrupt and held up his hand to make him pause before continuing, 'Please. Your government has invested considerable time, resources and diplomatic goodwill in us, would you want to prejudice all that?'

Max watched as this sunk into the American's mind. He could almost hear the Ranger's brain working out the ramifications on his own career prospects. Durwachter's expression was set in opposition. 'I get all that, but whilst this murdering bastard is out there, I'll be waitin' for a knife in my back.'

Penjo held up one hand. 'Trust me, Herman, I have your back covered,' the Dapon said, staring him down. With an impatient twitch of his head, Durwachter opened both hands palm upwards in resignation and sat back in his chair. Looking around at the others, Penjo said, 'Herman was the target, but Max and I bore the brunt of the attempt.' He looked at Max and added, 'I should say that you sheltered me from it.' He gave a little bow before announcing, 'And so it is he and I who have decided how to handle the situation. Everyone will resume their duties as planned. When the Chief visits us this evening there will be no mention of the grenade attack. I guarantee that the threat to Herman will be gone before the Chief gets here. To say more would jeopardise my plan.'

'So, you're not goin' to tell me who it is?' Durwachter could barely contain his fury. His fists were tightly balled and his chin jutted out like an Orang-Outang.

'I asked you to trust me...,' Penjo said softly but firmly, 'I don't want to make that an order.'

'Hey General, trust is a two-way avenue,' Durwachter retorted, 'I don't see nothin' coming my way.'

Penjo smiled, 'You trust me to handle this situation and I trust you to comply with my instructions.'

'Goddammit, you people,' the man thundered. He stood up, thrusting his chair backwards so that it fell over, then stalked out of the room.

'You people,' Norbu mimicked the American. 'That's where the problem lies.'

'Enough,' Penjo ordered. 'The story for general consumption, especially Major Jha, is that a live grenade was mistakenly switched for a dummy and when I was playing with the pin, Max recognised it for what it was, and the rest is history,' he said. 'Not a story that puts me in a favourable light but that is a small price to pay to keep this under wraps.'

With Durwachter gone, everyone else in the room knew the truth.

'Orders have already been issued for Choki to report to Chakrata,' Penjo said, looking at his wristwatch. 'At this moment he is being escorted there. On his arrival, he will be transferred immediately to a training battalion in Pune. There's no need to demote him, being posted to a low-grade training unit from a combat unit speaks volumes.' The Dapon paused as though making his mind up about something, then added, 'I have already spoken to the training unit commander, an old friend. Choki will never hold a position of trust or command in future.'

The meeting broke up with all four company commanders paying their respects to Max before they left. Eventually only the Gurkhas remained behind. Prabhat hunkered down next to Max's chair. There was a grim expression on his face that Max recognised only too well. 'We would have disposed of him,' Prabhat said.

Max smiled, 'Thanks, but not necessary. Remember, we're guests here.'

Kesarsing added, 'Paljor wanted to gut him, so did Choden if Pema hadn't got to him first.'

'She knows?' Max asked.

'They all know.'

Max laughed to himself, so much for their secret plan. Deepraj took a cloth package out from under his shirt unwrapped it and handed the CZ75 to Max. 'I retrieved it from your cabin, saheb, fully-loaded,' the Gurkha said.

He felt the weapon's perfect balance in his hand. He had no fears for his own safety but had felt undressed when he had reached for it and found nothing there.

'You have some visitors,' announced Deepraj. He half turned as the door opened and Pema, Choden and Paljor walked in ahead of several of the smiling team leaders, all carrying a *khata*. Each of them made namaskar before placing the white silk scarves around Max's neck.

Pema made a gesture that embraced all of them. 'The *ye-she* saheb told us that we could come,' she said. Her smile still managed to carry concern and the unasked question.

'Thank you all. It's nothing serious,' Max said, 'I'll be chasing you all around tomorrow.' They laughed and Shanaaz suddenly appeared in her white coat. Max pointed to her and said, 'See, the ye-she saheb wants to throw me out.' There was more laughter and each of the Tibetans took his hand in both of theirs before leaving. The Gurkhas stood to attention and left, Deepraj wearing a knowing grin.

Shanaaz put her hands on her hips and surveyed him. 'You look none the worse for wear.'

'I didn't hear you leave last night.'

'I stayed beside you until you fell asleep.'

'Have you got anything on under that protective white coat?'

'That is a highly improper question for a patient to ask of his attending physician and don't misinterpret me when I tell you I want you back in bed.' She frowned playfully.

'Yes doctor, I mean, no doctor.' He stood up and walked carefully towards her. 'If I don't push it, is it OK for me to get back to my desk? There's a mass of paperwork to catch up with.'

'I'll examine the wound first and then we'll see.'

He gave a theatrical sigh. 'Whatever you say, Doctor.'

*

'What are you not telling me?' General Mullick looked Penjo straight in the eye. 'I haven't survived in this country for this long without developing a nose for things that don't strike me as right.' Fernandes had briefed the special secretary about the informant's report of an explosion in the American's office though there had been no further detail.

Penjo inclined his head forward a little in acknowledgement. 'We've had an unfortunate training accident,' he said. 'I've dealt with it, nothing that affects our operational efficiency.' Then as an afterthought he added with a self-conscious expression, 'It didn't reflect very well on me.'

'I have your assurance on that?'

'Certainly.'

Mullick let that response sink in. If Penjo had decided not to enlarge on it, so be it. It was not his job to micro-manage the SFF unit. His personal obligation to the prime minister was nothing more than his job required but he had developed a strong affinity with Penjo and the 22s, a responsibility for them that went beyond his place in the hierarchy.

'The foreign advisors? The American?'

Penjo's immediate reaction was to wonder whether the Chief had an informant amongst them but reminded himself that the problems caused by Durwachter's character were already documented.

'Personally, the American is difficult, inflexible, but his work is greatly respected,' Penjo said.

Mullick decided to leave it alone. The Dapon was a shrewd and highly capable commander who had overseen the SFF achieve a remarkable level of proficiency. He tapped the operation folder on the table in front of him and asked, 'What are the weaknesses in the plans?' He added quickly, 'I mean, the risks of our people getting in and out, not the political fallout, that's my problem.'

'Communications. Once they're over the border, even using transmissions risks the signals being intercepted, so they will have to be the bare minimum UHS signals of coded co-ordinates, other than which we'll have no contact,' Penjo explained. 'The only information we will have as to their positions will be the GPS locator that the CIA have provided, that will tell us where each of them are.' His expression darkened as he added, 'We're told it gives off a false signal except to the receiver for which it's matched.'

'You have doubts?'

'The Chinese probably have the most advanced hacking expertise in the world. I want us to be able to switch off the device until it's needed. I prefer our people to rely on their basic skills to evade detection.'

Mullick saw the logic in this. 'Leave it with me.'

'Good,' Penjo nodded. 'Will you join us for dinner tonight?'

The Chief shook his head. 'No thank you, I have to get back to Delhi. Perhaps a drink in the mess, with the company commanders and the advisors?' He looked at his watch and said, 'In half an hour?'

Penjo allowed the relief to sink in. Enough time to get Max from the clinic to the mess. Doubts about how Durwachter would behave still niggled at him. Nothing more he could do at this stage. 'Certainly,' he said.

They both stood up and as Penjo walked around his desk, Mullick added as an afterthought, 'Nasty business for Dr. Khan in Mussoorie.

Extremists, both Hindu and Moslem, are becoming a big problem for us, I'd like her to stay on here, at least until this operation is over.'

'We're very glad to have her here.'

'Some local bigwigs are putting pressure on the Uttarakhand state police,' the Chief said, 'two of their young men were killed up at the Kempty Falls and they're trying to link it to Dr. Khan.' He put one hand on Penjo's arm and assured him, 'Nothing for you to worry about. We'll deal with that, but I thought you would like to know.'

Penjo digested this, wondering why Mullick would even mention it if it was unimportant. He dismissed it. It did not concern him and his plate was already overflowing.

'Incidentally, I believe Colonel Devlin was in Mussoorie at the time that those young men were killed,' Mullick said. 'It may be that the police would want to interview him.' He turned to face Penjo, blocking his way out, and said, 'That will not happen. You understand.' It was a statement, not a question. 'If Jha is approached to arrange an interview, you contact me immediately,' he added.

The Dapon's expression registered understanding: 'Ahh. Yes, of course.'

*

Mullick would dearly have liked to have a quiet word with Devlin but he was surrounded by the Tibetan officers and it would have been too obvious to cut him out of the herd. Durwachter stood in a corner of the room in animated conversation with Lobsang. He would have to make another visit or fabricate some excuse to get Devlin on his own somewhere. He refused the offer of another drink. 'I must go,' he said, touching Penjo's elbow. 'Thank you for your hospitality, Dapon, I have to present the operational plan to the inner cabinet.' Indicating the folder under his arm, the Chief said, 'Wish me luck.'

Penjo shook his head. 'It is our *karma*.' Pointing to the photograph of the Dalai Lama on the wall, the Tibetan said, 'His Holiness was forced to flee, so it is we who must keep the flame burning, even if it is only flickering at the moment.' Mullick nodded in appreciation.

'I'll see you to your car,' Penjo said. He turned and announced that the Chief was leaving. All the Tibetans made short bows and Max joined them in namaskar. Durwachter managed a curt nod of the head.

Shortly after Mullick left, the mess emptied except for Max and Herman. The American walked over, a glass in his hand.

'Here, from my private store of Black Label.'

'That's kind.'

'Kind? Hell no. I want to know how you knew,' said Herman as he leaned aggressively over Max, his face inches away.

'Knew?'

'Yeah. How'd you know there was a grenade in my drawer?'

Max toyed with the satisfaction of knocking the man's teeth down his throat. 'If, as you suggest, I knew it was there, how come I allowed myself to get injured?' He spoke slowly, separating the words as though talking to someone either deaf or retarded. Herman's expression was so full of fury that it was impossible to tell whether the words had registered. Max took the proffered glass and raised it in salute.

'*Slainte.*'

'That some of that shit Tibetan you're always talkin'?'

'No, it's Gaelic, it means good health in Irish.'

Herman stood back and surveyed Max in silence.

'I heard the typical sound of the lever as it flew free. I'd also heard of an identical booby trap that was laid for an unpopular Gurkha officer some years ago,' Max explained. 'You fit the unpopularity bill.' He saw the anger come back into the American's eyes and held up his free hand to signal peace. 'You and I were posted here to help prepare these people for a potentially fatal cross-border operation,' he said. 'I have the distinct advantage of familiarity with their language and culture but you, and I may as well be blunt, don't give a rat's arse for them or their way of life and you show it in the way you treat them. If they were Rangers or Seals, you'd never dream of treating them with the open contempt you show for them.'

'I…' Herman began but Max cut him off, 'I'm not here to debate with you, it's a fact.' He stood up out of his chair, using his extra height to lend weight to his words. 'You're an expert at what you do, they all know that and respect your skills. So why not get alongside them and teach what you know. It could save lives.' He knocked back the whisky and said, 'Isn't that what you and I are paid to do?'

The most difficult thing he had to do now was walk out of the mess unaided and without appearing to limp. Halfway to the door Herman was suddenly by his side.

'Need a hand?'

'No, thanks,' Max grimaced and reached the door in three strides, worried that the stitches would part. The door opened just as he reached for the handle and Si-thar, the paramedic, pointed to the *Sisu-Nasu* that was used for casualties.

'The doctor-saheb told me to bring you back to the clinic, Kushog-saheb,' Si-thar said.

The sense of relief at not having to walk all the way there softened his mood. Max looked back at the American who nodded slowly to him and raised his glass in salute.

'I hear you, *hombre*, I hear you,' Herman said.

*

She tutted at the dried blood that had leaked from three pulled stitches. 'I'll have to re-do these, it'll leave you with an irregular scar,' she said, 'so don't let anyone know that it was me who sewed you up.' She worked quickly and he marvelled at the deft way in which she repaired the tears before strapping the dressing firmly in place.

'How do you know that it wasn't the effect of the kiss on my blood pressure yesterday?' he joked.

'Because this blood is fresh, Dr. Watson, elementary,' she retorted dismissively.

'So?' He let the question hang in the air.

She studied him for a moment, a tiny frown puckering her eyebrows. 'I want you under my control for another 24 hours,' she said, 'so you sleep here tonight.'

He toyed with the idea of commenting that the bed wasn't big enough for two but decided against it. 'A kiss is just a kiss, a sigh is just a sigh...'

'Goodnight, Rick,' she said, pointing to the recovery room, turned and left.

HQ Research & Analysis Wing
Chakrata

'According to the assistant commissioner, they're threatening to take it to the party's national committee,' Fernandes said. He wondered how the special secretary would react but as Mullick was staring out of the window with his back towards him, the expression on his face was hidden.

'He seems to think that they want to use it to attack the government, screaming cover-up,' the intelligence officer continued.

Mullick nodded his understanding. 'To make political capital out of the death of their sons,' he said and turned round to face Fernandes before adding, 'That's just about their style.'

'But by saying nothing, aren't we giving substance to their suspicions?'

Mullick shook his head. 'They can't make the connection between the deaths and the Khan sisters without explaining just what that connection could be,' he said. 'What association would be drawn between the presence of an attractive girl all on her own and four men at the Kempty Falls?'

The half-smile on his face told Fernandes that his boss was unperturbed. 'We have no real authority to prevent the state police from insisting on interviewing the young sister, she's not military personnel,' Fernandes said. 'Once they have her locked away, God knows what they'll do to get her to talk.'

Mullick's expression hardened. 'I don't give a damn for their power; the national interest trumps a bunch of bustee cops,' he said. 'They're not getting within miles of Baniyana Forest and she's not leaving it until we relocate Dr. Khan and her sister well out of their reach.'

'Sir.' Fernandes was apologetic.

Mullick waved his hand, dismissing criticism. 'The last thing that the state police want is any inquiry into the activities of young political hoodlums. Have you seen the statistics for sexual attacks on young women in Uttarakhand in the last 18 months? If they allow the local heavyweights to stick their greasy fingers into this incident, they'll only draw attention to their record of abject failure to protect young women. It would be almost as though they endorse it.' Fernandes nodded acknowledgement. The special secretary massaged his face then added, 'Make sure Jha throws the national security regulations at any attempt to get access to the Khan girl.'

'Sir.' Fernandes recognised that the discussion was over and took his leave.

Left to himself, Mullick suspected that one or possibly both the Khans had been attacked by local party princelings but they had not reckoned on Devlin being in the vicinity. Once he knew that Devlin had been in Mussoorie that night, he guessed it was probably the major and one of the Gurkhas who had rescued the Khan girl. Devlin was known for never taking half-measures, that was one of the reasons they had asked for him. Doubtless the assailants got what they deserved, even if it was vigilante justice. Let others worry about legalities, he did not have that luxury. It did not serve the national interests for Devlin to be identified, there was far too much at stake.

*

Fernandes had the enormous satisfaction of having his suspicions confirmed by Mullick's insistence on shielding Devlin. He had just acquired knowledge that gave him powerful leverage for forwarding his career. It needed careful balancing to ensure that whatever course he took, he came out smelling of rose water.

Baniyana Forest

'Six teams will go in, three from Norbu and Jhampa's column to Aksai Chin and three from Pema and Paljor's to Doklam. Selection of the teams will be up to the company commanders, but I will review the choices with Herman and Kushog-saheb.' Dapon Penjo looked around the faces, registering the satisfaction reflected in the knowledge that the rehearsing was over, and they were 'going home'.

Norbu pointed to the other company commanders and asked, 'What about us?'

'One company commander from each column will go in, to co-ordinate the three teams,' Penjo said. 'We can't take the risk of losing all our senior and most experienced officers, you can decide amongst yourselves who goes.' He could almost hear them working out how to justify their inclusion. 'Co-ordination on the ground will be particularly dangerous,' he added. 'The greatest risk will occur if one of the commanders is captured because he or she will know the locations of the teams so I want you to arrange RVs that can't be compromised.'

Norbu gave Penjo a black look. 'You seriously think we would rat on our people?'

The Dapon shook his head. 'Hanging you by a hook from the ceiling, pulling out your fingernails, no, I don't think for a moment you'd give away any of our people,' he said. 'But if they pump you full of sodium pentothal you will no longer be in a position to control events. So I want double cut-outs.'

Norbu's expression still registered some reservations. Penjo continued, 'No, my main concern is if you get bumped by a regular PLA unit, we can't help you, you'll be on your own.'

'We know that.' Pema's response was curt. 'That's what all this extra training is about.' She softened her voice a little and added, 'This is what we volunteered for; we accepted the risks.'

Penjo nodded; then Max spoke.

'What the Dapon is not telling you is that I'm not happy with the extraction protocol. Gurkhas were involved in cross-border incursions during *Confrontasi* against Indonesia. Some of our soldiers teamed up with indigenous *Dayaks* and *Ibans* on operations that were supposed to be unattributable to the British. The government insisted that they would disown any of our people caught on the Indonesian side of the border. That was official policy. But we had our own secret protocol which we didn't tell either the general commanding or the intelligence people who had planned the operations. If any of our people were bumped, they'd signal us, and we'd go and pull them out.'

He looked at Penjo apologetically and added, 'I've proposed that we operate the same secret protocol for your operations.' Pausing, he pointed at his American counterpart: 'He agrees with me.' Durwachter nodded. Max continued, 'But the Dapon has overruled us.' His tone conveyed his despair. 'We…' he said, indicating Durwachter, '…are compelled to accept that the long-term interests of the Tibetan people takes priority over the safety of individual personnel.'

Max hoped that the way he said it conveyed to them that he did not agree with a word of it. He felt genuinely conflicted: his loyalty to the people he was training and his respect for Penjo. The Tibetan gave him a look which he interpreted as signalling that he was being disloyal. Then he resumed the briefing.

'Norbu, you and Jhampa will select the passes in the Barahoti district through which your teams will infiltrate,' said Penjo. Turning to Pema and Paljor, he said, 'Similarly, you must choose the entry points for your teams.' Gesturing towards Max, he added, 'I've accepted the Kushogsaheb's recommendation that you all go in through a variety of points of entry rather than one.' He gave a sarcastic laugh before saying, 'The PLA have done us a favour. Their recent helicopter incursions into Barahoti have given our political masters sufficient courage to allow us to use a chopper for the deepest incursion in each of our operational areas, that is for planting the NDDs.' He held up his hand and said, 'Don't get too excited. We only have permission for a 10-minute inbound flight, 20 minutes in and out, total.'

'Desmond will use up all 10 minutes just in landing,' Norbu groaned.

Penjo nodded. 'Yes, we know his limitations,' he said. 'The Chief agreed to replace him.' He drew in a long breath. 'He says he understands our concerns, but he can only offer us the Mad Monk.' This produced laughter all round and Pema covered her face with her hand as some of them looked at her.

'The Mad Monk?' Pema queried. Max looked at her. She gave an uncharacteristic giggle and explained, 'He used to be a monk, but the abbot threw him out of the monastery for...' She began to laugh again before resuming, 'He made two of the nuns pregnant, so he had to flee. He joined a Khamba guerrilla band, came over the mountains and joined the 22s. He turned out to be a natural flyer and they posted him to Aviation Research Centre.'

'So why isn't he part of the SFF?' Max pressed her.

'Because he's crazy...,' Norbu grinned, '...about women, but he's the best chopper jockey in ARC.'

'Don't let Ulan hear you say that,' Pema joked. Then becoming serious she answered Max's question, 'The 22s HQ in Chakrata think that we get the best of everything, they're a bit envious and as we already had Ulan, they gave us Desmond.'

'But if the Chief says we can have him, I assume you'll say yes?' Max asked, looking at Penjo who smiled and nodded before turning to Pema.

'You'd better warn all the girls to keep out of his way,' Penjo said.

'I'm not their nurse maid,' Pema said. She frowned, then grinned at Penjo. 'He's a good-looking man but if he tries it on with Choden she may cripple him for life.'

The Dapon let the laughter die down before continuing, 'According to the weather forecasters, conditions will be ideal for Aksai Chin in 10 days and Doklam in 12, so I want you to make your team selections within the next 48 hours.'

Prime Minister's Office
Raisina Hill, New Delhi

'The situation today is very different to what it was in 1962, Prime Minister,' General Chaudhari said softly but leant forward in his chair, to emphasise his words. 'Our status as a member of the non-aligned nations led Krishna Menon to deal with Russia for our equipment, most of which was out of date and ineffective,' the chief of defence staff told Kaur. 'All that *Hindi-Chini bhai bhai* rubbish meant that we were unprepared, badly equipped and our intelligence was virtually non-existent.' The CDS paused, trying to read the PM's face. In his opinion, Kaur's fixation with striking a deal with the Chinese was dangerously similar to that of Nehru; and look where that had led them. Equally, the general knew that he could not push the man too far, he had a stubborn streak that could derail his plans.

'Today we have our own satellite images as well as those from the Americans. We know that the Chinese are building roads deep into the Aksai Chin and Doklam areas,' Chaudhari continued. 'But what we don't know and must find out is which of these roads are defence quality and even more important, where their missile launch bases are so that we can take them out in the first phase of hostilities.'

For the third time, Kaur looked up from the file he had been reading. 'General, you told me they have mobile launchers that can be positioned anywhere they choose?' he asked. 'So why is it necessary to locate fixed launch sites?'

'The mobile launch vehicles can be identified by satellite and taken out before they can be deployed but the well camouflaged fixed sites will only be located once they commence firing,' Chaudhari explained.

'Those vehicles also need motorable roads and we need to distinguish them from tracks.'

Kaur digested this, then directed himself to Mullick. 'How good are the prospects of the SFF getting this intelligence?' he asked, raising his hand to indicate that he had not finished. 'I admire your loyalty to them, but I want a worst-case scenario.' The intelligence chief had anticipated the question but he allowed a few seconds to elapse before he responded, to give the impression that his answer was carefully weighed.

'Of locating them, better than fifty-fifty, Mentri-ji...,' he paused to allow the significance of his next words, '...but less than fifty-fifty of a successful extraction of all personnel.'

'They know this and are prepared to accept the risk?' Kaur pressed him.

'Ha-ji,' Mullick said. 'They are patriots, as they see it, fighting for their own land.'

'But for the benefit of ours?' Kaur did not conceal the sarcastic edge to his question.

'They see it as mutually beneficial.' Mullick judged it necessary to correct the PM's jaundiced view of the SFF. 'If I may be permitted to recall the critical contribution the Tibetan 22s made during the Indian Army's operations that resulted in the creation of Bangladesh,' he said, 'on behalf of a people with whom they have no cultural ties whatsoever.' Mullick registered the affirmative nod from General Chaudhari.

'The SFF Tibetans are the cream of the 22s, totally loyal to us and grateful for our country's generosity towards their people,' he continued. 'If anything does go wrong, they will be the ones who will pay the price whilst we hope to reap the benefit at no cost to ourselves.'

General Chaudhari pointed to the Aksai Chin region on the map on the table, focusing attention back to detail. 'The proposed incursion route is from western Nepal; the entire line west is too closely monitored by the Chinese,' the CDS said.

The PM sat upright and remarked, 'The Nepalese won't permit that, you can forget it.'

'We won't ask them, officially,' said Chaudhari, wearing a wolfish smile. 'Unofficially, I approached the Nepalese general in charge of their army's western command, we were at Wellington together, it's not just knowledge of strategy that can be acquired at the Joint Services Staff College. He'll depute a confidential team to see our people into Nepal's territory.'

'Outbound and inbound?'.

'Certainly.'

The PM digested this slowly as General Chaudhari drew attention to the Doklam plateau. 'We can't get our people into Doklam through the Chumbi Valley, there are more troops there than a Republic Day parade in Delhi,' he said. 'No, we'll use two access points in Bhutan.'

He looked up when Kaur said, 'We'll keep Thimphu informed as a courtesy, but we don't need the Bhutanese government's permission.'

Mullick frowned. 'May I suggest that Thimphu is informed after the event, we have concerns about the level of security of information in Bhutan.'

'Agreed.' Kaur was even more anxious than they were about maintaining the secrecy of the operation. He removed his glasses and peered through the lenses as though looking for a smear, then waved them at Roy and addressed him, 'You're external affairs, it's your responsibility.'

General Chaudhari's loud intake of breath prefaced his next words. 'At the end of the day, the security of India is paramount,' said the CDS, giving Mullick an apologetic glance. 'I regret to have to say it, but your people are expendable.'

The special secretary winced inwardly whilst recognising the bald truth. The SFF meant no more to the cabinet than *Bhata* on a *Chaturanga* board. Kaur was the *Rajah* and the rest of them were *Senapati*. His mind played with the analogy and he allowed himself the indulgence of wondering how Devlin and Durwachter would be represented on the game board, there was no historical role for them. The proposals for the infiltration routes had been theirs, Durwachter would have technical oversight of the Aksai Chin teams and Devlin those going into Doklam. Mullick had deliberately chosen not to refer to the foreign advisors in his briefing to the inner cabinet, a course which Chaudhari had endorsed. On paper, responsibility in the field lay with Dapon Penjo. If anything went wrong the Tibetan's would be the first neck on the block, followed – he did not doubt – by his own. The politicians seated around the table were a devious collection of self-serving opportunists, all searching for power that could be monetised whereas he and Chaudhari represented the best of the imperial legacy, the army and the Indian civil service. They were the rocks in the shifting sands of India's politics.

'Secretary-ji,' Mullick snapped out of his thoughts as the PM asked him, 'Do we still have full co-operation from CIA and SIS?'

'Absolutely,' he replied. Kaur nodded his satisfaction. Mullick continued, 'GCHQ will provide a live feed on military communications in the border areas during the operation and NSA have given us their latest non-traceable GPS modules. We will have electronic oversight throughout.'

'Very good,' the PM said. Waving his spectacles at foreign minister Roy, Kaur continued, 'Let them know how much we appreciate their help.' He closed the briefing file and ordered, '*Tik hei*, send them in.'

Mullick and Chaudhari exchanged a brief lift of eyebrows to acknowledge their satisfaction. As the meeting broke up, the CDS gripped Mullick's arm and whispered, 'Let's get out of here before they change their minds.'

The special secretary frowned as they left the room together. 'General-saheb, do you know the Uttarakhand police commissioner?'

'Dixit? A bit,' Chaudhari said. 'Why? Is there a problem?'

Mullick indicated an alcove to their right and they stepped out of the corridor. 'Possibly.' He then gave a brief account of the inquiries being pursued by the assistant commissioner and the BJP's hold over him. 'I have no proof,' Mullick said, 'but I'd bet the farm that it was Devlin who meted out swift justice on the two thugs who attacked a girl at the Kempty Falls. The dead men's families are stirring up trouble, claiming that the authorities are complicit in the deaths.'

'Sounds as though we're well rid of them.'

'The girl was the young sister of Captain Shanaaz Khan.'

The CDS's eyes opened. 'The 22s' trauma surgeon?'

'Yes. There was also an attack on the doctor's bungalow which went badly wrong for the attackers. Dr. Khan was escorted to Mussoorie by a team from the SFF. The thugs were bound and gagged and dumped on the ground of the ITBP Academy.'

Chaudhari smiled, 'It doesn't sound as though our friends need any assistance.'

Mullick nodded but added thoughtfully, 'No, but the commissioner has two unsolved murders on his watch and a bunch of angry politicians looking for blood.'

Chaudhari closed his eyes for a second or two. When he opened them, Mullick felt as though he was being drilled. 'Let the damned commissioner deal with his barbaric friends,' the CDS decided. 'If he gets close to your people, I'll make him feel like a first-year recruit. Understood?'

'Understood. My concern is to keep things under wraps.'

Chaudhari pointed his cane at him and said, 'You do that.'

Baniyana Forest

After three nights Max could not justify staying in the clinic any longer. He was already back in his office going over the operational details with Pema, Paljor and the three team leaders, Kalsang, Palden and Choden.

The situation was complicated by disagreement between India, China and Bhutan as to the location of the tri-boundary point. This had led to conflicting claims over the Doklam plateau, primarily between China and Bhutan, with India playing a support role. The Chinese claimed that the border was centred on Gymochen, significantly south of Bhutan's claim to Merug-la. From India's point of view, the important defensive position of the Jampheri ridge would fall within China's control if the line ran through Gymochen. Even though, strictly speaking, the Jampheri ridge was in Bhutan's territory, if the Chinese occupied Gymochen, they would be able to command the vulnerable Chumbi Valley which led to the narrow isthmus of land that connects the bulk of India from Assam, Manipur and Nagaland.

From Max's point of view, the teams would have a legitimate excuse for being in the contested area but once they moved north of the ridge line above Batang-la, they would be incontestably in Chinese territory. Delhi was already anxious about Chinese construction work on roads and a planned rail link in the conflicted area, all of which the Indians interpreted as aggression. But what the Indian Army needed intelligence on was preparations behind the Jampheri ridge. Once the teams crossed the LAC, they would be in Tibet proper and at maximum risk.

He passed the magnification reader to Pema. 'These satellite images are vague,' Max said. 'Can you make out whether that is a motorable track from Doklam?'

'We call it Zhoglam,' she corrected him.

'So long as we are talking about the same place,' he said, smiling at her, the last thing they needed was a debate about place names in different languages. Her expression lightened as she bent over the reader and examined the image. Straightening up, she pushed the reader to one side.

'These are useless, that's why we're going in, isn't it?' Pema said.

He nodded. 'But you need to be as fully prepared as possible and that includes all the routes in and out. Once you're across the border…'

'Ours or theirs?' she asked, giving him a lopsided grin.

'Let's look at it from their point of view, so theirs.'

She acknowledged this and used a pencil to trace a rough line starting from Gymochen, about three kilometres south of Doka-la; she studied the map for a few seconds. 'I'll bring my teams in from the north, over the Sinche-la Pass,' Pema said. 'It's a longer route, more mountainous but we'll be on our home ground and the PLA will be focussing on their front.'

Max nodded. 'Motorable roads are top priority because they can move mobile launchers along those easily but even the below ground fixed launch sites need a track for re-supply. That means that every site of interest to us has to be on a transport network of one kind or another.' He then pointed to the ultra-highspeed transmitting device and told the Tibetans, 'This is the safest means of getting the co-ordinates back.' He paused to lend weight to his words before adding, 'I know you have been instructed to photograph all the fixed locations but if you're caught with cameras and incriminating photographs…'

'We're stuffed,' Pema supplied in English, with a smile, then back into Tibetan. 'You're not suggesting that we disobey our orders, are you, Kushog-saheb?'

'*My* orders are not to carry cameras,' Max told the teams. 'I'll deal with the command.'

Her eyes flicked up for a fraction of a second as she realised that he meant what he said. 'But the Dapon-saheb…' she began to ask.

'Agrees with me,' Max said, cutting her short. Pema stared at him in the cold porcelain beauty that he could not quite reconcile with the ruthless efficiency with which she commanded her teams.

'No cameras,' she said with a little dismissive wave of her hand.

Laya, Gasa Province
Northern Bhutan
(12,500 feet above sea level)

❦

Dawn broke over the magnificent Gangchen-ta Peak, the sky an intensity of blue that lifted their spirits as the final checks were made. Paljor busied himself tightening straps that were already firmly in place and was given friendly punches for his pains. He had recovered quickly from the disappointment of not being selected and thrown himself into assisting the teams going in.

Choden watched him with a smile on her face. 'Why don't you take my place?'

He turned to look at her, waving his hand in admonition. 'Don't fool yourself that I wouldn't.'

The atmosphere amongst the three teams was as expectant as the brittle morning breeze, nervous tension enveloping their impatience to be off. Max pulled back his sleeve to expose his watch, then looked at Pema.

'Two minutes to zero hour,' he announced. She signalled Ulan and the helicopter fired up, the rotors turning lazily before settling into their steady beat. Kalsang directed his Red team on first, followed by Palden's Blue, and Choden's Green boarded last.

Pema hitched her Bergen over her shoulder and turned to Max. '*Cha-ka chey ah koo-la,*' she saluted.

'Every minute,' he returned the salute and watched her jog under the rotors and climb into the chopper. The beat of the blades grew heavy and the machine tilted forward as it fought for purchase in the thin mountain air. Yes, he would most certainly keep an eye on them as she had requested.

'I've never heard Pema call anyone uncle before, Kushog-saheb,' Paljor said quietly as they watched the helicopter gain height and make a course for the north. It was precisely that which was running through Max's mind. From her early near hostility, Pema had modified her attitude through one of professional detachment to one almost bordering on affection. He guessed that saving Penjo had wrought the real change; even though she maintained a respectful distance from him, Max was in no doubt about her feelings for the Dapon. As he reflected on it, it occurred to him that she may have been asking him to keep an eye on Penjo. No matter which, she had dropped her guard of restraint and he was pleased.

'I'm a Dutch uncle,' he said in English.

'A what?'

'Never mind. It doesn't translate well.' He cuffed Paljor on the shoulder and said, 'Come on, we can follow their progress on the LED screen.'

Together, they loped back to the temporary forward base they had established in an abandoned village. Max had insisted on siting their communications as close to the border as practicable and as luck would have it, it turned out that Laya was the base for a Royal Bhutan Army battalion commanded by someone who had been at Sandhurst with him. Colonel Wangdi was delighted to see his old chum and Max had to scale back on the extent of co-operation he was being offered. There had been a fierce debate in Baniyana over where to monitor the teams. Fernandes, who was responsible for both forward bases, had insisted that monitoring be done from Baniyana's communications centre. Max saw this as a political decision to enable Chakrata to maintain control over the teams. Both he and Durwachter objected to what they saw as interference with Penjo's strategic operational command. Eventually Prabhat persuaded Fernandes that there had to be separate centres for the Aksai Chin and Doklam regions, located as far forward as possible and as he was the communications expert, the intelligence officer was obliged to accept his advice, but Fernandes did it with bad grace. What had angered Max most was his querying the location of the command centres.

'Why have a command centre so close to the border?' Fernandes asked.

'You can't mount a recovery mission if things going wrong.'

'That attitude sends a message of abandonment to the people in the field,' Max countered. He allowed his contempt to colour his tone.

'There is no need to shout at me, Colonel, I'm not one of your soldiers,' Fernandes protested.

'More's the pity.'

'What do you mean by that?'

Max made a determined effort to restrain himself, poised to either punch the man in the teeth or dress him down in parade ground terms, he was not going to get what he wanted this way. He conjured a smile onto his face and said, 'Mr. Fernandes, forgive me if I'm mistaken but I believe you have never been a field officer.' He held up his hand to prevent being interrupted before continuing, 'It is impossible to convey the sense of isolation experienced by those operating behind enemy lines. It may only be a psychological support but just the knowledge that your own people are right there on the border gives massive comfort.'

Fernandes stared at him before stating the obvious, 'You speak from experience?' Max nodded. Fernandes looked at Durwachter who also nodded, then turned back to Max and said, 'I will get the clearance you wish.' The way he said it conveyed 'you'll wish you hadn't asked' but Max put it down to sour grapes at not getting his way. Nonetheless, the man had been as good as his word. What was really troubling Max was the communication equipment the CIA had provided. Prabhat had been briefed at GCHQ prior to their departure and had come away with the impression that the British communications experts were less confident than the NSA about the untraceability of the transceivers. To Max's mind, if he could locate the teams, it was inconceivable that the Chinese couldn't.

Durwachter dismissed his concerns. 'It's field-tested, best goddamn thing we ever had,' the Ranger said. Max sent up a silent prayer that for once the American was right.

Mussoorie Gateway Hotel

The assistant commissioner of Uttarakhand police strode towards the table around which the local heavyweights were seated, a double measure of Johnny Walker Red Label carefully positioned in front of each man, the bottle prominent on the table like a badge of office. He knew them all well and kept his facial expression neutral to disguise his contempt for them. One convicted murderer who had bribed the appeal judges to acquit him, two convicted of various corrupt practices and on bail awaiting their hopeless appeals and the last one the biggest un-convicted smuggler in the northern state. But this collection of bed lice held his career in their hands. He threw them a lazy salute, took off his cap and laid it with his swagger stick on the centre of the table. The greetings were uniformly flabby.

'What news commissioner-saheb?' Ghosh's blubbery lips gave him a lisp so that the words seemed to run together.

'I regret that we have no further evidence to identify those responsible for your sons' death,' the AC said, looking into the deep-set eyes of both bereaved fathers and still only saw criminals.

'But they are Mussulman women, what more do you want?' Flecks of spit rimed Ghosh's lips as he spoke.

'Being Moslem is not yet a crime, Ghosh-ji.' He managed a crooked smile to soften his response, unwelcome though he knew it was.

'They must pay!' The retired murderer's voice cut the air. The AC nodded his agreement. 'Ha-ji, those responsible for crimes must and shall be brought to justice.' He adopted his official face as his gaze swept the table. 'That is our duty.'

'Bhaia,' Ghosh acknowledged curtly. His eyes were almost hidden behind the folds of fat but they still reminded the commissioner of a rat, never more so than when he adopted this assertive tone as he continued to dictate, 'We have decided that a message must be sent.' Ghosh looked from left to right, sweeping them all into his words. 'This is no time for *evidence.*' The politician loaded the word with contempt. 'You will make an example of them.' The AC stared at the badge on his cap. The pride that he had experienced when first gazetted into the force had not weathered the years of climbing up the ranks. The sense of duty that his father had instilled in him from his years in the colonial service had evaporated, burned off by political expediency. Dancing to the tune of these *aparaadiya* demeaned him but he had family to support, both his sons to see through university, the bungalow in Dehra Dun that his wife had set her eyes on. *Bapa's* days were long gone, this was the new India. The country's criminals were the new colonialists. He pushed his chair back, stood and retrieved his cap and stick.

'Understood.' He gave them a half-hearted salute and marched away. Getting a search warrant for the Baniyana Forest encampment would be easy, Magistrate Poudyal did not want his sentencing scam investigated. But enforcing the warrant would put him on a collision course with the Chakrata people and they would squash him like a fly. The man, Fernandes, had seemed sympathetic, but he would be a last official resort. Out of sight of the aparaadiya he shook his head in frustration. For a mad moment he did consider approaching the Research and Analysis Wing and leaving it to them to deal with the problem but that would mean disclosing his relations with the politicos. No, there was far too much history there and he was the one most compromised. What his investigation had discovered was that an Englishman giving his address as the Forestry Department at Baniyana had stayed in this very hotel on the night in question. He also knew that the Forestry Department was a cover for an ultra-secret 22s unit and it did not take rocket science to see the link. The manner in which the four thugs had been dealt with pointed to a highly trained special operations operative, someone off-limits to the police. Though there was obviously some connection between him and the women, the foreigner would not be around permanently. They were Moslem women, and as such, expendable. Mentally, he shrugged his shoulders in despair, this was going to be another off-the-books operation.

Laya

The Mi-17's distinctive engine note carried from far away in these mountains.

'*Ai pugyo,*' Deepraj indicated with his head.

'No, it hasn't arrived, you silly bugger, it's still on its way in,' Max said and gave the Gurkha a friendly punch. The imprecision in the language never failed to amuse him and Deepraj always rose to the bait, complaining about English words that sounded the same but were spelled differently. Max was in one of his most buoyant moods, the mountain air was bitingly cold but sitting in the sun he could feel his skin bronzing. He had no way of knowing whether Shanaaz would be on the helicopter, the note he had written to her had been cryptically short: 'Scenery and weather magnificent, come and practise alpine medicine.' He could not sit in the communication tent all the hours that God gave and there were signallers maintaining a 24-hour listening watch. Once Laya had been selected as the jump-off point, he had made a quick trip to the bookshop in Mussoorie where he had found two books on the history and anthropology of the Layap people who populated this extreme northerly region of Bhutan. He convinced himself that Shanaaz would find this place and its people as fascinating as he did.

Paljor walked around scratching his head in wonder. 'These people have everything that the Chinese are committed to depriving us of,' he observed.

'Including a fairly mediaeval socio-political structure,' Max reminded him.

'But they're happy, don't you see?'

'Oh, I do,' Max said, 'but don't you think they would like to have had the opportunity to go to a school like St. Augustine's?'

Paljor grinned. 'That's not fair,' he told Max. 'You're not comparing like with like. Tibet was coming out of the middle ages before the Chinese invaded.'

'I agree with you, but time and Beijing's imperial appetite were against you,' Max said. He stood up, pointed towards the landing zone with his chin and said, 'Let's see what the postman has brought.'

'Postman...? Oh, I see.'

The helicopter swung in smoothly, landing lightly on the makeshift helipad and the pilot cut the motor. The door opened and Deepraj jumped down, followed by Shanaaz wearing a huge smile. She opened her arms as though embracing the surrounding mountains.

'This is stunning,' she said.

'Told you so,' Deepraj said. He was removing kit from the cabin but she took what looked like a pilot's case out of his hand.

'I'll take that,' she said. 'Thank you, Deepraj.'

Max held out his hand. 'May I?'

'No, you don't separate the medic from her tools,' Shanaaz said.

A loud voice greeted him from behind them. '*Tah-shi de-leh, Kushog-saheb!*' Flight-Lieutenant Linka walked towards them, a huge grin on his face. Pointing at Shanaaz, the Tibetan pilot said, 'I would like to be ill so that I can have such a beautiful doctor.' They all laughed.

'He's incorrigible,' Shanaaz complained, shaking her head. 'Never stopped asking questions about Nisha and me, pretending to be solicitous for our welfare when all he wanted was information for his little black book.'

'What is little black book?' Linka, aka the Mad Monk, made a show of sounding offended. 'Why would I not be concerned when the Kushog-saheb was not around to protect you?'

'I read you like an open book, Captain,' she smiled at him and he bowed.

'Let's get some lunch,' Max said, pointing to the mess tent. 'We have some wild boar coated in green chilli. It'll help you take off.'

*

After lunch the helicopter returned to Chakrata and Max took Shanaaz for a hike up towards the monastery that overlooked their campsite. In the late afternoon, they sat on a low stone wall in contented silence, surveying the surrounding mountains as the sun began to sink behind them.

'From the smiles on the faces of the teams in Baniyana,' she said, 'I guess that our people are doing well.' Putting her hand on his sleeve, she added, 'I'm not asking what they're doing, it's just good to know that everything you have worked for is coming good.'

He put his hand over hers. 'You're not being nosey, it's natural wanting to know that everything is working out and that they're not in trouble,' he assured her. 'Not being able to be with them is frustrating. It's the curse of higher command. The higher your rank the further away you are from the people for whom you're responsible. That's why I envy what you do, it's so direct.'

'So that's the contradiction of the ambitious soldier?'

'Well, that's how I see it.'

'Is that why you stay up here, to feel closer?'

He nodded. She frowned.

'I'd love to stay but I can't justify more than a day or two,' she said.

'Well, let's enjoy it.'

He took both her hands and stood up, pulling her towards him. She freed one hand and put it behind his head, drawing him to her. They kissed hungrily and without restraint. Then she leaned back a little, a smile dancing around her mouth. 'I hope you'll keep me warm tonight.'

'Just what the doctor orders.' They both laughed and set off walking hand-in-hand until the track narrowed.

*

Max woke at his habitual 05.30 but there was no way he was going to get up. Their bodies were contouring with each other and her hair lay just off her neck so that his eyes could follow the fine down at the base of her skull up into the rich brunette that ended part way down her back. The scent of her skin, heightened by the slight film of perspiration, filled his nostrils.

She sensed that he was awake and turned to face him. He opened his mouth to speak but she placed a finger across his lips. 'Fuck me again, Max.'

He checked his watch some time later. 'It's nearly 6.30. Do you want to slip back to your tent before anyone sees you?'

'I don't give a damn,' she laughed softly. Then her expression grew serious. 'I have to leave after breakfast,' she said. 'Any chance you could find an excuse to come with me?'

He had been turning just this idea over in his mind since their first night together. What genuinely troubled him was her stated intention of going back to Mussoorie to supervise vacating her bungalow. He had tried to dissuade her but without success. She said seriously, 'I can't run from these people forever. They know who I am and where I live.'

It was this that worried Max more than anything else. 'But don't you remember that the last time we went, even though your bungalow was supposed to have police protection, they lay in wait for you. It's a pound to a penny that the police are involved too.'

She laughed, 'What's a pound to a penny?'

'It means that I bet these thugs are politically connected.'

'Well, I'll ask Dapon Penjo to lend me a couple of the team members to look after me.'

'Hmph.' Though that was light years better than the so-called police escort, he still felt uncomfortable.

'So, it's settled,' she decided. 'Now I must risk hypothermia taking a shower in your camping contraption. It's not too bad after the sun has warmed the water but at this hour, I'll be lucky not to be pierced by ice needles.'

She climbed out of the sleeping bag, wrapped his sheepskin coat around her and grabbed her clothes. 'I'll return it after I've showered.' With just her head and legs visible, he was tempted to get her back into the sleeping bag. 'I can read your expression, Colonel, I'm out of here.' She blew him a kiss and manoeuvred herself out of the tent.

He sat upright and draped a spare blanket round his shoulders. The teams had been in position for just over a week and highly useful data had already been recovered from both the operational regions. The fact that there had been no problems so far did not mean that this satisfactory state of affairs would continue. But as he had to remind himself, even if anything went wrong, they were prohibited from going in to help. All he was doing was salving his conscience by staying close to the theatre of operations. As against that, he could not rid himself of the nagging doubts about Shanaaz going to Mussoorie, even for a short time. This was a present and immediate fear and supplied an excuse to accompany her.

Gyantse, Tibet

Pema looked out of the window at the Mandala restaurant watching the people outside go by. She was conscious of something being different, somehow it jarred but the reason for it had only struck her after some minutes: no one laughed. Not even the young people. There were more Han Chinese than she remembered from previous visits and she knew that some of them had married Tibetans. What began as an occupation was already beginning to assume permanence and with it the dissolution of their traditional way of life. What did she hope to achieve, realistically? The Chinese were here to stay and her endeavours and those of the people under her command were as flea bites on an elephant's hide. If they carried out their task successfully the benefits would go to the Indians. She could persuade herself that she was keeping alive the spirit of a free Tibet but, in her heart, she knew that she was shoring up false hope. That very thought angered her, driving her to hurt the Chinese in any way she could.

'*Noo-moh*,' she greeted the elderly man sitting opposite her, his kind eyes were in marked contrast to a face into which pain had ploughed deep furrows.

'You look troubled,' he said softly, his voice rasping like canvas across stone. He had always been able to read her, ever since she had been a little girl. It was pointless trying to conceal anything from him.

'All the information you have given me about the fresh influx of PLA units into the region…' Pema began only to stop. She wanted to say that it had reinforced her sense of the futility of their opposition, but it was vital intelligence and essential for her to plan the movements of her command. She continued, '…is like gold dust.' She squeezed him a smile before adding, 'It will help me keep my people from harm.'

She never asked him for the source of his information, she did not want to know but it obviously came from the PLA regional headquarters. Not only were they increasing the number of infantry battalions assigned to the Gyantse district, they were bringing in some militia units too. Formed from ethnic Tibetans, nicknamed 'the Filth', she hated them with a vengeance. As if to prove their loyalty to China, they were twice as brutal as the regular PLA soldiers and people feared them because they could pass unnoticed amongst the population when not in uniform. The most vital and worrying information was that they had begun to impose what amounted to martial law over the area from Gyantse down to the border with India.

'I am most grateful,' she said.

He nodded, then his expression resumed its look of concern. 'You should not have taken the risk of coming into Gyantse. I could easily have found you in the mountains.' Glancing around at the almost full restaurant, he added, 'You are safe here, the Chinese don't come, they say our food is only fit for dogs.' He gave a short, cracked laugh. 'We served them shit, it fed their prejudices and we gained a safe house.'

'And the Filth?' Pema asked, raising one eyebrow.

'We can smell them,' he said. Looked at the ancient clock on the wall, he added, 'Walk with me to the truck stop on Lhasa Road, we have people there who will take you safely out of the city.'

*

As the elderly truck bumped and lurched its way over the poorly maintained road, she pieced together the information her uncle had given her, locating in her mind's eye where each of the three teams was in relation to the PLA and militia units. The main infantry concentration was garrisoned at Yadong, as were the mobile missile launch teams. The border was manned by border guard units, mainly low-quality personnel who were required to stand hour after hour with their minds in neutral, staring at the snow. Until now, their dispositions had enabled her teams to move relatively safely south of Shigatse and north of Batang-la, reconnoitring the tracks and searching for subterranean launch sites. In the two weeks that they had been operational, they had fed back the co-ordinates of 11 sites and four heavy duty motorable tracks. Palden had directed his Blue team to position the nuclear detection devices but she could not verify whether they had been activated. So far, they had been lucky, but the increased PLA presence and introduction of the militia units argued that it was time to pull out, before luck ran out on them.

'*Ah-cha!*' The driver's voice cracked her awake. He was pointing through the dirty windscreen as the truck slowed down. The figures in the road were unmistakably PLA infantry soldiers, the distinctive fur hats, the long grey greatcoats and the AK 52s.

'Just behave normally,' she said reassuringly.

The driver gave her a frightened look and said to her, 'Papers, you have papers, show them.'

She smiled at him and pulled out her identification documents. The soldiers waved them down and the driver wound down his window, allowing the freezing air into the cabin. A soldier held up a gloved hand and the driver handed over his papers. A second soldier tapped on the passenger side window and Pema opened the door. She pointed to the window and laughed, 'It doesn't work.' The soldier's face was impassive as he held out his free hand. She offered him her papers which he took and signalled her to get out of the cabin. Both soldiers then walked over to a tent that had been erected beside the road, handed the papers to someone inside and then held their rifles pointing loosely at her and the truck. The flap of the tent was pushed aside, and an officer emerged studying the papers. He walked straight up to Pema and said in schoolboy Tibetan, 'Where are you going?'

She pointed to her travel permit and said, 'Batang-la.'

'What you do there?'

'Visit my mother, she's ill.'

The soldier stared at the document, then tapped the open page. 'It does not say your mother is ill.'

'No, but it says I go to visit my mother.'

He stared at her in silence, then a smile crept around his mouth, 'I go with you, to visit sick mother.' He laughed as he shouted to the soldiers, then pointed to the truck's cabin. 'Get in.' She put one foot on the step and suddenly felt his hand on her bottom. She pulled herself up quickly into the cab and he swung himself up to sit pressed against her. He commanded the driver, 'Drive, go.' She sat tense as the truck sped along the road, every bump and pothole being transmitted into their bodies. She was conscious that the hand on her bottom had been a first move. After only about three minutes he put his hand on her thigh and squeezed it. She tried to remove his hand but he just squeezed more tightly, smiling. 'You like it, no?'

'No.'

'You should be grateful, I'm a Chinese officer.' He continued to press her thigh, moving his hand up into her crotch. Suddenly he barked at the driver, 'Stop!' As the truck lurched to a halt, he opened the door and pulled her out. 'You know what you have to do.' He undid the flap over his holster and took out his pistol. She recognised it as a standard issue Soviet Makarov. Waving the semi-automatic weapon at her, he ordered, 'Take your clothes off.'

She made a gesture of hopelessness. 'It's freezing cold.'

'I make you warm,' he sneered. She looked around her. Just off to the side of the road was a patch of scrub. Pointing to it, she said to the man, 'Over there's more comfortable.' Her voice was submissive. He nodded and grinned approval.

She moved a little ahead of him, picking her way slowly across the broken ground to allow him to get close up behind her. She bent down as though she was stumbling, reaching forward with her hand to steady herself. As she collected her balance and began to stand up, she pivoted on her right foot and the stone she held in her extended arm struck him in the side of the right temple. Both his hands reached for his head and she kicked him in the crutch, jack-knifing him forward so that she could bring both hands gripping the stone down on the back of his neck. He sprawled forward, still holding on to the pistol. She stomped on his pistol hand, the heel of her boot driving into his wrist and the weapon fell free as he cried out in pain. Sweeping it up she released the safety catch and checked the magazine before slamming it back into position and then shot him twice in the head.

'*Wah! Wah!*' The truck driver's face was ashen. 'What have you done?' The driver was wringing his hands.

'Reincarnated him.'

She motioned him to get back in the cab. Swiftly she searched the dead man, recovering her papers, a spare magazine and a shortwave personal radio, then stuffed them together with his Makarov inside the fold of her bhaku.

'My number, they have my number,' the driver said, pointing a shaking finger at the vehicle's number plate.

'If they question you, tell them you dropped us off here and the officer told you to leave,' Pema said. 'It's mostly true. Come on, get in and let's get out of here.' She was shouting at him, knowing that she had to frighten him into obedience.

Back on the road, she now had to re-think the plan. Once the dead officer was discovered, a search operation would be put in hand. The bulk of their operation had been completed, leaving Palden's Blue team too far west to withdraw through the planned exit points, she would order them to try their luck into eastern Nepal. Those passes were high, risky and bitterly cold but not well-guarded. Kalsang's Red team was closest to Kala Tso, so his and Choden's Green team would head for the Jampheri ridge, towards the Sinche-la pass. But first she had to recover her communication equipment. She calculated that they were still about 10 kilometres from Kangma. Now that her freedom of movement was circumscribed, she wished that she had found a cache closer to Gyantse, it was urgent to contact the teams. As the truck bumped and lurched its way noisily through the increasingly stark land, she began to question her own judgment. Pushing the doubts aside, she scanned the ground ahead and suddenly saw what she was looking for.

'Stop here,' she said. 'I'm leaving you now.' She felt along the fold of her sheepskin until her fingers met the loose stitching. She held out a misshapen gold coin to him and said, 'Here, this is for your trouble. Remember, you left us back there, close to the checkpoint.' She gestured behind her and said reassuringly, 'They can't prove otherwise.'

The gold was enough to buy him another truck if he had to abandon this one. She raised her hands in Buddhist salute. 'To a free Tibet. Now go!'

He needed no further encouragement, grated the gears savagely and accelerated away down the road, leaving a trail of filthy smoke. Five hundred metres ahead was the goat track she recognised where she struck off at a tangent to the main road. The sky was overcast, threatening snow, when it came it would hide her tracks but first, she had to make really good time to the cache. The dead Chinese officer's shortwave radio crackled, and her heart missed a beat, surely, they had not found the man already? Then silence.

Penjo's voice kept repeating in her ear: 'Always travel in pairs.' Why did she always think she knew better? Her lack of care for herself had now put everyone at greater risk. Why did she allow her self-confidence to override basic caution? Was it really so necessary to prove herself to everyone? She bit back on her anger; she would need all her energy to see this through successfully. She broke into a loping stride.

North-northwest of Batang-la

'**A**re you sure?'

Jigme, the Green team's signals operator, was offended at Choden's tone of voice.

'Certain,' he told her.

'Shit.'

Jigme nodded agreement. Choden cuffed his shoulder by way of apology and he recovered his dignity.

The coded signal ordered them to get out using the same route they had used on the way in but in half the time. The instructions were intentionally limited to a one-second burst, no room to explain what had prompted an emergency exit. All Choden knew was that Pema wanted them out of Tibet as fast as they could make it. Five minutes was all it took to strike their camp close to the turquoise water of the river. Choden had to make an instant decision whether to detour to their cache of arctic clothing without which they would risk freezing to death on the high passes. But it would cost them half-a-day's march and they did not have that amount of leeway. 'Improvise,' she heard Kushog-saheb's voice in her ear and it made her smile. Staring at the distant snow-mantled Himalayas that would soon engorge them, she did not have a clue how she was going to improvise.

'Here,' said Jamsung as he handed over her backpack and turned away before she could get a good look at his face. Over the past two days he had been much less himself, no joking around, little or no banter. Choden suspected he was ill but hiding it from the rest of the team. Deciding not to draw attention to it, she pointed to their direction of travel and set off at a sharp pace. She calculated that they would reach the outer perimeter of the area, normally manned by the Shigatse garrison troops, just before nightfall. By moving all night, they should reach a point within striking distance of Batang-la. The trick would be to avoid the PLA positions in the long corridor towards Yadong so that they could hit the Bhutanese border.

Within two hours her suspicions proved accurate. Jamsung's noisy breathing was signalling his distress and the others had to support him. She called a rest halt and squatted down in front of him. His face was grey, even the scarlet sunburned cheeks were drained of colour. He summoned a smile that barely widened his mouth. 'Sorry, *Noo-mo*,' he said. 'I'm a burden. You must leave me here. I'll find shelter and recover.' He made a weak gesture towards the mountains and added, 'Leave me some *tsampa* and *cha*.'

Choden shook her head. 'We're not leaving you, *Ah-ku*.'

'But…'

'No,' she said, standing up to signal that it was not open for discussion.

They needed transport, preferably a vehicle but failing that a horse or even a yak. She opened the map concealed inside the pages of a prayer book: the village of Tedong was about four kilometres due east of their position, she remembered having attended a festival there several years earlier. Walking over to where Sonam was heating some cha on a couple of fire pellets, Choden tapped him on the shoulder.

'Go to Tedong,' she said, pointing in its direction. 'Get us a motor, anything will do, buy, beg, borrow or steal if you have to.' She took two battered gold coins out of her belt purse and gave them to Sonam. 'No, don't steal but pay whatever they ask for. Fill it up with fuel and get back here as soon as you can.'

The young man stood up grinning. 'Suppose there's no motor.'

'Wipe that stupid grin off your face,' she told him. 'We're going to need transport if we're to get out of here alive.'

Sonam's expression turned sheepish and he set his shoulders back in salute. She shook her head in mock disapproval. 'OK, horses or worst case a yak, for Jamsung, understood?'

His carefree attitude irritated her sometimes, but he could be trusted to use his initiative and he had a way with people that made them trust him.

'See if you can buy sheepskin *chubas* too.' She had noticed dried sheep turds scattered about on the ground. Sonam swung his Bergen onto one shoulder and picked up his Uzi. 'And don't get into a fight,' she reminded him. 'I don't want you bringing the PLA down on our heads.' Pointing at the weapon, she added, 'Conceal that.'

'Yes, *Ah-ma*.' He stuffed it into a fold of his chuba and waved a lazy salute.

'You'll wish I were your mother if you don't get me that transport, get out!' she said, kicking at his bottom. He jumped out of the way laughing, then started to jog away.

The wind was steely cold, anaesthetising her face and she cast around for a burrow that they could shelter Jamsung in whilst they waited. A stand of stunted juniper amongst some buckhorn bush caught her eye and she walked over to it. Hidden behind the foliage was the broken corner of what had been a low stone wall. She pulled the branches aside to reveal a space big enough for the three of them to crawl into. The others realised what she was doing and moved towards Jamsung to help him but he waved them off angrily and stumbled towards the burrow.

'*Di-gi-ray, di-gi-ray.*'

Even that display of bad temper told Choden that he was not OK, no matter what he said. He crawled slowly into the space and collapsed against the broken wall. As the paramedic for the team, she examined him as best she could. His teeth chattered as he spoke. 'I think it's malaria again, Noo-mo.' She nodded. There was already a film of sweat on his forehead. Once they got into the mountains the sweat would freeze and expose him to hypothermia and his chances of survival would be zero.

'We're getting some transport,' she told him with an encouraging smile.

'Tcha!' Jamsung tried to spit but it was dry. 'You must think about the others, I can hide up somewhere on the road.'

She shook her head. 'We're not leaving anyone behind.'

He retreated into his pain, too weak to argue. She gave him two Tylenol and he drank them with his tea then sank back, resting his head on his Bergen. Huddled over the Tommy cooker, the rest of them sipped the butter tea as she explained her plan, for what it was worth.

Southeast of Kala Tso

Kalsang's Red team found the ruins of a fortified monastery that Pema had selected as the last RV on the exit route. When they received the signal to get out, it was the nearest to their position. They rested up amongst the rubble of what, he guessed, had been the main hall, the night sky visible through the fire-charred beams. The night was relatively light, and he calculated that they could use their fuel pellets to make cha without risking their position. It would help wash down the cold tsampa. He checked his watch and noted that Dawa was listening for any messages on his earpiece as he sharpened his long-bladed hunting knife. The last codeword from Pema meant that she was in trouble. Kalsang estimated that she must be somewhere between Gyantse and their current position. Standard operating procedure was for each team to make its own way out and the company commander would do likewise. But it went against the grain to abandon Pema to her own devices if she was in trouble. He leaned over the kettle.

'We wait for 48 hours in case Pema gets here, agree?'

'No need to ask.' Dawa did not stop sharpening his knife. The other two, Loshay and Tenzing, nodded silently. Though Kalsang was the leader, they worked as a team. It was also acknowledged that he would take the blame if anything went wrong; that was the price of leadership.

'I'll take first watch,' Kalsang told the others. 'Get some sleep.' He picked up his Galil sniper rifle and changed the Nimrod ×6 sight for a night sight. Dawa stopped stropping his knife and grinned at him, 'Can you get us a nice fat ewe?'

'Only if it's a *gyah-nakh*,' he quipped.

'How can you tell?'

'They have a little red star printed on their forehead.' Kalsang laughed at his own joke and walked over to a broken stone staircase in the northern corner of the hall and climbed to the highest point of what had once been a tower. It gave him an almost 360° view of the terrain. He opened the bipod and positioned the Galil so that it commanded a maximum field of fire, settled himself comfortably against a pile of stones and popped a piece of *choorpi* into his mouth. In two hours, the rock-hard dried yak milk would still only have yielded a little.

State Highway No. 208

The goat track meandered at a rough 90° angle to the Gyantse-Kangma road and Pema followed it to where she had cached her transceiver and .44 Magnum Desert Eagle handgun. Recovering her own equipment, she buried the dead Chinese officer's Makarov, kept his radio, then continued on for several kilometres until the track bisected the motorable road that led to Samada. She needed to make as much distance as possible from the corpse. She felt her luck was improving when a battered bus heading south picked her up. She squeezed in beside an old woman who was sitting on two sacks of what looked like millet.

Samada was a small town, spread thinly across a Himalayan foothill. Its small temple had escaped the ravages visited by the Chinese upon larger buildings and it was the base of a Rinpoche to whom she was distantly related. Her estimate that the bus would arrive just after dark proved correct. They passed through the clumps of two-storey mud-and-stone houses that marked the edge of the town, then entered a narrow street, almost brushing the buildings that hemmed them in on both sides before it pulled into an open rectangular square. The front windows of the bus were caked with dust and filth so it was only when it did a U-turn that she could see a small crowd of people waiting at what she assumed was the terminus. To her dismay, a number of uniformed militiamen stood waiting to receive the vehicle.

Pema spoke to the old woman beside her. 'Let me help you with these, *Ah-mah*.' She took hold of the two sacks and lifted them out to allow the smiling old woman to extricate herself. Pema held back, allowing the other passengers to clamber over the assorted chickens, goats and baggage. Under cover of the pushing and shoving around her, she undid the loose rope that secured the neck of one sack and let a little millet spill onto the floor.

'Oh, sorry,' she said, turning her body to conceal what she was about to do – she pushed her handgun, transceiver and the dead man's radio deep into the millet before securing the sack again.

Together they shuffled along the aisle. Pema disembarked, depositing the sacks on the road before she helped the old woman negotiate the steps down to street level, chatting away as she did so. Holding a sack in each hand, she turned to find a militia officer standing right in front of her.

'Where are you going?' he demanded.

'We're…,' she began, only to be interrupted by her new friend. 'Where d'you think we're going, *choong-rah*? Home, of course.' Not content with calling him a young goat, the old woman's voice was dripping with contempt when she added, 'Just because you've sold yourself to the gyah-nakh doesn't entitle you to harass women.'

The old woman pushed herself between Pema and the militiaman and stepped up close to him; the contrast would have been funny if Pema had not been worried about what was going to happen, especially if they stopped and searched her. She knew she would have to take responsibility. Her new friend was not only short but hunched over and the militia officer towered over her, yet she appeared not in the least cowed by him. Some residue of the innate sense of humour possessed by her people must have been ignited in the man. He threw his hands in the air in mock surrender and backed off. 'Whoa! No need to be so *loong-lahng*. I apologise,' he said. He then made a sweeping theatrical gesture with his arm, indicating that she should proceed.

'Hah!' was all the response she gave him as she flicked her head at Pema. 'Come, *phu-mo*.' Leaning heavily on her walking stick, she set off down the road that continued deeper into the town.

Pema gave the militiaman a little nod and was about to follow when he said, 'Not you.' His voice arrested her. 'Papers.'

Conscious that she had given Batang-la as her destination when she was stopped at the checkpoint, she had decided to leave her permit in the cache. Now all she had was her resident ID card which showed that she was registered in Gyantse. She dug the tattered ID out of her bhaku and handed it over. She was reasonably confident that the dead PLA officer had not yet been found or if he had, the news would not have been circulated this quickly. She kept her eyes down, acting as most of her countrymen and women did when faced with authority.

'Where's your travel permit?'

'Permit?' She played dumb. 'I'm still in the Gyantse region, no?' Before she could reply, the old woman was back beside them, tapping the man's legs with her stick.

'She's seeing me safely home, if you people did your job, we wouldn't need escorting.' To Pema, she said, 'Come on, hurry up girl, I'm tired and I want to go to bed.' The militiaman looked at his nearest colleague who shook his shoulders helplessly. Putting her card in his pocket, he scowled at her, 'Report to the police in the morning.' She gave another submissive nod and then hurried after the old woman who was now hurling more insults at the militiaman. Catching up with her, Pema said quietly, 'Perhaps we shouldn't provoke them.'

'Filth, that's all they are, filth. But they know to leave me alone.' She turned a triumphant face towards Pema and said, 'I'm a Khamba, they're terrified of my people.' That, Pema knew to be correct. 'You have somewhere to stay tonight? No, don't tell me, you're staying with me.'

Pema was weary and the invitation was enticing but she worried that despite the old Khamba's feisty contempt for the militia, they would know exactly where to find her if they came looking. Without her ID, she would be arrested.

'You're very kind.'

'Nonsense. I saw you put something in the sack. If you have to hide from the militia, you're a true daughter of Tibet. Say no more, we're here.'

They had stopped in front of a big wooden door and she banged on it with her stick. Almost immediately it opened onto an inner courtyard. A man and woman bowed respectfully before closing the door and dropping a heavy wooden bar across it.

'Come, come,' the old woman beckoned her in. The man took the two sacks of millet from Pema, smiling as he did so. To her surprise, her host suddenly straightened up, losing her hunched stance. She laughed,

'They're easily fooled.' Her face became serious as she said to the man, 'Empty the sacks and bring our guest what you find inside them.'

She turned to Pema. 'You don't have to tell me what you're doing. We Khambas have been resisting the gyah-nakh from the time of the occupation. We must believe that one day we will get our country back, until then we shall resist.'

The man re-appeared bearing the handgun, transceiver and radio on a wooden tray.

'I see that I was right,' her host said, giving her an amused looked. She then became serious. 'For several days we have been expecting the militia to impose martial law, controlling movement in and out of the town. Obviously, they arrived whilst I was away. Our information is that more military are moving into the region, concentrating on the border with India.' This confirmed the intelligence that Pema had received in Gyantse.

'Even with your ID you will not be permitted to travel,' she said, glancing at the gun. 'We must find a way to get you out, *Noo-moh* but first I expect you would like to wash and then we shall eat. Doma will show you to your bedroom, there is a bathroom next to it.' She smiled, 'Oh yes, we are very modern.' Pema steepled her hands in appreciation.

'Thank you, *A-roks*, I am in your debt.'

'After you have washed, we shall discuss how to get you out safely.'

*

Standing in the shower with the hot water running down her body, Pema felt a sense of guilt. Her teams were out in the bitter cold, probably with phö-cha as the only hot thing they dared to brew up, yet here she was enjoying comparative luxury. Suddenly something Kushog-saheb had said to her at the end of a gruelling day when, though exhausted, she had declined his offer of a lift. 'Only a bloody fool is uncomfortable when she doesn't need to be.' She reflected that, fed and rested, she would be in a better state of mind to plan getting both herself and the teams out safely. Nonetheless, she was now seriously worried in case her description had been circulated, the fact that the militia had her ID would make their task easier. She fired up the transceiver and sent the code for the RV.

*

The room was warmed by an iron cooking stove over which Doma was busy and from which a delicious aroma filled the air.

'You look a lot better,' said Dekkie, her host who was indicating the chair beside her. 'Come and have some *thuk-pa*.'

Pema made namaskar and sat down. 'I'm very grateful but I'm afraid that being associated with me will cause you problems,' she said. 'I think I should leave as soon as possible; they might come looking for me.'

'Not before you have eaten something,' Dekkie decided.

The door opened and the male servant entered and bowed. When he straightened up Pema could see the look of concern on his face.

'My brother says that a gyah-nakh officer was murdered on the Gyantse road, they are looking for a man and a woman,' Dekkie explained. 'Ragpa's brother is in the militia, we needed to have inside information.'

There was a momentary silence as they both looked at her. Pema instinctively trusted Dekkie but was disinclined to say more than was necessary.

'You don't have to tell us anything,' she patted Pema's hand reassuringly. 'We'll do whatever we can to help you.'

'I killed him. He was trying to rape me.' Pema felt that this was more than enough to explain her urgent need to escape from the town and it had the great advantage of being the truth.

'Ahh.' Dekkie canted her head at a sympathetic angle. 'He chose the wrong woman.' She was thoughtful for a moment. 'In which direction do you want to go?'

'Due south.' There was no need to burden them with more information.

Dekkie turned to face Ragpa. 'After we have eaten, take our guest through the town by the secure route and set her on the old road.'

'I'm very worried, your association with me...'

'What association?' Dekkie interrupted her. 'You helped an old woman with her load, then you went on your way.' She raised one eyebrow. 'You did say you were heading north?' Pema smiled.

'Now, eat or Doma will be most upset.' Dekkie pointed at the woman and Pema nodded appreciatively as she wolfed down the thick, home-made noodles swimming in the meat stew. She was not going to get the sleep she had hoped for and getting to the RV would make massive demands on her physical and mental strength.

'Will there be mobile patrols on the old road?'

'You should be safe once you hit the snow line, the Filth rarely go up there.'

'In about 25 kilometres,' Ragpa added.

'Are there any checkpoints I need to avoid?'

Dekkie and Ragpa looked at each other for a moment.

'Stay off National Highway 318, they often put up surprise checkpoints along it all the way to India,' Ragpa said.

'And the new PLA units are between here and Lake Yamdrok,' Dekkie added, lifting a warning finger. 'But as you're not going towards the west, they shouldn't trouble you.' She pursed her lips to indicate that she was not taken in by Pema's declared route. 'No,' she confirmed. Dekkie looked at her sideways for a moment. 'Can you ride?'

'Of course.'

'There's no *of course* unless you're a Khamba, we were all birthed on horseback.'

Dekkie looked at Ragpa. 'The young Mongolian pony.' He nodded. She turned back to Pema. 'It's built for endurance not speed,' she said, flicking her head towards Ragpa. 'Like him.' They all laughed. 'Try to find him a good home when you're done with him.'

Pema knew better than to offer to pay for the pony. She put her hands together and bowed deeply.

An hour and a half later, she gave Ragpa a wave of salutation. He said softly, 'Free Tibet and return.' Then he smacked the pony's rump and she trotted through the stand of trees that concealed the hidden gateway into the town.

Northeast of Batang-la

The frigid light of dawn's anaemic sun crept over the mountain tops and sparked a million reflections from the snow that clothed the sparse treeline, marking the beginning of the frozen ground out of which the Himalayan giants rose up as though waves of rock and ice had been petrified as they crested the land.

'*Kahk!*'

Pema dragged herself out of nowhere. Exhaustion had finally overtaken her, lulled by the gentle motion of the pony she had fallen asleep in the saddle.

'Kahk! Kahk!'

She automatically pulled on the reins to bring the pony to a halt in compliance with the threatening tones of the order. Several members of a militia patrol barred her way, their rifles raised to their shoulders and pointed at her.

'*Tah-shi de-leh.*'

Still trying to gather her wits it was easy to play stupid and greeting them with a simple hello bought her time to assess her situation. Behind a semi-circle of six militiamen, between the road and the trees on the left an old-style Russian jeep was parked which, together with their .303 Lee-Enfield rifles demonstrated their lowly status in the Chinese pecking order.

'Where are you going?' The two stars on his collar signified they were commanded by a sergeant.

'Sakya.'

'Hah.' He gave a derisive snort. 'Well, this is the wrong road.' He lowered his rifle and walked up to her.

'Papers.'

This was what she had hoped to avoid. She could not outrun them nor could she draw her Desert Eagle and hope to shoot them before one of them got her first. She reached behind her, lifting the flap of a saddlebag and making it look as though she was searching. She turned towards him, anxiety in her expression.

'They've gone…I know I put them here but now…' She gave a little whimper of despair. The sergeant took two paces towards her, gesturing with his rifle for her to get down.

'Should I go back?' She adopted a frightened tone of voice. He took two paces towards her and swung the butt of his rifle against her back. She slumped forward over the pony's neck, the blow had caught her in the kidney, she could hardly breathe. Gritting her teeth, she slid out of the saddle. One of the other militiamen grabbed a handful of her bhaku and pulled her towards the jeep.

'You're going nowhere, stinking Khamba bitch.' It dawned on her that her three-quarter length bhaku, together with the Mongolian pony, was enough for him to classify her. He pointed at two of the militiamen.

'Search her saddlebags, they're all thieves.' He spat in her direction and waved towards the jeep. 'Sit over there.' The pain made her walk slowly, she kept her head bowed down. Her escort kicked her from behind. 'Move.'

Still half-walking, half-stumbling she slipped one hand inside her bhaku and switched the transceiver on. She pressed the pre-set indicating that she was in trouble and activated the positional signal, then pushed the device deeper inside her clothing. The Desert Eagle was tucked into her waistband behind her back but underneath the bhaku. She was grateful that the rifle butt had caught her on the left, if it had been the right, he might have detected the hidden weapon.

One of the militiamen led the pony to the side of the road and started to search the saddlebags. He gave a little triumphal grunt. 'Cha…and butter.'

The sergeant leered at her, then told the one with the tea to light a fire. Turning back to her, he pointed to the ground beside the jeep. 'Sit.'

She walked the few steps to beside the jeep and hunkered down beside the wheel-arch, the wheel taking her weight so that she could keep on her feet. If they started to search her, she would kill as many of them as possible before they took her.

Red Team
West of Batang-la

❦

Dawa had been on watch for just over an hour when he heard the
sound of a motor vehicle approaching. He selected a small stone
and aimed it at Kalsang's sleeping form.

'Eh?' Even as he woke, Kalsang's keen ears detected the ragged note of
the motor. He woke the others and ran quickly up the staircase.

'It's not gyah-nakh. They drive modern vehicles. Listen to it, it's a heap
of shit,' Kalsang said.

Dawa nodded. 'But who drives a heap of shit along this cattle track at
this hour of night?'

They looked at each other and grinned. 'Choden?' Kalsang hazarded.
Dawa used the night sight to look for the vehicle, it did not take long.

'Got it. Only showing sidelights,' Dawa reported. 'The main beams
must be broken, no point trying to hide from anyone if you're making a
racket like that.'

'It's one of ours, just signalled V with its lights,' Kalsang said and
pointed his heavy torch towards the oncoming vehicle and repeated the
Morse signal. Minutes later they had the open back utility vehicle inside
the broken walls of what had been the courtyard of the monastery.

Choden slid out of the front passenger seat. 'Why are you still here?'
she asked.

Kalsang raised his hands in surrender. 'I know, I know, but if Pema's
in trouble, she'll head here so...' He left it to Choden to draw her own
conclusion. She pursed her lips for a second, then nodded.

'Jamsung's sick, I risked getting some transport but we're sitting ducks
if the gyah-nakh intercept us,' Choden said.

Kalsang nodded. 'Especially in a load of shit like that.' He gestured towards the vehicle.

Choden grimaced, 'Beggars can't choose.' She stared at him. 'Trouble is we don't know why Pema ordered us out.' She looked around. 'Good spot. You can see anything approaching from far off.' She was torn between getting Jamsung up into the mountains as quickly as possible and letting him rest for a few hours to gain strength. 'Got your arctic gear?'

'Yes. You?'

'No,' Choden said. 'Sonam got us three filthy old sheepskin chubas but Jamsung needs thermals.'

'He can have mine.' Kalsang opened his Bergen and handed her his set.

'OK.' She made her mind up. 'We'll stay together until tomorrow night, then I'm leaving, Pema or no Pema.'

Kalsang acknowledged the reasoning. 'Come nightfall tomorrow, we all pull out. Till then we'll harbour up here.'

They doubled the lookouts, made Jamsung as comfortable as possible, then huddled together for warmth.

Choden was mentally exhausted but sleep eluded her. She checked the time: the next possible contact window would shortly open. Lifting her head, she noted that Jigme was already up, wearing both earpieces. As she walked towards him his head moved fractionally, he was receiving. He pressed the toggle momentarily, then took one of the earpieces out.

'Pema.' His finger was caught in the low beam of his torch, pointing to a spot on the map he had balanced on a stone balustrade. 'Here.'

'Trouble?'

He nodded, 'Just the emergency signal and her location.'

Choden studied the map. She calculated that they were less than 15 kilometres away. Kalsang was beside her now, running his fingers through his hair. As she gave him the news, the others gathered round.

'Load up. We'll drive to within two clicks of Pema's position, then scout forward on foot.'

Kalsang dipped his head in agreement. 'I hope Sonam's rust bucket can get us all there.'

'Hmm.' Choden gave a dismissive grunt.

Mussoorie

Saturday, 9 February

The assistant commissioner did not recognise the number on his cell phone. 'Yes,' he barked. There was the slightest pause before an educated voice he recognised inquired, 'AC Narendra?' The use of just his forename confirmed the caller's identity. The tone of his response was deferential: '*Ha ji.*'

'Persons of interest to you are presently at the Gateway.' The pause this time was for effect. 'This is a gesture of goodwill, from one service to another.' The line went dead.

The assistant commissioner had not really expected his backdoor inquiry to the Research and Analysis Wing to bear fruit. In truth, he was more than a little suspicious that it might lead to him being entrapped. He deleted the phone call as a precautionary measure. Using his police walkie-talkie, he was put through to the superintendent of serious crime.

'Saheb?' Reception was, as always, dreadful. Why couldn't they have some decent equipment? Maybe, he reflected, he could parlay this into the state government providing them with state-of-the-art radios. Even as he thought of it, he dismissed it. Those fat bastards only looked after themselves. He kept his message cryptically neutral.

'Ajay, the Gateway has foreign guests.' He killed the connection.

*

They sat beneath the parasol on the veranda of Gateway Hotel, Shanaaz in the shade whilst the sun struck his arm reminding him that, like so many Asian women, she prized a fair skin and avoided its rays. Her smile was half-hidden behind her cappuccino. 'Your worries were quite unnecessary.'

'So far.'

True, the army's furniture had been returned to the Quartermaster's Department and the bungalow had been emptied of her and Nisha's belongings, all without incident. But he still had a nagging concern: it was too easy.

'Stop looking as though the heavens are about to fall, I shall have to call you Henny penny!' She laughed and wiped a thin line of foam off her upper lip. He scratched the back of his head but there were some itches that wouldn't go away. She looked behind him and smiled.

'How y'all doing?' Herman sat down. He had joined them at the last minute, grateful for the opportunity to get away from the constant monitoring of the Aksai Chin teams. At first, Max had quietly resented the intrusion into their private space but, contrary to his expectations, the American had proved surprisingly considerate, giving them space as he soaked up everything about the place and its people. A waiter bustled over.

'Get me one of them cappuccinos, if they're any good.'

Ignoring the doubt in his tone, the waiter gave a little bow before adding, 'We are having Illy, very good coffee, saheb.'

'Next thing you'll be looking for is a Big Mac,' Shanaaz joked. Herman's expression acknowledged his preference for the familiar.

'You ever been to the States, doc'?'

She nodded. 'I did an internship at Johns Hopkins, incredible. But we don't have those resources in the Indian Army, we have to improvise.'

'I guess in our line of business, that's one helluva lot more useful.' He glanced at his watch. 'OK if I just finish my coffee, then we start back?'

'No problem, Deepraj will be here in about 10 minutes,' Max said.

*

'They're sitting on the veranda; another foreigner has joined them.' The receptionist was using his own mobile as he watched from inside the hotel.

'Call me as soon as they leave.'

'Yes, sir.'

He was scared of the superintendent-saheb. When the policeman had found the illegal still that he and his brother were running, spying on the hotel's guests was a cheap price to pay for the police turning a blind eye to their business. That and the free drinks for senior police officers which he hid from the hotel's accountants.

The guests were standing up now, he decided to wait until he saw them actually leave the premises before calling back, the superintendent-saheb had a bad habit of smacking him on the back of his head if not satisfied with the information.

*

The Pajero hugged the bends as they contoured around the hills. Max inhaled the rich combination of new growth and decomposing vegetation that filled the air, shutting his eyes and savouring the moment. Shanaaz sat beside him in the back seat, leaning against him as the vehicle swayed gently around the series of S-bends. Deepraj was an accomplished mountain driver and enjoyed the luxury of the Pajero rather than the aged ex-US Army jeeps that he was accustomed to coaxing up and down Darjeeling's roads. Herman broke the silence. 'Well, I reckon we count that mission accomplished.' Max said nothing. Herman turned around to look at him and asked, 'What d'you say?'

Max gave him a dismissive wave of the hand. 'So far so good.'

'That the best you can do?'

'These bastards' influence is what prevents India from progressing.'

On the drive into Mussoorie he had briefed the American on the Kempty Falls incident. Herman's response had been a slow smile. 'Wish I'd been there.'

'Trouble is, I risked prejudicing our work in Baniyana.'

'Hell, they had it comin'.'

Whilst Max agreed, he knew that they had had the misfortune to disturb a feral animal. Indian politicians were a breed apart, especially the corrupt ones, which meant most of them. Uncaged, they knew no boundaries.

'Saheb.' Deepraj's worried tone snapped him out of his thoughts. They had just entered a straight stretch of road and ahead, blocking it, were two knife rests, staggered to force vehicles to slow to a crawl in order to negotiate them. Two uniformed armed police officers with automatic rifles waved them down.

'Shall I crash through?' Deepraj asked.

'No, let's play this straight.' Even as he said it, Max queried whether it was the right decision. Deepraj brought the car to a halt just in front of the officers but left the handbrake off.

Pointing his rifle at them, one of the officers shouted, 'Get out of car, everyone, out!'

This was definitely not normal protocol.

'Stay put,' Max said quietly.

'Out! Out!' Both officers now shouted at them.

Max tapped Deepraj on the shoulder. 'Try talking to them nicely. Is your gun under your seat?' The Gurkha gave a nod and leaned out of the window talking to them in Hindi.

'What's the problem, officer-saheb? Do you want my driving licence?'

Another figure stepped out of the trees, not in uniform but carrying an AK 47. Max spoke softly, 'This is no police operation.' He looked in the rear-view mirror and saw two more armed men approaching from the back. Under cover of Deepraj's seat he cocked his CZ75. 'Herman, take the guys coming up behind us.'

'Got it,' Durwachter grunted.

Speaking softly and wearing a smile, Max said, 'Keep talking, Deepraj. Smile at them. When I say now, shoot the one nearest to us and hit drive...Shanaaz, drop to the floor.'

Deepraj held up his empty right hand in mock submission, withdrew it and called out, 'OK...OK...OK.'

Max put his head out of the window, smiling at the one with the AK 47. 'Now!' He raised his hand, rough aligned and pulled the trigger. Deepraj got off a shot before the Pajero lurched forward and he grabbed the steering wheel.

The sound of the guns inside the car was deafening. The windscreen shattered as the second officer fired at them from the front but as the vehicle shot towards him, he took fright, stumbled backwards and fell. Deepraj drove straight over him. The rear window shattered, showering Max with glass particles. He twisted around, one of the attackers was lying on the floor, the second was firing at them. Max's aim was knocked off when the Pajero hit the knife rest, jolting the car which Deepraj was now swerving erratically down the road.

'Can't you keep this fuckin' thing steady for a second,' Herman shouted as he fired. 'Gottim!' The remaining rear attacker spun round, his rifle falling from his hands.

'I rather think I got him, actually,' Max said. 'Everyone OK?' He squeezed Shanaaz's shoulder and brushed some of the glass particles off her head. She struggled to get up and back into her seat, sweeping it clear.

'Are we safe?' Her voice was unsteady.

'From that little effort, yes.' He put one hand on Deepraj's shoulder. '*Syabas!* Now let's get back to base as quickly as we can. I hope to God there are no other surprises en route.'

'Man, you take no prisoners.' Herman was reloading his gun. 'Think there may be more trouble?'

'Can't rule it out, but my guess is that they thought they had enough firepower to knock us out, so hopefully not.'

Herman continued feeding bullets into a magazine. 'Sure have a way of making friends and influencing people. Not sure it's safe to be around you.'

'That's the pot calling the kettle black.' They both laughed.

Max's mobile started to ring. It was Penjo.

'On our way.' He rang off. 'Shit! Pema's teams are in trouble.'

'Any details?' Herman twisted around to face him.

Max shook his head. 'Sitrep on arrival.'

With both the windscreen and the rear window smashed, the air rushed through the vehicle making them uncomfortably aware of the speed.

Southeast of Batang-la

Kalsang studied the scene through the Nimrod ×6 sight. The militiamen were hunkered down around a small fire except for one who was guarding Pema. She was sitting on the ground, her back against a rear wheel of the jeep, knees drawn up so that her chin rested on top. He whispered to Choden, 'She looks OK, the one guarding her keeps looking towards the fire, so he's not particularly alert.'

'I can see,' Choden said. They were only 150 metres away, concealed in the trees on the same side of the road as the militiamen. 'See any lookouts?'

He traversed the area left to right looking for anyone on the high ground. 'I need to move right to get a view of the trees, what d'you think?'

There was virtually no cover once Kalsang moved out of the treeline. He passed Choden the sight and she checked for herself before passing it back so that he could attach it to the Galil.

'Six is the normal capacity for those Russian jeeps,' she observed, 'but one of those around the fire glanced up towards the trees slightly ahead of their position. Could be a lookout up there.' She calculated that it would take them about one minute to close on the militiamen. 'We could disarm them, tie them up, take the jeep and leave them. They wouldn't last long out here.'

'But if someone comes looking for them?' Kalsang wondered.

She continued talking whilst watching her front. 'You don't want to kill our own people.' Her voice carried no criticism, simply stated a fact.

'No.'

'They chose to work with gyah-nahk against us,' Choden said, 'they're worse than the PLA.' She squinted at the scene ahead of them. 'That jeep's in better condition than our truck. We take them out, load them into the truck and push it over the mountainside. We can squeeze into the jeep and if we run into any more patrols, we'll be on them before they know that it isn't one of their own.'

'Agreed,' Kalsang said quietly.

'I'll go up close through the trees with the others. Give me three minutes, then take out Pema's guard and any lookout.'

They checked watches, then Choden wriggled her body backwards, rose to her feet and briefed the others. She looked at Kalsang, tapped her watch, then led the team forward, slipping quickly from tree to tree.

When the second hand hit the mark, Kalsang rolled right putting him at the base of the hypotenuse to the treeline. As he brought the Galil up into his shoulder he heard gunfire and snapped off a shot that felled Pema's guard. Then just as he rolled right again bullets kicked up the soil where he had just been. Scanning the lower branches of the trees he spotted an irregular shape. Just as he focused on it, he felt as though he had been kicked in the left shoulder and the Galil fell out of his hands.

*

Pema was watching the forest through half-open eyes. If either of the teams were going to rescue her, their only covered approach was through those trees. When she detected the first hint of movement she looked up into the tree where the lookout had been positioned but it was impossible to tell if he had noticed anything. Her guard was more interested in the tea-making, only glancing towards her occasionally. When the first shot sang out, a militiaman fell forward into the fire. Tugging the Desert Eagle out, she threw herself into the prone position. Her guard fell backwards heavily. Now she heard shots being fired by the lookout and she took a careful two-handed aim, the recoil from the .44 round lifted the target momentarily off her vision but she was satisfied to see the man tumble out of the tree. Jumping up, she registered that the other militiamen were all on the ground. She ran towards the fallen sniper who was still clutching his rifle and trying to get to his feet. She kicked his legs away from under him, kicked him in the head and snatched up his rifle.

Choden ran towards her, issuing instructions. Pema noted that there were members of both the Red and Green teams checking on the militiamen.

'Kalsang?' she asked.

'Back there, he took out the one guarding you,' Choden said. Looking back, she called out, 'Dawa, go back, I can't see Kalsang.'

After Choden had given her a brief report, Pema said, 'Better get the truck and Jamsung here quickly.'

Sonam came up as they were talking. 'Four dead, three wounded,' he reported.

The sound of a hawk's cry drew their attention back to where they had left Kalsang. Dawa was pointing to the ground. They both ran over to where Kalsang lay, blood soaking his shirt. Choden called for her medical kit as she cut the shirt away with her knife. Kalsang's face screwed tight in pain as she explored the wound. Her face was totally without expression as she spoke, 'I think the round is lodged inside and the upper end of the humerus has taken a hit. I'll strap you up, feed your morphine addiction...'

'What...?' He managed and she laughed.

'Joking. Once we're up there...' said Choden, pointing to the mountains, '...the air's thin, you won't feel a thing.'

'Liar!' he spat back, then groaned as she cleaned it up as best she could. She handed over to Dawa to finish bandaging the shoulder.

'Stay here, we'll bring the jeep over to you,' Choden told Kalsang. Out of earshot, she said to Pema, 'The bastard was using a soft-nosed round, Kalsang's shoulder's a fucking mess.'

The four dead bodies were lined up and the three wounded militiamen were seated with their backs to each other in a triangle. The one Pema had shot was rocking backwards and forwards moaning and holding his leg from which blood was oozing. She kicked the foot of the wounded leg. He cried out and looked up at her. Then she shot him in the chest.

'Now,' she said quietly, 'die slowly.' Pema pointed at the two remaining wounded militiamen and spoke to Choden, 'Dress their wounds, then tie them back to back on the pony. If they're lucky they'll survive.' She looked at their identity cards and bent down to speak into their faces,

'We know who you are. You can choose, but if you stay in the militia, we'll hunt you down. We shoot traitors.' She made a show of putting their ID cards in her bhaku.

Choden shouted at Dawa, 'Don't waste that cha.' He grinned and lifted the pot high in invitation. Whilst they crowded around, sipping the cha, Pema drew Choden aside and gave her a brief account of what had happened since she left Gyantse.

'All the information is that the PLA are strengthening their garrison over this whole area. We need to get out as quickly as possible.' Pema looked up at the darkening sky before continuing, 'There's a heavy snowfall coming. We need to get into the mountains fast.'

Choden frowned, 'Kalsang needs urgent medical attention, I've done all that I can, but he's lost a lot of blood and there's only so much we can do out here.'

Pema nodded, 'Jamsung will slow us down. Even if we use the jeep for the road, we still have a three-to-four-day trek to the nearest pass. If you sedate Kalsang, is there enough plasma to keep him alive?'

'Maybe.' Choden wanted to sound hopeful but she knew it was against the odds.

Pema spoke her thoughts out loud, 'Kalsang won't feel much and we can give Jamsung a shot of morphine if we have to.' Choden nodded.

The militia radio suddenly crackled to life asking for a situation report. Pema pointed at Dawa who picked it up and gave a garbled response. The radio repeated its message and Dawa covered the microphone with his glove before saying 'poor reception…can't hear.' He kept this going for a minute, then the caller gave up.

'Bring that with you,' Pema said.

The commander was in a quandary: in their condition, Kalsang needing urgent medical attention and Jamsung a deadweight, her operational efficiency was significantly reduced. Additional PLA forces in the region added to the potential hazards and they had lost their major advantage of being fast moving. In a conventional situation she could call for a chopper, but higher command had ruled that out. She toyed with the idea of detaching two men to carry Kalsang to the nearest clinic but discarded it for sheer impracticability. That would put all three at risk with no guarantee of getting Kalsang treated. Provided they could move undetected, they would get back in one piece but Kalsang's condition was critical. Worst case, she would lose him but get everyone else home. She cursed Delhi for its proscription on a CASEVAC. Durwachter had assured her that their transceiver messages were undetectable, so now was the time to signal Chakrata. The teams would do their best but some of the responsibility needed to be shared. If command tied her hands, they must at least know what they had committed her to. She beckoned Jigme over and dictated a brief message for him to encode and transmit. She closed her eyes, seeking a moment of calm in which to make her decisions but she had a sudden vision of a black Tara. She snapped herself out of it. Prayer had its place but not here, not now.

The truck with Jamsung arrived. 'Get Kalsang and Jamsung into the jeep, drain the truck's tank, then set fire to it,' Pema ordered.

Soon after the heavily loaded jeep took off, the truck exploded and the pony took fright, its wounded passengers shouting out in pain as it cantered over the broken ground shaking them like cloth dolls.

PLA Regional Command
Shigatse Prefecture

Lieutenant-General Liu Peng was a career soldier who had navigated the political obstacle course of the party and now found himself in a command where all his staff officers were party appointees. The decision to double the combat establishment and bring the missile sites to an alert status increased his responsibility but had nothing to do with any threat posed within Tibet or any fresh Indian activities in the Doklam area. Denied access to the party's plans, he could only conjecture that it was another example of the central committee's posturing in the long-running confrontation with its southern neighbour. Lifting his head to look at the colonel of engineers sitting opposite, the regional commander of Shigatse asked, 'Two silos?'

'Yes, General, here and here,' said the engineer colonel, tapping the map and pointing to the north of Batang-la.

'Right on the perimeter of the area claimed by India and Bhutan?' Lieutenant-General Liu did not attempt to disguise his incredulity.

'I am only following orders,' the engineer said with a straight face.

The commander was not going to draw out an opinion. Either the engineer was a committed party apparatchik or a good actor. Constructing two subterranean missile silos in that sensitive area was upping the stakes by a large measure. Did the party really want to go to war with India again? Undoubtedly, they would overwhelm them, but those mountains were a cruel killing ground and heavy losses were inevitable. What for? To gain a few kilometres of uninhabitable Himalayan vastness?

The door opened and the intelligence directorate major stepped in, broke his stride in a momentary pause of salute, then advanced on the table waving some signals in his hand.

'The missing captain has been found. Shot in the head,' he reported. 'The truck was abandoned outside Doka-la. The man and the woman have disappeared.'

Lieutenant-General Liu lifted one eyebrow, waiting for some positive news.

'A militia patrol southeast of Batang-la is not responding properly to calls,' the major added. 'I've sent a Harbin Z-19 to search the area.'

'Why the worry, the militia is as reliable as a paper bucket.'

The intelligence officer paused, anxious not to annoy his commander but also aware that ignoring the information would rebound on him. 'The militia in Chayu…'

'Militia again,' the general interrupted sarcastically.

'…report that a woman associated with known Khamba terrorist sympathisers escaped, despite a curfew,' the major continued. 'The woman who murdered a PLA officer sounds very similar. Now this militia patrol has dropped off the radio net.' He paused, waiting to see if his commander showed any interest.

'The militia are a liability, they're part of the price we pay to convert these uncivilised people to accept that they are part of the greater China,' Lieutenant-General Liu said.

'This particular patrol is one of their most effective units.'

'What are you suggesting?'

'We may have a new guerrilla team operating in that area,' the major replied while pulling at his ear lobe, a nervous sign that his commander recognised.

The general sat in silence for several seconds consulting a wall map showing the distribution of military units under his command, then got to his feet and pointed to Yadong. '128 Mountain Rapid Reaction Regiment is based here. Tell Colonel Wei to deploy some units to search the area and report back.' He turned to face the major and said, 'The murder of one of our officers, surely that's for the PSB to investigate?' He raised an eyebrow.

'General.' The major gave a deferential nod. His gut instinct was that there was a connection between the murder and the missing militia unit, but it was only his intuition. He was reassured that special forces would be involved, but on his own map he had drawn lines between the three events: they were telling him something. His commander's attention was back on his papers. He withdrew, closing the door quietly behind him.

Lieutenant-General Liu paid little attention to the political officers attached to his command and because the major respected his commander, he tried to keep them off the general's back. But this pig-in-the-middle role was exhausting him. Reporting everything to the party hacks was disloyal so he had been tailoring what he told them. But now the area was being reinforced and the missile silos were under construction, he needed to look after number one.

'General.' The signals staff officer snapped Liu out of his thoughts. 'The Z-19 has found five of that militia patrol – all dead. Two are missing, so is the jeep.'

'Could they have turned rogue?' It wouldn't be the first time that militiamen had turned their coats.

'We don't know yet. Do we tell the PSB to investigate?'

'No,' Lieutenant-General Liu said. '128 MRRR are being deployed. Let's keep it in the family for now.' He started writing out the orders for Colonel Wei Zhongxi, the 128 MRRR's commanding officer.

Colonel Wei was a nasty piece of work. A soldier who genuinely believed in the party, he would shoot anyone for deviating from the party line. But his ruthlessness stood him in high repute with Beijing. If the militiamen had defected, no one would want to be in their shoes when the colonel caught them.

HQ 128 Mountain Rapid Reaction Regiment
Yadong

Colonel Wei's adjutant watched his commanding officer read the message from the Harbin Z-19. A narrow, angular head with sharp features, not a scrap of spare flesh on his hard body, just like his mind. When the message came in, the adjutant and the radio operator had laughed but Wei would not see the funny side of it. Nor did he. Looking up, he screwed up eyes that were almost slits in their normal configuration.

'Tied to a horse? How could they allow this to happen?' He did not expect a reply. Their attackers were obviously trained military, intelligence had no reports of guerrillas based in the region so this signified foreign-based forces in the area. Had the truck not been set on fire, the Z-19 might not have found the dead militiamen or the idiots on the horse. If it was foreign operatives, they would almost certainly use radio to contact their base.

'Get on to Gyantse command, tell them to search for illegal transmissions in this region, in or out.'

Mountains northeast of the Doklam Plateau

The road had petered out long ago, but the jeep's 4-wheel drive had carried them up into the foothills, further than Pema had anticipated, for which she was grateful.

'We're running on air,' said Sonam as he gripped the wheel as though he could will the vehicle to keep moving. The needle of the fuel gauge had been dead at the bottom of the curve for almost 15 minutes, not even the broken ground that shook the vehicle violently could make it flicker.

Pema had been scanning the land ahead of the goat track that they were following, looking for a suitable place to abandon the jeep.

'There, next to that jagged rock.' She pointed to a shallow depression in the face of the mountainside about 50 metres ahead. Sonam grunted surly acknowledgement, he was not a wizard. As the thought struck him, the engine coughed and the jeep jolted before it caught again for a second, then died. Their momentum was just enough to get them within 10 metres of the spot and he applied the brake before it began to roll back downhill. She gave him an appreciative clap on his shoulder, then turned to Choden who was pressed up next to her.

'We need to get well above the snow line before dark,' Pema said. They both automatically looked at the sky which had turned a threatening grey. Raising her voice as the team clambered stiffly out of the vehicle, she said, 'Weapon check.' Pointing to two of them, she added, 'You take the first turn on the stretcher. Twenty minutes a shift.'

Dawa untied the two bamboo poles from the roof, then cut the canvas cover from the rear of the vehicle. 'Here.' Choden handed him a coil of parachute cord which he threaded through holes he cut in the canvas to form a sleeve on each side.

Pema spoke to Jamsung who was squatting beside the jeep, 'Good?'

'Good,' he smiled. 'Perhaps you'll listen to me.' He glanced in Choden's direction and said, 'I'm a deadweight, leave me behind. I'll get into a local village and wait till I'm fit again, then I'll follow.'

'From here?' She gestured about her impatiently. 'You'll not make it to the nearest human habitation. I need every pair of hands.'

He threw his hands up despairingly: 'These?'

'Yes. You're weak now but getting stronger.'

He shook his head sorrowfully. 'No, *ah-cha*. But I'll do my best.'

'We can't move faster than the stretcher bearers, I think you'll be OK.'

Pema noted how his eyes were bloodshot and his face was filmed with sweat. Her people called it the black fever, its recurrence was irregular, and it could be fatal. He probably had not taken any Mepacrine either. She caught Choden's eye, jerked her head in the direction of the goat track behind the jeep. They walked out of earshot and she pretended to be identifying features in the surrounding hillside. 'Jamsung is struggling, carrying Kalsang is reducing our operational efficiency to a really dangerous level,' she said.

Choden answered slowly, 'I know a CASEVAC was ruled out but we're almost inside the territory claimed by Bhutan. Why don't we call it in?'

'I've been thinking about it too, but there's no point,' Pema said. 'Delhi's ruled it out, no matter what Penjo wants.'

Choden allowed her frustration to colour her words. 'So, they abandon us, just like that?'

Pema shook her head. 'Penjo said that the Chief fought for us but he's in the middle of a political struggle between the PM and Amitab Roy,' she said. 'The PM has this dialogue with China, we're expendable.'

Her face set in rigid contours as she considered their situation. Suddenly, she decided. 'Tell Jigme to call it in. You encode it. Minimum information. Better hope that the CIA is right about it being untraceable.' Her expression was angry as she turned to face Choden. 'It's their responsibility, they need to know.' Choden's expression was grim. If they got out of this, Pema would be open to massive criticism.

'Sure?'

'Certain.'

Pema's tone reminded Choden of her own doubting response to the commander's order to abandon the operation. What goes around comes around.

PLA Regional Command
Shigatse Prefecture

The divisional signals officer wore a smug look as he handed the intelligence directorate major the report. 'Get this to 128 MRRR.' The major read the analysis. A UHS message had been detected. The communications geeks' interest had been sparked because it was faster than anything they had. Investigating further, it appeared to originate from a source in Uzbekistan, but they knew that could not be correct because they would never have picked it up. It was a complex algorithm concealing its origin. Then they went back to the original message and used two satellites to triangulate it. They were convinced it came from a point northeast of the Doklam Plateau. It had to be foreign special forces, most probably the CIA. The major congratulated the signals officer, 'Good work. Contact Colonel Wei at Yadong.' Once the intel was relayed, he would get great satisfaction from breaking the news to General Liu. Later, he would inform the commissar. Much later.

North face of the Zhompalti Ridge

The wind screamed, slicing like knives at what little of Choden's face was left exposed as she crawled out of the tent and trudged through the snow to the other tent where they were huddled around the Tommy cooker, brewing endless mugs of cha. Pema looked up. Choden shook her head.

'If we don't get him to a surgeon soon,' she told Pema, 'we'll lose him. His arm has to come off.'

'Gangrene?' Choden nodded. 'Jamsung?'

'I don't know how he got this far, even with Dawa virtually carrying him.' Choden tugged her scarf down, freeing her mouth so that she could sip on the mug of cha thrust into her hand. The hot butter tea spread its warmth. She pushed her sleeve up to check her watch. 'Time to spell Dawa.' The lookout had been in position for 30 minutes.

'My turn,' said Loshay as he struggled out of his sleeping bag.

'I'll go with you.' Choden pulled the tent flap aside and they both crawled out.

Positioned on an ice ledge, they had built a low walled snow berm to protect the tents from the worst of the wind, but the lookout position was 40 metres away, secreted in a snow burrow from where to observe any approach from the north. Dawa heard their boots crunching the snow, looked back and raised a finger to his masked mouth. Choden and Loshay lay down and wriggled up either side of him. Dawa pointed down to either side of where the track lay under the snow. He put his mouth next to Choden's ear and whispered, 'Movement.'

'When?'

He raised his gloved hand and spread his fingers.

'How many?'

Two fingers.

Two of them there for five minutes meant they were scouts, an ordinary combat unit would have advanced in line, combing the area. More likely, specialist mountain units with one pair reconnoitring ahead but if they were not moving, they must have spotted something and were waiting for the main patrol to move up. Choden knew that the tents were not visible from the track below because she had selected the lookout site herself and she was confident that in their Alpine coveralls they were virtually invisible. What the hell had they seen? She tapped Loshay and slid backwards, he followed suit. She whispered to him, 'Tell Pema-la, bandits about to bump us.'

As Loshay eased himself backwards from their position, Choden pulled herself up next to Dawa, patted him and pointed over to their right, then slid back out of the burrow and moved up to a position from where she had a 45° angle to the track below them. Once in position, she pushed the snow very gently up in front of her, leaving a gap wide enough to give her a field of fire, then taped a spare magazine to the one already locked in to her AKSU. At this short range its accuracy was good and if they were charged, its unselective firepower would do most damage. Now it was just a question of whether Pema could get the others out of the tents and into position before they were hit. A snowflake landing on her forward sight was the forerunner of a fall of snow that quite suddenly reduced visibility to three to four metres as curtains of snow were blown across from side to side. She adjusted her fur hat so that the front of it sheltered her eyes.

As Loshay pulled the tent flap open, Pema caught sight of the conditions outside. He gave her the message. Her immediate instinct was to strike camp and withdraw higher up the mountain, but it would take too long, the enemy's strength was unknown and their rate of march too slow. She gave her orders quickly and quietly. Leaving Jamsung to guard Kalsang, the rest moved out into a defensive crescent with the right point sited on Dawa. She wriggled forward beside him and asked, 'Choden?'

He pointed away to his right, but Pema could see nothing through the thick veil of snow. She crawled away until she was about 10 metres to his left and burrowed gently into the snow, inching forward to give herself a view of the approach and prepared to sit it out. Even if something had caused suspicion, they still had the advantage of concealment, the high ground and the added firepower of their two Minimis. She shut her mind to the outcome, this is what they did, and these were the best of the bunch.

Dawa had lost all sense of time. He tensed and released his body periodically to fight off the paralysing cold, rolling his shoulders independently. Switching hands, he exercised his fingers to prevent them cramping up inside his gloves. Periodically he swept the snow off the barrel of the Galil. His vision was barely three metres, but he alternated between looking through the Nimrod ×6 sight and using his natural eyesight as he searched for any sign of movement. Silently, he urged the attack to come in.

Almost imperceptibly, the wind began to drop and the density of the snow thin out. He quartered the ground more carefully. The ice plateau on which they had encamped was quite broad, snow dunes rose behind him, concealing the tents; but as the ground fell away in front, the dunes became mere ripples running away to the track now concealed beneath a thick layer of snow. He put his eye to the sight again and as he did so, the ground in front of him seemed to rise up, transforming itself into a ghostly figure. He traversed a centimetre left and then right, other figures were appearing out of the ground. He lifted his eye from the sight to allow him a full field of vision. He counted eight figures and kept them under observation hoping that one would do something to indicate that it was in command.

His patience was rewarded when a figure more or less in the centre of the advancing line made an arm gesture signalling for those on its right to spread out.

'Got you,' Dawa whispered to himself.

They were advancing slowly, a mixture of caution and having to high step through the thick snow on the ground. He focused on the commander through the sight, their arctic gear lent even more uniformity to their appearance, but he identified the PKS light machine gun that the man was carrying, another sound reason for taking him out. He wriggled his fingers again to ensure his touch would be sure.

As the only sniper in their group, it was standard operating procedure for him to take the first shot and he knew that it would have to be at short range in these conditions: there was no foliage to help him gauge the strength of the cross winds and the snow's reflection glared into his eyes. A series of snap shots, to give them the best chance of knocking out all their pursuers. He focused on the man's head, only the snow goggles visible.

The dark lens filled the image as he took first and then second pressure, the image exploded. He switched fractionally to the left and another pair of goggles, another image exploded. Now the Minimis opened up and return fire was coming in, he abandoned the sight for straight over the barrel. The attackers had dropped to the ground, nestling into the snow for extra cover.

A couple of hand grenades would have been perfect at this point, but a decision had been taken not to equip the teams with them. Now that the enemy were prone, they would spot his muzzle flash more readily even though his muzzle brake acted pretty well as a suppressor. He could roll to his right, but the bipod would make the rifle unwieldy to handle. Lifting the barrel slightly till the bipod feet cleared the firm ground, he slid back until he was below the level of the berm and manoeuvred himself into a new position.

As he grounded the bipod, an object flew into his left field of vision and then the snow around him erupted and the blast rocked him. He hugged the ground with every muscle in his body, forcing himself to squint through the thick cloud of snow that was settling back down. An indistinct block took shape as a figure with a raised arm: he took aim at the central mass and the shape collapsed. Instantly, the cries of alarm that screamed out were cut off by another explosion. The grenade intended for them had taken out whoever was close to the would-be thrower. Now the bulky grey shapes were hurling themselves forward, but the snow was impeding them, and they were falling down under the hail of fire from the Minimis. He scanned his front for a target, but no one was standing.

A movement in the snow over to his right caught his attention, he was staring into the muzzle of a rifle that filled his sight. As the image in his sight burst, his head recoiled and a line of pain seared his skull, then he lost consciousness.

Dawa came round as blood trickled down his face, dripping off his chin and staining the snow. Reflexively he touched his head, his fur hat had come off. Instinct took over and he looked to his front just as he became aware of the silence. He grabbed a handful of snow to wipe his face and heard Choden ordering two men forward to check on the bodies. Getting to his feet, he advanced cautiously just as she came into sight calling out their names.

'Sit down,' she told Dawa as she tallied up the team. 'Tenzing?' She called out but there was no response.

'Here, over here.' Sonam was pointing at the ground.

Choden hurried over to where Tenzing lay face down in the snow beside his Minimi. As she bent over him, he raised himself up on one arm, the other arm was pumping blood into the snow. They sat him up and she cut open the sleeve of his coat revealing the mess of blood and bone that had been his right arm.

'It's just a flesh wound, *ah-cha*,' Tenzing laughed.

Choden smiled at him and told Sonam to get her Med-kit bag. She estimated that the combination of shock and the freezing temperature would act as a short-term anaesthetic, allowing her time to administer some morphine. Tearing the arm of his shirt into two, she applied a tourniquet just above the elbow to arrest the flow of blood. Sonam arrived and she opened the Med-kit and handed him a field dressing and bandages. 'Wrap up Tenzing's flesh wound.' He looked at her for a second, his expression suggesting that she had lost the plot, then it dawned on him and he laughed.

Choden got up and walked over to where Dawa was holding some compacted snow against his head. 'Let me see.' As he took his hand away, the snowpack fell off.

'Scalp wound,' she said as she was examining his head. 'A centimetre lower and it would have gone straight through the empty space.' She grinned as she pulled out a field dressing and bound it in place. Dawa nodded, retrieved his hat and put it on. The crack of a gunshot made his head snap round.

'Last one,' Loshay called out.

'Where's Pema?'

Dawa looked behind him to where he had last seen her. 'That hand grenade,' he muttered as he hurried towards the debris of broken rock and snow. 'Here.' He pointed to where Pema lay in a catatonic position, parallel to a ridge of snow, earth and rock.

Choden knelt down and put her ear to Pema's mouth. 'Breathing.' She put Pema into the classic recovery position and began to examine her, turning her gently as she searched for a wound. Finding nothing she tested for vital signs. 'Pulse is slow but steady.'

'Concussed?' Dawa asked.

She nodded. 'Let's get her back into the tent.' She told Loshay to collect the white camouflage coveralls and anything else useful from the dead PLA soldiers. She then hurried after the others, taking stock of the situation as she did so. They were down to five combat fit, but if they had to carry Kalsang, Tenzing and Pema, their effectiveness was virtually zero. She assumed the Chinese would redouble their efforts to locate and destroy them. Instinctively, she looked up at the sky, the *Chögyal* was smiling on them, search helicopters could not fly in these conditions but once it cleared, they would be easy prey. She offered up a silent prayer for Pema's swift recovery, at least that would restore them to a minimum of battle readiness.

*

An hour later Pema still showed no signs of recovery. Choden knew they could delay no longer. She looked at Dawa, lifting her eyebrows in a silent question.

'A bad hangover without *chahng*.'

Jamsung was still struggling but at least he was caring for Pema and Kalsang in the other tent. She looked at the faces of the rest of the teams. 'We have to move out now, but we can only manage one stretcher.' She looked at Tenzing. 'Can you walk?' He nodded vigorously and she felt a pang of guilt that she was grateful that it was him, anyone else with a wound as bad as his would never contemplate pressing on but she would still have to keep an eye on him.

'Ready?' They all nodded. Loshay shrugged his shoulders. 'I can carry Pema-la if someone takes my pack.'

'I'll spell you,' Dawa added.

Choden nodded slowly. 'Everyone, take turns.' Pointing to the map spread out on the ground, she added, 'If we can get over the ridge, even to Sinche-la, at least we'll be in the disputed territory.'

'They'll still say we're in gyah-nakh territory,' said Dawa with a bitter laugh.

'True, but we can insist we're Bhutanese, it gives us some legitimacy,' Choden said, even though she knew he was right.

They were surviving on nothing but themselves at this point and she needed everyone to stay focused. Loshay leaned forward, an earnest expression on his face, as he asked, 'If we get to Sinche-la, will the Dapon-saheb lift us out?'

She shook her head firmly. 'Not a chance. Delhi forbids any rescue, the Dapon made it clear before we left.' Turning to face them all, she said, 'We're on our own but this is what we do. We'll make it.' She wished she had the confidence that she injected into her words. 'We leave in 10 minutes.'

As they busied themselves sharing out the loads, she drew Jigme to one side and gave him a note. 'Send this now.'

He looked at it and gave Choden a lopsided grin. 'You've already encoded it?'

'Do it again.'

'They'll not understand.'

'I think they will.'

What she said and what she expected were not necessarily the same, but Choden guessed that their radio was not the untraceable miracle the Americans had promised. She had to rely on Penjo remembering that they had once used this double encoding trick on an escape and evasion exercise. It added another layer of security to the message which, if she judged correctly, would influence their commanding officer, provided he remembered the trick. She knew she was playing on Penjo's carefully concealed relationship with Pema. It was the only hope she had of getting them out alive.

Laya

Sergeant-Major Prabhat squeezed the bridge of his nose between his fingers trying to decipher the message. He glanced up at Paljor and asked, 'You've checked it for mistakes?'

'Three times.'

The Gurkha shook his head in frustration. He was confident that the teams' communications skills were impeccable, but as it stood, the message was gobbledygook. It had Choden's normal call-sign; if she had been under compulsion, she would have used the tell-tale call-sign, so they had not been taken prisoner. On a hunch he gave the slip back to Paljor. 'Scan it to Penjo-la, ask him if he knows what it means.'

Paljor blinked for a second and was about to ask how their commanding officer, hundreds of miles away could possibly do more than they had. Prabhat spoke brusquely and pointed at the fax/scanner. 'Do it. Now.' He walked out of the tent and over to the mess tent where Max was studying a map with Durwachter.

'We can't decipher Choden's signal, saheb,' Prabhat told Max, who frowned, wondering what he was supposed to do. The Gurkha explained, 'I've sent it to Penjo-saheb, in case he can make sense of it.' He made a little facial expression as if to say they had nothing to lose.

Max had marked an arrow with a china-graph pencil on the talc overlay and tapped its point with his finger. 'Is this the latest fix we have on their position?'

Prabhat nodded. 'They're moving again, very slowly but still outside the disputed area.' The Gurkha paused before adding, 'Chakrata says that PLA radio traffic in the area has intensified.'

'What about the SATINTEL?' Durwachter asked.

'Chakrata is pressing CIA Delhi for a quicker feed but they just say they're still interpreting it.'

'Goddamn!' The Ranger stood up angrily. 'We have eyes on the ground with the best intel but we could lose it all.'

A ringtone interrupted them, and they looked towards the comms tent. Moments later Paljor walked out with his mobile in his hand. 'It's Penjo-la for you, Kushog-saheb.'

Max identified himself and listened without interrupting. 'OK.' He ended the call and handed it back to Paljor. 'The PLA hit them, they've taken casualties and Choden's asked for a CASEVAC.'

'Not Pema?' Durwachter queried.

'She's one of the casualties.'

'Will he agree?'

'No,' said Max. His voice bitter. 'Penjo's coming here. He said nothing more.'

'Any details on the casualties?' asked Shanaaz, who had arrived as Max was repeating Penjo's message.

'Two seriously wounded but not yet life-threatening, one concussion and a potentially fatal malaria,' Max said. He guessed that the news about Pema was putting a massive strain on Penjo. Though the pair of them were exceptionally discreet, he had no doubt about the strength of their feelings. But Penjo's personal life was now hitting the buffers of his orders. Durwachter interrupted his thoughts.

'Fernandes, the Indian spook, he comin' too?'

Max shook his head. 'He didn't say.'

'How long will it take them to reach the border?' Shanaaz asked as she studied the map.

'With a stretcher case, about two to three days, assuming they're not bumped again.' Even that was optimistic, Max knew. 'We move our base forward, right on the border,' he addressed Shanaaz. 'It's that place we recce'd, next to the monastery. That flat land where they thresh the rice will make a good helicopter LZ. You'll have to set up a field surgical unit there too.'

She frowned. 'I really need to be with them, not waiting behind the lines. I'm a frontline trauma surgeon.'

Max nodded apologetically. 'I know but this is the problem with covert cross-border operations.'

She set her mouth in a grim line. 'Ask Penjo to bring Si-thar and a field O.T. kit with him.'

He nodded towards Paljor.

'On it.' Paljor had the mobile to his ear. Shanaaz was looking angry.

'Problems?' Max asked quietly.

'Received wisdom in military medical circles is that massive progress has been made in mortality/morbidity rates by getting the wounded attended to as close to the frontline as possible.' She shook her head. 'We're not doing that.'

Max shrugged his shoulders. 'It's an accepted risk in this type of operation, I don't like it any more than you do but the politicians make the rules.'

She stared at him in silence for several heavily weighted seconds before adopting an accusatory tone. 'But they're your troops and they've asked for help.' Giving her the official line made Max feel like shit.

'The politicians are terrified that the Chinese will seize on it to launch a full-scale attack, a handful of Tibetans can be disowned, they're expendable.'

'You're all such hypocrites.' Her eyes were full of anger as she turned away. She looked quite magnificent even though he was the butt of all that animosity. Nor did it help matters that he agreed with her.

'That's one angry lady,' Durwachter observed dryly.

'She's a doctor first and a soldier way second.' Max's tone conveyed that he approved of her priorities.

*

It was dusk when Ulan, the Mongolian pilot, brought the Mi-17 in. They were all standing on the rim of the LZ when Penjo jumped out, followed by Fernandes. The Tibetan's expression was inscrutable as he returned the salutes. Fernandes looked suitably sombre as he moved forward to shake hands with them.

'Gentlemen.' The atmosphere was as cold as the night air. Max indicated the interior of the mess tent. 'We have some hot rum.'

They trooped in in silence and a mess waiter poured out their drinks. Penjo crossed over to the situation map pinned to a board. 'Their latest position?'

Max nodded. 'They haven't made much progress laterally but judging by the contours I'd say they're about 2,000 feet higher.'

'No further sitreps?'

'They're maintaining radio silence.'

Max guessed that Penjo wanted to know if there was any more detailed information on the condition of the wounded, especially Pema.

'We'll move our base right up to the border tomorrow.'

'How can you be sure that they will come out over this pass?' asked Fernandes, tapping the map.

'We can't, not for certain,' Max said, 'but given their current position that's almost inevitable.'

'And if they change?'

Max stated the obvious. 'We'll move accordingly.'

'It is imperative that no one else crosses the line of control,' Fernandes told everyone assembled there. 'This order comes from the prime minister himself. You understand.'

Looking at the man, wrapped up in his oversize puffer coat with the flaps of his hat pulled down over his ears, to Max, the intelligence officer resembled a beached penguin. Nor did the man's magisterial tone of voice endear him to them. Max was tempted to ask why they had been permitted to fly the teams going in but not getting them out, but he could see that it was pointless trying to argue with someone this far down the chain of command. Perhaps it was the expression on Max's face that made Fernandes suddenly perk up. '*Nuntius non interficere*, isn't it?'

'We don't shoot the messenger,' Max countered, 'even one from Cambridge.' His words were weighted with contempt. He directed himself to Penjo. 'I assume the helicopter will be attached to us for the duration?'

'Certainly,' the Dapon said. 'Bhutan Army have a fuelling point at Chayu that we can use.' He turned to Paljor. 'Find me a cot.' He paused, then added, 'Oh, and one for Mr. Fernandes too.' The Indian was never going to win a prize for popularity.

Shanaaz ducked into the mess tent and Penjo gave her a worried smile.

'Have we brought everything you need, doctor?'

'I've checked the list and it looks complete, thank you for bringing Si-thar.'

'How do you people stand this cold?' Fernandes, still cocooned in his padded coat and a hat, was warming his hands over the portable room heater.

'We can fly you back in the morning,' Penjo said, a little too quickly.

'No, no, my duty is here.' There was no need to ask him what that was.

A hot meal was eaten in a tight, spastic atmosphere, each of them pre-occupied with their own thoughts. Penjo toyed with his food, leaving most of it on the plate, then got up and stood staring at the map. Durwachter joined him. The American spoke quietly so that his voice did not carry to the table. 'I have a WhatsApp link to Bob Boyce in our embassy, he's feeding me the satellite intel.' Penjo nodded his thanks and Durwachter continued, 'There's a heavy snow blanket over the whole of the Doklam area and no sign of major troop movement.'

Penjo answered quietly, still facing the map, 'It doesn't need a large-scale operation, just a few special forces. They're hunting a wounded animal.'

'Yeah.' They stood in silence for a while before Max joined them.

'I suggest we turn in, we've an early start, before dawn,' Max said. 'Prabhat will wake us if they make contact.' He left them, crossed over to the comms tent and gave instructions that any information had to be delivered to him first.

Shanaaz was waiting for him as Max ducked out of the tent. 'We'd better sleep separately tonight,' he told her. She screwed up her face and it reminded him of a naughty girl. 'I don't care about myself,' he said, 'but I suspect our Indian friend has a Victorian sense of the proprieties.'

'I don't think he approves of Muslims, moral or immoral.'

'He's a curious creature, a hidebound Hindu wrapped in a high-class English education, public school and Jesus College, Cambridge. Very bright but I suspect very ambitious.'

'Let's not offend his susceptibilities.' She gave a scornful little laugh. 'We have to remember that he's our paymaster.' She looked around, seeing no one, she kissed him. 'Sleep well.' Then she was gone.

Max stared up into the night sky, but it was Shanaaz's face framed by the fur hood of her Parka that was fixed on his retina.

He racked his brain for some means of helping the team, but every option ran up against the order from Delhi. It was the soldier's curse, always marching to the tune played by the politicians and their insistence on avoiding the harsh realities: the war in Malaya had been 'The Emergency', the war with Indonesia 'Confrontation', anodyne descriptions to cover the death and mutilation faced by the poor bloody infantryman. What would they be calling this, 'The Doklam Standoff'? There was the ultimate irony, the Indian politicians standing off rather than rescuing their troops, troops they would disown when they were captured or killed. Or would it be 'The Chakrata Incident'?

The whiff of cigarette smoke made him turn to find Prabhat standing a few feet away.

'I thought you'd given up.'

'I did but now I haven't.'

'You should turn in, your signals team are good.'

Prabhat took a deep drag on his cigarette and blew smoke rings before answering, 'Can't sleep.'

'I'm not surprised, smoking those bloody *biri*, if you have to smoke, buy some quality tobacco.'

'It's because they are so bad that it helps me not to smoke.'

It was typical Nepalese humour, extracting fun out of something serious. Max wished he could see something comical in Choden's situation but that was impossible.

HQ 128 MRRR
Yadong

'What do you mean, disappeared?' Colonel Wei's left eyelid twitched like a butterfly's wings when he was irritated. 'Disappeared? Like being arrested by the PSB?'

His staff officer could not tell whether the 128 MRRR commanding officer's right eye was open or closed, the slit was so narrow, but he felt as though his facial muscles were paralysed. He searched for a sensible answer.

'Gone…both Knife and Stone teams, sir…gone,' the staff officer said, his voice trailing off.

The colonel touched his eyelid with his fingers to steady the fluttering, but he could feel the muscles moving under his fingertips. He had deployed two of the best teams, though he admitted they had not completed their training in the semi-arctic conditions on the high Himalaya. The staff officer knew that he had to anticipate Wei's inevitable queries about aerial reconnaissance.

'The Z9Bs Squadron commander swept their last known area, but they had to return to base because flying conditions deteriorated.' Wei shook his head in disbelief. The staff officer ploughed on, 'Apparently the Z9Bs performance is limited to a 4,500-metre ceiling in those temperatures.'

Wei pointed his free hand at his second-in-command, Major Xan. 'I will order the air force to take the 1st and 2nd companies as far forward as conditions permit,' he said. 'See if you can get some road transport provided from there. If the weather permits and the fairies can find their way in the snow, I'll send you some air support.' The colonel stared at the major silently, making him feel uncomfortable. 'Just make sure that you don't disappear,' he told Xan, 'or don't bother to come back.'

Xan, who had served with Wei for many years, was not inclined to point out that those who disappeared would not be coming back. He did a quick calculation in his head, even at maximum speed he could not reach the missing teams' last known location in under 36 hours. Perhaps the weather would improve. He looked out of the window, perhaps not.

High on the Zhompalti Ridge
East of Doka-la

Choden's joints ached and her muscles burned. She heaved her shoulders a little to ease the weight of Pema's body which she was carrying in a fireman's lift. No matter how often she adjusted it, the magazine on the AKSU slung around her neck kept hitting her knee each step she took. She had stopped brushing the snow away and a thick layer had formed across her face mask. She muttered a short prayer to the God of the mountain, grateful that all she had to do was step into the tracks that Sonam was making as he led them higher and higher. She had already shortened the lifts between breaks, any less and they would lose the momentum that they needed just to keep going. Each time she felt like stopping, she thought of Tenzing and Jamsung who had insisted on carrying a stretcher bearer's pack as well as their own. Where Jamsung drew the sheer will power to keep him going, she could not fathom. He was mute, as though even speaking would rob him of what little strength he needed to carry on. She stumbled, nearly lost her balance and could not prevent Pema slipping off. Looking down she realised that she had almost tripped over Sonam who was lying prostrate in front of her. He climbed ponderously to his feet, turned and muttered, 'Sorry, *ah-cha*.' As he re-arranged his load, she saw that he was carrying one of the Minimis and a stretcher bearer's AK-47 as well as his own Uzi. She managed as much of a smile as her frozen features would allow.

'Wha…?' Pema's voice was faint. Kneeling down, Choden lifted her head gently, noting with a flood of relief that her eyes were open.

'You can see me?'

'Of course.'

Choden looked back at the others who had come to a halt. 'Break! Cha, quick as you can. Dawa, tail-guard.' She turned her attention back to Pema, realisation spreading across her features. 'You've been out for over two days.'

The rest of the team crowded around, the fatigue lines etched in their faces seemed to dissolve as each of them greeted her. One of the stretcher bearers knelt down to tell Kalsang but his eyes remained closed. Choden gave Pema a brief summary of their situation; Sonam came up with the steaming phö-cha as Choden was talking.

'I've added some sugar, the Kushog-saheb says that it's the British Army's best kept secret,' Sonam said, 'for a rapid recovery.'

'They have phö-cha in the British Army?' Pema looked at him over the mug.

He laughed, 'It's their version.' She sipped on it and felt the combination of hot tea, butter and sugar filtering down through her body. Gazing around, it dawned on her that she must have been carried. Feelings of guilt consumed her and she closed her eyes to regain control. She opened them and looked Choden in the eye. 'You carried me?'

'We all did.' Choden took one hand out of its mitten and held it up. 'How many fingers?'

'Not necessary.'

'You made the rules, obey them.'

Choden tested for brain damage, to her relief the basic tests were negative.

'No sign of brain damage, but are you physically up to it?'

Pema pushed herself to her feet and took a few steps. 'If I can do this, I'm fit to go.' She had a headache that she kept to herself and felt a bit dizzy.

'Hmm.' Choden was dismissive. 'We have to keep going whilst the snow provides cover. Once it stops, their choppers will be looking for us and our rate of march is dictated by the stretcher.' She pulled out the map and spread it on the snow between them. Pema checked her GPS then located their position. She did a quick calculation. 'If we limit our rests to two hours, we could hit the Zhompalti Pass in about 48 hours.'

'We've had less than two hours' sleep in the last 36,' Choden said. 'Jamsung is living on borrowed time. I don't know what's keeping Tenzing on his feet and the rest of the team is exhausted. Sonam was on point and he collapsed, that's when I dropped you.'

Pema looked apologetic. 'Sorry, I forgot I was a passenger.' She looked up but the sky was impenetrable. 'Think we could take two hours here?'

Choden nodded slowly. Pema would need more time to gather her wits about her. She decided that now was as good a time as any to break the news. 'I've asked for a CASEVAC,' Choden told Pema, who looked at her quizzically.

'They've agreed?'

Shaking her head, Choden said, 'Kalsang isn't going to make it like this, nor is Tenzing.' She swept her arm around and added, 'You were unconscious. Jamsung is...' Pausing, she made a hopeless gesture, '...he needs help.' She threw her hands up and asked, 'What choice did we have?'

Pema controlled her anger, breaking radio silence put them at much greater risk, but she had to acknowledge that under any other circumstances it would have been the right thing to do. Her features softened. 'They won't come, it was futile,' she told Choden, 'but you'd run out of alternatives. Now I see the imperative of keeping moving.' She gestured with her head towards the others. 'Can they do it?'

'Why not ask?'

Together, they walked over to where the rest of the team was hunkered down around the Tommy cooker. Choden looked at Pema, yielding the command back to her.

'I know you're all out on your feet and I've been sleeping,' Pema began. There were grunts of laughter. 'But we need to make as much distance as possible in the cover this weather provides, two more hours could get us high enough to hide from aerial search. Agreed?' No one said anything but they looked at each other, waiting for someone else to speak first. Choden had expected her to give them the two hours she had mentioned, when Pema didn't, she made the decision.

'Good. We'll leave in one hour from now,' Choden said. 'Rest up.'

Pema drove herself to the limits and expected everyone to do the same but she had not seen the men struggling to keep Kalsang steady on the stretcher, unable to wipe the snow away from their faces, their rhythmic grunting as they stepped into the tracks made ahead of them. It was one of those occasions when the junior officer knew best. To cover for any temporary embarrassment, Choden said, 'Come, take a look at Kalsang.' Pema paused, aware that Choden had taken the initiative but instead of feeling angry there was sudden relief as part of the responsibility was lifted off her shoulders. As she had been speaking, a slight dizziness had made her feel light-headed and the headache was pounding behind her eyes. She did need time. She knelt down beside the stretcher. A triangular canopy had been erected to protect his face, she lifted one corner and felt his forehead. Kalsang was running a fever.

'The antibiotics don't seem to be working,' Pema observed.

'I'll give him an IV methicillin, it's all I've got left,' Choden said. 'I was keeping it for Tenzing.'

Pema felt for his pulse. 'Shit.' She stood up. 'Where's Dawa? On lookout?'

Choden pointed back down the fast-disappearing track. She squeezed the tiredness out of her eyes and said, 'I'll take this watch.' A few paces away she called back over her shoulder. 'Keep some phö-cha for me.'

*

It was just over an hour into their climb when Pema realised that the snow had stopped falling. The wind continued to whirl the surface powder around, and the night sky was clouded over. She sent a prayer to the God of the mountain to protect them.

'It's stopped.' Dawa had taken point and he turned round, pointing up at the sky.

'Yes.' Pema checked her watch. 'Can you keep going for another 10 minutes?'

He gave a flick of his head, turned and ploughed on. He was as tough as a yak and broke the path for them. Choden had been right to give them the hour's rest, they had made good time so far.

North face of the Zhompalti Ridge

'This contour?'
'Yes, sir.'

Major Xan studied the map with the young Z9B flight-lieutenant. They had made good time to the place where the militia unit had been attacked and now the snow had lifted, a flight of Z9Bs had been attached to him. The same flight had airlifted two units in and watched them set off up the mountain following the contour the airman was indicating. Xan studied the mountain: the snow carpet was deep and no track was visible.

'Can you take me up there?' Xan asked, pointing to where the mountain disappeared into the cloud.

The airman shook his head. 'Not into the cloud base, sir, you'll see nothing. Better wait until daylight, we can't fly above 4,500 metres.'

'No,' Xan said. 'We're going now.'

The major detailed Sergeant Guo's team to board the helicopter and 15 minutes later they were climbing slowly through the thin air, contouring the side of the mountain as they searched for signs of their comrades. The searchlight swept the terrain, the light bouncing back off the surface snow and being sucked into the bare rock and black ice. Each crevice felt as though it drew them closer and closer and Xan could not resist an overwhelming fear of being dashed against the mountainside. He turned sharply towards the pilot. 'Not so near, stand off more.'

The response was a superior smile. 'It's an illusion…sir.'

'Back off!' Xan shouted.

The pilot shrugged and their view broadened as he lifted them up. Xan scoured the cruel face of the mountain, the relentless expanse of snow and the blue-black shards of bare rock and ice, it was pointless looking for people for whom this land was home, who had the ability to blend into a geography as savage as themselves. He checked his watch: 30 minutes. He could legitimately report that there was no trace of their men.

Sergeant Guo tapped the pilot on the shoulder, leaned forward and pointed a little ahead of their flight path.

'See something?' Xan shouted.

'Irregular surface.' Guo used his hand to indicate.

Xan leaned forward to speak to the pilot. 'Take us down, closer to the ground.' The pilot looked at him as though he didn't know what he was doing but descended even lower than previously. As they passed over the area Guo had indicated, the force of the wind from the rotors blew the top snow away, revealing dark shapes in the snow which they quickly recognised by their uniforms which had been stripped of their white arctic coveralls. Xan reasoned that the guerrillas must have climbed higher.

'Can you land anywhere near here?' he asked the pilot, who shook his head. 'Hover over a space the team can drop onto,' he said.

'We're above my hover ceiling,' the pilot said. 'I'll have to descend about 2,000 feet.'

Xan tried to control his temper. 'We'll lose hours!'

The pilot shrugged his shoulders as he said, 'The air's too thin, sir.'

The major disliked the man's insubordinate tone which was not improved by the mechanical addition of 'sir'. 'You can't land here, nor can you hover, is there anything you can do?'

The pilot replied without turning to face Xan, 'Descend to a height at which I can hover and you can abseil down unless you can find me somewhere to set down.'

Xan made a mental note to file an adverse report on the pilot, then turned to Guo. 'We've been given the wrong kit for this terrain.' He was tempted to add that they also had the wrong pilot, but he resisted it.

'He'll take us down a couple of thousand feet, then you'll abseil in,' he told Guo. 'Follow the contour of the mountain, the other team will follow as soon as I can get them up here.'

The aircraft lifted away from the mountain side in a sickening manoeuvre then began to drop rapidly. Guo was glad that he would soon be on the ground.

Minutes later the pilot turned around to face them. Pointing down, he asked, 'Will this do?'

Guo peered out of the window and inspected the mountainside above. 'It'll do.' There was no love lost between the MRRRs and the aviators, nor had he missed the insubordinate manner towards Major Xan.

The door slid open and the full force of the Himalayan air hit them like walking into a wall of ice. The rope tumbled out, unravelling as it fell, the first man was over the edge of the opening even as the end hit the ground. Guo chalked that up to the pilot's credit, not many could estimate that accurately. It was an auspicious sign.

South face of the Zhompalti Ridge

They were distributing the loads amongst themselves as Choden walked back from the lookout post. Pema was arguing with Dawa as he bent to pick up her Bergen.

'No. I'm carrying it,' Pema insisted. Her face was an unhealthy grey, but she held firm to the straps. Dawa held his hands up in surrender.

'*Ah-cha*,' Sonam said as he touched Choden's elbow and led her over to where Jamsung still lay in the snow. As she bent over him, she was already calculating how much it would slow them down for someone to support him on the march.

'*Ah-phu?*' Jamsung did not respond. '*Ah-phu?*' Still nothing. She knelt down and worked her hand under his clothing until she could feel his carotid artery. The skin was cold, and nothing moved beneath it. He had slipped away into the mountain. Pema had to be told but Choden knew that the decision would be hers. 'You carry him for 20 minutes, then Dawa will take over.' Sonam gave a little bow.

Pema turned to face her as she came up. 'Let's go.'

'Jamsung's dead,' Choden said quietly.

'Oh God.'

'We'll carry him.'

'Yes.'

Pema made a little helpless gesture then quickly recovered. She stared at Choden for several seconds, then her expression hardened. Softly, she said, 'Send a signal.'

Choden nodded slowly. Their situation was deteriorating by the minute; she was coming to terms with the reality that she would die out here. Even if they never got off the mountain, the politicians must be made aware of the price her people were paying. She allowed herself a moment's pause as she looked around: if this was the end, she could not have asked for better companions and it would be in their homeland. She composed the signal in her head, signed off with Pema's call-sign, then sent it herself.

Advance Base Camp
Bhutan-Tibet border

The low-lying early morning cloud clung to the mountains making their movements ghostly, the dramatic stillness threaded with the chuntering of the generator. Max was grateful for the steaming mug.

'Will they come today?' the mess waiter asked anxiously.

Max sipped his coffee as he pondered the question. 'Probably not, too soon.'

Penjo and Durwachter materialised out of the mist. The Tibetan's face was grim.

'Fernandes up?' the Dapon asked.

'Don't think so,' Max said.

Durwachter held up his hands to indicate a quote. 'PLA traffic is busy,' he said, looking at Max.

'Prabhat says GCHQ has identified activity by 128 MRRR out of Yadong and there's air-born chatter over where we've located our people,' Max said.

He had always known that there was one side of his character that did not conform to military discipline. A soldier's duty was to obey the orders of his superior officers, but he had never been able to reconcile that with his own sense of right and wrong. He was conscious of previous occasions when he had questioned orders that would have broken his own moral code if they had been carried out. By judicious means he had avoided head-on collisions and observations on his military record which might sink his prospects of promotion. Yet there was nothing that he would have done differently in any of those circumstances. Chief of his principles was his duty to the people over whom he exercised command.

It was acutely clear that Pema's team faced overwhelming odds whilst here they were, drinking hot coffee on the mountainside.

'Saheb.' Prabhat handed Max a message form. He read it and passed it to Penjo. Durwachter leaned over to see what it said. The Dapon stared silently into the cloud outside the tent as all of them digested the curt message. He turned towards Prabhat. 'Which code?'

'The same one Choden used to you, huzoor, I recognised it, but this time it's Pema-la's call-sign.'

Penjo nodded slowly, then turned to face the mountains, his expression unreadable. It reminded Max of a picture he had once seen of an American Indian who led his tribe into Canada to escape the ethnic cleansing pursued by President Jackson. Penjo looked around as if ensuring that no one else was there. 'I'm going in to pull them out.'

Max stared at him then shook his head slowly. 'You can't, you're in command. I'll go.' The words slipped out, automatically.

Raising his hand to stop being interrupted, Max continued, 'Two seriously wounded and a dead body, they're not an operational unit, we need to extract them before the PLA wipe them out.'

He paused. Penjo's face was grim as he pointed his finger at Max. 'You're British, if you're caught or killed,' the Dapon said, 'there'll be an international furore.' He shook his head determinedly and decided, 'No, I can claim to be a local guerrilla.'

'But who'll defend your unit against the Indian politicos and anyway,' Max said, 'I'm Irish.'

'Maybe just send the chopper?' Durwachter interposed.

'No.' Max was adamant. He had been weighing the consequences overnight, his career prospects versus his personal responsibility for the people in the field; ultimately, he had to answer to himself. 'They're on the run, exhausted, carrying wounded men and a corpse, it's no longer a fighting unit,' Max said. 'The PLA's hard on their heels and Pema was concussed, a fresh mind is called for. I'm not getting caught and if I'm dead you can say that they crossed the border and snatched me.'

Penjo stared at him, shaking his head slowly from side to side. 'You're serious?'

'Never more so.'

The Tibetan massaged his chin in his hand, anxiety etched into his forehead. 'OK.' He looked towards the entrance to the tent. 'We'll try to keep Fernandes in the dark until we have you back.' He frowned. 'Ulan will co-operate?'

'He's a mad bugger,' Max laughed. 'But you'd better ask him.'

Durwachter raised one eyebrow. 'Two mad buggers.' Looking at Penjo, the American added, 'Get the other chopper up to Laya? Make it three mad buggers.' Penjo forced a half-smile and the American continued, 'Just in case.' His eyes creased to a half-close. 'Better arm it, the Chinamen have a history of hot pursuit.'

*

The early morning sun gave no warmth but the sky was clear and duck egg blue. Deepraj reported quietly to Max, 'I've loaded my Carl Gustav and two spare magazines of mixed HE and flechettes, saheb.' When Max said nothing, the Gurkha's expression changed to one of slight puzzlement. 'I can't come?'

Max frowned, 'I'm already deep in the shit for going, I'm not dropping you in it too, that's final.'

'What's final?' Shanaaz had come up unnoticed. Max touched her elbow and walked over to where the ground fell away steeply below them. She followed.

'We're going in to evacuate the wounded.'

'We, meaning you?'

He nodded.

'And me.' She put her hand lightly across his mouth. 'I'm a combat trauma surgeon, at least I can justify going, I'm needed but you...?' She hesitated.

'I'm just a bloody foreigner?'

'That's not what I meant.'

'But it's true. Look.' He placed his hands on her shoulders. 'In terms of military discipline and international politics there's no possible justification for me to go. On the other hand, soldiers answer to a more basic code of conduct.'

'But...' Now it was his turn to stop her interrupting.

'If you're determined to go, all the more reason that I do.' He smiled as the conflicting emotions travelled across her face.

'So, Delhi relented?' she wondered.

'U-huh.' He shook his head and put his finger to his lips. 'Not a word to Fernandes. We'll head back to Laya to throw him off the scent, then swing back round. We'll be illegal both there and here. Still coming?'

She gave him a contemptuous laugh. 'Ever heard of the Hippocratic oath?'

The Zhompalti Ridge

They were on the edge of an ice field when Jigme called a halt. Pema turned round, about to tear him off a strip for usurping her command. She halted mid-sentence as he indicated the transponder. He had been the rear stretcher bearer and unable to respond to the communication until he had set down his burden. The pain in her head had increased and she had been toying with the idea of handing over command to Choden, all too conscious that her judgment was being impaired by some sort of head injury.

Choden came up to her from the front where she had been on point. 'Stay here, I'll get it.' Choden tramped back through the part trodden snow wondering what on earth Chakrata would be asking of them now.

Jigme had pulled his face scarf down and wore a look of disbelief. 'They're coming for the wounded.'

She made him repeat the signal word for word in case he had only read what he wanted to hear. Confirmation triggered a fresh train of thought. The chopper's load capacity limited the number it could take out so they must have opted to evacuate the wounded and Jamsung's body. A quick mental calculation told her that the chopper was operating very close to its operational ceiling which also affected the load. She hurried back to report to Pema who was crouched down, resting against her Bergen. She looked up and asked Choden, 'Got any Ibuprofen? I can't think straight.' Pema's face was drawn with pain, the skin looked jaundiced in the moon's light reflected off the snow. Choden struggled out of her Bergen and gave Pema the news while rummaging for the painkiller.

'Really? Pema sounded dubious. 'You're not telling me this just to lift us over the ridge?'

'No. That's the signal. ETA in about 20 minutes. Here.' She handed Pema the tablets. It was no time for niceties. 'Rest here, I'll get a T marked out in the snow,' Choden said, 'we can illuminate the points with torches as soon as we hear it approaching.' Pema nodded and closed her eyes. Choden shouted, 'Dawa.' The big man lumbered over to her.

'How's the wound?'

He cocked his head to one side. 'Forgotten about it.'

'Good, guard the rear.'

Choden directed Tenzing to brew some cha whilst the rest of them marked out the T for the chopper. Identifying the wind's direction was difficult because it was swirling around like a ghost. As she trampled the snow flat, she revised her estimate of how long it would take the balance of the team to make it to the pass over the ridge. Making allowances for their condition, if they cracked on, they ought to cross into the disputed territory within 24 hours: always assuming the Chinese didn't bump them.

It took longer than anticipated to mark out the T and the sound of the chopper's rotors carving their way through the freezing Himalayan night coincided with its completion. Pema was still struggling with the pain in her head but the fear that it might be the Chinese rather than their own made her shout a warning. 'Cover! Take cover!'

Jigme looked up from trying to get some cha down Kalsang's throat. He looked around, smiled and shrugged his shoulders as if to say it was pointless. She got to her feet but even as she tugged the Desert Eagle out of her jacket, Pema recognised that it was a futile move. Jigme was straining to identify the aircraft.

'It's ours,' he announced. For a moment, the relief pushed the pain out of her head.

She must have passed out momentarily because the next thing she knew Shanaaz was talking to her. She shook her head, now she was imagining things. She felt someone steering her towards the chopper and then she blacked out again.

Out of the corner of his eye Max saw Pema collapse against Jigme. Choden briefed him as they loaded Kalsang and Tenzing onto the chopper. Shanaaz had a drip connected to Kalsang and was putting one up for

Tenzing as Jamsung's frozen corpse was fed unceremoniously into the rear of the aircraft. Together, they lifted Pema into a seat and buckled her in. It was difficult to hear Choden's voice against the whoomph-whoomph of the rotor blades. Max reached in and tugged out a haversack.

'Some energy bars and chocolate,' he said. 'Need any ammo?'

Choden shook her head. 'We've redistributed it amongst ourselves, don't want more weight.'

'The chopper can carry two more, d'you want to detail anyone?'

Choden thought about it for a moment, turning over in her mind whether to give them the choice, then discarded the idea. They were a team and if they were to survive, it would be as a team. Automatically the converse occurred to her. 'No, without the casualties we're up to speed.' Choden gave him a mischievous grin. 'Want to take a bet on us?'

He smiled back. 'Only if I can collect.'

'All aboard the Delhi Mail,' Ulan bellowed through the open door. Max saluted Choden and climbed in. The door was barely shut before the chopper tilted forward and began to climb.

Less than five minutes into the flight Max detected a change in the sound of the engine. 'Do I hear something I shouldn't?'

Ulan was fiddling with something beside his seat. 'Fucking Russian junk.' The Mongolian glanced up at Max, worry lines etched on his face. 'It's over fucking complicated, too many things to go wrong...something's interfering with the cyclic.'

'You're speaking Mongolian.'

'Huh? Yeah, well it's what controls the pitch, what makes us go up and down, right now we're going down when we should be going up.'

'Serious?'

Ulan said nothing, concentrating on trying to correct the glitch but Max was conscious of them descending. He turned round to Shanaaz who was changing Kalsang's dressing, the smell from the wound filled the cabin.

'Don't like to add to your problems but strap yourself in,' he told her.

'What?' She was fully focused on her work, he barked out an order. 'Strap yourselves in! We're going to crash land.'

The aircraft was now falling at a speed that sent his stomach into his mouth.

'Shit! Shit! Shit!' Ulan was tweaking various controls without any noticeable effect. He flashed Max a look of desperation. 'Brace yourselves!' More terrifying than the rapid descent was the vision through the cockpit glass of the mountainside rushing up beside them. The shock of the rotor blades' impact against the rockface, hurled them all violently to the left, causing the seatbelts to bite painfully into them accompanied by the sound of the Perspex window cracking and then the smell of aviation fuel.

Max grabbed hold of his seat as he unbuckled but still fell onto Ulan who lay against the left-hand side of the chopper. A shriek of metal against stone accompanied a further shift in the machine and the pilot screamed out in pain. Max tried to orient himself, working out which way was up. Both Kalsang and Tenzing were motionless but Pema was moving.

'Max...' Shanaaz was suspended from her seat by the seatbelt. He got a foothold then took her weight. 'Release the buckle but move carefully, I don't know how precariously we're balanced.'

'OK.'

He had to get them all fast, any spark from the shattered electrical equipment would ignite the fuel. Shanaaz was checking on Kalsang and Tenzing.

Pema was fiddling with the release on her seatbelt. Max tapped her on the knee. 'Grab hold of something and I'll free you.' She nodded, found a handhold and he opened the clasp.

Ulan was moaning with pain. Max crouched down beside him.

'Can't move,' he gasped. 'Get out, it'll go up any minute.' The pilot's left arm was trapped between the fuselage and the rock face. He screamed as the chopper suddenly shifted its position.

'Ulan's arm is trapped under the chopper,' Max shouted to Shanaaz.

'They've both survived.' She said it in a tone that suggested that this might not last. Max reached up and pulled against the door which was now over their heads. It stuck. He got a precarious foothold on the side of the seat, grabbed the door handle with both hands and wrenched at it with all his strength. Suddenly it gave, sliding open and making him lose his balance for a second. He steadied himself and reached for Shanaaz.

'I'll get you out on top then pass the others to you.'

'Let me.' Pema navigated her way over the obstacles and stood under the opening. Max helped her up onto the seat and she pulled herself out of the cabin, then sat on the side of the fuselage her feet dangling. With no proper foothold it was difficult to keep his balance as he manhandled Tenzing up. Part way through, Tenzing came round and used his good arm to help Pema get him out, then together they pulled Kalsang up as Max fed him into the opening. Max caught a whiff of aviation fuel in his nose. He called up to Tenzing.

'Help Pema-la drag Kalsang away, this damn thing will go up any minute.'

Shanaaz was counselling Ulan who was trying to tear his arm free. 'Save your strength, we need to find a way to get the pressure off.'

Max was beside her, shaking his head. He gripped her arm. 'Can't you smell it? Aviation fuel, it's leaking. We have to get out before this thing goes up in a ball of fire.'

He could see she was still thinking of trying to lift the weight off Ulan's arm. Angrily, he shouted, 'We don't have time. Amputate the arm... now!'

She was wide-eyed with shock for a moment, then her face set into her professional mask. She stood up and made for the rear of the aircraft. She talked to Ulan as she searched amongst the jumble of kit at the rear for her trauma case.

'I'll use local anaesthetic. The pain won't be worse than what you're in now.' She gave Max directions as she clambered back. 'Put a tourniquet on his upper arm.' He cast around for something to use, then tore out some of the exposed electric cabling and wrapped it round before tugging it tight and twisting it closed. She unrolled her surgical kit and pointed to a syringe and two ampoules. 'Load both into the syringe.' As she was speaking, she cut Ulan's clothing away to expose the shoulder and the short length of upper arm that was not trapped. 'Two shots into the bicep, here and here.' She indicated with her finger as she selected a scalpel.

As Max inserted the needle, he became aware that the aviation fuel was soaking into his clothes. 'Look away,' Shanaaz told Ulan, 'it's easier for both of us.' She went to work, her hands moving with quick firm strokes. Most of the joint was exposed by the time Max had administered the second shot. She gripped the brachial artery between her fingers as she pressed a pack against the upper face of the wound with her free hand.

'Hold that pack firmly while I clamp off the artery.'

'I think he's passed out.'

'Good.'

Max watched, fascinated as she worked, ignoring the blood that was everywhere.

She synchronised her commentary with her hands.

'Sit him up.' She handed Max a roll of bandage with her free hand and held the pack in position whilst he wound it round and round. Watching her strong sensitive fingers plying their trade had mesmerised him but now it was over he was overwhelmingly aware of the air being heavy with the stink of the aviation fuel.

'We need to get clear, now!'

He coughed as the fumes caught in his throat. Together they manhandled Ulan out through what was the roof, Pema pulling from above and Max feeding the inert body up.

'Drag him away.' He began to cough, and the fumes filled his head. He gripped Shanaaz's arm.

'Out, now!' He lifted her bodily and shoved her towards the opening.

'My case!' she shouted down. He shoved her surgical roll into the bag, closed it and passed it up to her.

'Smoke! There's smoke!' He smelled it as Pema yelled her warning. He climbed towards the rear of the cabin, grabbed two bags of kit and his Bergen and started back to the front.

Shanaaz's voice was high-pitched. 'What the fuck are you doing, Max. Get out!'

In his head he replied that he was rescuing the fucking essentials for keeping them alive, but he kept his mouth shut because he could hardly breathe. He heaved the Bergen out followed by the two bags.

'Leave the kit, get the fuck out, it's going to blow!'

Suddenly Tenzing was leaning down with his one good arm. Max shook his head. 'Take the bags, run!' He launched himself up, grabbed the edge of the opening and hurled himself out, landing on his chest, half in, half out. He yelled at them, 'Go! Go! Go!'

As they ran, stumbling away, Shanaaz kept glancing back over her shoulder. A gust of wind blew the smoke over Max and he disappeared from view. A lick of flame shot up, illuminating the heart of the smoke a fraction of a second before an explosive 'whoomph' consumed everything in a fire ball.

'Oh God, oh no.' She grabbed Tenzing as the blast hit them, knocking them over. Dazed, she fought to hang on to her senses as she struggled to her feet and started back towards the blazing helicopter. She had taken no more than two or three steps when the ground appeared to rise up in front of her, stopping her in her tracks. The realisation that it was Max threw her into a confusion of shock, relief and anger. 'You...you, stupid, stupid bastard!' Fighting back tears, she pummelled his chest with her fists whilst he stood there saying nothing.

Slowly he raised his hands in surrender. 'The Gods smiled on me.'

She took a step back, relief fuelling her fury. 'Whose Gods?' she screamed at him.

'Yours, theirs...' Max said, gesturing towards the Tibetans, '...has to be, I haven't got one.' He reached out and held her by the arms, his expression grimly sympathetic. 'I think we need to get your patient warm and some plasma into him after which he needs some needlework rather urgently,' he said, staring around him, momentarily disoriented, '...and I have to think how to get us out of this fuckup.' She shook her head in a gesture of despair, turned and hurried over to where Ulan lay on the ground.

'There are high altitude sleeping bags in the kit I pulled out.' He extracted two and opened the zippers. 'Let's get Ulan and Kalsang into them, fast.' Looking around for Tenzing he saw him on his knees facing the burning outline of the chopper. As he got closer, he could just detect the sound of a Buddhist *mantra* above the whine and roar of the fire and he remembered that Jamsung's body had been with them. Tenzing was bowing but he could not join his hands in prayer. Max knelt beside him and placed his own palms together in silent tribute.

'He has returned to the mountains, Kushog-saheb.'

Max nodded. He admired the Buddhist concept of constant reincarnation and especially their philosophy, but he had shed all formal religious belief after his initiation into the absolutes of war. He pushed himself to his feet and patted Tenzing on his shoulder. 'Back to work.'

Half an hour later all three wounded were bagged against the elements. Shanaaz had sedated them and given intravenous antibiotics. She had put the bag of plasma under Ulan's body so that his own weight was infusing him. Kalsang's condition was perilous but she had done everything she could to make him more comfortable. All the textbook techniques for Pema's condition were premised on a full neurological examination which was as practicable as baking a soufflé on Everest. Pema was still trying to make light of her symptoms but Shanaaz wasn't deceived.

She paused to sip some cha that Pema had brewed up for them. 'Thanks for the help,' she said to Pema, 'but you need to rest too.' To Max, she confided, 'I really ought to take Kalsang's arm off, but I suspect that the gangrene has already penetrated his shoulder and there's no way I can operate on that here.' Nodding towards Tenzing, she continued, 'I might be able to save his arm in a fully equipped theatre, but I can't tell without an MRI.' She then glanced at Pema and said, 'And she needs an MRA.'

It was all delivered with clinical detachment which was reinforced when she said to Max in a voice that he sensed was fighting delayed shock, 'That's my report. Now, what's yours?'

'I signalled Laya with a brief sitrep.' He nodded in the direction of the burnt-out helicopter. 'That was intended to be a covert rescue mission, in and out before anyone got wind of what we were doing,' he said. 'Now, sadly, we've doubled the problem.'

'My patients aren't going anywhere in a hurry.'

They sat in silence, the tiny blue flame from the Tommy cooker the only sign of movement in the deep shadow of the mountains at night. Max kept running the options through his head: the only certainties were that short of a miracle, the wounded men would die and only Shanaaz, himself and possibly Pema had the ability to try to walk out. He stared up at the Zhompalti Ridge which was behind them.

'You know that we're in the disputed territory here,' Max said to Pema. 'A rescue mission wouldn't amount to more than a minor border incident.'

'Penjo disobeyed his orders.' Pema's distress was personal.

'No, I disobeyed the orders,' Max cut in. 'He didn't know we were coming in.'

Pema snorted disbelief.

Shanaaz put a hand on her arm and added, 'That's our story and Ulan was happy to go along with it.'

'Poor devil, he hasn't got much to be happy about now.' Max lifted his eyes in the direction of the sleeping bags. He tried to think himself into Penjo's shoes: having agreed on the rescue operation, logically he would be trying to devise a solution now that there were two groups at risk. He would not be able to shrug off the thought that his strategic planning was clouded by his relationship with Pema. Unprofessional, true but decidedly human and, in Max's view, all the better for that. Factoring in his own assessment of the man, Max was prepared to bet the house on a second attempt to get them all out. He had memorised the map of the terrain between their base and the far side of the Zhompalti Ridge where they had left Choden and the others. He had also gone over their flight path with Ulan, now he had to estimate how far they had flown before their crash landing.

'Have you got your map?'

Pema looked askance at him for a moment, then undid the top of her fleece and untied the silk scarf around her neck. She handed it to him in silence. He spread it across his Bergen, took out his torch and examined it carefully, smoothing out the creases. Pointing, he said, 'Look, I calculate that we are about here.' Max continued as he moved his finger, 'We left Choden's team at about this point; the pass to which they're headed is here.' He traced a straight line between the two furthest points. 'Where we are now must be close to Choden's exit route.'

He stood up and surveyed the surrounding hills, much of which was illuminated by moonlight. He pointed to the silhouette of a saddle on the ridge. 'That's the natural route over the Zhompalti from where we left them.'

They both stood up, following his explanation. Pema's expression lightened as she said, 'Without the wounded, they can make good time.' She paused, calculating in her head, then continued, '12 to 13 hours will see them over the LAC.' A quiet note of cautious hope coloured her words.

'There's still the enemy,' Max said. Automatically, he looked up at the sky, which was painted with dark quilts of cloud, threatening but not delivering the snow that would hinder aerial pursuit. A plan was forming in his mind, larded with qualified risk but in their extreme situation, worth the candle. Might as well be cashiered for a sheep as for a lamb, but would Penjo buy it? He sent a revised signal.

Advance Base Camp
Bhutan-Tibet border

Confident that Fernandes would avoid the freezing early morning temperature, Penjo had quietly roused everyone out of their sleeping bags at 04.30. They had followed him through the glacial mist along the track to the monastery where they were shown into a chamber decorated with beautifully painted thangkas hanging on the egg-yolk-yellow painted walls. Monks in their magenta-coloured robes served them with mugs of phö-cha. Herman sniffed his and put the mug on the table, untouched.

'At least try it,' Penjo encouraged him.

'Can't get past the smell.' The American shook his head, making Linka, the Tibetan pilot, and the two Gurkhas laugh.

Penjo opened a map on the table and they crowded around him to look at it. The grim timbre of his voice said it all. 'As of last night, we have a potential double disaster. My gamble was based on the hope that, faced with a successful rescue, Delhi would grumble but accept the *fait accompli* with a bad grace.' He looked at Durwachter and said, 'I apologise for not telling you before, but Max and I agreed that the story would be that he took off against my orders.'

The American's eyebrows flicked acknowledgement. 'I guess one Limey colonel was less important than protecting your outfit.'

Penjo nodded and continued, 'Fernandes still doesn't know where they went but we can't keep it from him much longer.' They all stared at him, each one speculating what was coming next. The Dapon looked at each of their faces in turn, then went on, 'Before I tell you what I propose, I want to make it crystal clear that it's up to each of you to make the decision for yourselves. I'm not ordering anyone to do anything, this has to be entirely voluntary.'

No one spoke even though they were beginning to guess what was coming next, simply from who was there. Penjo paused to lend weight to his next words. 'The key objective is to evacuate the wounded and to reinforce Choden's team to fight their way out, if necessary.' Pointing to the map, he looked directly at the Tibetan pilot. 'Linka, you pick up the doctor and the wounded, drop the Kushog-saheb and Deepraj at Choden's location, then turn round and get back here. I estimate the whole operation can be completed within half an hour to 40 minutes.' He held up one finger and added, 'Provided the weather holds.'

His expression was unreadable as he continued, 'Collecting the wounded and the doctor is no great risk, they're just on the Bhutan side of the LAC but once you cross the Zhompalti Ridge you're on the wrong side of the disputed area by anyone's judgment. I don't need to remind you that the Indian government has forbidden us to cross into Tibetan airspace.'

Again, he looked at them all in turn. 'If you agree, I'll take full responsibility for the operation.'

Durwachter massaged his face between his thumb and forefinger. 'You're betting the house.'

Penjo ignored him, staring at a grinning Linka.

'We don't know why the chopper went down but I can guess, the Russians wouldn't give us anything decent,' the Mad Monk said, then paused and smiled. 'And, of course, Ulan's not as good a chop-jock as me, I'd like to rub his nose in it by picking him up.'

'Is that a yes?'

'You people say *I* am mad!' He laughed, 'This is crazy.' Penjo started to speak but Linka interrupted him, 'Course I'll go, sir. I'll be irresistible.' The smile dropped off his face. 'LZ, is there an LZ? I can't winch the wounded.'

Penjo traced his finger along the contour on the map. 'Where they are is a cliff face above an ice slope. It's not ideal but Max says he'll mark out a makeshift pad.'

The smile crept back into Linka's face. 'OK.'

Penjo turned to face Deepraj. 'The colonel asked for you, he says it's not an order.'

'Makes no difference,' said the Gurkha, shaking his shoulders. 'He needs me.'

'But not me?' Prabhat asked, frowning.

'Yes, to monitor the emergency communications here, in Gorkhali, just to add a layer of security.'

'Ah, understood,' said Prabhat. He looked at Deepraj and said in English, 'The saheb's your *dhoko* now, bhai.'

The Gurkhas exchanged high fives.

'What's a dhoko?' Durwachter inquired.

Prabhat looked at Deepraj who nodded. 'When we're being tested to see if we're good enough to be recruited into the Brigade of Gurkhas,' explain Prabhat, 'one of the tests is a race but each of us has to carry a cone-shaped wicker basket, a dhoko, suspended by a hemp strap from the forehead.'

'Loaded with 25 kilos of rocks,' Deepraj added with a grin.

Durwachter studied them for a moment before turning to Penjo. 'I'd like to go too.'

'But you're American.'

'So?'

'If you're caught or killed, the Chinese will go ballistic.'

'Any more than the Brit you've already got out there?'

'But another liability...'

'Liability? Hell no.' His tone was almost threatening. 'Some of those guys are my trainees and anyway...it's what I do.'

Penjo closed his eyes momentarily, his head half-cocked to one side. When he opened them, he gave a curt nod. 'Against my orders.'

'If that's how you want to play it, General.'

'Your funeral.'

'Maybe, maybe not.'

The Zhompalti Ridge

It was less than a hundred metres from the rock face but dragging Kalsang and Ulan there in their sleeping bags proved exhausting. Tenzing managed on his own and Pema ignored Shanaaz's instructions to rest, insisting on carrying some of the kit. Max laid out the silver sleeping bags in an arrowhead pointing in the direction of the wind. He told Tenzing to get inside his bag. 'Keeps the arrow formation from being blown away.'

It occurred to Shanaaz that he even made the wounded work, but she could not decide whether it was admirable or an inhuman way of treating her patients. Checking on them throughout the night, she had not slept, the cold and the stress had exacerbated her sense of frustration at the little she could do to improve their condition. Max had explained the need to move to enough space for the chopper to land but she was loath to move them more than absolutely necessary. Kalsang was holding onto life by the merest thread and Ulan was in danger of hypovolaemic shock from all the blood he had lost. Turning them into a human signpost tested her patience to the limit.

As if he could read her thoughts, he gave her a tired smile. 'No one could have done more for them under these conditions, you'll soon have them back where you can attend to them properly.'

'*Ins'allah.*' Her response was automatic.

'Whatever.'

Occasionally, like an automatic reflex, one of the liturgical prayers of his early Catholic upbringing escaped his determination never to invoke the divinity, but he never criticised others for their faith. What he believed in was the bond between men and women in extreme adversity. That was about to be tested.

'What we could do with now is a shot of rum.'

'I don't drink,' she said sharply.

'Purely medicinal, doctor.'

She was on the point of an angry rebuke when she saw that he was grinning. 'Oh, you're mad!'

He gave her a bear hug and the hood of her Parka slipped back a little. As he held her, looking down onto her hair, a snowflake fell on to it. He looked up and more flakes landed on his face. 'Better cover their heads.' What really concerned him was the prospect of the snow preventing the chopper from seeing them. He checked his watch: roughly another four minutes before its ETA. He was calculating whether to risk transmitting long enough for them to home in on their position when the unmistakable beat of distant rotors approaching lifted his spirits. He was confident the burnt-out chopper would be visible, then the arrowhead would be spotted.

'Brush the snow off the sleeping bags.'

The flakes landed heavily on his face as he strained for sight of the aircraft.

'Will they see us?' Shanaaz called out anxiously.

'Certainly,' he lied.

*

'We should be over them now,' said Durwachter, peering out of the window then back at the console mounted GPS. 'Can you sweep a bit lower?'

'Can't risk flying blind this close to the rockface,' Linka said. 'The mountains have a magnetic draw.' The pilot held the collective as lightly as a conductor's baton. The aircraft tilted forward and hovered. 'We're above the hovering ceiling so I can't hold this for more than a few seconds. Can you see now?'

'There,' said Deepraj, indicating to their right. 'The helicopter wreckage.' The aircraft jerked up and away from the wreck.

'Sorry, too close for comfort,' Linka apologised.

'OK, they have to be within a 100m radius,' Durwachter shouted. The pilot turned into a 45° angle and started to sweep right.

'Train your searchlight over there,' said the Ranger, waving to the left. 'Think I saw something. Back up about 50 metres.'

The light reflected off a shiny surface. Deepraj pointed through the cockpit window. 'There, 11 o'clock.'

'Got it.' The chopper banked further left, righted itself to the vertical and descended just north of the point of the arrowhead. Deepraj swung the door open and jumped down.

'Jesus Christ, it's cold,' said Durwachter as he followed the Gurkha.

'Over here,' Shanaaz shouted and directed them to where Kalsang lay. 'This one first.'

The loading was completed in just over a minute and Shanaaz helped Pema up before being pulled in by Linka. Max handed up her medical case and followed her in. 'Let's go.'

As he climbed in with Deepraj, the American called to Max, 'Mind if I join the party?'

'You're as welcome as the flowers in May,' Max laughed then moved forward to sit just behind the pilot.

'D'you have a fix on Choden's position?' Durwachter asked.

'The one thing this pile of Russian garbage doesn't lack is electronic equipment for us to home in on their signal,' the Mad Monk moaned.

'Good,' said Max as turned round to Deepraj, 'You've got the Carl Gustav, so I hope you've brought me something useful.'

The American jerked his thumb to the back of the cabin. 'He's got an armoury in back.'

Shanaaz looked back questioningly over her shoulder as she hung up a plasma container she had connected to Kalsang. Max was unscrewing the top of a thermos flask as he responded, nodding in the direction of Herman and Deepraj, 'We're dropping off to help Choden's team, you go straight back.'

She shook her head in despair before concentrating on hooking another I/V to Ulan.

Max turned back to Linka. 'Can you hover over Choden's position for us to abseil down.'

The pilot shook his head. 'Way above my hover ceiling. If there's no sort of LZ, I'll fly in and skim the ground very slowly, two to three seconds? You'll have to tumble out.'

Max turned to face Durwachter and Deepraj. 'Did you get that?' They both nodded.

Apart from the engine noise, the only sounds were as they each checked their weapons.

'One minute,' Linka shouted back.

Shanaaz worked her way forward until she was pressed against Max. She spoke softly into his ear, 'Why do you have to go, haven't you risked enough?'

He wanted to hold her, but he could not afford either of them the luxury. Staring ahead through the windscreen, he spoke just loud enough for her to hear. 'This is my call. I have to see it through.'

'Doors open, 30 seconds to target, good luck!' Linka yelled.

She squeezed his arm as he shoved two equipment packs out, swung his legs over the sill, then he was gone, with Deepraj and Herman right behind him. She caught a glimpse of the three of them rolling in the snow as she heaved the door closed.

'Help!' Pema was struggling to close the door on the opposite side, the angle of the helicopter tilting her away from it. Shanaaz climbed across and together they shut the door.

Linka waved one arm in the air. 'Thank you, ladies.'

She felt Pema fall against her and registered her sickly pallor. 'Let's get you strapped in.' How many of her patients would survive? She worked back until she was between Kalsang and Ulan, now it was up to their will to survive but she would talk them through, it was all that she could do until they reached full surgical and support facilities. Try though she might, she could not get the picture of Max emerging from the explosion out of her mind. His luck was due to run out.

*

'Give me one good reason I don't have you arrested for refusing an order?' Major Xan was livid with anger towards the pilot who stood mutely, pointing at the sky which looked almost low enough to touch. 'Nothing's happening, you can still fly in these conditions.'

The pilot shrugged his shoulders. 'Up there,' he said, pointing towards where the mountaintops were concealed by the dirty, snow-laden eiderdown, 'visibility is zero. Standing orders forbid me to fly under these conditions.'

'What about my team that's already up there?'

The pilot opened his palms as if to say, 'What's that got to do with me?' Xan wanted to punch him in his supercilious face, but he knew that would only complicate matters. Out of the corner of his eye he saw his radio operator hurrying towards him. That could only mean that fuckface Wei wanted a report.

'Command...' Wei cut Xan off.

'Must wait. Get Sergeant Guo for me.'

It took a few minutes and once connected the line was affected by static.

'...following tracks...heavy snow...visibility five metres...stop...'

'No, don't stop, keep after them.'

'...support?'

'When weather breaks.'

Frustrated, Xan tossed the handset back to the radio operator. Staring at the mountainside, he anticipated what that shit Wei would say if he didn't commit all his teams. He stepped up close to the pilot.

'Your operational hover ceiling is 2,500 metres.' It was a statement couched as a question.

'Yes, sir.'

'Take us up to that limit and we'll abseil in.'

'But the cloud...'

Xan pointed his finger between the airman's eyes. 'I'm not debating with you, that's an order.'

The pilot glanced up at the sky then looked Xan straight in the eye. 'Yes, sir.' He took a deep breath, then added. 'I need your order in writing...sir.'

Xan pulled out a message pad and pressed so heavily that the ball point punctured the paper. The characters were barely decipherable, but he tore it off and pushed it into the airman's chest. 'Take off in 10 minutes.'

*

Choden's tired smile of welcome changed to one of astonishment when Durwachter came into view. He even managed to greet her in Tibetan. She led them back up to where the team had a snow bivouac and the ubiquitous phö-cha.

Max saw the strain in their faces, but they all got to their feet, smiling. He waved them all back down as he addressed Choden, 'Any idea how far they're behind you?'

'We estimated about three hours when we stopped, about an hour ago,' she said. Everyone nodded agreement.

'Numbers? Formations?'

Choden glanced at Dawa for an answer.

'Looked like two teams, about 30, they were moving pretty fast, faster than us,' said Dawa, looking around and the others all nodded in tired acknowledgement. 'Then the snow came, and I lost sight of them,' he added.

Max did some quick calculations; dawn was breaking but the overhead cloud still held them in comparative darkness. 'We're about four hours march from the disputed LAC,' he said, looking to Choden for confirmation. She nodded slowly so he adjusted his estimate. 'Four and a half.'

Deepraj was translating for Durwachter, who frowned as he pointed to their route. 'We'll be exposed for about two of those hours.'

'Unavoidable,' Max responded in English. 'Any other route would add at least 24 hours and we don't know how long the weather will keep their choppers grounded.' He looked at the tired faces. 'I know, fatigue's a real problem at these heights, you're all doing a great job.'

Durwachter had been doing his own calculations. 'So, we hit the route up to the ridge, then what's the plan, keep going or defend?'

Max looked to Choden as he said, 'It's your call, we're here in support.' He had already decided what they should do but equally he knew that she was the glue holding them together, he could not risk undermining their confidence in her.

She waved an arm, including the team members in her response. 'We're good for whatever the situation calls for. We've been adopting the IA drills that you taught us so far but if we come under attack by two or more of their teams, we'll need better defensive positions. It depends on the terrain.' She flicked her head towards the ridge. The others nodded. She paused a moment, then, noting Max's quiet smile, she gave her orders.

'Let's go. Sonam, take point.' She faced Max. 'He has an instinct for the best route.'

Durwachter pointed to the Minimi that Sonam was carrying. 'I'll take that.' He held out his Uzi. 'This is lighter.'

Sonam glanced towards Choden for permission. 'Good idea.' She directed Herman, 'You shadow him.'

'Yes mam,' the American smiled, 'guess I know who's in command.'

Max turned to Choden. 'Let Deepraj relieve Dawa as tail-end Charlie, fresh ears and eyes.' She signalled Dawa to change places with the Gurkha. They shouldered their packs and moved off in the tracks broken by Sonam and Durwachter.

Choden fell in just behind Max. After a few minutes she moved up to his shoulder. 'You're deferring to me, why don't you just take command?'

Without breaking step, he replied, 'They're your men, they trust you, that's more valuable than rank and anyway I agree with your decision.' He did not add that her brief exchange with Durwachter had probably amused and inspired them to make the extra effort demanded of them.

They quickly settled into a comfortable pace. After 40 minutes he allowed himself the luxury of visualising them hiking down the path beside the monastery. Minutes later he wished he hadn't because the snow stopped. Choden grunted and he took stock of their situation. They were about halfway to their destination, carving a path parallel to the ridgeline but exposed to observation from below. Instinctively, he looked back down but the spur they had just negotiated blocked his view. He stopped beside the track and Choden looked at him in anticipation.

'Let's call in our back marker.' She waved those behind him forward until Deepraj appeared.

'Seen anything?' Max asked.

The Gurkha shook his head. 'The pace is too slow, saheb.'

'They're tired.'

'I sense the *Dushman* closing on us.' Deepraj simplified the world into friends and enemies. He also had an uncanny sixth sense that Max had learned not to ignore.

'Can you drop back a bit?'

'Huzoor.'

The hillman would have no problem in catching them up but the earlier warning would give them just that little bit more time to deploy. Max and Choden worked their way back up their line until they caught up with Durwachter.

'Deepraj thinks they're gaining on us,' Max said.

The Ranger shook his head slowly. 'No way we can go any faster, Sonam's busting a gut already. I'm gonna relieve him in two minutes.'

'That's not what I have in mind.' Max turned to Choden, 'We'll have precious little time to establish a defensive perimeter and as Herman's on point he's best placed to read the terrain, scan the way ahead for a feature we can hold.'

Durwachter raised one eyebrow as he looked at Choden. 'You OK with that?'

'You have the experience and the point,' she replied. He threw her a salute, turned and headed back up the mountain.

Choden waited until Durwachter was out of earshot, then smiled at Max. 'I'm glad you're here, watching the front door and the back door.'

'We're just adding our fresh minds to the problems.' In his experience, the Chinese would have deployed more than just two teams in pursuit of a force that had wiped out an MRRR unit. The PLA always relied on superior numbers. He guessed they might face upwards of 60 well-trained special forces, odds heavily in favour of the Chinese. Having to break ground had slowed them down significantly whereas the PLA had the benefit of marching in their tracks. It was time to make another suggestion.

'If we can find a solid defensive position, we can let them walk into it. They're expecting us to keep running till they catch us, so we'd have the advantage of surprise and the high ground.'

'Can you...?' She hesitated but he guessed what concerned her.

'Yes, I'll go to point with Herman.' Despite the fact that Durwachter had taken the enormous risk of coming over to join them, clearly, she still had reservations about him. They had to make the mountain work for them. He scanned the high ground above, searching for a feature that they could exploit.

'Who's your most experienced mountaineer?'

'Dawa – he's even tried K2.'

'OK if I take him up front with me?' She turned round and passed a message for Dawa to come forward. 'Thanks.'

His scrutiny of the mountainside above them had revealed a particular geophysical feature. When Dawa came up, Max outlined his basic idea as they worked their way forward. The Tibetan's eyes brightened.

Forward Base

Bhutan-Tibet border

Penjo had his back to the communications tent entrance as he spoke into the microphone. 'Get air traffic control, Paro, to give you clearance through to Chakrata.'

Prabhat was signalling him urgently with his eyes. Penjo glanced in the direction of the entrance and saw Fernandes standing there.

'When you have a minute, General.'

Penjo nodded and turned his attention back to the radio.

'I'll signal Chayu to give you an emergency refuelling stop. Your ETA Chakrata should be in about one and half hours.' He gave the microphone back to Prabhat.

'Any update from Max-saheb?' the Gurkha inquired.

'No.' Penjo put his finger to his lips and Prabhat acknowledged it with a quick smile.

Fernandes was waiting outside the tent clapping his hands together to keep warm. 'Where is Doctor Khan? I don't seem to be able to make myself understood to her assistant.'

Hoping that he could spin things out until the team arrived – if they arrived, Penjo embarked on a half-truth. 'She's accompanying the wounded to the base hospital in Chakrata for emergency surgery.'

Fernandes's face registered astonishment. 'You mean they've returned? When?'

Penjo shook his head. 'Just the seriously wounded.'

'What about the others?'

'We anticipate them in about 24 hours.'

'How…?' Fernandes started, then his expression changed and Penjo decided to eke out a bit more of the truth.

'You're wondering how the wounded got out? Once they were south of the LAC, I sent a helicopter to evacuate them.'

Fernandes stabbed his finger towards Penjo. 'You were under strict cabinet orders not to allow the helicopter to cross the border.' The man's magisterial tone rubbed him up the wrong way and Penjo's built-up resentment at civilian interference coloured his words.

'May I remind you that they were within Bhutan's border, the border supported by India.'

Fernandes fired back angrily, 'You're playing with fire, General, it's disputed territory, you know full well that flying over the Zhompalti Ridge will be regarded as provocation by the Chinese. You have exceeded your authority.'

Penjo's eyes opened and closed as the words bounced against his brain. Speaking with slow deliberation, he said, 'As the general officer responsible for the operation, I judged it expedient and necessary to save lives.'

'But you are disobeying an order from the cabinet itself, isn't it,' Fernandes shouted in disbelief.

Penjo drew himself up to his full six feet and looked down on the man he regarded as nothing more than a flunkey. Then he cast caution to the winds. 'Soldiers under my command undertook an extremely dangerous mission to carry out a covert operation that was commissioned by the self-same cabinet that issued a morally bankrupt prohibition on any rescue attempt,' the Dapon said. 'As their commanding officer, I am responsible for their lives and I exercised my discretion as the commander in the field.'

Fernandes took a step back, plainly never having been addressed in such a fashion before. Penjo watched the man's Adam's apple bobble up and down as he tried to summon up a response, then decided not to give him that opportunity.

'They have obtained vital intelligence on Chinese missile launch sites, road construction and troop movement, all critical to the defence of India,' he said. 'Did you really think I would allow them to be wiped out?'

Fernandes's eyes closed to slits. 'On my authority as the senior RAW officer here...'

'You have my permission, Mr. Fernandes, to stuff your RAW authority up your arse.'

Penjo restrained himself from spitting at the man, turned on his heel and marched away, allowing himself the luxury of a grim smile. What would the officious little bastard say if and when he learned that they had lost a helicopter and both Max and Herman were inside Tibet? Well, he had burned his boats, or should it have been his helicopter? He had to smile. Max had not minced words in his last report, the odds were heavily stacked against them getting out. He looked up towards the monastery perched on the side of the mountain, a prayer would not be out of place and it would put him out of Fernandes's reach for an hour or two. He needed to make peace with himself.

*

'There.' Dawa pointed to just below the ridgeline above them where the snow bulged out from the side of the mountain. Max scrutinised it carefully, looking for a route that would take them above it. The mountain contoured round in a soft curve that would position them at about a 60° angle to their line of approach if they occupied positions above the bulge.

'How precarious do you think it is?'

'Can't really say from here,' Dawa said, 'but firepower onto the position might shake that bulge loose.'

Durwachter followed the line that they were both pointing at. He slipped his Bergen off his shoulder, dipped his hand into a side pocket and withdrew two No. 36 Mills Bombs.

'Those things went out with the ark,' Max joked.

'Can't get much more unattributable than World War I grenades.' The American turned to Dawa. 'Think they'd work?'

The Tibetan canted his head to one side, pausing before saying with a grin, 'One did, sir, in your desk.'

'Sonofabitch!' Durwachter's laugh was hollow.

'What's the plan?' Choden walked up to them.

Max pointed to Dawa. 'Get everyone here and I'll spell it out.'

Whilst Choden was calling the members of the team over, Herman pulled Max to one side. 'Just over there.' He pointed to what looked like a horizontal crevice in the side of the mountain just below the bulging snow. 'I could get a real good field of fire from there.'

'True,' Max said. 'Ask the boss, tell her I agree with you.' He watched the slow smile on the American's face – he had undergone a significant change of attitude from the early days. It was apparent in his body language as he talked to Choden, there was none of the superiority that he had exhibited previously. As she nodded, Max reflected on Herman's idea.

It would expose the American to the force of the explosion. That made him revise his plan. Herman stared at the mountain and then looked back at Max. 'You gonna try create an avalanche.'

'I've seen much less than a hand grenade trigger a major fall.' He turned towards Dawa. 'So has he.'

'Neat...if it works.'

'Nothing's for sure, but we need to herd them in, create a mass killing zone, otherwise...' Max shrugged his shoulders.

Choden pointed to Dawa as she spoke to the men gathered around her. 'He's going to drop the mountain on them,' she explained. Turning to Max and Durwachter, she traced an imaginary line across the crevice. 'Together with Dawa and Deepraj, I'd like you to form the frontline using the crevice, the rest of us will be up there, in the shooting gallery.' She directed their gaze to an imaginary line in the snow some 10 metres above the crevice. Addressing them all, she said, 'Kushog-saheb opening fire will be the signal to commence firing. Let's go.'

As they trudged up beside the crevice, she turned to face Max. 'How d'you intend to avoid being carried away with the snow?'

Max screwed his face up. 'That's the trick.' He pointed to the middle of the crevice. 'We'll dig a vertical channel against the rock face, a bit like a chimney and drop the grenades into it. We'll be in the crevice.'

She shook her head in disbelief. 'Good luck.' Then she turned and set off after the others.

Durwachter was regarding him steadily. 'I get the chimney trick but what happens if I get to take up that position I mentioned?'

'If it works, you'll be exposed.'

'So will you all,' the American countered.

Max acknowledged that Durwachter's choice of position for the Minimi gave him an ideal field of fire which they needed if they were to do as much damage as possible whether or not the mountain co-operated with them. Herman gave him a grim nod but did not suggest an alternative. 'OK,' Max said. 'Don't say I didn't warn you.'

He walked back down to survey the ground over which the attack would come in. Assuming Choden's dispositions above them were good and if Deepraj held the left of their position with the Carl Gustav, they could do a great deal of damage. Whether it would be enough was a different issue. He selected a spot that would give the Gurkha both maximum cover and an uninterrupted field of fire. Setting up the Carl G required that the rear position was clear, the backdraught from the recoilless rifle needed space to dissipate. Then he checked the position from the front. Satisfaction at his handiwork was short-lived as Dawa came up and handed over an extendable entrenching tool.

They worked their way along the rock crevice until they reached the point where the chimney had to be dug and both set to work, tunnelling down vertically against the ice face. Max calculated that three to four metres deep would afford them enough protection against the exploding shrapnel. He had wanted to carve out a hole in the ice face to compress the force, but the tool made little impression on the ice and the most he could achieve was a shallow cavity. They packed the snow tightly around the funnel shape at the base of the chimney, then climbed back up, tamping the snow against the walls to narrow the channel.

Dawa hauled himself over the lip of the tunnel and took up a position a few metres to Max's left, lying on the floor of the crevice that sloped very gently back towards the mountain. They would be far enough back to be concealed from their attackers. As he lay there, Max experienced a sudden sense of claustrophobia. He had been so concerned with maximising the effect of the grenades that only now did the thought strike him that they might be too successful and bring the entire bloody mountain down on them. Further speculation along this line was interrupted by the sight of

Deepraj hurrying along the path that crossed the terrain before swinging back to the extreme left.

Max crawled out of the crevice and met the Gurkha on the path. Jerking his thumb behind him, Deepraj said, 'Eight minutes, maybe less.'

'Good.' Max pointed to the position he had prepared for him.

Deepraj looked at it and grinned. '*Hawas huzoor.*'

Max relieved Deepraj of his Kalashnikov. 'Open fire as soon as I do,' he told the Gurkha. He took one last look at the approach, turned to view their position from the perspective of the attackers, then crawled back to his place above the chimney.

The ground sloped gradually down in front of him forcing the attack to come uphill. Surprise would only be for a very short time and he counted on the Chinese spreading themselves across the icefield where the Minimis could do maximum damage before the assault went to ground. He was not going to fool himself that their chances were even 50:50. Heavily outnumbered and with no practicable route to withdraw under cover, they were committed to holding out. Time favoured the opposition who could work around and enfilade them eventually too. Durwachter, over to his right, would catch sight of them shortly before he did. No matter, he had to draw them in. He adjusted his firing position, exercised his fingers to fight off the cold and removed his padded mittens, leaving only the thin leather gloves. A quick check of the Kalashnikov that he had zeroed in before leaving Baniyana ensured it had not iced up and he tested the pressure of the spring in the spare magazine. He turned the retaining pins in the grenades just to make sure that they would come free easily, then placed them between Dawa and himself. He was counting on their pursuers being over-confident, a quality he was not burdened with. He smiled across at Dawa, then Durwachter's hoarse whisper carried across the crevice.

'Jesus Christ, they've brought half the fuckin' Chinese army.'

Max put his eye to the sight and half a minute later the first Chinese soldiers came into view, making efficient use of the ground. The scout paused, kneeling in the snow for a minute before he was joined by another figure Max guessed must be an officer or NCO. Had they been spotted?

His concern fell away as the commander gave a hand signal to advance. He wanted them as fully committed as possible before commencing fire.

The line of figures filled more and more of the track and now he could see the heads of those following as they snaked around the curvature of the mountain. The more there were, the longer he needed to delay before firing. He switched his view to the immediate front noting that the scout was now no more than three metres in front of Deepraj's position. He steadied the figure of the commander in the cross-hairs and squeezed the trigger, then moved the optic to the right, searching for the scout. Even as he filled the sight, the image fell backwards. The Carl G must have hit him dead centre.

Now the gunfire was everywhere, bullets striking the rockface causing splinters of ice and stone to fly off. Max centred on another moving figure and fired again. The Chinese opened up with a light machine gun, raking the crevice, the rounds striking the rock above his head and forcing them to lie low. These were professionals and he knew that they would be advancing under the covering fire. The hollow whoomph of a mortar told him that time had run out.

'Dawa!' Max shouted to be heard above the gunfire. Dawa put down his rifle, picked up one of the grenades, then in near synchronisation they both pulled the pins, threw them down the chimney and moved back from the edge of the crevice. The dull explosions were less than a heartbeat apart and the shockwave shot up out of the mouth of the chimney throwing snow up in the air. Then, nothing.

He waited, holding his breath in anticipation but still nothing. Ah well, he mused, the best laid plans. Grey figures were collapsing in front of his position but those behind were coming on, undeterred. He picked his targets deliberately, two more down and lining up another one when he was struck by splinters of stone coming off the overhead rock.

It felt as though he was in a bubble of time, the realisation that he would die on this mountain was not worrying but a sudden sense of guilt that he had brought Deepraj down with him made it imperative to check on the Gurkha. He risked taking his eyes off the oncoming Chinese as he looked for Deepraj.

Time to evacuate the crevice and try to climb up to join Choden. He shouted to Dawa and pointed up. As they wriggled back deeper into the crevice an explosive crack heralded a sudden shift of the rock beneath him. A creaking noise as though a steel girder was being torn off a building drowned out the gunfire temporarily. A muffled roar like a giant breaker striking the shore drowned out every sound. His immediate thought was that the Chinese had brought up some artillery as the floor shook under him. He dug the toes of his boots into the rock, trying to get enough purchase to stop himself being thrown around. The floor moved again, tossing him towards the back of the crevice.

Scrabbling for a handhold to prevent being shunted down the crevice he dropped the Kalashnikov over the edge, keeping hold of the sling so that the rifle acted as an anchor, stopping him from falling further. Gingerly, he inched himself up until he had both hands gripping the edge of the crevice and could take stock of the situation.

Dawa lay spreadeagled across the floor. Max lifted his head just enough to see out of the crevice. Where there had been an undulating terrain of snow climbing up to their position, now there was nothing. It dawned on him slowly that the firing had stopped. Inching forward he looked down onto the naked face of rock and ice, as though the mountain had been shaved, leaving a sweating blue-black skin.

'Max, you OK?' Durwachter's face, upside down, peered at him from above.

'Think so.'

He called in the direction of Deepraj's position and was rewarded with an answering shout. As he crawled out of the crevice onto what remained of the track, he took his first real look down the mountainside. There was neither sight nor sound of the Chinese.

Durwachter was taking cautious steps across the ledge above the crevice.

'Shit, man, don't do that again.'

They made their way slowly up to where Choden and the others were gathered. Sonam pointed at a field dressing bandaged on his head.

'Looks worse than it is.' He managed a grin. Choden's gaze swung between the lightening sky and the crest of the saddle before she turned to Max.

'I think we were lucky.'

'I *know* we were lucky,' Max said, 'but we can't count on it holding.'

The faces around him reflected the exhilaration at surviving and the stress of knowing just how close they had been to disaster. The mountain had shown its cruellest face towards their enemy but as the light faded, the giant shards of darkness served as an immediate warning of peril. Max looked to Choden and Durwachter.

'I suggest we push on to the border before we're caught by the Chinese or the weather,' he said. 'No breaks for cha.'

Further words were unnecessary.

Forward Base

Bhutan-Tibet border

❧❦❧

'They're coming in,' said Kesarsing as he handed the binoculars to Prabhat. 'You'd better tell saheb.'

'I know.' Prabhat's voice was weary. He had been on radio watch for over 48 hours, but it was the reception that awaited Max that really weighed most heavily. Still, first things first.

'Make sure that there's hot food ready for them.'

'Huzoor.'

On his way back, Kesarsing met Norbu and Paljor and gave them the news. Norbu shook his head slowly and said, 'I'll escort the Kushog-saheb.'

Now that Penjo had been relieved of his position, the grim-faced Kham was acting commanding officer, Kesarsing could not tell whether he was there to take Max into custody or would accompany him out of respect.

For Max, the sight of Prabhat was the best sort of greeting but the sergeant-major's expression boded ill.

'I'm so happy to see you, saheb,' Prabhat said.

'And I'm happy to see you too,' Max said, 'but you don't look very cheerful.'

Drawing him aside, Prabhat explained, 'Really bad news, huzoor, Penjo-saheb has been relieved of his command, the *feta-wallah* is giving the orders.' His reference to Fernandes was as welcome as a dose of dysentery. 'Norbu is acting commanding saheb and I think he'll be here in a few minutes.'

Max nodded slowly. He was physically and mentally exhausted and this much bad news drained what little reserve of patience he might have had. He was grateful to Prabhat for giving him advance notice.

'Thank you huzoor for breaking the news to me first. I'll see all our people back to base and then deal with the problems.'

Norbu came into sight along the narrow path, exchanging greetings with Choden and the others. Max caught Herman's eye.

'Trouble.'

'Hell, we all knew that before we left.'

'They've relieved Penjo.'

'Bastards.'

'Fernandes is here too, so I'm well in the shit.'

The American gave him a rueful smile. 'Eyes wide open, man, eyes wide open.'

As they turned back onto the path, Norbu barred the way. The big man's darkly bronzed face was inscrutable as he bowed slowly to both of them. Then, speaking in Tibetan, he addressed Max, 'Kushog-saheb, on behalf of the SFF, we ask that Sakyamuni bless you for bringing our people back. We cannot express ourselves as we would wish to and so we ask you, here and now, to accept the gift of our friendship for all time'. He bowed low and as he straightened up a sadly apologetic smile lit his face. 'I'm ordered to inform you that you must accompany me back to Chakrata.'

Max translated for Herman, including him in both the blessing and the gift but not the summons to Chakrata.

'Let me see Choden and the rest of the team back to base first,' Max said to Norbu, who nodded.

As the two of them walked back, Max asked for news of the wounded only to be told that they had all been flown directly to hospital in Mussoorie. Kalsang and Tenzing were on the danger list, Ulan was back in surgery and Pema was waiting for the results of her brain scans. The welcome at the Forward Base was colder than anything they had experienced on the mountaintops.

Fernandes strode out to meet him, his facial expression managing to capture his *schadenfreude* at Max's situation.

'Who the hell did you think you were to ride roughshod over your orders?' he thundered. 'You've done irreparable damage to relations between Delhi and Downing Street. I sincerely hope that you're cashiered, at the very least, you richly deserve it, especially in the light of your activities in Mussoorie.'

Max was tired and angry. 'Coming from someone with your poverty of experience, I regard that as a compliment.' He deliberately ignored the reference to Mussoorie.

'I expressed my reservations about you to the Chief from the very start,' Fernandes said, 'and I was right.'

'Somehow, I don't think the Chief would regard you as qualified to judge anyone.'

'It would have been better for everyone if you'd died out there.'

'Please don't restrain yourself.'

The urge to punch the man's face out the other side of his head was overwhelming, but Max clenched his fists and clung onto the thinly stretched threads of his reserve. The rest of the team had gathered round and the atmosphere was turning hostile towards Fernandes.

'Devlin, consider yourself under formal arrest.'

Max shut his eyes for a moment to keep control of his temper. Something was wrong here; if he was going to be arrested for Mussoorie, it would have been a policeman, not an intelligence officer. From what Norbu had told him, he was still answerable to the Research and Analysis Wing setup.

'First, it's Colonel Devlin to you, Fernandes,' Max said as he stepped up very close, towering over the Indian. 'And I can only be arrested by a *military* officer of equal or superior rank.' Poking the spook in the chest, Max added, 'You don't qualify on either count.'

Fernandes stepped back, momentarily thrown off balance, then he blustered, 'My orders come from General Mullick.'

'Show me.'

The senior RAW officer looked taken aback at being challenged, opening and closing his mouth, yet no words emerged.

'I thought so,' Max said, while turning to face Norbu. 'The acting commanding officer of the SFF unit, Colonel Norbu Khamba has requested me to accompany him to Chakrata, which I shall do voluntarily, as soon as I have had a shower, a sleep and a change of clothes.' He repeated this in Tibetan which made the atmosphere relax a little.

Norbu, however, looked uncomfortable. 'I apologise, Kushog-saheb,' he said, deep lines furrowing his forehead, 'but my orders are to take you there immediately.'

Max's instinct was to tell Norbu that his orders would have to wait on his convenience, but he was also anxious to give the acting commander face, especially in the presence of Fernandes. He responded in English, 'Alright then, unfoddered and unwashed it shall be.' He then translated a simple acquiescence in Tibetan.

Prabhat intervened, 'We should come too, saheb.'

Max turned to Norbu. 'Are the Gurkhas summoned?'

He shook his head. 'Only you, Kushog-saheb.'

Good though it would have been to have travelled together, Max was relieved that Deepraj had not been singled out. At least he was not being implicated in the Mussoorie mess. Now it was important to make proper arrangements for the Gurkhas. 'Very well. Can you arrange for my men to be billeted in Mussoorie until their travel orders come through?'

Norbu nodded slowly, recognition in his eyes. Max spoke to the Gurkhas, 'You three come to Chakrata, collect your kit and then Norbu-saheb will transfer you to Mussoorie to wait for your orders from London. Keep a close watch on the doctor-saheb and her sister until her new posting comes through.' They drew themselves to attention in acknowledgement. A signaller passed a message to Norbu which he read slowly. When he spoke, he was looking grimly at Fernandes but talking to Max.

'My orders have been changed. I have to give you into the custody of this...man.' Norbu almost spat the word into the ground, his dark features holding back a storm. Quite apart from giving the RAW man a quick victory, this was definitely a change for the worse. Max smiled reassuringly at Norbu, 'That's OK, you have greater responsibilities.'

Max gestured towards Choden and the others who had closed in around them, their mood ugly and threatening. He joined his palms together as he looked at each of them.

'*Kah-leh-peh.*'

Their response was automatic.

'*Kah-leh-shoo.*'

Each of them shook hands with him.

Choden's eyes were welling as she gripped both his hands in hers – a silent farewell.

*

Shortly after lift-off, Max fell into an exhausted sleep. That saved him from any form of conversation with Fernandes, who had been prevented from boarding into the rear seat until Max was seated up front next to Linka.

Max was fearful that he would be spotted or that the snow under him would creak and give away his position as he clung to the reverse slope. He kept reaching forward for his CZ75 which lay perilously close to the ridgeline but every time his fingers reached the butt, he slipped backwards and had to claw his way back up slowly again and again. Over the ridge he could just see Choden, Pema and the others ahead and below where he lay, they were all on their knees, PLA soldiers behind them with rifles pointed at the back of their heads. He knew that it was a hopeless gamble but if he could just shoot the officer commanding the execution detail, perhaps they could turn on their captors. His forefinger touched the hatching on the grip and his fingernail sought purchase to ease the weapon back into his hand.

Then, he felt someone grab his arm. 'We're coming into land, Kushog-saheb.' Linka shook Max out of his nightmare. Still desperate to rescue the Tibetans, he struggled to gain purchase on a different reality. The cabin of the helicopter was cold, but Max was sweating. The Tibetan pilot managed to convey a message of fellow feeling before turning back to the instrument panel. The damp barbecue smell of the avionic electronics was unreal after the clarity of the mountain air, reminding Max that he was the one with the gun metaphorically pointed at the back of his head. He looked out of the window, not recognising any of the familiar landmarks.

'Where are we?'

'Palam,' Linka said.

Max looked back at Fernandes in the rear seat. 'You said we were going to Chakrata, why are we in Delhi?'

'Change of orders.'

'Whose orders?'

'That's none of your business.' The Indian's eyes were full of the same contempt as his words.

'Actually, I think it's very much my business.'

'We've had a signal from London,' Fernandes said, 'if you must know.' The intelligence man looked like the cat that had the cream.

'SIS or MoD?' Max asked, still nursing the improbable hope that the damage to his career would be limited to the intelligence world.

'You're not authorised to know,' Fernandes said. With a supercilious smile fixed on his face, he added, 'You don't answer to any authority.'

Max wanted to put the arrogant bastard back in his box, but he knew that it would achieve nothing other than give him momentary satisfaction. Despite feigning any concern, he was worried about being handed over to the civil police. Once caught up in the Indian criminal justice system, he could serve a life sentence before ever getting to trial. Compared to that, justifying himself to London was a cake walk.

Linka set the chopper down as lightly as a feather. Max reached across and shook hands. 'I didn't even have a chance to congratulate you on your work over the Zhompalti.'

'It's what I do,' the Tibetan grinned, 'Kah-leh-peh, Kushog-saheb.'

'Kah-leh-shoo and thanks for everything.' As he unbuckled and got out of his seat, Max added, in English, 'Remember, you were always following my orders.'

An Indian Army staff officer ducked under the rotor blades and gestured for Max to follow. As they got clear, the officer turned round to Fernandes, who was behind them. 'Not you, gentleman,' the spook was told. 'Please follow this officer to the civil area of the airport.' Another greatcoat-clad officer appeared and shepherded the intelligence man away. The look of affront on Fernandes's face gave Max a moment's pleasure.

'This way, Colonel, please.'

Max looked around him. It appeared to be a remote corner of the airport, there were military helicopters and an IAF Embraer Legacy parked in front of a row of hangars. Though Delhi was freezing, it was a balmy evening compared to the Zhompalti Ridge. There were sentries guarding the entrance to a brick building with red and blue military designations on signboards. Wrapped up in greatcoats, with khaki balaclavas under their helmets, the sentries came sharply to attention and his escort acknowledged it with a salute. Holding the door open, he beckoned Max inside, indicating a half-open door just to the right.

'Please, sir.'

Still wondering whether this normal military civility was simply a prelude to being clapped in irons, Max pushed the door open and stepped into an outer office. A sergeant clerk stood up and gestured for Max to enter an inner office. Giving a peremptory knock, he walked in. Seated at a table were two uniformed Indian Army officers, a lieutenant-general and to Max's pleasant surprise his old Staff College colleague Colonel Sidartha Chopra. The third occupant was General Narayan Mullick, who stood up and came forward to greet him.

'I must apologise for the manner in which you were brought here, Colonel,' Mullick said, 'as you will appreciate, things are not always as they seem.' Max said nothing, waiting for the bomb to drop. Mullick turned towards the officers. 'General Chaudhari,' he addressed the chief of defence staff, 'may I introduce Colonel Devlin.' Max stood to attention, feeling conspicuously filthy.

Chaudhari regarded him with a detached air of amusement as he indicated a chair opposite him. 'Please. I asked Colonel Chopra to join us, he's been bending my ear ever since you arrived.'

Chopra stood up and reached across the table to shake Max's hand.

'Max.'

'Sid.'

'I gather you two have a shared history,' Chaudhari said with a smile.

'Gentlemen,' Mullick frowned, his voice serious. 'Please understand, this meeting never took place.' He looked at the officers, who nodded. Max held his tongue. 'What the SFF accomplished was a major intelligence coup and bringing everyone home would, in normal circumstances, have been what I think you would describe as the icing on the cake,' the special secretary said, before adding, 'Unfortunately, one of my senior officers, in an excess of zeal…'

'Bloody stupidity,' Chaudhari interposed.

'…disclosed to the SIS duty officer in London, that you had entered Tibet illegally.' Without pausing, Mullick continued, 'It is a matter of greatest personal regret, for which I owe you a profound apology, that Fernandes broke the chain of command by not reporting to me first. Most regrettably, that led to a frantic exchange of diplomatic signals between Downing Street and Rashtrapati Bhavan.'

Mullick inclined his head down a little as he looked at each of them. 'The fact is that the shit hit my fan and I could not prevent it splattering you,' he said. Pausing and tapping the tabletop with his fingers as though undecided, he then took a deep breath and continued, 'There is a sharp conflict of opinion within our cabinet and this information gave valuable ammunition to the powerful member who disapproved of the operation from the start. But, of course, I did not tell you that.' He waited for them to acknowledge his caveat before adding, 'The risk of hostilities with China is, even now, a possibility.'

General Chaudhari gave a dismissive wave of his hand and observed, 'But the intelligence that your people gathered has greatly strengthened our defensive capability and the Chinese know that we're ready for them this time.'

Mullick gave a deferential shrug of his shoulders. 'I'm just a soldier parachuted into a civil service position, General and I'm anxious to protect my department and the SFF.'

'What the Chief is about to tell you is that you're being fed to the political lions,' Chaudhari interposed, making no attempt to conceal his disgust. 'The politicos here and in London need scapegoats, here it's Brigadier Penjo and you're London's. There's no way that this can be dished up attractively.'

'But I disobeyed Penjo's orders, why should he bear the blame?'

'Nice try, Max,' Colonel Chopra smiled grimly, 'but no one's buying that.'

'Would you have abandoned your men in that situation, Sid?' Max threw caution to the winds.

Chopra looked suitably discomfited. 'Fortunately, I wasn't faced with that dilemma.'

'No, Sid, but if you had been, would you have mounted a rescue?' Max persisted.

The colonel scratched the back of his neck and said, 'I'd like to think that I would have.'

'Of course, you damned well would!' Chaudhari exploded. His hair shot through with grey, the chief of defence staff was an imposing figure who commanded respect as if born to it. Turning to Max, he shook his head. 'We'll do what we can for Penjo,' he said, 'and I'll have a word in the ear of your CIGS for what it's worth but...' He looked Max directly in the eye. 'I'm embarrassed to have to say that we've let you down.'

Looking at Mullick, Chaudhari said, 'You and I have our work cut out to protect the RAW from the political aftermath.' He stared at him for several seconds before adding, 'And you'd better watch your back too, Mullick.' Then he stood up, jammed his service cap on, walked around the table and gripped Max's hand. Flicking his head in Mullick's direction, he said, 'As you said, this meeting never took place so I'm off to prepare an alibi.' The ADC opened the door and the CDS walked out, waving them a salute.

Mullick shook Max's hand firmly. 'I must do likewise, it's hard to know who to trust these days. We are indebted to you, Colonel,' he said. With a twinkle in his eye, Mullick added, 'As are Dr. Khan and her sister. But, as you are aware, you were never officially in India.'

As the door closed behind him, Max turned to Chopra. 'That greasy shit Fernandes clammed up when I asked him about our casualties, can you tell me, Sid?'

'It's mostly bad news, I'm afraid Max,' Chopra said. 'The two Tibetan troopers didn't pull through but the brilliant surgery on the pilot by that remarkable lady doctor seems to have saved his life at the cost of one arm.' Max knew that Shanaaz would derive as much enormous professional satisfaction from saving Ulan as regret at the death of Kalsang and Tenzing. He wanted to share it with her, but it was clear that he would not be afforded that opportunity. The loss of Kalsang, especially, would be a kick in the gut for the members of the team after their heroic efforts to save him.

'Pema?'

'The operational commander on the ground?'

'Yes.'

'She'll pull through, but I doubt she'll return to active service.'

Momentarily, the loss of life, the cost to the careers of outstanding officers left Max without words. That he had been deprived of the chance to talk to Penjo, Pema and most especially Shanaaz compounded his sense of injustice.

'They're a remarkable group of people, both dedicated and professional, it was a privilege to serve with them. I'd be grateful if you would let them know how much I respect them.'

'*Tik hei*,' Chopra nodded gravely.

Max thought for a moment then decided. 'I'd be grateful if you'd put Dr. Khan up for an *Ashoka Chakra* for operating on Ulan when the chopper was about to go up any minute.'

Chopra gave him a twisted smile. 'You always were a clever bastard. The decoration for gallantry off the battlefield, even though she was actually on the battlefield, but no one will question it.'

'Precisely. What happens now?'

'You're on a special Indian Air Force flight to RAF Stansted. As Mullick said, officially, you never arrived and so you never left.' Chopra looked at his watch. 'ETD in half an hour. Sorry, there are no movies or amenity packs on board, but I've made sure you'll get some decent grub and a bottle of Glenfiddich.'

'As long as I can get my head down.'

Chopra called to the clerk, 'Sergeant, you can bring that bottle in now.'

The clerk walked in with a bottle of Johnny Walker and two glasses which he put on the desk. 'Shall I pour, sir?'

'No, I think we can manage that, thank you.'

Chopra poured two generous measures, handed one to Max and raised his own glass in salute.

'Here's to the poor bloody infantryman, who always gets shafted.'

They both drank and Max felt it going straight to his head.

'Anything else?'

Max really wanted to speak to Shanaaz, but he was anxious not to cause her embarrassment.

'Yes, please make sure that my three Gurkhas get home safely.'

'Wilco.' Chopra's eyebrows lifted for a second. 'Max, there is one thing I'm curious about.'

'What?'

'Do you know anything about some thugs in Mussoorie getting their comeuppance for attacking a young Moslem girl who just happened to be the sister of your Dr. Khan?'

Max widened his eyes in response and adopted a theatrical tone of voice. 'Now, why on earth would I know anything about that, Sid?'

'Nothing, other than that you were in Mussoorie that night and whoever it was who took out two of the bastards, he knew his job.' He shrugged. 'Just curious.'

'Sounds like rough justice, Sid.'

'Something you definitely wouldn't know anything about,' Chopra nodded sagely.

They walked out on the tarmac together in comfortable silence broken only by the occasional roar of a large passenger plane taking off. When they reached the foot of the mobile steps up to the aircraft's entrance, Chopra put his hand on Max's shoulder.

'I'm truly sorry, Max. I hope to God this doesn't spoil your prospects of promotion.'

'I'm no summer soldier to shrink from the service of my country,' Max smiled at his friend. 'You used to quote from Thomas Paine when we were at Camberley.'

'Oh, yes, I remember that. "These are the times that try men's souls." You accused me of being a philosopher soldier.'

They shook hands and Max mounted the stairs. He paused at the door into the fuselage and looked back.

'I'll see thee at Philippi.'

Office of the DAG
The Ministry of Defence
Wilton, Wiltshire

❦

Max had rehearsed what he was going to say once he had been summoned to the DAG's office, but now, sitting in front of Major-General Macrae, everything struck him as completely unreal. He was being carpeted because an Indian spook felt that his nose had been put out of joint. Why wasn't the army protecting its own? Bitter? God almighty he was bitter, the army could go and fuck itself. He had chosen to wear Number One dress, his cross-belt gleamed and the silver RGR insignia on it caught the skimmed-milk sunlight that was the sole source of warmth in the room. The core principle of his chosen profession was loyalty to your own, so he kept asking himself the same stupid question: 'How had it come to this?' Whitehall had put him in an invidious position, requiring him to apply his uniquely qualified skill sets to the SFF, teach them everything that would enable them to carry out their mission and survive. That had entailed earning their trust, a two-way process. His superiors in the army, at least those who had seen active service in one or more of the world's trouble spots, knew that the heart of soldiering lay in that bonding between those at the sharp end. It was axiomatic that an officer always prioritised the interests of those under his command. This, he was satisfied in his own mind, he had done. But it ran counter to political forces who were rarely, if ever, aware of the cost in human terms.

'Thank you for coming in, Max.'

Major-General Macrae's tone was friendly, making the order sound as though it had been an invitation. Uncommon familiarity was a sure sign that all was not well.

'When you were asked about this post, I observed that everything political carries risks.'

'You were candid, General.'

The DAG blinked as he nodded, and his tone of voice became more serious. 'It's an unfortunate fact that the political risk materialised.' He made a little throwaway gesture with his hand. 'But before I say anything else let me assure you that the army's unofficial view is that you acquitted yourself with distinction and, if I may add my personal observation, honourably and courageously.'

Max was impatient for the 'but'. It was not long in coming.

'Your service record is outstanding.' He gave Macrae credit for the reluctance in his tone. 'I'll not beat about the bush. When we engage with other government departments, their comments become an integral part of the record.' He raised a hand to stop Max from interrupting. 'As it happens, SIS are full of praise for the work that you did and especially for the intelligence gathered by the teams under your training. James Chalmers actually told me that he'd like to recruit you.'

Max shook his head in disbelief.

'He's apologetic. It seems that a report from an RAW officer was handled by the duty officer in London during the wee small hours so that it was forwarded to the principal secretary to the Joint Intelligence Committee before Chalmers had a chance to intercept it,' the general said. 'From the JIC it was only minutes before it was on the PM's desk. A serving British Army officer on a covert and unlawful entry into a sensitive part of China's territory…' Canting his head to one side, he added, 'You know the rest of the story.'

Having it all set out in simple terms, including the ill-fated happenstance of the signal not first passing over Chalmers's desk increased Max's sense of his luck having run out.

'And all this goes onto my personal record, sir?'

The DAG nodded. 'Today's Army is relatively small and posting of Gurkha battalions is politically very sensitive. For that reason, Gurkha battalion commanders need political approval.' He opened his arms in a gesture that left nothing to the imagination as to Max's prospects for command. 'You would have been the army's choice for the next battalion command. I cannot say more than that.'

Max digested this with all the relish he would have had for a meal of shit. 'I appreciate your blunt appraisal, General,' he said. 'In truth, I think it's clear that I have no future in the brigade which, in effect, means the army.' He made it a statement, not a question.

Macrae frowned. 'Both the brigade and the army would be anxious to retain your services, but the cruel truth is that you have hit a promotional glass ceiling in the Brigade of Gurkhas, politically,' he said. 'But before you make any unconsidered decisions, perhaps I should add that I do not see this as excluding you from promotion in an administrative role.'

'Thank you for that, General.'

'Unconsidered' was a polite word for intemperate. An insuperable hurdle had fallen across his chosen career path and all at once he was shut out of the world that he had lived and breathed to the exclusion of almost everything else for all these years.

There was no disguising that this was the end of the road.

Epilogue

London

One week later

An unsatisfactory and frustrating long-distance phone conversation with Shanaaz had convinced him that she valued her career more than sharing her life with him. He was hyperconscious of his sudden loss of self-worth as he faced an uncertain future. Probably he had transmitted, unconsciously, his feelings of insecurity, she was far too acute not to have sensed it. He had barely contained his own emotions when she became tearful.

That night he had gone out with Bruce Rose and the pair of them had drunk themselves to a standstill. They both shared a history of identifying themselves with the people with whom they served and for whom they were responsible and had done what they believed was right. But outside the extraordinary context of their peculiar circumstances, they knew their actions would be judged to be wrong by 'normal' standards. As Bruce had put it, 'We didn't sign on for the fucking normal'.

The following day, nursing an evil hangover, it had been time to take stock of what the future held for him. He sat down at the desk in his small Chelsea flat and started to write the letter resigning his commission.

For the umpteenth time, he examined his motives. It was a counter-intuitive process, turning his back on a way of life that had more than satisfied his need for challenges against which to pit himself. But remaining to watch others step into the shoes that he might otherwise have filled would only lead to bitter frustration. He only had himself to blame, the lure of that step into uncharted territory was his Achilles heel, but he knew that it was just the way he was.

He finished the letter, signed it carefully and folded it.

Next, he turned on his laptop and examined his finances. A quick calculation disclosed that he could raise his share of the investment that would be necessary if he went into partnership with Chuck, an ex-special forces veteran venturing into the travel industry. All that remained was to contact the American to find out whether the offer of a partnership in Nepal was still open.

As a soldier, he knew a rat's fart about business, but Chuck would take care of that side of things. What he would bring to the party was his knowledge of the people, languages and cultures of the Himalayas and South Asia, now he had to monetise such skills as he had. Together, they had the potential for a successful and rewarding enterprise.

Would the fates smile kindly on them? In his mind's eye, he saw Shanaaz saying *Ins'allah*. He was equivocal in his attitude to superstitions: living so much amongst the peoples of the Orient, he had learned to respect the inexplicable, but luck had been an unreliable companion of recent days. Despite his ancestry, it was not something that he reflected on that often. Had he, he wondered, taken for granted what his ancestors called the *ádh mór* of the Irish? Good luck or not, it remained to be seen.

He put the letter in its envelope, wrote the address neatly on the front and added a 1st Class stamp. Leaving the flat he walked to the corner of the road and dropped it into the letter box.

The die was cast.

Acknowledgements

The Tibetans' struggle to keep alive their faith in Buddhist philosophy under the leadership of H.H. the Dalai Lama is a constant inspiration.

This may be a work of fiction, but it is interwoven with reality. The story pays tribute to the courageous roles of women in the Indian subcontinent where chauvinism permeates.

The Special Frontier Force, established in November 1962 to draw on the talent of the Tibetans-in-exile, has played a significant role in the defence of India's border with the PRC's Autonomous Region of Tibet. The fragile ceasefire in the disputed regions of Aksai Chin in the west and the Doklam Plateau in the east descended into murderous hand-to-hand combat between Chinese and Indian soldiers as recently as June 2020.

My fascination with India is seamed with the joys and frustrations generated by close association with that magnificent yet turbulent country whose rich cultural tapestry beguiles one minute and infuriates the next. Max and Deepraj epitomise Kipling's 'two strong men who stand face to face, though they come from the ends of the earth'. Those who follow their escapades may hope to hear more of them in time.

I am indebted to Squadron Leader (retired) Dai Evans, most recently of the Hong Kong Government Flying Service, for his invaluable advice on the performance of helicopters at high altitudes and Colonel James Robinson (retired) for advising me on the Royal Gurkha Rifles and the current MoD nomenclature.

My grateful thanks and appreciation to Giulio Acconci for yet another inspired cover design and a huge debt of gratitude to Angel W Lau for her patient editing and proof-reading of my egregious errors.

A special thank you to Pete Spurrier at Blacksmith Books for his professionalism and support.

The characters and events that occupy these pages are all conjured out of my imagination and bear no likeness to anyone living or dead.

Errors of every description are all of my own manufacture.

Neville Sarony
May 2021
Hong Kong